"YOU ARE THE VERY DEVIL OF A WOMAN, MISS O'CONNELL

🐚 🐚 🐚

"You run rampant through a man's sensibilities—dashing about the countryside flashing your legs like a gypsy, then trouncing a fellow's self-regard by humiliating him at cards—not a friendly social game, mind you, but a bloodletting session of poker. You bait the wolves, then when they come after you, you indignantly declare they should be locked into cages."

"You exaggerate."

"Only you would say so. You invite more trouble upon yourself than you know."

"I invite nothing."

"Not true. You invite this."

He caught her hand as she started to walk away. His mouth descended upon hers gently but firmly. His lips coaxed, demanded, played, commanded, and she hadn't the iron in her soul to contest him.

🐚 🐚 🐚

"Alive with adventure, this spirited tale will leave the reader with more than *Gold Dust* fever."
—*Affaire de Coeur* on *Gold Dust*

🐚

please turn the page for more reviews

"This one is full of humor, action, adventure, and loving. A must read."
—Rendezvous on Gold Dust

❧

"Katy is . . . all girl and a wonderfully interesting and complex character. . . . The action is never-ending. The description of the trek to the Klondike reads as if the author's been there and done that."
—Publishers Weekly on Gold Dust

❧

"TRUE WESTERN BUFFS."
—Dorothy Garlock, author of Larkspur, on Lawless

❧

"One heck of a good, intense, emotional read."
—Romantic Times on Lawless

❧

Windfall

EMILY CARMICHAEL

Windfall

WARNER BOOKS

A Time Warner Company

WARNER BOOKS EDITION

Cover design by Diane Luger
Cover photo by Herman Estevez
Hand lettering by Carl Dellacroce

Warner Books, Inc.
1271 Avenue of the Americas
New York, NY 10020

Visit our Web site at
http://pathfinder.com/twep

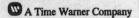 A Time Warner Company

Printed in the United States of America
First Printing: August, 1997

10 9 8 7 6 5 4 3 2 1

CHAPTER 1

Paris had been a nightmare. England, in its gloomy, drizzly way, was merely an annoyance. But the annoyance was approaching genuine aggravation now, as sheets of rain and wind battered the old-fashioned carriage that was carrying Ellen O'Connell to the railway station. The carriage was not only old-fashioned—it was old. The cast-off of some wealthy family who had moved up to a newer, more fashionable vehicle, it was a pensioner with threadbare upholstery and fatigued springs. Enough rain leaked through the roof and blew in around the windows and door to get the women inside almost as wet as the driver who rode the box.

"This is dreadful!" Jane Browne declared. She huddled deeper into her wool redingote and grimaced apologetically. "I'm so sorry, Ellen! What a way to end your visit to England! I've been at Papa for absolutely years to replace this old thing, but he insists that the new carriages don't have the 'presence' of the old ones."

Ellen knew very well that Dr. Browne could not afford

a new carriage on his income as a rural surgeon. He was doing well to maintain his home and educate his five daughters.

She managed to smile at her friend, though her teeth were chattering. "I suppose we should have delayed until morning. This storm has been threatening all day. I should have known, the way my luck has been running, that it was simply hovering in wait for us to leave before it lashed the countryside with wind and rain."

"Tsk! Now you're thinking that Mother Nature herself is persecuting you. Such a fancy! There's another blanket beneath the seat," Jane told her. "It won't do for you to get chilled. Wrap it around yourself."

Ellen did as she was told. She had never been a person who took kindly to being mothered or ordered about, even in a solicitous fashion, but lately her fierce independence had guttered like a flame that was starved for fuel. She hugged the blanket tightly about her, and her shivers calmed a bit. "Somehow, when we came from the station in Stafford two weeks ago, it didn't seem this far."

Jane shrugged. "It is far enough—the price we pay for Papa's penchant for the country. But one never minds the distance when the day is fair."

Whatever the distance was, it was going to seem like double today, for the carriage slid about the road as if ice, not mud, were beneath the wheels. Thomas, the driver, was one of two Browne domestics. He served as gardener, groom, handyman, errand boy, and anything else the family required of him. The bad road would not have been such a delay if Thomas had been an expert coachman, but he wasn't, and his difficulties became more apparent as the rain and wind measureably increased for every mile they progressed.

"Don't fret," Jane advised at the worried pucker of Ellen's brows. "We have two full days before the ship leaves. If we miss the train this evening, there will be another tomorrow. Missing the shops in London will not be a loss. I can little afford to indulge myself with new fripperies."

Two days, Ellen reflected. Two days before she would truly be on her way home. How she needed the comfort of familiar places and a loving family! The longing was so great she felt it as a physical ache. That ache had prodded her to the brink of unseemly impatience to leave Jane's family behind, although Dr. Browne and Jane's four younger sisters had been all that was hospitable and generous.

Would they have been so hospitable, a freshly cynical voice inside Ellen's head asked, if they knew about Paris? Would Dr. Browne have allowed his daughter to accompany Ellen to America if he'd known about Paris? Ellen burrowed more deeply into the blanket and sighed. The dark sky, the rain, wind, mud, cold, and leaky carriage were a fitting end to her sojourn on foreign shores.

Just as Ellen was working up a good case of depression, the carriage slid precipitously to one side.

Jane cried out in alarm, then sighed as the vehicle righted itself. "This mud is awful! Perhaps we should return home and go down to London tomorrow. We're both wet as—what is that dreadful expression you use?" She flashed an impish smile at Ellen.

"A duck's behind. Wet as a duck's behind." Ellen had picked up the expression from her less than proper father, though behind wasn't as colorful a word as he used.

"Wet as a duck's behind," Jane repeated with a smile. "We're both that, and cold as well. Shall we turn around and try again tomorrow?"

They had entered a woods. Tree branches whipped in the wind, surrendering the last brown leaves of fall. A small whirlwind of twigs and leaves clattered against the carriage. The storm was getting worse. Ellen sighed. "That seems the reasonable thing to do, I suppose." She hated the thought of delay, even though they had two days before the ship left London for New York. She was headed home, and like a horse headed for the barn, she was reluctant to go any other direction. Yet if their progress continued to be this slow, they might well miss the train, and spending the night at some inn would strain her resources. She'd spent nearly her last shilling to pay for their passage across the Atlantic.

Jane thumped the roof of the carriage as a signal to stop, and they slowly slid to a halt. Thomas slid open the little window between the interior and the driver's box, allowing a cold spatter of rain to get them even wetter.

"Aye, miss?"

"Let us go home, Thomas. The storm is too strong."

"Whatever you say, miss."

The window snapped shut. Ellen could hear Thomas shouting at the two horses. The wind had spooked them, she suspected, but shouting was hardly the way to calm them. Finally the team dragged the carriage around and headed back the way they had come. The wind was behind them now. The pace picked up. The horses knew they were going home.

Suddenly a splintering crack sounded above the wind—almost as loud as a rifle shot. A prolonged, rumbling crash followed, accompanied by a screech of tortured wood. The carriage lurched and slid sideways. Thomas shouted.

Jane screamed and Ellen held on for dear life. Time

seemed to stretch in a dreamlike elasticity as the two women bounced from one side of the carriage to the other. When they finally came to rest, the seats were canted at a sharp angle. One set of windows looked out upon mud and crushed vegetation, the other set upon pelting rain and gray sky.

Ellen straightened her hat and untangled herself from the blanket that had twisted around her. Jane was wrong and she was right. Mother Nature was out to get her.

Jordan Chesterfield was about to wear a path in the bedroom's expensive Oriental carpet. Hands clasped rigidly behind his back, brows lowered dangerously, he worried a route from the window to the bed and back to the window, where the rain beating upon the panes perfectly matched his mood. In the big four-poster lay his brother George, eyes closed, breathing shallow, skin waxy and pale. And fidgeting in a nearby chair was the earl of Tindale, who was rather pale himself.

"I don't know how it happened, Chesterfield. Really I don't. I'm not even entirely certain it was my shot that did the deed."

Jordan sent the earl a look of glacial contempt.

"It . . . it could have happened to anyone, really!" Tindale insisted. "He should have known better than to be bolting out ahead of the party like that!"

"I agree," Jordan conceded. "My brother is a fool. And he runs with fools."

"I beg your pardon?" The particular fool being chastised stiffened in umbrage. "Are you calling me a fool, Chesterfield?"

"Anyone who trots off into the woods with a gun in his hands and liquor clouding his brain is a fool. Can you think of a better term for it?"

Tindale bristled, but he didn't answer. The unconscious man on the bed was evidence that could not be denied.

"Where the hell is Martin?" Jordan demanded. "Loftus went to fetch him two hours ago."

"Off feeding some widow headache powders or tending the sneezes of somebody's brat, no doubt."

Jordan shot him a quelling glance. He was tired of Tindale's whining excuses and fed up with his haughtiness. The man had nothing to be haughty about. He was an empty-headed fool and a vain, useless parasite. The only reason he was a guest at Endsfield Park was his great good fortune of being the son of the duke of Marlowe. That and the fact that Lady Chesterfield, Jordan's mother, thought Tindale was vastly entertaining at card parties and balls. He wondered how entertaining his mother found the earl now that the blundering dunderhead had accidentally shot her younger son.

"Really, Chesterfield." The earl loosened his collar. Possibly he was feeling the heat of Jordan's scrutiny. "Don't worry so. I hit him with buckshot, not a carronade. I daresay he'll recover right enough."

"The holes in his thick hide don't worry me as much as the head injury. He's not gained consciousness since hitting that rock."

"It's just a little knock on the head. With as thick a skull as George has, he'll be right as rain soon enough. Wait and see."

"Thank you for your considered opinion," Jordan said sardonically, "but I think I will consult a physician just the same."

Tindale sniffed at Jordan's tone. The son of a duke had far more social consequence and rank than a mere baron, no matter how ancient and honorable the baron's family might be. And as the son of a duke, Tindale wasn't accustomed to being spoken to with such disdain. Jordan, however, didn't give a damn.

A discreet knock on the door jolted through the tension between the two men.

"Yes?" Jordan called.

The door opened to reveal the bent form of Codgkins, the butler. "Sir, Lady Chesterfield has retired to her suite in extreme agitation over Master George's injury. I believe she wishes me to inform you of her distress."

Jordan clenched his jaw.

"Miss Moorsmythe is trying to calm her, sir."

Hillary Moorsmythe, Jordan reflected, had a job on her hands if she thought she could soothe his mother out of a set of flamboyant histrionics.

"Also, the gamekeeper, Mr. Carey, has brought in a party of poor souls whose carriage slid into a ditch down the road a bit."

"Are any of the party injured?"

"No, sir. But one of them claims to be a physician." Codgkins related this claim with a slightly pained grimace.

"A physician? Good God, man! Why didn't you say that at the outset? Bring the doctor up here."

Codgkins hesitated.

"What's wrong?" Jordan demanded.

"Sir . . . this person does not seem to be the same caliber of physician as Dr. Martin."

"Right now I'd settle for a horse doctor, Codgkins. Bring him up. Now."

The butler raised a disdainful brow. "Very well, sir."

Jordan wondered at Codgkins's supercilious expression, then concluded that butlers were paid to be supercilious. Two minutes later, however, his own brows arched upward as Codgkins brought the physician into the room. Behind him, Tindale shot from his chair and exclaimed softly, "I'll be damned!"

"This is Miss O'Connell, sir," Codgkins said impassively. "She is a physician." Only the barest hint of a smile revealed the butler's enjoyment of Jordan's reaction.

"Miss O'Connell," Jordan repeatedly blandly. "Really." He groped for words and found nothing intelligent to say. Standing before him, bedraggled as a wet cat dragged in from the storm, petite, slender, but with curves enough to leave no doubt as to gender, the self-proclaimed physician looked him straight in the eye just as though she weren't—outrageous though it seemed—a woman.

"By damned!" Tindale said. "A woman doctor! Where did you learn your trade, madam? Tending your sick old father at his bedside?"

The woman's gaze shifted to the earl. From a pair of green eyes that put emeralds to shame, she gave him a look that should have inspired him to keep his tongue still in his mouth. "My father is neither old nor sick, sir. Your butler indicated you were in need of assistance. I see that is not true." She turned to leave, back straight and spine stiff.

"Wait!" Jordan commanded. "Forgive our manners, please."

"Or the lack of them?"

"Precisely." Jordan glowered at Tindale. If the earl had been a rooster, his feathers would have ruffled in annoyance. "Tindale, I will let you know how things progress."

At the clear dismissal, the earl left, ruffled feathers and all. Jordan was alone with the damp doctoress. With midnight hair escaping her braided coif in damp ringlets and a pert nose reddened by the cold, she certainly did not look the part of a physician. The idea of a woman taking on such a masculine calling was rather ludicrous in itself, though not unheard of. That aside, however, this particular woman, whose slender curves were disconcertingly accented by the clinging dampness of her gown, looked more like a disheveled seductress than one of the militant "new women" who were charging out of the home and into the male-dominated professions.

Still, Jordan realized, at this point, any help was better than none. "Please don't think me rude for asking, Miss O'Connell, but are you indeed a licensed physician?"

She sighed, and some of the starch went out of her spine. "I am not on England's Medical Register, sir, for one must complete medical training in Great Britain to qualify for that honor, but I graduated from the Medical College at Cornell, in New York, and just recently was in Paris for graduate clinical study."

"Then I am fortunate that the storm brought you to Endsfield." Jordan moved aside, giving her a view of the bed and its occupant. "My brother was accidentally shot several hours ago in a hunting accident. The wounds themselves are slight enough, I think, but when he fell, he hit his head on a rock. He hasn't regained consciousness since the incident."

When the woman saw George lying on the bed, her demeanor immediately changed. Jordan could have sworn she grew at least two inches in height and ten years in age as she moved to the bed and took charge. If her appearance was that of a temptress, her manner, Jordan noted with relief, was confidently professional. She felt George's pulse, lifted an eyelid and looked into his eye, and pinched his cheek. "Someone should have been called to see this man hours ago."

"Our family physician was sent for. He has not yet appeared."

"Then you are a fool to have kept me standing there reciting my qualifications while your brother is very obviously in need of help."

"I cannot very well let just anyone treat him," Jordan said, a definite edge to his voice.

"It seems you have very little choice," the woman snapped.

"It seems so."

Ellen moved easily into the routine that had become so familiar in her work as a clinical student at the Paris École de Medicine, except that now there was no experienced clinician watching her every move to ensure she didn't fumble or make an error of judgment. It didn't matter. This young man's condition was straightforward. Straightforward and dangerous. The shot wounds didn't concern her unduly. A swift glance at the bloody little holes showed most of them to be superficial. The head injury was another story entirely. The boy's continued unconsciousness was not a good sign. Not good at all.

The arrogant Lord Whatever-his-name-was stood across from her and frowned mightily, no doubt sensing her concern. If Ellen had been one who rattled easily, she would have been rattled. The Englishman's doubts about her were stamped upon his aristocratic features, and the man delivered enough heat with his scrutiny to steam the water right out of her clothes. He made the spacious chamber seem very small, somehow, and the air within seem very warm, despite the inadequacy of the fireplace that was the only source of heat. Ellen was accustomed to a skeptical attitude in both patients and their relatives, but this relative was more commanding than most. His presence was like a charge of energy in the room, setting it to sizzling with both his skepticism and his masculinity.

Ellen was not easily discomfited by men. She had been raised in a rough, masculine world, had chosen to train and work alongside men in a profession they regarded as their own, and regarded men as friends, sometime adversaries, occasionally attractive, often annoying, and seldom anything to become flustered about. But something about this Englishman raked across her senses in a most disconcerting manner.

Forcing herself to concentrate upon the business at hand, Ellen met the Englishman's visual dissection with a level gaze. "Help me to turn him to his side, please, so I can get a better look at the back of his head."

Silently, he did as she requested, his relentless eyes resting not upon his brother, but upon her.

"Hold him there for a moment, please."

The scalp was broken nastily over the point of impact, and worse, a purple and blue bruise surrounded the area. The hair was matted with dried blood that someone had tried to wipe away, and a small amount of fresh scarlet seepage was present as well. She wished for eyes that could see through the flesh to the skull beneath. Whether or not the skull was cracked, the brain had obviously suffered a serious concussion.

"You can let him down now," she told his lordship.

He did so, very gently, then brushed a strand of hair back from the younger man's brow. Momentarily, the depth of his concern cracked through the stony composure of his face. When he wasn't scowling, Ellen noted, he really was quite arrestingly attractive. He turned his clear gray eyes back to her, and she felt a surprising jolt of sensual awareness—very unprofessional, given the circumstances! A thread of anxiety tightened his voice as he questioned her. "Well, *Doctor* O'Connell?"

Ellen rallied her composure. "Exactly how long ago did your brother hit his head?"

He glanced at his pocket watch. "Probably four hours or a bit more."

Ellen tried to keep her expression neutral as she once again looked at the boy's eyes to determine the level of consciousness.

"How bad is it?" the Englishman asked.

"Bad enough." She sighed. "I brought a medical bag with me. I believe your butler put it with my other baggage. Would you please send down for it?"

"Yes."

"And also ask my friend Miss Browne to come up. She can assist me."

"I can—"

"No, you can't." She frowned up at him, then took pity on the fear he was unsuccessfully trying to conceal. "He's your brother, isn't he? And you're worried about him?"

"Naturally."

"Then let Miss Browne help me." She reached out and took the man's hand. It was warm, dry, and surprisingly callused for an aristocrat's hand. Ellen ignored both the Englishman's startled expression and the odd tingle that shivered through her own veins as she held the hand up before his face. "Look at your hand, sir. It's a man's hand. Big. Wide fingers. There's a reason why women do fine needlework and men commonly do not. I don't want your clumsy fingers getting tangled in my thread or bumbling about the wound site and making things worse."

His lordship's frown made it clear that he was unaccustomed to being called clumsy and bumbling, but he merely lifted one brow. Distrust was etched deeply into his expression, but he conceded her point. "Whatever you say, Miss O'Connell."

"Dr. O'Connell," she corrected.

A skeptical smile twitched his aristocratic mouth. "Dr. O'Connell, then."

He returned with Jane and the medical bag in less than two minutes. Jane had changed into dry clothing, Ellen noticed, and had managed to rearrange her hair into its usual pristine flawlessness. In addition to being dry and clean, she seemed inordinately in awe of their host. She looked as though she might kneel down and kiss the hem of his coat at any moment.

"Jane!"

Jane snapped her head around. "Yes?"

"I need your help in stitching this laceration, if you don't mind."

In a tone that barely skirted sarcasm, the Englishman inquired, "I suppose Miss Browne is a physician also?"

"Oh no, sir!" Jane turned back to him with a deference far in excess of what the fellow's manners deserved. Her eyes were wide, and her fingers twisted in the folds of her skirt. "But I have some small experience in assisting my father, who is a surgeon."

His lordship harrumphed, and poor Jane visibly jumped.

Ellen sighed. Her friend was usually such a sensible, down-to-earth person. It was one of the qualities Ellen had admired most about her when they had met in Paris. Jane had been visiting a cousin there and had attended a charity fund-raiser for the clinic where Ellen studied. The kindhearted English girl had subsequently started volunteer work at the clinic, and she and Ellen had become close friends. Normally, Jane was a woman who combined intelligence, common sense, and a self-assurance that let her deal smoothly with almost any situation. Any situation, apparently, except being scrutinized by a person who bore a silly title in front of his name.

"Jane!" Ellen repeated sharply.

"Sorry." Jane visibly struggled to break the spell of her awe. "The laceration. Of course I'll help." Her face was flushed, she turned her attention to Ellen's patient, and her eyes softened with compassion. "Oh, the poor man!"

"He's been buckshot," Ellen told her, "but the real concern is his head. I need you to hold it just so while I stitch the laceration closed. Then we'll see to cleaning up the shot holes."

Jane immediately settled down to business. She poured disinfectant over Ellen's hands, then clipped the hair from around the young man's wound while Ellen got a needle, catgut, and gauzes from her bag. Their host stayed close behind her, looking over her shoulder from his impressive height, weighing down her every move with his leaden mistrust.

"Mr . . . uh . . . pardon me," Ellen said, "but I didn't catch your name."

"Chesterfield," he supplied coldly.

"Mr. Chesterfield . . ."

Jane shot her a warning glance. Apparently, even in a crisis situation, Brits were expected to adhere to social correctness. All right, Ellen thought sourly. She could be as silly as the rest of them.

"Excuse me, Lord Chesterfield," she corrected with exaggerated courtesy. "If you want your brother's head to be properly stitched, then kindly refrain from hovering over my shoulder like the grim reaper. Your brother is not in immediate danger. If you would care to go downstairs, be sure I will call you if you are needed."

His scowl grew almost as black as his raven's wing hair, but he nodded coldly. "If my watching discomforts you, Miss O'Connell, then I will confine myself to the chair and stay out of your way."

"Thank you," she replied with every bit the same hauteur. As she returned to work, Jane's brief look was a silent plea to behave herself.

Once Lord Chesterfield was not breathing the cold breath of disapproval in her ear, Ellen accomplished the job neatly and quickly. She cleaned and disinfected the area around the wound and stitched the laceration neatly closed. Her cold, wet clothes, the squish of her soggy shoes and stockings, and the annoyance of having Lord Chesterfield glower from his throne in the corner faded from her awareness. From the time she had first entered medical school at Cornell, her attention to detail, her focus, her ability to tune out any and all distractions, had won her praise from her teachers and envy from her fellow students. Her twin sister Katy had often accused her of being a perfectionist, and Ellen conceded that it was true. She expected perfection of herself in all things, whether she was cooking, sewing, or diagnosing and treating a patient.

That was why her failure in Paris had been so shattering. Never before had she fallen so short of the mark.

"That should keep him," Ellen said as she tied the last stitch.

Lord Chesterfield jumped from his chair as if a spring had launched him from the seat. "Is he going to be all right?"

"I should think so," Ellen said, but her frown was not

as confident as her words. She lifted her patient's eyelid and looked for signs of returning consciousness. "Jane, hand me the smelling salts, please."

The salts had no effect.

"Lord Chesterfield, what is your brother's name?"

"George."

Ellen slapped the patient lightly on the cheek. "George? George, can you hear me?"

Of course he didn't. If her taking a needle to his scalp hadn't brought him around, a little sting on his cheek wasn't going to do the trick. Ellen wished one of her teachers from the École de Medicine were here. Even Henri—Henri of the unflappable confidence, warm smile, sharp wit, and talent for making her believe in herself. But Henri was not here. The thought caused a sharp pain in the vicinity of her heart.

"Why hasn't he come around?" Lord Chesterfield demanded, as if the whole situation was due to her incompetence. He began to hover again.

Ellen pulled herself back into focus. She didn't want to tell him what she suspected. One thing she had learned in her clinical experience in Paris was that it was best not to voice bad news until the bad news was a certainty.

"We will watch and wait, Mr. . . . Lord Chesterfield. At least he will not feel the pain of me digging the shot out of him. I wonder if I might have some tea sent up for myself and Miss Browne, though? My hands are growing quite stiff with the cold."

The Englishman took her hand as if it was his proprietary right. He scowled at the iciness of her flesh, then looked her up and down as if he had just noticed that she was a person who might feel damp, cold, and weary.

The deliberate perusal sent a flood of warmth to Ellen's face despite the icy chill in the rest of her.

"No wonder you're cold," he told her. "You're a soggy mess." Again his tone seemed to place fault for her situation squarely on her shoulders. "If George's shot wounds can wait a few more minutes, you should dry yourself and change. That will warm you up."

"I'd rather tend to your brother first."

"It was the head wound I was most worried about," he told her, as if he were the doctor and she a bystander. "Surely the buckshot can wait."

"All the same—"

"Go change, Miss O'Connell, and I will ring for your tea."

Lord Chesterfield obviously was accustomed to having his orders followed without question. He would have been right at home in the Middle Ages, Ellen thought peevishly. But she obeyed. Only, she told herself, because she was cold.

When she returned, warm and dry, wearing one of the plain gray dresses she had used in the Paris clinic and a minimally frilled cap that hid most of her hair, a tray had arrived with tea and biscuits. There was no time to enjoy the warming drink, however, because young George suddenly came to life and vomited all over the bed and poor Jane, who desperately tried to turn him over so he would not swallow and choke on the foul effluent. Lord Chesterfield demonstrated his good sense by jumping in to lend his strength to the task, ignoring the mess that immediately soiled his spotless and flawlessly fashionable jacket and waistcoat.

Ellen immediately sprang to their aid. "Hold him up! Yes, like that. Good."

"He was conscious for a moment while you were gone

from the room," Lord Chesterfield told her. "He tried to talk, but the words were nonsense. And his right hand when he tried to raise it was weak as a baby's."

Ellen tried to keep her distress from her face, for keeping a confident mien around a patient and his family was crucial. George's vomiting ceased. They cleaned him, and Ellen did a brief examination. The boy had sunk into an even deeper unconsciousness. She tried to tell herself that what had to be done could wait until the family physician appeared, that her brief clinical experience in Paris did not qualify her to perform such a drastic procedure, that no one in the world would condemn her for simply maintaining the patient until a more experienced physician arrived to take the responsibility off her hands.

No one except herself.

Ellen sighed. "Lord Chesterfield, I must have a word with you. Is there a place we may speak in private?"

His eyes searched her face, and he grew very still. "I take it this is news I'm not going to like."

Ellen hoped the fearful pounding of her heart did not show in her expression.

"Very well," he said sternly. "Come to my study."

CHAPTER 2

"**Y**ou want to do what?"
Chesterfield's voice shook with incredulous anger. He had removed his soiled jacket and waistcoat, and in his fine linen shirt and tailored trousers he looked even more imposing, if possible, then before.

Ellen bit her lip. She didn't want to do this. She didn't want to talk this intimidating autocrat into letting her do it. But she must.

"I believe you heard me correctly, Lord Chesterfield. I know it sounds drastic—"

"It sounds outrageous!" His face grew pale. His mouth became a furious slash above the tightly clenched, square jaw. "Did you study in Paris or in Bedlam? Any sane person knows that a hole in the head spells death, madam! It is bad enough that my brother has a bloody goose egg the size of my fist!" As if to illustrate, he clenched his fist—sizable indeed!—and brought it down upon the desk.

Ellen jumped back. "Please calm yourself, Lord Chesterfield!"

"I am perfectly calm!" he shouted.

Her determined composure collided with his furious aggravation. The standoff was much like staring down one of her father's mean-tempered bulls back home on the Thunder Creek Ranch in Montana. In those contests, the bulls had generally won.

It would be so easy to give in, to say "Whatever you wish, sir," and hope the boy could recover without such heroic intervention. In a childhood and youth full of crisis and adventure, Ellen had never been one to rush into dramatic action. She didn't care for grandiose gestures. Her sister Katy had been the one who staged spectacular rescues and defied odds to save the day, while Ellen had stood quietly on the sidelines and cleaned up the mess.

Yet here she was, standing up to a man who looked as though he ate nails for breakfast and knives for dinner, telling him she could save his brother with as dramatic a procedure as the medical arts had ever devised. She swallowed back the urge to retreat. George Chesterfield's life depended upon this procedure. Ellen was as sure of that as she had been sure of anything in her life.

She took a deep breath. "Lord Chesterfield, surely you're a modern man with an open mind."

"I am a modern man, madam. Not a madman!"

"I have seen this procedure done in Paris very successfully."

"Trust the French to come up with something so atrocious."

"It is not atrocious, sir! And not insane! In fact, this procedure is a lifesaver, and it can save the life of your brother!"

"You said, Miss O'Connell, that my brother would do well enough."

"That was before I observed the decrease in his state of consciousness."

"You were mistaken, then?"

"Yes."

"Perhaps you are mistaken again."

"No, sir! I am not. Your brother is bleeding inside the skull, and the accumulating blood is putting pressure on the brain. That is the reason for his prolonged unconsciousness and the weakness on his right side. The bleeding is impinging the left side of the brain."

Chesterfield's jaw tightened, and he exhaled in a great gust of frustration. "You expect me to believe this . . . this unlikely medical mumbo jumbo?"

Ellen was silent.

His eyes raked her scathingly. "You expect me to trust this wild story from a total stranger and let you drill a hole in my brother's head?"

"In his skull, Lord Chesterfield. You make it sound as though I propose to enter on the left side and drill through to the right. I assure you this is quite safe, and he's deeply enough unconscious to not feel a thing that is done to him."

He glared at her until her skin prickled, then suddenly turned away. "Have you ever done this thing?"

"No. But I have seen the surgery performed. It is not complicated."

The air between them seemed to stretch thin in another long silence. Lord Chesterfield stared at the formal garden beyond the study window, but the bright colors of the late autumn flowers did not soften his mien.

"Did Miss Browne mention that her father is a surgeon?" he asked.

"Yes."

"Perhaps we should ask his opinion."

"Dr. Browne lives outside of Darwood, more than two hours from here, and the rain is still steady. If this procedure is to succeed, it must be done now."

Ellen had never seen a man look quite so agonizingly torn. His hands curled into fists, as if he wanted to hit something.

"Do you have the instruments you need to do this?"

"No," she confessed. "But in an establishment of this size, I'm sure we can find enough to make do."

He turned. His eyes found hers and held them. Glittering metallic gray, sharp as a knife's edge, they seemed to cut past her shell of precarious confidence and dissect her soul to examine her true worth. His gaze was so intense, it hurt, yet Ellen could not look away.

"All right, Dr. O'Connell. Do it."

Three hours later, Ellen and Jane collapsed on the bed in the room that had been assigned for Ellen's use.

"It's over." Ellen sighed. "I didn't think it would ever be over. I thought we were going to be in that room, bending over that poor man until our backs broke."

Jane took in her friend's pallor, the shadows that made her usually bright green eyes seem to disappear into her skull. Jane was tired, but she knew that Ellen was exhausted. They were both spattered with blood and aching in each and every muscle, but Ellen had borne the burden of responsibility, and therefore most of the tension. Ellen had been the one who could not afford to straighten and stretch to relieve cramped muscles. She had scarcely blinked her eyes, so intensely had she concentrated on her vital task.

Jane was so proud of her friend that she couldn't find words strong enough to express her sentiment.

"You were absolutely wonderful," she told Ellen. "I

can't wait to write my father about what you did. He'll be so proud that he knows you."

Ellen opened her eyes wearily. "Pray God my patient is as pleased with the results."

"Surely he will be fine now."

"Yes, surely." Ellen's tone didn't convey the confidence her words implied. "And if he isn't, Lord Chesterfield will no doubt hang us both up by our thumbs. I thought he was going to have a fit when I banned him from the bedchamber during the surgery. If his brows had dropped any lower he would have tripped over them."

Jane laughed at the image, then choked in horror at her own temerity, not to mention Ellen's. Jordan Chesterfield was, after all, a member of the nobility. He wasn't someone to be laughed at. "You should show more respect," she chided Ellen.

"Oh bother! You'd think having a title made the man into something better than the rest of us. He's ill-tempered and stuffy, and he puts on insufferable airs. I'll laugh at him if I see fit."

"Really, Ellen. It's customary for commoners to tiptoe around the sensibilities of the upper classes. They expect it, you know."

"He can expect it all he likes. One of the things my pa always told me was that a man has to earn respect, and an O'Connell doesn't knuckle under to someone just because he has money and a big house or a fine line of talk."

Jane shook her head. Ellen was smart and sensible, with a generous heart and compassionate spirit—a true jewel of a friend. But sometimes Americans were very difficult to understand. They had so little sense of social order.

Ellen struggled tiredly off the bed and started to remove her bloody apron and dress. "I'll just change and go back to sit with George. I have no confidence at all in the young chambermaid who is watching him. She looked much more capable of dusting furniture than recognizing the signs of postsurgical distress."

"Lord Chesterfield is there."

"I'm sure he knows less than the maid."

Jane helped Ellen get out of her clothes, then pushed her friend back onto the bed. It didn't require much effort. She could have done it with one finger. "I'll sit with the young man. You're much too tired."

"You're tired, too."

"Not as tired as you are. After all, you did all the work and most of the worrying. Look at yourself in the mirror. I can see right through your skin to the bones. I vow, if you looked any closer to death, we'd have to bury you. You will not do young Mr. Chesterfield any good if you drop dead from overtaxing yourself."

Ellen made a rude noise. "I've been more tired than this and survived. Back in—"

Jane interrupted with a laugh. "I know, dear. Back in wild Montana you and your sister used to ride the range all day and do chores all night. That's when you weren't dragging silver ore out of some mountainside, punching cattle—or whatever one does in Montana to make the poor cows behave—or fleeing some posse with that wild father of yours."

Ellen gave her a crooked smile. "I may have exaggerated just a bit."

"Really?" Jane asked in mock astonishment.

Ellen rolled onto her stomach and buried her face in her hands. "How do you have enough energy left to laugh?"

"I'm fine, you see? You wash up and go to sleep. It's not good for you to get so tired. If it weren't so late I'd ring the kitchen and have them bring you up a tray."

Ellen groaned. "The patient is my responsibility."

"I promise I'll call you if he as much as quivers an eyelash. Truly I will. Don't worry so. I've done this for Papa many times. I'll monitor his pulse, check his color and breathing, listen to his heart, keep track of his temperature."

"Thank you, Jane. There's no better friend in the world than you."

Jane changed into a clean dress, washed her hands and face, and spread a quilt over Ellen. She was already asleep, her hands still soiled with her patient's blood, her tightly shut eyes bruised with weariness. Jane took a moment to indulge in good-natured envy of Ellen's exotic half-Irish, half-American Indian looks. Her beauty was strong enough to shine through fatigue, just as Ellen was strong enough to weather her unfortunate situation—Jane hoped. It was a shame that the world was so cruel to someone so innocent and trusting.

Lord Chesterfield nodded to her when Jane silently slipped into the patient's chamber. Sitting beside his brother's bed, the baron did not look surly or sour tempered as Ellen had accused; he merely seemed worried. The chambermaid was gone.

"I will sit with him, sir, if you would like to rest. I don't think he'll wake for a while yet."

His lordship's eyes didn't leave his brother's face, which was almost as pale as the snowy bandages that swathed his head.

"I'll call you if there's any change. Really, Lord Chesterfield, I think he'll be fine. Dr. O'Connell was very highly thought of in Paris."

"Was she indeed?"

"Yes, sir. My father says she has a special healing touch that can't be learned. One must be born with it."

"I can only hope that your father is right, Miss Browne."

With a weary sigh, he squeezed his eyes shut and pinched the bridge of his nose. "I suppose sitting here brooding does little good. I should talk to Lady Chesterfield and reassure her. Call me if he so much as moves."

"Yes, sir."

Jane breathed easier when the door shut behind the baron. The man seemed larger than life, somehow, and made her feel stammery and stupid when he looked her way. She'd never seen gray eyes that were quite so piercing, nor observed a manner so—not arrogant, really—but more than merely confident. All in all, the baron was a fine-looking specimen of English nobility. Perhaps that was the reason that Ellen spoke of him with such determined disdain. Ellen was not in charity with fine-looking men right then, thanks to Henri Chretiens.

Lord Chesterfield, however, was in a completely different class from Henri, in Jane's opinion. Superiority was bred into the man. It was obvious. The Chesterfields were well-known in Staffordshire. They were one of the great families, not terribly high in rank, as nobility went, but of such an ancient and honorable lineage that even an earl or duke would hesitate to snub them.

Jane's family did not mix with such highly ranked personages. In England, surgeons were more respected than they once were. A few decades earlier they had been considered little more than glorified barbers. Gentlemen physicians never indulged in such unseemly and plebian work as cutting and stitching and bloodying their hands as a surgeon did. Medicine was becoming more of a science and less of an art, though, and the boundaries between physicians and surgeons were blurring. Yet a surgeon was still considered a mere tradesman, and he and his family were not acceptable in gentle society.

The nobility and gentry were people who moved through a sphere as far removed from Jane's world as the land of fairy tales. They were beautiful, rich, and powerful, and the rules in dealing with them were every bit as cast in stone as the rituals of High Church. Jane had never considered that the upper classes might endure pain, loss, and worry just as ordinary people did. Logic dictated that they must, of course, but such a thing had made no true impression upon her mind until she walked into George Chesterfield's bedchamber, had seen such a perfect young man in danger of losing his life to a senseless, stupid accident, and had cringed before the pain and anger radiating from the very imposing baron.

For all their wealth, influence, and pedigree, the Chesterfields were as vulnerable to malicious Fate as anyone else. Jane could spare only a bit of sympathy for Lord Chesterfield, for he seemed strong enough to take Fate by the throat and shake until events fell out more to his liking, but for George—the beautiful young man lying so pale and helpless on the bed, her heart ached.

A younger, softer, gentler version of his handsome brother, George Chesterfield seemed infinitely vulnerable, like some fairy-tale prince banished to the netherworld of dark dreams until he should be saved by a pure and loving maiden. Jane had to smile at her flight of fancy. She was known by family and friends alike to be a sensible girl who had both feet planted firmly on solid earth. The rarified social atmosphere that surrounded the Chesterfields must be making her giddy.

Still smiling, she sat down in the chair beside the bed

and took the young man's limp hand in hers—just in case he should wake up frightened and need someone nearby to comfort him.

Very early the next morning, when Ellen saw how the color had returned to her patient's face and felt his strong steady pulse beneath her fingers, whatever fatigue that remained after her few hours of fretful sleep washed away in a flood of relief. Shortly after she entered the room, George finally woke. Jane was bending over the bed straightening the covers when his eyes opened. At first they merely slitted, as if he were uncertain about wanting to wake, then they came to rest on Jane's face and opened wide.

"I've died and gone to heaven," he whispered reverently. "Who would have thought I'd get there."

Jane actually blushed. Ellen couldn't remember ever before having seen her friend blush.

"You're certainly not dead, sir," Jane informed him. "And while Endsfield Park is very nice, I don't think I'd call it heaven."

George tried to sit up. Jane firmly pushed him back down. He didn't resist very strongly.

"Right," he said, giving her a smile that was more of a grimace. "If this were heaven, it would be vastly disappointing, for I have the devil's own headache." His gaze traveled appreciatively over the parts of her he could see without moving his head. "Whoever you are, however, you would certainly qualify as an angel."

His eyes twinkled as he sent Jane a smile of boyish charm calculated down to the last appealing curl of his mouth and flash of white teeth. It was quite a feat, Ellen conceded, considering the fellow had a goose egg on the back of his head, a hole just behind his left temple, and had spent the last day hovering between life and death. Poor Jane looked as though she didn't know whether to laugh or simper. Ellen decided the time had come to step in.

"Welcome back, Mr. Chesterfield."

He turned his head, then grimaced as he paid the price in pain. "I . . . uh . . ."

"I'm Dr. O'Connell. And this is my good friend Miss Browne, who's been helping me care for you."

"Uh . . . you're a doctor?" George asked incredulously.

"Yes. I'm afraid you had a nasty accident while you were hunting with your friends. I'm sure you're quite uncomfortable right now, but you shouldn't worry. There's been no permanent damage, and in a week or ten days you'll be quite all right."

"You . . . you're a doctor?" he asked again. He seemed to find that the most alarming part of the situation.

Ellen was accustomed to such a reaction. "Jane, would you please find Lord Chesterfield and tell him that his brother is awake?"

"No need," Lord Chesterfield announced from the doorway. "I can see for myself."

Ellen jumped at the unexpected sound of the baron's voice. She turned as he strode into the room. With the haggard anxiety gone from his face and a new strength in the set of those broad shoulders, he was enough to give any susceptible miss pause. Not that Ellen was at all susceptible. Nevertheless, she was suddenly conscious that the clean dress she had put on when she woke was both drab and wrinkled, and her hair had received only the most cursory attention from her comb.

"I say, Jordan! This is real, then? I'd begun to think I

was dreaming." George gave Jane an impish smile. "It's not every man who wakes up to find two such dazzling women hovering over his bed."

Lord Chesterfield sent his brother a quelling look. "You were lucky to wake up at all, you idiot."

"Really! What happened? I don't remember a thing past walking out with Tindale and Farley to get some grouse."

"You and your friends were doing more weaving than walking. I gather you dashed off to do something or other—no one was quite sure—and allowed yourself to get in front of the party. Tindale mistook you for a bird and filled you full of shot."

"Be damned! Did he?"

"You fell and hit your head on a rock."

"So that's what hurts so much. Good thing the old noggin's hard as stone, or it would have cracked like an eggshell."

"I'm not sure it didn't," the baron said darkly. "If you want the gory details, you'll have to ask Dr. O'Connell."

Ellen smiled. She couldn't help but notice that his lordship was not quite so reluctant this morning to apply the title Dr. to her name.

"You're going to be fine, Mr. Chesterfield. You had a very serious concussion, and your head is going to feel as though someone's pounding it with a sledgehammer for a few days, but that will ease up soon."

"You're certainly an improvement over old Martin." George gave her the same breezy once-over he'd given Jane. "Prettier by far."

Unlike Jane, Ellen didn't blush. Though no older than her friend, she was long past such tender sensibilities.

"Martin will be here soon," the baron assured his brother. "I sent for him, but something's held him up."

George grinned at Ellen. "Fate is kind."

Ellen refused to surrender to the smile that pulled at her lips. "Mr. Chesterfield, you should rest now. In a few hours, we'll see if you can hold down some broth. I'll sit here with you while Miss Browne gets some sleep."

Jane opened her mouth to protest, but Ellen wouldn't allow it. "Jane, dear, you were in here all night so I could sleep. Go to bed, or I will have you as a patient as well."

Ellen didn't miss the quick, wistful look Jane gave George as she left. If Lord Chesterfield hadn't been in the room, she would have been tempted to lecture her fresh patient about keeping his flirtatious smiles away from her friend. She contented herself with giving him a disapproving look while she rechecked his pulse and felt for fever. When she was through, Lord Chesterfield took her arm and drew her away from the bed. His long fingers nearly circled her slender upper arm as he subjected her to his frank inspection.

Ellen scowled, annoyed at the jolt his touch once again gave her senses. Of all the women in the world, she should be immune to such silliness.

"You're still exhausted," he concluded. "You should rest as well. I'll stay with George."

"He shouldn't be left alone," Ellen cautioned. "Not even for a moment."

"I'll see to it. If I'm not here, then someone else reliable will be."

"And you'll call me immediately if there's a change?"

"Yes."

Ellen started to move away, but he held her, gently but firmly. He frowned down his straight, aristocratic nose at her, and she wondered what she had done to set him off. "You'll stay at Endsfield until Dr. Martin arrives, Miss O'Connell?"

"Of course I will. I don't need to be in London until Friday morning. Surely your physician will have come and the storm abated by then."

"I would certainly hope so. If you wish, I'll send you and Miss Browne to the railway station in my carriage as soon as Dr. Martin arrives, even if the storm still blows. Jamison is an excellent coachman, and he'll ensure you get there."

"Thank you." Once again she tried to draw away. Once again he held her fast. His brows collided in a thundercloud that cast his deep-set eyes into glowering shadow.

"Lord Chesterfield?"

He cleared his throat, then said firmly, "It seems I owe you an apology, Dr. O'Connell."

She lifted her brows slightly, trying not to smile. His Most Arrogant Lordship apparently found it difficult to choke down the crow he should rightfully eat, and she wasn't about to make the task any easier.

He took a deep, steadying breath. "It occurs to me that I was most rude in my cynicism."

"Were you?" she asked guilelessly.

"I should not have called you a madwoman."

"Indeed."

"I should not have cast aspersions upon your professional dignity, just because you're a woman."

She couldn't keep back the smile. "You don't say?"

"And I thank God most sincerely that you were right and I was wrong. I and my entire family are considerably in your debt for saving my brother."

In Montana, the only apology Ellen would have gotten

would have been a breezy "Way to go, Ellen," or a slap on the back that would have come close to knocking her over. In this one thing, she decided she preferred English verbosity to Montana directness. The English style of apology required more squirming, and Ellen thought she was entitled to a fair amount of that from Lord Chesterfield.

"I'm accustomed to muleheadedness in men regarding my profession," she told him. "Don't give it another thought."

His hackles rose with indignation. Probably no one else had ever had the temerity to call him mule-headed—to his face, at least. Whatever biting retort sprang to his lips, however, he held it back and gave her a tight smile instead. "I'm sure you are well acquainted with . . . 'muleheadedness,' Dr. O'Connell."

Ellen had to give the man credit. Lord Chesterfield might be a starched, disdainful, overbearing jackass, but he had the guts to say he was wrong—and to say he was wrong to a woman. In Ellen's experience, a man would rather pull out his own fingernails than humble himself in front of a female. After the nightmare of the day before, this day was starting on a much higher note.

The high note didn't last long, however. With George in the care of his brother and Jane getting some much needed sleep, Ellen decided to seek out the kitchen. The basket lunch that the Brownes' housekeeper had sent with them in the coach had been the last thing Ellen had eaten. Now that her patient's situation had eased, her stomach was growling in protest of its fast. Ellen was not familiar with the schedule kept in noble households, but at this early hour, surely someone would be in the kitchen preparing breakfast. At the thought of sizzling sausage and poached eggs, her mouth watered. Even a heap of kidneys—an English dish she usually found completely unappealing—would have tasted good right then.

The problem was that the kitchen was nowhere to be found. Such an important part of a household shouldn't be hidden away where even a bloodhound couldn't find it, Ellen reflected irritably. She found the dining room, the library, and three rooms that could have been designated as parlors. She found a gallery that might have been a room lifted from an art museum. The walls were hung with portrait after portrait of unsmiling, stern-looking Chesterfield ancestors. Having one's portrait painted must be a deadly serious business, Ellen mused. Not one of the august lords and pristine ladies looked as though they had ever cracked a smile or laughed at a joke.

This tour was very entertaining, but it wasn't getting Ellen fed. Exasperated, she tried to backtrack to George's room and got thoroughly lost. Since she was a small girl, Ellen had known how to find her way through the wildest reaches of Montana, but she couldn't find her way in this silly, useless maze the Chesterfields called a house! There was no one around to direct her, even though the dawn had expanded into full morning. Not only did they build houses that were senseless and confusing, these people apparently lazed in bed until all hours of the day.

Finally Ellen found someone in what appeared to be a family salon. A cozy fire was crackling in the fireplace, and in front of it, in an oversized wing-backed chair, sat a young woman reading a book. She looked up when Ellen cleared her throat.

"Yes?" the woman inquired with slightly raised brows.

"Excuse me, but I appear to be lost," Ellen said. "Could you direct me to the kitchen?"

The woman's eyes conducted an icy survey of Ellen from head to toe. From the expression on her face, she found much lacking.

"You're lost," she commented, sounding as if Ellen had confessed to a dreadful sin. "How long have you been here?"

"Only since last night."

"Well, I'd think you would have learned where the kitchen is, at least."

"I've been a bit busy," Ellen said tartly. "Just direct me to the kitchen, will you?"

"Really! You've quite a bit of lip, haven't you?"

The woman was going to have quite a bit of lip herself—a fat lip—if she didn't show some manners. Ellen had taken just about all she could take on an empty stomach. "The kitchen, please?" she prompted crossly.

The woman sniffed and gestured with a disdainful wave of her hand. "Go to the morning room and take the stairs down to the basement."

"The basement?"

"Yes, of course. The basement."

"Thank you," Ellen said with exaggerated courtesy. A kitchen hidden away in the basement. She would never understand these people.

The kitchen, when Ellen found it, made up for the lack of activity in the rest of the house. Three cooks bustled here and there, and twice that many maids, plus a young errand boy who seemed more a pest than a help. Baking bread filled the air with its warm aroma. Pies were already in the making. A bucket full of eggs sat on a worktable. The infamous kidneys were being cleaned in the sink, and a slab of bacon was being sliced by a maid. All in all, Ellen thought, a very hopeful picture.

"Hello," she said.

One and all they looked up from their work. A maid gaped. The cooks scowled. Only the young errand boy smiled.

"I wonder if I might bother you for a bit of breakfast. I could fix it myself."

"I beg your pardon, miss?" a plump, gray-haired woman asked. She had a rolling pin in one hand and a smudge of flour on her chin. The homey little smudge didn't do a thing to soften her expression.

"Uh . . . I could fix it myself. You don't need to take the trouble. I'd try not to get in the way."

"Breakfast is at ten," said the girl who was slicing the bacon. "It ain't yet eight."

"I know, but you see, I missed dinner . . . uh . . . maybe if I could just boil an egg?"

"I'll bring some coddled eggs and shortbread up to the dining room, if it please you, miss." The cook wiped the flour from her chin and fixed Ellen with a polite but chilly stare.

"Please don't take the trouble. I'll just fix something for myself and eat it here."

"Here?" a maid asked in an astounded whisper.

What was wrong with these people, anyway? Ellen wondered.

The housekeeper put an end to everyone's confusion and consternation by sweeping into the kitchen like an English ship-of-the-line under full steam. "What is this?" she demanded. "Here now, miss? What can we do for you?"

"Something to eat?" Ellen answered hopefully. This

eminently reasonable request was seeming more and more impossible.

"Certainly. I'll see that a tray is sent up to your room."

"But—"

"Run along now, miss. Cook is very particular about her domain being intruded upon, I'm afraid. I'll see that a tray is sent up directly."

"Yes." She sighed. "Of course." Ellen was not at all sure she could find her room.

The housekeeper seemed to sense her problem. "I'll just see you on your way. All of you back to work, now." She raised an imperious hand at the kitchen staff. "Lady Chesterfield will have your ears if her eggs and kidneys are late."

Apparently, Lord Chesterfield's wife had no better humor than her husband, Ellen mused as she followed the housekeeper out of the kitchen.

Hours after Ellen had consumed her breakfast and returned to bed for a much needed rest, Jordan, Lord Chesterfield, stood in his mother's sitting room and wondered why men had ever deduced that they, and not women, were the world's masters. He wasn't afraid of his mother. Not really. He did, however, respect her talent for making his life miserable—as she was about to do now. She peered at him from narrowed, glittering eyes. The boudoir chair in which she sat was luxuriously plush, but her back was much too straight to touch the back cushion, her chin too high to allow for any relaxation.

"A woman?" she queried disdainfully.

"A physician," Jordan explained again. His mother seemed to have difficulty with the concept. He'd had a bit of difficulty himself at first, Jordan admitted. What man wouldn't pause at the notion of so feminine a creature having the competence and courage for the thing Ellen O'Connell had done. And Miss O'Connell was feminine. Even rainsoaked, muddy, and disheveled she was feminine—enough to make a man ache in places that he shouldn't ache for a physician.

"A woman physician? How preposterous!" Lady Chesterfield pursed her mouth sourly, then took a sip of her afternoon sherry, as if the sweet wine might make the odd notion more palatable. In the mornings she drank tea, but in the afternoon she allowed herself one glass of sherry for her nerves. After dinner she did not drink at all. Tea kept her awake; wine unsettled her stomach; and milk was for children.

Apparently the sherry didn't do the trick, because she gave Jordan a singularly displeased look. "The creature can't be English!"

"I believe she is American, Mother."

"Indeed," she said, as if that explained it all. "And what is this blather you say about her performing surgery on George? What exactly did she do?"

"I doubt seriously that you want the details."

"Perhaps not, but I do want the details of why you allowed her to touch dear George instead of waiting for Dr. Martin, who has treated the ills of the Chesterfield family for thirty years and more."

"I fear the situation was quite urgent, Mother. We couldn't wait."

"And this person told you this? Really, Jordan. I would have expected you to have more sense. You usually are very sharp about things. No doubt this . . . this charlatan wanted to push herself forward and prove herself at poor George's expense."

"She did prove herself, Mother. And not at George's

expense. He's doing very well. In fact, we can scarcely keep him abed. He had Tindale up in his chamber playing cards a bit earlier. Won a good amount from him, I understand."

Lady Chesterfield sniffed. "Serves that horrible man right for shooting him. If he weren't the duke's son, and if the duke weren't so vital to your political career, I'd throw the fool out."

"Some of the blame must be laid at George's feet," Jordan reminded her. "He was behaving recklessly."

"He's just a boy."

"He's twenty-four. A man. But he's hopelessly spoiled."

"Are you implying that I have pampered him?" She managed to look down her nose at him, even though he was standing and she was sitting. "At least George makes friends among his social peers and condescends to be an agreeable host, which is more than I can say for my eldest, who holds the title and therefore has more social responsibility. I have put myself out to plan an amiable gathering at this house—inviting people who are important to your advancement both personally and politically." She speared Jordan with a daunting look that he knew all too well. "They have been here a week—riding, shooting, fishing, playing cards and charades. And have you kept them company? Not at all!"

"Mother, I have other matters to attend to than amusing myself."

"Poppycock! Your little games with your ships are not as important as being properly convivial within Society."

Jordan sighed. There was no arguing with her, for his mother refused to acknowledge that he was deeply involved with the steamship line in which he was a partner. She had very old-fashioned ideas about the unsuitability of the upper classes engaging in trade. "Common," she called it. True gentlemen did not make money from commercial ventures, and if they did, only as investors. Soiling one's hands with business was simply not acceptable.

Therefore she refused to admit that Jordan's half interest in the Atlantic and Mediterranean Steamship Line was anything more than an investment, despite the fact that it occupied almost all of Jordan's time.

"Well now," Lady Chesterfield continued. "Back to this . . . Person . . . who is supposedly treating our poor George. How long must we endure her being here?"

"She will be here until Dr. Martin arrives."

"Dear Dr. Martin. I do hope that is soon. I really can't abide these so-called modern women. Do you know this O'Connell person was in the kitchen this morning causing all kinds of confusion with the servants? Of all things! She has no decorum at all."

"She's an American, Mother. Americans are known for their lack of decorum."

Milady exhaled in a disdainful humph. "No doubt she's little more than a country midwife—really not suitable company for the rest of the house party. And her friend, Miss Browne—I know of that family. Very common. Her father's a surgeon, but at least he's an honest man, I've heard. Really, Jordan, you can't expect refined women like Hillary and her dear mother to endure such company."

"I think Miss Moorsymthe and her mother are sturdy enough to survive Dr. O'Connell and Miss Browne. While they are here, Mother, I expect them to be treated with courtesy."

Lady Chesterfield huffed indignantly, but on this point

Jordan was firm. "Mother, I insist. We as a family owe Dr. O'Connell an enormous debt, and I don't want a single discourteous look or word to travel her way. Do you understand?"

"Don't talk to me as if I were a child, young man!"

"I'm not talking to you as if you were a child, but as the one-time dragon of London society who still has plenty of fire left in her breath."

"One-time, indeed!" Lady Chesterfield chuckled. "If I didn't have to look after you out here in the country, I'd still be setting them on their heels in London."

Jordan smiled. "Just don't try to set Dr. O'Connell on her heels, Mother. She's a bit of a fire-breather herself."

"Doctor indeed!" Lady Chesterfield scoffed irritably. "Americans!"

Jordan found himself almost hoping that Dr. Martin would be further delayed. He was rather looking forward to seeing the inimitable Miss O'Connell come face to face with the formidable dowager baroness. That should add a bit of spice to his mother's very proper house party.

Chapter 3

Late that afternoon, the storm abated, leaving in its wake freshly washed blue skies and roads that were little better than quagmires. Dr. Martin did not make his appearance that evening, so Ellen sat the evening and night with George, relieving a weary Jane, who had risen midmorning and spent most of the day sitting at the patient's bedside. George had to be watched constantly, not only because of the head injury, but because he had no discipline in following orders. He was ordered to stay in bed, and found a hundred excuses to be up walking around. He was ordered to eat broths and bland bread, and he sent messages to the kitchen for hearty meat pies, cheese, and sweet biscuits.

Ellen had to pry Jane away from her duties when evening came. She couldn't decide if Jane was simply an overconscientious nurse reluctant to surrender her charge or if the twinkle in George's blue eyes and his charmingly impish smile had turned her head, but Ellen was firm.

"There's a dinner tray in your room," Ellen told her.

"Eat and go to sleep. If you don't get some rest, I'll be nursing you all the way across the Atlantic."

That was if they managed to get on the Atlantic in the first place. If they didn't leave first thing the next morning, they would certainly miss their boat.

"I'm really not tired, Ellen. It's you who should be resting."

"Go!" Ellen insisted.

The smile on George's face faltered when Ellen gave him an equally firm look. "Now, Mr. Chesterfield. Let's have a look at those bandages."

Dr. Martin did not come the following morning. Ellen momentarily entertained the thought of leaving anyway. These were modern times, after all, and though Endsfield Park was far from a city, there must be physicians other than the elusive Dr. Martin who could care for George. When she hinted at her thoughts to Lord Chesterfield, however, his skeptical smile told her that he'd suspected all along she had no devotion to her Hippocratic oath, and what could one expect from a woman and an American? That smile got her back up.

"Of course I will stay until your physician can take over," she said stiffly.

Lord Chesterfield gave her a brief bow. "I expected no less of you, Doctor."

Like hell, Ellen thought huffily. Was that glint in his lordship's eye amusement?

Later, Jane reassured her. "I'm sure we can get a refund and buy passage on another ship," she said. "There's no reason to be in a hurry, is there?"

No reason except that Ellen longed for the comforting bosom of her family. But perhaps, after all, she should not be in such a hurry to burden them with the knowledge of what she had done. A delay of a week—even two—was not going to matter.

"I suppose not. But this is an imposition upon you as well."

"Dear Ellen! Think nothing of that!" Jane's eyes positively shone. Her friend was having a better time here, Ellen realized, than she would have visiting Montana, for true to her English heritage, she was fascinated by all the pomp and circumstance of the nobility. Jane had lived all her life looking at the great houses and their wealthy denizens from afar, and now she had the opportunity to see them up close.

"Very well," Ellen conceded with a smile. "But don't let George Chesterfield charm you with that smile of his. I suspect that young man is the very devil."

The Brownes' man Thomas was sent out with several sturdy lads from Endsfield to pull the carriage from the ditch and to convey the news to the Browne family that Jane and Ellen would be guests at Endsfield Park for a few days. Jane insisted upon taking on the majority of the burden of tending George. The young man was resting very comfortably and showing no hint of infection or further epidural bleeding. Ellen had little to do other than be available in case her patient should develop a sudden complication. She slept, walked in the garden, and brooded upon how different the formal designs of shrubs, trees, and flowers were from the wild and natural beauty of her home.

Late in the afternoon, she was arguing with her patient on just what he could and couldn't eat during his recovery when Lady Chesterfield made her first appearance.

"George!" She advanced to the bedside without favoring Ellen or Jane with so much as an acknowledging glance. "I see you are still with us, no thanks to that fool Tindale."

"Mother!" George countered her scowl with an engaging smile. "You're looking lovely, as usual."

"It's how you look that I'm concerned about!" she sniffed, but her manner softened perceptibly under the onslaught of George's smile. "Considering you've been peppered full of holes and cracked your head like an egg, you appear to be amazingly chipper."

"Thanks to an excellent doctor and nurse," George told her. He expanded his smile to include Ellen and Jane. "Mother, allow me to present Dr. O'Connell and Miss Browne."

Lady Chesterfield managed to look down her nose at the younger women despite the fact she was a half head shorter than both of them. Jane promptly curtsied. Ellen merely nodded her head. So this was the ill-tempered Lady Chesterfield with whom the housekeeper threatened the servants—Lord Chesterfield's mother, not his wife. The Lord of Endsfield Park came by his stiff-necked arrogance honestly, Ellen observed. His mother could have demonstrated rigor mortis if she'd held herself any more stiffly. She'd given her eldest son her dark good looks as well as her intimidating manner. The straight, aristocratic nose was his, as were the thick, arched brows and uncompromising chin.

"How do you do?" Lady Chesterfield acknowledged finally.

"Quite well, thank you," Ellen replied evenly. She saw Jane grimace as her friend straightened from her curtsey. No doubt she'd committed a cardinal sin by meeting her ladyship's gaze without so much as flickering an eyelash in deference. "Your son is recovering nicely, ma'am," she continued. "But I hope you can convince him to restrain his energy—and his appetite for rich food—during his recuperation."

"Indeed." Lady Chesterfield's eyes traveled down Ellen's plain brown dress and then back up again to her face. "You are American, are you not, Miss O'Connell?"

Ellen had seen her father evaluate a horse with more warmth. "I am." *And proud to be,* she added silently.

"You have very dark coloring," her ladyship commented with an infinitesimal lift of one brow.

"My mother was of the Blackfoot people."

The brow shot the rest of the way up. "An Indian?"

"Yes, ma'am."

"And I would venture, from your name, that your father is of Irish descent?"

"Yes, he is."

"How unusual." With mouth pressed into a tight line, she shifted her gaze to Jane, who seemed to visibly grow smaller beneath her regard. "Miss Browne, are you a nurse?"

"No, ma'am. I . . . I simply have experience helping my father, who is a surgeon. We live at Rose Briar Cottage outside the village of Darwood."

"I know of your father." Nothing good, her tone said.

The lady's expression softened when she turned back to her son. "Well, George, I hope you have learned your lesson about paying attention to the business at hand when you are out shooting. Miss O'Connell seems to have done a good job by you, and you must do as she says, at least until Dr. Martin answers Jordan's summons. Miss O'Connell, you must come down to dinner at eight."

The sudden, tartly issued invitation took Ellen aback.

"I . . . uh . . . thank you, ma'am, but I should stay with George. I'm sure Miss Browne—"

"Nonsense. Miss Browne can stay with my son. Lord Chesterfield wishes you to be shown every hospitality." Her grimace was so subtle as to almost not be there, but it showed exactly how she felt about the matter. "He is master of this household, and his wishes will be observed. I will see you at eight, Miss O'Connell."

She gave them all a frosty smile and made a regal exit. Ellen exhaled a sharp breath that combined wonder with exasperation. "And that is that!" she said, mimicking the tone of Lady Chesterfield's words.

"Now, Ellen!"

"Oh bother, Jane! The last thing I want to do is spend the evening chit-chatting with the upper crust." She glanced a brief apology at her patient. "No offense intended, Mr. Chesterfield."

"None taken," he said with a grin. "I'll admit that most of us are crashing bores."

"Well, I am excited for you!" Jane insisted. "One of the guests in the house is the duke of Marlowe. He's a confidant of the queen herself! And Mrs. Moorsymthe and her daughter are very well placed in Staffordshire society, and in London, too, I daresay, for Miss Moorsymthe is very beautiful and extremely smart, I'm told."

Ellen rolled her eyes. "Oh do tell!"

"You must go, Ellen, if only so that you can tell me all about it!"

"I don't believe I have a choice, seeing that the mistress of the castle has issued her ultimatum."

It was Jane's turn to roll her eyes. George smiled at both of them. "I say, Doc, but would you mind smuggling me up some of the lemon cakes that'll be served for dessert? I've been smelling them all day long."

* * *

Family and guests met in the drawing room thirty minutes before dinner. A formally dressed footman guided Ellen to the correct salon and left her at the door, where Lord Chesterfield spotted her and rather unexpectedly came to her rescue.

"Good evening, Miss O'Connell. I'm glad you decided to join us."

"Your gracious mother issued a command for my presence in a manner that a general would envy."

"She is known for that talent." He offered his arm. Gingerly, Ellen took it. His black evening habit and superbly tailored trousers with their silk side-braid and sharp front crease made him look more imposing than ever—imposing, urbane, and incredibly handsome. His tailor—and Ellen was sure it was a very exclusive tailor—must delight in fitting such an athletic physique. Were she a woman susceptible to fine masculine looks, Ellen might have attributed her weak knees to girlish giddiness. But after Paris, she would never again be either girlish or giddy, so the sudden weakness was no doubt due to hunger.

As Lord Chesterfield guided her toward Endsfield's glittering guests, Ellen became aware of how drab and frumpy her best clothing must appear. The tailored green skirt with matching jacket was more appropriate for traveling than for wearing at a formal dinner. "I'm sorry I hadn't something more suitable to wear," she said.

"You needn't worry about it." He regarded her with a warmer appreciation than her appearance warranted.

"Lord Chesterfield, you devil! Who do you have here?" A middle-aged lady with faded blond hair and washed-out blue eyes fixed Ellen with a look that belied her playful tone. The only thing about her that was not faded was the glitter of diamonds at her throat, her wrists, and pinned to her bodice.

"Mrs. Moorsymthe, allow me to present Dr. O'Connell, from America. She is the physician who has been treating my brother."

"Doctor?" The woman stared as if Lord Chesterfield had just announced Ellen was from the moon.

Ellen's smile was strained. She was accustomed to people's surprise, shock, skepticism, and rudeness, but her patience was stretching thin.

A younger, much prettier version of Mrs. Moorsmythe joined them. She was the young woman who had so impatiently directed Ellen to the kitchen. Her eyes widened when she recognized Ellen, and a flush rose to stain the perfect milky skin of her cheeks.

"Dr. O'Connell," Lord Chesterfield said, and Ellen was surprised to observe that his smile held a hint of devilment. "This is Miss Moorsmythe. She and her mother are close friends of our family."

Miss Moorsmythe's eyes flashed in brief anger at their host's choice to present her to Ellen rather than presenting Ellen to her, which would imply her own social superiority. Within seconds she had herself under control, however. The glitter in her eyes calmed to a mere feminine brightness, and the embarrassed flush softened to a hint of English rose in her cheeks.

"We've met," she said blandly. "Yesterday, when . . . Doctor is it? Yes. Extraordinary . . . When Dr. O'Connell was having difficulty finding her way to the kitchen. I'm afraid I mistook her for a servant. So sorry." She offered a stiff smile.

"Since you ladies are acquainted, then, I'll leave you to chat."

Skunk! Ellen thought after Lord Chesterfield as he retreated and left her to the Moorsmythe women's mercy. The younger witch's smile signaled that she was ready and eager for battle.

"A woman doctor," Miss Moorsmythe began. "How unusual. And an American as well."

"Indeed," the older version agreed.

"Not so unusual," Ellen replied. "My stepmother is a doctor as well."

"Really?" the Moorsmythe ladies said at the same time.

"How . . . interesting," the mother said.

"Interesting indeed," echoed the daughter.

Ellen felt like a zoo exhibit beneath their scrutiny. They elevated supercilious disapproval to a subtle art form. A slightly lifted brow. A certain curl to the smile. A rime of frost coating polite words. Every intonation and expression artfully withered and deflated.

But Ellen was not so easily cowed. She mentally pictured the ladies trying to do something useful, perhaps pulling a bogged cow out of a mud hole during a messy Montana spring, as Ellen and Katy had often done on their father's ranch. Mrs. Moorsmythe would push on the cow's rear with the tail slapping generous quantities of unmentionable cow by-products in her face. Lovely Miss Moorsmythe would pull on the front end, up to her knees in muck, speckled with foam flying from the animal's mouth. Her smile would not be so superior then.

Ellen smiled tolerantly. "I'm afraid the English medical establishment is a bit behind the times in modernizing their views concerning women. In America women have been allowed to study for medical degrees for decades, and Europe is even more liberal-minded."

Mrs. Moorsmythe sniffed. "In England, women follow the example of our good Queen Victoria, who believes that the sphere of women is in the home."

"Really?" Ellen did a fair job of matching her haughty tone. "And yet Victoria doesn't limit herself to such a confining role."

Miss Moorsmythe countered: "I'd hardly call it confining to guard one's modesty and try to excel at pursuits that are appropriate for a woman."

"Medicine is an entirely appropriate calling for a woman. Women have been the nurturers and healers since the beginning of time."

"Yes, but—"

"Hello!" An excited, childish voice drowned out Miss Moorsmythe's reply. The voice belonged to an impishly smiling sprite who looked up at them with startling blue eyes reminiscent of George's. "Cousin Jordan said Andrea and I may dine with family tonight! He gave old Miss Todestan the evening off."

"Prissy! You know it's rude to interrupt adult conversation, and you promised to behave." A striking young girl not quite yet into womanhood took the child's shoulder and tried to pull her away. She was a slightly older version of the little girl—impish charm growing into true beauty. Tight braids could not hide the luster of her dark hair, nor could the girlish pinafore hide a figure on the brink of maturity. "Please forgive her, ladies. Her manners haven't quite caught up to her mouth."

Ellen smiled, glad for the interruption. "Don't worry about it."

"Miss Todestan is our governess," Prissy told her. "She has a wart on her cheek that looks like an old squashed raisin."

"Prissy!"

Mrs. and Miss Moorsmythe gave the two girls withering looks, and Ellen instinctively leapt to their defense. "Our conversation could use some younger viewpoints. Please join us."

"It seems they already have," Mrs. Moorsmythe said coldly.

Prissy was undeterred. She gave Ellen a huge smile. "I'm Priscilla Chesterfield. I'm ten. My sister's name is Andrea. She's fifteen. We're Jordan's cousins."

"Prissy!" Andrea scolded. "You shouldn't call Lord Chesterfield by his Christian name in public."

"This isn't public. We're in the drawing room."

"That's public. And unless you behave, Aunt Elizabeth will banish us upstairs."

"Jordan won't let her. He likes me."

"Jordan . . . Lord Chesterfield, I mean . . . has to do what she says. She's his mother."

"He doesn't have to do what anybody says! He's a baron and he sits in the House of Lords. So if Jordan lets us stay, we stay."

"I must say!" Mrs. Moorsmythe commented disdainfully. "Lord Chesterfield certainly does let you run wild, young lady! I'd say it was past time you and your sister were sent to school to acquire some polish."

The sparkle in Prissy's eyes faltered. Ellen wanted to tell Mrs. Moorsmythe that her own polish could use some buffing, but instead, she smiled down at Prissy. "When I was your age, my sister and I ran wild all the time. We didn't have a governess or a nursery, and we grew up just fine."

The smile returned to Prissy's face. "Really? Where did you live?"

"Watch out!" Andrea whispered in an urgent, hushed tone. "Here comes Aunt Elizabeth!"

Lady Chesterfield regarded her nieces with pursed mouth. "Are you minding your manners, young ladies?"

Before Mrs. Moorsmythe could complain, as she seemed about to do, Ellen jumped in. "They're delightful."

Her ladyship turned her pursed-mouth regard on Ellen, but her eyes quickly slid away, as if Ellen was not really worthy of her notice. "We are about to go into dinner. Hillary, dear,"—she gave Miss Moorsmythe a brief smile—"you will go in with Jordan, of course. Mrs. Moorsmythe, the earl of Tindale will escort you. Miss O'Connell, if you would please follow along with Andrea and Priscilla." She gave her nieces a stern look. "You young ladies behave yourselves, or you'll be sent upstairs."

The words might have been addressed to Lady Chesterfield's nieces, but her warning glance included all three of them, Ellen suspected. For her part, she would like nothing better than to retire upstairs for a quiet meal in peace and solitude. How these people cut through all this protocol to find their appetites was beyond her understanding. They couldn't simply take time out of their day for good fellowship over a friendly dinner table. No. They had to make a ritual out of everything. First they met in the drawing room to play silly 'who is superior to whom' games, and then they marched into dinner like a regiment going to war, strictly in order of rank. It was really a shame that these people had nothing more important to occupy their lives.

Ellen believed she was hiding her exasperation fairly well, but her expression must have revealed her feelings, for Prissy sent her a conspiratorial smile and rolled her eyes. Ellen laughed softly, earning her a stern look from Lady Chesterfield. Andrea hissed a caution at her younger sister, who responded by sticking out her little pointed tongue the minute their aunt was not watching. As they fell into their assigned place in the dining-room parade, Prissy took Ellen's hand and smiled. Thinking back to her own less than decorous childhood, she returned Prissy's smile full measure.

When she looked up, Jordan Chesterfield was regarding her with measuring gray eyes from his place beside Miss Moorsmythe far up the long dining-room table. His expression was veiled. Only a small upward curl at the corner of his mouth hinted at a smile. Following the direction of his attention, Hillary puckered her perfect brows in a tiny frown and shot Ellen a resentful glance.

Ellen sighed as they all sat. How she longed to be back in Montana.

Two days later, late on a rather dreary morning, Ellen was in George's room with Jane, checking on the dressings on her patient's head wounds—both the one the rock had inflicted and the one she herself had wrought. They were all enduring the company of Wesley, earl of Tindale, who had not yet tumbled to the fact that neither Ellen nor Jane was impressed with his fatuous flirting.

"George, you devil!" the earl teased. "You've landed in a bed of roses, eh? Two beautiful women to tend your every need. You owe me one for this, old boy. If not for me, you'd never have gotten to meet these lovely ladies."

"If not for you," George replied, "I'd have brought home a brace of grouse instead of a lump on my head and a load of buckshot in my . . . in my"—he looked apologetically at Jane, who was unwrapping the bandage from his head—". . . my back."

"Not to mention several other parts," Ellen said with a smile.

Jane blushed. Ellen didn't think she'd ever seen her friend blush before they came to Endsfield Park.

"Well, that's a mess!" Tindale observed of the exposed surgical site.

"It's healing very nicely," Ellen said.

"Of course, dear Ellen, I didn't mean to imply that your skill is less than exemplary. I may call you Ellen, mayn't I?"

"You may call me Dr. O'Connell," Ellen said bluntly.

The reproof gave the earl no pause. "Of course. How very proper of you. Perhaps upon closer acquaintance, we may be more familiar. I must say, it is very novel, such a beautiful woman taking a profession. One can understand, perhaps, that women not having the looks or grace to capture any man's regard might form such ambitions, but a lady with your gifts of femininity and charm must have many gentlemen competing for your attention."

"You're in my light, sir."

"What? Oh. Sorry." Oblivious of Ellen's irritation, Tindale leaned over her shoulder to look at the rapidly healing puncture where she'd drilled a hole in poor George's skull. "How ghastly! It's amazing to me how one could ever develop a stomach for viewing such things."

"Well, then, old man," George said. "Perhaps you'd like to stop viewing it. I'd appreciate it if you'd leave my physician to do her work."

"Don't be so touchy, George. After all, I only put a little harmless buckshot in you. She's the one who decided to ventilate your head."

Ellen was grateful for the interruption when Lord

Chesterfield appeared at the door. "I see you're entertaining quite a crowd," he said to George. "You must be feeling well."

Ellen automatically did a comparison between Tindale and Jordan Chesterfield. She couldn't help but notice, seeing the two titled blue bloods so close together, that the English aristocracy encompassed a great variety of quality, and that quality did not necessarily increase with rank. Lord Chesterfield might often be starched and stiff-necked, not to mention humorless and narrow-minded, but at least he behaved like an adult. He did not preen in public, despite his compelling good looks, and he did not talk merely to hear the sound of his own voice.

George grumbled at his brother. "I'm well enough to get out of this blasted bed—if you can convince my two watchdogs."

"Perhaps Dr. Martin can render an opinion on that," replied Lord Chesterfield. "He's finally arrived. The storm caught him in Stafford and he just now returned."

Ellen's heart gave an uncomfortable lurch. It was unlikely that the family physician would approve of either her or her methods, and she found herself not wanting to endure an embarrassing set-down in front of Lord Chesterfield. She felt like a student again, waiting for an instructor to belittle her work just because she was a female. Certainly not all of them had done that, but enough of them had to make her expect the worst.

"Dr. Martin," Chesterfield said over his shoulder. "Are you coming up?"

"Yes, yes," said a breathless voice. The speaker followed a few moments later, panting and red in the face. He was a grandfatherly looking fellow with thick white hair, dancing eyes, and a pudgy build. "Why does no one put bedrooms on the ground floor, I ask you? Young and old, fit and feeble must trudge up these endless staircases. Not that I'm feeble, mind you, but I'm not as young as I once was."

He paused for breath at the doorway and looked around. "My goodness, young George! I didn't know you were so popular. Hello, Lord Tindale. How is that nasty rash you were suffering last summer, eh? And what lovely ladies. Which one of you is the American physician Lord Chesterfield has been boasting about?"

Jordan Chesterfield had been boasting about her? Unlikely. Ellen hesitantly raised her hand. "I'm . . . uh . . . Dr. O'Connell."

Dr. Martin gave her a sharp-eyed once over. "Ah. I see you're every bit as beautiful as Jordan claims." He smiled. "I hope you're going back to America, my dear. With a lovely young thing like you in the country, no one would call upon me for doctoring, would they?"

Ellen smiled weakly. Was Lord Chesterfield flushed because Dr. Martin had revealed the compliment, or because the courtly physician had put praise in his mouth that he had never uttered?

"Now all of you leave Dr. O'Connell and me to discuss the patient." He made a sweeping motion with his hands as if he would physically whisk them out the door. "You, too, Lord Chesterfield, and don't give me such a dark look, sir. I've known you too long to be intimidated by your growling." He turned to Ellen with a fatherly smile. "He's quite a likable fellow beneath all that bluster. Don't let him fool you into thinking he's not."

Lord Chesterfield shot Dr. Martin a black look as he left. The physician merely chuckled. "Now, let's take a look at your patient, Dr. O'Connell. Come from Irish stock, do you?"

Ellen dragged her attention away from the door that had closed upon Jordan's retreating back. "Uh . . . yes. My father was born in Ireland."

"Good, solid people, the Irish. My grandmother was from Galway. Stubborn as a stone wall, but good-hearted."

Ellen didn't know what to think of the man. He certainly wasn't what she had expected. He peeled off the fresh bandages that Ellen had just wrapped around George's head.

"Jordan told me about the procedure you performed," Dr. Martin said. "Quite incredible, really. Never seen one done, myself, but I've read of it. Let's see here . . ."

He looked closely at the surgical site, the impact size, tested George's reflexes and peered into his eyes. Then he quizzed Ellen on the symptoms she had observed when she had first seen the patient.

"Interesting," he concluded. "Remarkable, I'd say. George is very lucky you happened by. Not everyone would have had the courage to perform the surgery. I'm not sure I would have. The results are certainly impressive. My compliments to you, Dr. O'Connell, and to your teachers. You were studying in Paris?"

"I received my medical diploma from Cornell and then traveled to Paris for clinical study."

"Well, my dear, you've accomplished little short of a miracle here. And all with a sanitized drill from the carpentry shed. Splendid work."

Ellen felt a renewed surge in a spirit that had been sorely beaten down in Paris. "Thank you."

"We won't say anything to the medical authorities about your practicing medicine without being on the British Medical Register. After all, the situation was critical, and you did what had to be done, and did it very well. But those stodgy old men can sometimes split hairs until all reason is abandoned. We English can be very hidebound at times."

"Yes sir. I mean . . . not really . . . uh . . ." She gave up and smiled.

"Let's admit the master of the house, shall we? He was looking a bit testy. It wouldn't do to try his patience overmuch."

Lord Chesterfield remained closeted with Dr. Martin in George's chamber for the better part of an hour, while Ellen sipped tea with Jane in one of the house's many salons. Ellen still couldn't keep all the rooms straight—the drawing room, the sitting rooms, the morning room, and so forth. Jane told her this was a sitting room. From what Ellen could see, it was little different from the drawing room or morning room. They were all grandly furnished, ostentatious, and uncomfortably cold in spite of a legion of fireplaces that must have taxed the local forests to provide fuel.

"My father knows of Dr. Martin," Jane told Ellen. "He's considered very able. Many of the best families use him."

"He seems more like an Irish leprechaun than an English physician."

"Don't let him fool you," Jane warned. "He's known as a great perfectionist."

Right on cue, the great perfectionist walked into the room, followed by Endsfield's master.

"Ladies," Dr. Martin greeted them with a wide smile. "What a great pleasure it has been making your acquaintance. Dr. O'Connell, I wish you every success in practice in America. I've heard that the colonies are in need of competent physicians, so I'm sure you'll be kept busy."

"Thank you, Dr. Martin."

He paid Jane a compliment or two about her father and then left. Jane immediately hurried to resume her duties at George's bedside. George had recovered past the point where he needed constant watching, but neither the patient nor the nurse seemed anxious to relinquish the excuse to spend hours together. Ellen observed the thoughtful frown on Lord Chesterfield's face as Jane practically ran from the room.

Annoyed, Ellen shot from the hip. "I wouldn't worry about Jane sinking her working-class claws into your brother. She is well and truly impressed by the enormous consequence of your family."

He turned his gaze upon her, one brow slightly raised. "Really? How gratifying." His arch look twisted into a wry smile. "You needn't bristle so on behalf of your friend, Dr. O'Connell. I was just thinking what an exceptionally sensible young lady Miss Browne seems to be. I can only hope that some of her moderation and sense influences my brother. And also that my brother does not amuse himself by playing with her affections, for she obviously has formed an attachment of some kind for him."

"Jane Browne deserves nothing but the very best," she said in challenge.

Refusing to pick up the gauntlet, he merely smiled. "Of course. She's an exceptionally fine young woman. You must think us a very ungrateful lot."

"Well, no. That is . . ."

He rang the bell, and when the maid promptly appeared, ordered more tea for Ellen and a pot for himself.

"We're also insufferably stuffy, incredibly stiff, offensively dour, annoyingly ostentatious, and unbearably stodgy."

Ellen wondered if Lord Chesterfield had somehow eavesdropped upon some of her conversations with Jane. She fought back a blush.

His mouth twitched. "Have I about covered it?"

"I . . . I—"

He waved her unspoken apology aside. "I'm afraid that's how we English appear to most outsiders. Still, you have been treated rudely. Lady Chesterfield's ideas of right and proper stopped evolving three decades ago. Our guests have shown you only the barest courtesy, and my own behavior at times has been quite frankly discourteous. I fear none of us is very progressive in attitude."

Ellen made a face. "You have that in common with much of the rest of the world."

"That's true. Given your controversial ambitions, I'm sure you've had ample experience with Society's inertia. Unlike most of the rest of the world, however, I would like to make amends. I know I've put you to considerable inconvenience—you missed your sailing date to New York, did you not?"

"The ship sailed two days ago."

"And you, honorable and conscientious as you are, stayed here to fulfill your promise to tend my brother. I admire honor and dedication in a person, man or woman. Therefore, I have a proposition for you."

"I beg your pardon?" The thought that immediately leapt into Ellen's mind was ridiculous, she knew. Still, harsh experience taught caution. "A proposition?"

"Indeed. A proposition. Isn't that what I said?"

Chapter 4

"**B**ut that's wonderful! How marvelous! Since I met you this summer I've had more adventures than in all the years that went before. Dear Ellen, you're truly a friend like none other."

Ellen indulged in a rather unladylike word. Jane's glowing smile turned into dismay.

"You did accept, did you not?"

"Not exactly."

"But, Ellen!" Jane bit her lip and visibly reined herself in. "Of course. You must be terribly disappointed at such a delay. We've missed our ship already, and I'm sure there will be troublesome argument required to secure a refund and book another passage."

Ellen sighed. "Not so much as you'd think. It turns out that our host owns a significant share of the steamship line I booked passage on. He's assured me a full refund."

Jane brightened. "How decent of him."

"And he's offered to take us as his guests on their

flagship, the *Mary Catherine,* when it sails for New York."

"Splendid! But then why do you look so gloomy, Ellen?"

"The *Mary Catherine* is just now having some sort of new steam turbine installed. It will not sail for three weeks or so. That is why Lord Chesterfield has invited us to remain at Endsfield Park with the rest of his house party."

Jane's enthusiasm bubbled over. "That *is* happy news! One can spend one's entire life in England without so much as receiving a 'good day' from someone as grand as Lord Chesterfield, and here we are invited guests in his home. Not the usual sort of guests, to be sure, but guests all the same."

"I'm overwhelmed," Ellen said sardonically.

"You needn't be such a gloomy goose! I know how you long to be with your family. And I know that your situation puts a dreadful damper on any enjoyment you might glean from this interlude. But think about it positively. There's no harm in spending a few weeks here. You can put aside your concerns for a short time and relax in a world that is quite removed from the one you will soon have to face."

The note of pleading in Jane's voice impressed Ellen with the vehemence of her friend's yearning. Typically, Jane never gave a thought to herself or her own desires.

"Your wish for me to accept Lord Chesterfield's invitation wouldn't have anything to do with a certain young man, would it? One with a wicked smile, bright blue eyes, and a hole in his head?"

Jane had the grace to look guilty. "His smile is not wicked! It's charming."

"My dear friend, you are treading on dangerously thin ice."

"You believe I've formed an attachment for George?" Jane waved the notion aside as if it were the farthest thing from reality. "I'm not so foolish, Ellen dear. George Chesterfield is as far above me as the moon is above the earth."

"I'd say it was the other way around. While you are one of the sweetest, most generous, and genuine souls I know, George Chesterfield is spoiled, self-indulgent, and probably hasn't done a useful thing in his entire life. And his brother the grand pooh-bah baron is little better."

Jane laughed. "Ellen O'Connell! You're a snob! I've suspected it for weeks, but now I know it's true."

"A snob? Me? Don't be ridiculous!"

"Certainly you are! To be worthy of your regard, a person must be serious, hardworking, and ambitious. And preferably, he must be able to climb mountains in a single stride and rope a cow with one hand while digging for gold with the other."

Ellen couldn't help but laugh. "You forgot several requirements, I'm sure."

"Ah yes. One must be orderly, but not regimented. Flexible, but not frivolous. Dignified, but not stiff. Europeans are too lax in their ways. The English are too stiff-necked and conventional." Jane raised a brow, questioning if Ellen recognized herself.

Ellen did. Painfully so. "I'm sorry, Jane. You're right. I'm a snob."

"A very sweet, generous, delightful snob."

"Not to mention gullible, naive, and witless at times."

Jane gave her a sympathetic smile. "We won't explore that right now. Really, Ellen." The teasing left her voice as she led them back to the original subject. "You shouldn't worry about me with George. I know my place in the scheme of things only too well. But perhaps we both deserve to forget reality for a small while and allow ourselves to pretend, just this once. Three weeks is such a short interlude. It will be gone before we know it. At the end we will go to your Montana, where I will see the sights and you will rejoin your family, and then I will come back to England to keep house for my father and sisters. And I will never again be in such society as we are in now."

There was a plea in Jane's words. Ellen wished she could refuse. She longed to ask Lord Chesterfield to deliver them to the railway station, flee to London, and secure passage on the first ship crossing the Atlantic. She didn't want to be a guest at Endsfield Park, where every day she would have to endure the snubs of these titled, wealthy popinjays who thought their pedigrees placed them above the need for manners, compassion, or decency. She didn't want to sit at dinner and watch the perfect Miss Hillary Moorsmythe fawn over the baron. She didn't want to feel her spirits sink even lower under the weight of Lady Chesterfield's contempt. She didn't care to watch the earl of Tindale preen himself or be polite when the duke of Marlowe patronized her as though she was some empty-headed ninny.

Most of all, Ellen did not want to have any further contact with the master of Endsfield Park. The magnetism Lord Chesterfield exuded sucked more good sense from her brain every day, fool that she was. She'd seen his arrogant armor crack under strain and been witness to flashes of compassion, warmth, strength, and courage that made the mighty aristocrat only too human. Human, fascinating, and tantalizing. Her reaction to him was cer-

tain evidence she'd been on these foreign shores too
long. She desperately needed to return to her own world
and yank herself back into line.

Yet Jane had a point. Ellen's longing to leave was a
purely personal desperation. There was no logic or reason to it. Everything Jane had said was true. Besides
which, Ellen owed her friend a mighty debt for lending
emotional support through these last trying weeks. The
English girl could have declared that she wanted no part
of Ellen or her problems. If she had adhered strictly to
Victorian propriety, that was exactly what she should
have done. But Jane had stood by Ellen when she had
desperately needed a friend—even to the point of crossing the Atlantic with her to hold her hand when she
faced her family.

How could she rob Jane of the opportunity to glean
a few pathetic crumbs from the upper crust? Ellen
couldn't understand the fascination with this trivial way
of life, but then, Jane was English and had lived all her
life in the shadow of these autocrats who thought themselves so grand.

She sighed. "All right, Jane. I'll tell Lord Chesterfield
that we'll stay, and we'll take the *Mary Catherine* when
she sails."

The glow of Jane's smile was almost worth the sinking of Ellen's heart.

A full day passed before Ellen realized how boring aristocratic life in the English countryside could be, although an invitation to Endsfield Park during the
hunting season seemed to be considered a social coup,
at least that was what she gathered from overheard conversations among the Park's other guests. The house
party had expanded by several of George's friends—a

young Mr. Henley (few of these people had first names, it seemed to Ellen, and if they did, they very seldom employed them, even among friends) and his sisters Miss Henley (another lack of a first name) and a younger girl, Miss Adele Henley, whose Christian name was available, Ellen deduced, only because she was the younger sister. There was also Lord and Lady Clifton and Sir Nigel Higgenbotham. All the men were enthusiasts of shooting everything with feathers or fur that had the misfortune to live in Endsfield Park's vast expanse of woods, and they spent much of their time in the company of Lord Chesterfield's pointers—though Sir Nigel had brought his own dog along—tramping through the damp brush, shotguns on their shoulders and the thrill of the hunt in their blood. Never mind that their prey scarcely had enough of a sporting chance to make the chase interesting, and that the larder and smokehouse were already well stocked.

Lord Chesterfield, Ellen noticed, did not often accompany his guests into the forests. He showed more enthusiasm for whatever occupied him in his study. The ladies of the party entertained themselves by walking in the gardens, even though the weather was brisk. Arm in arm they strolled, heads together, talking of fashions, friends, family, Society, who was courting whom, who was marrying whom, which London ball was a disappointment and which a success. Literature, art, and music were also acceptable topics. When the weather was absolutely too damp to stroll the garden, they socialized in the music room. Hillary Moorsmythe played the piano with surprising talent and feeling while Mrs. Moorsmythe beamed with pride. Miss Adele Henley sang with a fine voice. And Lady Chesterfield presided over all with condescension and grave dignity. Ellen couldn't help but wonder if the dowager baroness relaxed her deportment even when she was attending to life's basic functions. A rude thought, she admitted to herself, but her medical training had channeled her thinking into rather elemental terms.

Ellen and Jane did not attempt to intrude on the elevated company of Endsfield's other house guests. Jane, for all her talk of mingling with Society, spent much of her time keeping company with George, who still spent most of the day resting in his chamber. Ellen preferred solitary walks in the garden or reading before the fire in the library if the day was too cold.

It was in the garden, exploring an old-fashioned maze of eight-foot-tall hedges, that Ellen once again encountered Lord Chesterfield's cousins. If she had not met them at dinner that one night, she wouldn't have known that children lived at Endsfield Park. Children were important in English upper-class families, Ellen gathered. They were the heirs to titles, the repositories of precious bloodlines, and the future of English tradition. They were not important enough, however, to actively share in the life of the adults. A separate part of the residence was set aside for their use, including bedchambers, a nursery, a playroom, and a schoolroom. Their days were directed by a governess and several tutors. Lady Chesterfield, dutiful and correct in all things, summoned the girls once each day for a short visit, Ellen had been told. The servants seemed to think the children had been lucky to be taken into the household at all after their parents had died in a boating accident.

Therefore Ellen was surprised to see Andrea and Prissy running free as street urchins through the complex paths of the maze. When they spotted her, Prissy waved enthusiastically.

"Are you lost, Miss O'Connell?"

Ellen smiled at the girl's wide-eyed concern. "No. Why would I be lost?"

"The maze has lots of twists and turns."

"But the true path is so well worn that it's easy to find your way."

"It is?"

Andrea interrupted. "Prissy, don't be impertinent. Miss O'Connell probably wants to be alone."

"No," Ellen denied. "That's all right. I was just taking a walk. I'd be glad of your company."

Andrea sighed with the melodrama peculiar to adolescents. Clearly she would be happy to be without her younger sister's company, if the opportunity ever arose.

"I thought you girls did lessons in the afternoons," Ellen said.

"Miss Todestan went to visit her sister who has the influenza," Andrea said.

Prissy grinned puckishly. "Miss Toadstool, you mean." She drew herself up stiffly and pontificated in a fair imitation of Miss Todestan's voice: "Young ladies do not slouch, Miss Priscilla. Young ladies do not run about and dirty their pinafores like young heathens, Miss Priscilla. Young ladies pay attention to their elders and do not speak unless they are spoken to." She broke off with a giggle.

Andrea gave her a withering look. "You're not funny, Prissy."

"You're just kissing up to Miss Toadstool because you think she'll tell Aunt Elizabeth to let you go to the dance."

"I am not. You're just a child. You don't know anything."

"I know more than you, Miss Perfect."

"What dance?" Ellen asked, trying to divert them from the little squabble. They reminded her so much of herself and her sister Katy that she had to smile.

"There's always a ball at Endsfield Park at the start of fox hunting season. Almost everybody in the county comes."

"It's not a *ball*." Prissy rolled her eyes and intoned the world 'ball' to give it the significance of a queen's gala. "It's just a dance. Everybody stands around talking about everybody else while other people prance around pretending they're having fun."

"How would you know? You've never been there."

"I've hidden behind the drapes and watched." Prissy quickly shifted her direct gaze to Ellen. "Do Americans have dances?"

"Oh yes. All kinds. From fancy balls to barn stompers."

"What's a barn stomper?" Andrea asked.

"Everyone cuts loose in somebody's big barn, square dancing, round dancing, and couples, too. There's always lots to eat—a side of beef or barbecued pig. There's straw bales to sit on, and the women makes pies, and some of the boys always drink too much whiskey or beer."

Both girls were looking at her as if she described the far side of the moon. Ellen jerked herself back from her memories and remembered where she was. She shrugged apologetically. "Where I grew up is a bit different from here."

Prissy's eyes were wide. "Cousin Jordan said you were from Montana. Where's that?"

Ellen was surprised that Lord Chesterfield had remembered, that he'd even paid attention when she'd told him. "Montana's in the northwestern United States."

"If you'd been paying attention during geography lesson," Andrea chided Prissy, "you'd know."

Prissy made a face at her older sister, but quickly returned her attention to Ellen. "Are there wild Indians in Montana?"

"A hundred years ago, all the people in Montana were Indians."

"One of George's friends told me that wild Indians scalped his great-great uncle who went to America. And they stuck people on stakes like they were pigs on a spit, and—"

"Prissy!" Andrea scolded.

"Well. It's true!"

"The Indian tribes were at war with the white people," Ellen said. "Whenever people are at war, all sorts of cruelties take place—on both sides."

"See!" Prissy goaded Andrea. "I told you it was true. Have you ever seen an Indian, Miss O'Connell?"

Ellen laughed. "Prissy, my mother was an Indian. She was a very beautiful Blackfoot woman named Many Horses Woman."

Prissy's mouth fell open. Andrea flushed and stammered over an apology.

"Don't worry about it," Ellen told them. "I haven't scalped anyone in weeks, other than shaving some hair off your cousin George's head."

The tension broke as both girls laughed. When their cousin Jordan appeared between the hedges of the maze, Prissy bounced over to him with the news.

"Did you know Miss O'Connell is a wild Indian? Her mama has black feet. But she says she hasn't scalped anyone in a long time."

"I'm glad to hear it," Lord Chesterfield said.

He smiled at his young cousins in a way that softened

his whole manner. If he ever turned that particular smile on a woman—complete with warmly crinkled eyes and a slightly lopsided curve to the lips—the poor female would probably melt into a puddle right where she stood. Ellen felt a bit soft and warm herself just standing in the reflected glow.

Then he looked up and directed the full heat of his regard toward her. The heat was her imagination, Ellen told herself. There was nothing other than a polite sociability in his expression. The slow burn in his eyes was merely warmth leftover from his greeting to Prissy and Andrea. Still, an unwanted response coiled deep inside her.

"Are you three ladies hiding?" he inquired. "I wouldn't have found you except for these two having a fit of giggles."

"Miss O'Connell was telling us about the Wild West," Prissy told him.

"More likely you were badgering her about the Wild West." Lord Chesterfield gently pulled one of Prissy's braids. "Where is Miss Todestan, Sprite?"

"Off visiting her sick sister in Merwyk. Mrs. Hawkins said we should get out of her hair, so we came outside."

"Why are you here, Cousin Jordan?" Andrea asked. "Mrs. Hawkins said you were busy in the study."

"I saw Dr. O'Connell come out into the garden and decided to join her." He cocked one brow at Ellen. "If she doesn't mind."

"Of course she doesn't . . . I mean, of course I don't mind." Ellen gritted her teeth. She was reduced to babbling in the man's presence. If she stayed here much longer, she would start simpering worse than Hillary Moorsmythe.

"In that case, shall we walk a bit?"

Ellen didn't miss the keen looks exchanged by the two sisters as Lord Chesterfield took her arm and escorted them down the maze path.

"This maze was built—or perhaps I should say planted—by the second Baron Chesterfield when Endsfield Park was first built. That was in the seventeenth century."

"The house doesn't seem that old."

"It's been updated, of course." He smiled. "These days one does want to have indoor plumbing. The house burned in 1851 and was completely redone. My grandfather was very fond of cigars. He fell asleep in the study one night with a lit cigar in his hand. He and my grandmother escaped the result of his folly, fortunately, but the house didn't."

"Aunt Elizabeth doesn't allow anyone to smoke cigars in the house," Andrea said from where she and Prissy walked behind them.

"I'm sure I agree with her on that," Ellen replied. "Anything that smells so bad can't be good for your health."

"Yes. Doubtless you're right." He didn't look at her, but kept his gaze straight ahead on the maze path. "I was very glad to learn from Lady Chesterfield that you've accepted our invitation to stay."

"It was generous of you to offer."

"It was the least I could do, considering. Dr. Martin was quite definite in his admiration of your skill and judgment."

"That's very gratifying."

The conversation degenerated into meaningless small talk—something Ellen despised and was not at all good at. Andrea and Prissy were quiet. Ellen sensed their watchfulness.

"Would you like a tour of the grounds?" her host finally asked.

"I wouldn't want to impose on your time."

"Not at all. I have nothing pressing this afternoon."

Ellen thought she heard a smirk from behind them.

Endsfield Park was a huge estate. Even a walk around the various outbuildings, which Lord Chesterfield called "offices," was more exercise than Ellen had taken in a long while. Her softness made her painfully aware of how she had changed since leaving Montana. She used to be almost as strong as the cowboys who worked on her father's Thunder Creek Ranch. Now she labored for breath taking a turn around an English country estate. Appalling.

The tour was interesting, however. Lord Chesterfield was not one of those aristocratic landholders who spent his time seeking pleasure in the city while his stewards ran his estates. He knew every nook and cranny of Endsfield and the name of every person they saw. Ellen almost expected him to know the name of the cows in the dairy. She was surprised at how self-sufficient the estate was—doubtless a holdover from a time when survival was more precarious. The dairy, the brewery, the smokehouse, the washhouse—all were hives of industriousness, far from being quaint holdovers from an earlier age. The stables were grand. Spotless and huge, they were home to horses that would have turned her father green with envy. Ellen knew many people who lived in quarters less clean and spacious. Andrea and Prissy both proudly introduced her to their horses. Andrea had a sweet-looking chestnut mare that was as much a stunner as the girl herself. Prissy's steed was a pony named Sir Socks. Next year, she announced to Ellen, Cousin Jordan had promised her a real horse. She was really too grown up to be riding a pony.

"I'm sure Sir Socks will miss you," Ellen said.

"Oh no. I'll still come see him every day and bring him a carrot." The girl kissed the pony on his velvety nose. "He's my friend."

The last stop on their tour was the kennel. Like the stable, it was spotless. Pointers, beagles, and foxhounds lived in the canine luxury of indoor/outdoor runs that furnished plenty of room for exercise. The kennel master, a Mr. Tarahill, was a lanky fellow who bore an uncanny resemblance to the hounds he tended.

"Lord Chesterfield 'as some of the finest huntin' dogs in the country," he told Ellen when they were introduced.

"Take her to see Maisy!" Prissy demanded. "Maisy's going to have puppies!"

Maisy was a lovely pointer with sweet eyes and a tongue-lolling smile, and very obviously about to be a proud mother. She came out of her kennel run for the introductions and gravely offered her paw when Ellen knelt down to pet her.

"She's beautiful," Ellen said, "and so sweet. Look at those eyes. They hold a wealth of intelligence."

"She's the best pointer I've ever had," Lord Chesterfield said. He knelt down beside Ellen, and a delighted Maisy launched herself at him, tail wagging, tongue flapping the air as she attempted to reach his face. He permitted a couple of wet kisses, then gave her a soft command. Instantly the dog sat, a model of canine decorum.

Lord Chesterfield, the stiffly proper autocrat, grinned like a boy. "Usually Maisy lives in the house, but with so many guests, she's better off down here where Tarahill can keep an eye on her. It won't be long before she delivers."

"And I get a puppy," Prissy claimed.

"We get a puppy," Andrea corrected.

"Only if you promise to train it to mind its manners," their cousin reminded them.

Ellen watched the foursome—Jordan Chesterfield, his two young cousins, and the pointer, and could scarcely believe this man was the same one who'd greeted her so tersely the day she arrived. The reticent, self-possessed, arrogant aristocrat with the warmth of a stone wall, once away from his grand house and his mother's haughty guests, rolled up his sleeves and melted down into someone quite human. He cut her a sideways glance, almost appearing embarrassed. "I fear we don't stand much on ceremony out here in the kennel."

Ellen would be willing to bet that Lady Chesterfield scarcely knew the kennel existed, or that her son the baron was happier sitting on a concrete floor with a dog and two children than in her drawing room full of blue bloods. She'd wager that Miss Hillary Moorsmythe didn't know either, and what's more, didn't care.

"Maisy's a lovely dog," Ellen told him.

"She'll no doubt deliver while you're here. I'll let you know, so you can come out and admire the puppies."

"I'd like that."

When they stepped from the kennel building, Ellen discovered that one of her suppositions was wrong. Hillary Moorsmythe did know the kennel existed, for she was waiting for them just outside the door. Actually, she wasn't exactly waiting for them. She tried to make it appear that she was out for a stroll and just happened along at the precise time they exited the kennels. Ellen wasn't fooled, however. She saw the predatory gleam in those crystalline blue eyes.

"Jordan! Shame on you, subjecting Miss O'Connell to your smelly old kennels."

Ellen saw Prissy's eyes roll toward heaven.

"Jordan and his dogs! Isn't that a man for you?" Hillary twinkled up at him engagingly. "You're not going to get out of tea this afternoon. Lord Clifton, Sir Nigel, and Henley are back from shooting, and they'll feel neglected if you don't listen to their stories of derring-do. And the duke is huffing and puffing about some message he received from London. One would think you men could put aside running the world for just a few odd days here and there to enjoy life, wouldn't you? I do hope you don't become so dull when you are secretary of something or other, Jordan."

The possessive note in Hillary's words set Ellen's teeth on edge, but she had no reason to be jealous. After all, Jordan Chesterfield was nothing to her. Less than nothing. He could let this witless female dither over him all he wanted.

"I suppose we must go up to tea," Lord Chesterfield consented. "Dr. O'Connell—"

He reached out to take Ellen's arm, but his hand was intercepted by Hillary, who appropriated it for herself.

"I think I'll stay with the girls, if you don't mind," Ellen said, drawing away. "Would you show me around a bit more, Andrea and Prissy?"

"We'd be glad to," Andrea answered with grown-up dignity. "You haven't seen the carriage house yet."

"Well, of course, tea would be dull for you, Miss O'Connell," Hillary acknowledged with a feline smile. "Pursuing such a demanding profession as yours must make one lose interest in more feminine social pursuits.

By all means, you and the children continue amusing yourselves. Come with me now, Jordan. Lady Chesterfield is waiting for us, I'm sure." She almost dragged her prey toward the house. Glancing back over his shoulder toward Ellen and the girls, Jordan gave them a wry smile along with a shrug of inevitability. Ellen had to squeeze hard on Prissy's shoulder to keep the little imp from laughing.

"What do you think?" Prissy asked Andrea.

They were in the children's playroom, which had been converted from Endsfield's unused nursery when Andrea and Prissy had arrived two years before. Mrs. Hawkins had brought their dinner to them and left them on their own to dine, a rare luxury. Usually Miss Todestan watched their table manners and deportment like a hawk, but on this evening their governess was still tending her sister in Merwyk.

"What do I think about what?" Andrea asked around a bite of potatoes.

"Miss O'Connell, silly."

"She's nice."

"I think she's pretty, even if her mama was a wild Indian."

"Indians aren't wild anymore, Prissy. I'm sure Miss O'Connell doesn't go about shooting arrows and taking scalps."

"I know. I'm not that dumb."

Andrea regarded her sister thoughtfully. Her cupid's bow mouth pulled upward in a slant of mischief. "I think Cousin Jordan is smitten with Miss O'Connell."

Prissy's eyes sparkled in delight. "Smitten?"

"Definitely smitten."

Prissy conceded that her sister should know. After all,

Andrea was fifteen—almost grown-up, and grown-ups knew about such things as being smitten. "I thought he was going to marry Miss Moorsmythe." Prissy grimaced. "Miss Bore-smythe. Yuk."

"That's what Miss Moorsmythe thinks." Andrea gave her sister a conspiratorial smile. "Perhaps if Cousin Jordan pays a lot of attention to Miss O'Connell, Miss Moorsmythe would get huffy and show Jordan what a witch she really is."

"Right!" Prissy bounced in her chair, something that definitely would not have been condoned by the governess. "Then Cousin Jordan wouldn't marry her."

"And we wouldn't have to worry about being sent away to school."

"Do you think Jordan would really let Miss Boresmythe send us away?"

"Mama once told me that men always do what their wives want when they're first married. It's not until later they get cranky."

"By then it would be too late."

"Jordan would have forgotten us by then. We're only poor cousins, after all."

Prissy's exuberance faltered. "We'd end up in some school that would feed us bread and water every time we blinked."

Andrea nodded emphatically. "Let's make a secret pact. We'll do everything we can to make Cousin Jordan become smitten with Miss O'Connell. And we'll make sure witch Hillary knows about it."

The sisters joined hands over the table. "Done!" they both vowed.

"What do you think?" Miss Moorsmythe demanded of her mother.

Hillary had come to her mother's chamber ostensibly to borrow a string of pearls that looked exactly right with her dinner dress, but more importantly to solicit Mrs. Moorsmythe's opinion on her current quandry.

"I think the woman is common and unattractively pushy. A doctor indeed! Unfeminine is what it is. Most unsuitable to be keeping company in this house. I suppose, under the circumstances, Lord Chesterfield had little choice but to let her stay, her and that friend of hers. But that doesn't mean we must associate with them."

"Well, the woman may be common, but Jordan is paying an uncommon amount of attention to her. I saw them strolling around the grounds this afternoon with those two little cousins of his trailing behind. I went to fetch him for tea, and I vow they were so engrossed in each other that he scarcely saw me." Hillary fastened her mother's pearls around her throat and regarded herself in the mirror. She was everything a proper young woman should be. Silky blond hair, rosy cheeks, a figure that showed to great advantage in her sapphire-blue princess-style evening gown with its enormous puffed sleeves of white net lace over dark blue satin. How Jordan Chesterfield could even look at that common black-haired American was beyond understanding, especially when everyone expected an announcement of their engagement before they returned to London.

Mrs. Moorsmythe came up behind her daughter and looked in the mirror at the perfect reflection of a proper English rose. She patted Hillary's arm. "Don't fret, my love. That woman is nothing. Men are easily diverted by such an exotic piece of trash, but when it comes to permanence, they stick to their own kind. You must not lower yourself to show jealousy. That will only make such a divertissement seem more attractive to him. Men are very perverse that way."

"If he embarrasses me," Hillary vowed, "I'll make him regret it."

"Not until after you're married. Then you can make him regret it all you wish," Mrs. Moorsymthe teased.

Hillary exhaled in a puff of frustration. "Men!"

"What do you think, my dear?" Lady Chesterfield queried Ellen. "Do they not look lovely together?"

Dinner was over. Guests and hosts were gathered in one of the salons to entertain themselves and each other. For Ellen, the evening had not been going well. Jane had deserted her once again to play cards with George, who was resting in his chamber. Mr. Henley and Miss Adele Henley were also with George, so even Lady Chesterfield could not complain of impropriety. Lord Chesterfield had overheard Ellen tell the earl of Tindale that she enjoyed chess and had immediately challenged her to a game. He had beaten but not trounced her. Ellen counted it as a victory that she'd at least put up a decent defense—and he'd not patronized her by letting her win. They had been setting up the board for a second game, one in which Ellen had vowed not to let Chesterfield's disconcerting gray gaze distract her into making stupid moves, when Hillary Moorsmythe had spirited the baron away for a game of cards.

Lady Chesterfield had immediately descended upon Ellen, like an eagle upon a helpless mouse, and plied her with a false and frosty smile.

"Does who look lovely?" Ellen asked as the grand lady condescended to take the chair beside her.

"Lord Chesterfield and Miss Moorsmythe, my dear."

Hillary had dragged Lord Chesterfield to the card

table to make a foursome in bridge with Tindale and the older Miss Henley. Jordan had resumed his aloof manner as he might put on a coat. While he had played chess with Ellen, an easy charm had warmed his smile and a keen wit glittered in his eyes. Now, however, he seemed supremely and fashionably bored. Hillary was all bright animation, teasing, laughing in a soft, mellow contralto, her white-gloved hand resting possessively upon Jordan's arm.

"They've been partial to each other all their lives," Lady Chesterfield confided to Ellen. "Mrs. Moorsmythe and I have known for years that they would make a match of it. They're well suited, don't you think, Miss O'Connell? I vow they'll be one of Society's most glittering couples."

So stay away from him, Ellen heard between the lines.

"They do seem absolutely made for each other," Ellen admitted. It was true. Jordan and Hillary were from the same world—both privileged darlings of a privileged set of people. Ellen wondered why the news sat like a stone on her heart. She might find Jordan Chesterfield attractive, compelling, enticing in a perverse sort of way, but she was in no position to be losing her heart to any man. She was done with men, once and for all, whether she wanted it that way or not.

With Henri, in Paris, she had ignored class barriers and social propriety. How innocent she had been, how easily impressed by Henri's sophistication and good looks, how readily awed by his medical expertise. Henri had made her forget who she was, where she was, forget that people on the eastern side of the Atlantic lived by a different code from the people of her beloved Montana. She'd known the code but thought it was ridiculous.

She'd known the code but thought she was above it—
and the code had burned her for the presumption.

At least, thanks to Henri and her own foolishness, it
would never happen again.

CHAPTER 5

"**H**enley bagged a brace of grouse yesterday," George complained to Ellen.

"Really?"

"Yes, really! By the time you let me out of this room, the season will be over, you know. Either that or those blighters who call themselves my friends will have bagged all the birds."

Ellen was unsympathetic. "I'm cheering for the birds. I can understand hunting for need. I've never understood hunting for sport. How many fingers am I holding up?"

"Three."

"Follow my hand as it moves from left to right. Without moving your head, please. Behave, Mr. Chesterfield. You know the routine."

"I'm *tired* of the routine." He directed an exasperated plea toward Jane, who watched from the foot of the bed. "Can't you convince Doctor Diligence here to let me out of this prison, Miss Browne? I'm right as rain, steady as a rock, strong as an ox."

"Is that so?" Ellen asked skeptically. "How long since one of your headaches?"

"Days."

Ellen cocked an inquiring brow at Jane.

"He had one yesterday morning," Jane admitted meekly.

George sent her a hurt look.

"But it wasn't as bad as the others," Jane added. "And it was over quite quickly."

Ellen gave George a stern frown. "Very well, Mr. Chesterfield. You may resume limited activity. But I expect you to show a bit of good sense about not overtaxing yourself."

"Thank you!" He grabbed Ellen's hand and kissed it with a laughing flourish. "Thank you!"

Ellen retrieved her hand impatiently. "That limited activity doesn't include tramping through the woods to shoot birds, I might add."

"Of course not! I wouldn't think of it." He gave her a look of offended innocence, then flashed a smile. "A quiet ride through the fields?"

"No," Ellen said.

"A bit of fishing?"

She shook her head disapprovingly. His jubilation began to fade.

"A slow walk in the garden?"

"That sounds like more the thing," Ellen conceded. "But not alone."

He slid a sideways glance at Jane. "Certainly not. Perhaps Miss Browne would take the trouble to stroll with me."

Jane was blushing again, Ellen noted. The girl did nothing but blush these days. It was getting downright annoying. Irritated beyond reason, Ellen folded her arms. Her keen-eyed look sent a separate warning to each of them. "Don't overdo it."

Less than five minutes after the doctor had left the room, taking her dull good sense with her, George was dressed in the warm and comfortably worn tweed Norfolk jacket and knickerbockers he generally wore for expeditions into the woods. If he was only allowed to march around the garden, at least he could look the part of having a sporting good time.

"You can come out now," he said with an indulgent smile.

Jane peeped from around the privacy screen in one corner of the chamber.

George grinned. "Miss Browne. One would think after all the time you've spent looking after me that the sight of me dressing would not be so frightening."

"You, sir, are a rogue."

He chuckled. "Life should be so exciting. No, Miss Browne. I'm simply a bored and restless fellow with too much time and money on his hands. I do hope that doesn't deter you from walking with me. I fear our sourpuss doctor friend won't let me out of my cage unless you consent to be my watchdog."

"Mr. Chesterfield!" Jane propped her hands on her hips and managed to look stern. "Ellen is not a sourpuss. She's one of the sweetest people of my acquaintance."

"Really?" George tied a necktie around his throat and inspected his reflection in the mirror. He grimaced at the nearly bald area above his left ear and sighed at the overall seediness of his appearance. "Not exactly easy on the eyes right now, am I?"

"You look fine," Jane told him.

He gave her a smile. Speaking of easy on the eyes, his

little nurse was a treat for any man's vision. She was a good sport as well, and a friend. Who else would have spent interminable hours with him in this room, playing cards and checkers, reading him Dickens and Yeats and H. G. Wells. Who would think a young woman would appreciate H. G. Wells? She was still in high color from her loyal defense of her friend. The flush in her cheeks suited her.

"You're quite mistaken, Miss Browne. Your friend Miss O'Connell is not the sweetest woman of my acquaintance," he said with a gentle smile. "You are."

Jane blushed furiously. "You're not seeing Ellen at her best."

"Indeed?" George dropped down in a chair. The curmudgeon physician had gauged his condition accurately. He wasn't quite up to galloping over the fields or marching through the woods. "Why am I not seeing her at her best, Miss Browne? The woman is easily aggravated and stern as a governess. Is that not her best?"

"You're ungrateful, sir! Ellen saved your life."

"I am extremely grateful. Believe me. I'm not sure how I would manage if I were dead at such an early age." He grinned at Jane's exasperation. When most women scowled, they looked like witches. When Jane frowned, she simply looked adorable. "Ah!" he exclaimed in revelation. "I have it! I'd wager the good doctor was soured by a romantic misadventure. Isn't it fashionable for ladies to pine and fret after an elusive gentleman?"

Jane blinked, for a moment nonplussed. He'd hit the target, George thought. The sharp-tongued Miss O'Connell had a weakness for a man. How unexpectedly human of her.

"You are very rude, Mr. Chesterfield. You shouldn't be talking about Ellen with such disrespect."

"I'm right, aren't I?" he crowed. "A classic romantic tragedy. The stuff of ladies' dreams."

"You are insufferable!"

She really was very attractive when her eyes flashed so, George noted. He held out his hand and tempted her with a captivating smile to take it. She did. A warmth that owed nothing to the fireplace spread its glow through his body.

"Am I insufferable, Jane?"

She colored at his familiar use of her name.

"I don't really mean disrespect to the estimable Dr. O'Connell. She seems a very good sort of person. Perhaps she is simply paying the price that women must pay when they take on the responsibilities and cares of a man's profession."

Jane snatched her hand from his care and glared at him. Apparently his words were miscalculated.

"George Chesterfield! Are you one of those hidebound men who believe that women should limit themselves to keeping house and raising children?"

"Who? Me?" He'd taken the wrong turn here. That was obvious. "I think . . . I merely think women should be protected."

"From what?"

"Well . . . from men!"

"I agree!" Her toe tapped the floor in staccato annoyance. "Women need protection from men who think they and they alone have intelligence, perseverance, judgment, and ambition. And women should be protected from men who think any female who steps outside the pale of domesticity no longer deserves the respect or courtesy due any human being. And men who believe that they and they alone have the right to define how women should live their lives. And—"

"Wait!" George held up his hands in surrender. "Mercy, sweet lady! I bow to your superior wisdom."

Her eyes flashed an even brighter anger. "Now you are patronizing me. I do not need to be patronized or placated, Mr. Chesterfield. And I am not your 'sweet lady.'"

She turned and swept regally toward the door, which was a conclusion that George had not anticipated. He stopped her with a plea. "Miss Browne, wait!"

Jane halted with her hand on the doorknob. The set of her shoulders and stiffness of her spine didn't bode well.

"Please, Miss Browne. Jane . . . I'm a stupid fool. My brother has told me so often enough. The truth is, I was deliberately provoking you to see the flash in your eyes and the flush of your face. When you talk about something you feel strongly about, your face glows with animation. Do you know that?"

She surrendered her grip on the knob and turned around, eyeing him warily.

"I confess I'm so accustomed to bantering with the ladies, paying them trite courtesies, that I forget some women mean what they say, and feel what they say. I'm sorry, Jane. Don't leave."

"Tell me why I should associate with someone so rude?"

He smiled. "Who else would be patient and generous enough to go walking with me? Who else is soft-hearted enough to put up with me?"

She tried to look unsympathetic and stern, but slowly her expression thawed and her true nature shone through in a rueful smile. George had not been facetious when he'd named her sweet and generous.

"You are a bad one, Mr. Chesterfield." Jane sighed.

He offered her his arm and opened the door. "I think you should call me George."

Ellen sat on a garden bench and gazed out over the hedges, flower beds, and fountains. There was a certain peace to be found contemplating Endsfield Park's regimented and neatly trimmed shrubbery. The order attempted to permeate one's soul, creating precise pathways of thought and pruning the wild chaos of emotion to a decorous sensibility.

She should prescribe a dose of garden-watching for herself, Ellen thought. Once or twice a day might do the trick and steady her back on the calm and even keel that was her usual approach to life. As it was, she was growing more testy by the day. The Ellen of old would have found George's irreverence appealing. Now he struck her as irresponsible and irritating. Six months ago Jane's susceptibility to George's charm might have been amusing. Now it annoyed her to the point she was snapping at both of them.

Ellen liked her old self much better than the curmudgeon she'd become. What she needed was a swift kick in the backside, she decided. After all, she wasn't the first person to make a mistake, nor the first woman to be betrayed by an unscrupulous man. Unfortunately, the person most expert at kicking Ellen in the backside—both literally and figuratively—was an ocean and most of a continent away. Ellen smiled as she pictured Katy's reaction to her sulking self-pity. More than ever she wished she was in Montana and could talk to her twin sister.

At a much closer distance, Andrea and Prissy—who were also quite accomplished at delivering blows to tender anatomical parts—watched from the concealment of a hedge.

"She looks sad," Andrea noted.

"She doesn't look sad; she looks cranky. That's the way grown-ups always look," Prissy said.

"Well, she ought to be sad. Jordan's gone off without her to fish with the duke and his dippy son."

"He hasn't been paying enough attention to her," Andrea said. "Hillary's never going to get mad the way things are going."

Prissy made a face. "Every time Cousin Jordan talks or walks with Miss O'Connell, Miss Bore-symthe drags him off."

"Hillary won't be anywhere close by while he's fishing." Andrea's mouth twisted in thought. "And Jordan couldn't really want to spend the afternoon with Lord Tindale. Wouldn't it be romantic if . . ."

The sisters looked at each other, their eyes alight. Finishing the sentence was unnecessary. "Yes!" they both exclaimed.

Their prey looked up unsuspectingly as they skipped around the curve of the hedge. Prissy waved.

"Hello, Miss O'Connell!"

"Hello there. Is Miss Todestan still with her sister?"

"No," Andrea answered. "She said we should get some exercise and enjoy the fine weather before the clouds and cold return."

"We're going riding!" Prissy announced. "Do you want to come with us?"

"I don't have a horse," Ellen said.

"Follett will give you one," Andrea said eagerly. "Do come!"

Ellen looked down at her attire, a serviceable brown

skirt, shirtwaist, and jacket that were not really suitable for riding. Andrea sensed her hesitation.

"We'll ride down to the river path," she invited temptingly. "It's very pretty there. Wild roses are still blooming in the sheltered areas by the river, and cooberries are on the bushes."

Ellen raised a questioning brow. "Cooberries?"

Andrea shrugged. "I've called them cooberries since I was little. They're delicious, whatever they are, and they don't make you sick unless you eat a whole bucket of them."

Ellen looked toward the woods while the girls willed the right answer from her lips. She smiled, and a gleam of longing lit her eyes. "Yes, girls, thank you. I'd like to go."

Andrea and Prissy exchanged a grin of triumph.

Ellen ignored the warning of her good sense. She knew this wasn't a good idea, especially given her present circumstances, but she'd indulged in enough moping and introspection to turn her hair gray, and the prospect of doing something other than brooding was simply too tempting.

Follett, the stablemaster, was only too happy to provide her with a mount—a pretty chestnut mare named Goldie with smooth gaits and a mannerly disposition. Despite her gentle nature, the mare had spirit and energy. When Andrea and Prissy trotted briskly away from the stable, she followed eagerly, and when the sisters urged their mounts to a moderate gallop that carried them over several low hedges and a muddy ditch, Goldie strained at the bit to increase the pace. Ellen couldn't resist the temptation, even though she hadn't quite gotten the hang of the sidesaddle she rode.

It wasn't that the sidesaddle was unknown in Montana. Many proper Montana women chose to ride them. Ellen and Katy, however, had never bothered much with propriety. They had always ridden astride. Katy had always laughed at sidesaddles as being sissified. Their father had called them ridiculous contraptions that didn't deserve to be on the back of a good horse or under the backside of a good woman. What a sidesaddle really was, Ellen could have told them, was uncomfortable, unstable, and a downright danger to life and limb.

Goldie broke into a canter, then increased her pace to a gallop, and Ellen thought of a host of less polite adjectives to describe the sidesaddle. She felt unbalanced and out of control. Her backside bounced against the saddle while her hands—and consequently the reins—flapped through the air in a manner that only incited the mare to more speed. There was no stopping her before the first hedge.

Ellen managed to survive the jump. Waiting for her in the field beyond two more hedges and a ditch, the girls cheered their approval. Ellen desperately reined the mare in. Too late. The horse faltered, then surged ahead to take another hedge. She came down without her rider, who had stayed behind to become part of the shrubbery.

"Stupid damned contraption!" Ellen sputtered as she untangled herself from the hedge. At least the landing had been soft, if a bit prickly. Goldie had stopped on the other side of the hedge and turned her head to regard Ellen with gentle equine reprimand. Andrea and Prissy rode to her aid, gracefully jumping the ditch and hedge that separated them.

"Miss O'Connell!" Andrea quavered. "Are you all right?"

"I'm fine," Ellen admitted ruefully. She plucked a

leaf out of her hair and emptied her sleeves of a few small twigs.

"You should have told us you don't know how to ride," Prissy said solemnly.

"I do know how to ride," Ellen said testily. "I've ridden since before I could walk. But that saddle is positively unnatural!"

"You ride astride?" Andrea's voice was breathless with the scandal of the idea.

Prissy's eyes grew wide with delight. "Really? Do you?"

"I do, and I will from now on!" Ellen declared. "This is embarrassing. I could've taken that hedge bareback when my legs were scarcely grown long enough to get a decent grip on the horse."

Both the girls smirked their disbelief.

"You don't believe me?" Ellen laughed. Suddenly she felt young again. Young, mischievous, daring, and loath to decline a challenge. "I'll show you."

She stripped the sidesaddle off Goldie's back, then transformed her skirt into pantaloons by bringing the rear hem between her legs and tucking it into the front waistband. The girls' jaws dropped as she took a handful of Goldie's long mane and vaulted nimbly up onto her bare back. Well—perhaps not so nimbly, or even gracefully. Several years had passed since she'd done this, after all, and she was certainly in no condition to be performing gymnastics. But at least she managed it without falling on her face.

"Be careful!" Andrea warned as Ellen urged Goldie into a canter.

"Of course!" Ellen shouted. "I'm always careful." She pulled up so fast that Goldie slid to a halt on her rear legs, then wheeled the horse toward the pesky hedge and tightened her legs to urge her forward. Goldie leapt into an instant canter, gathered speed, and easily sailed over the obstacle. A few strides out, Ellen spun the mare on her rear legs and took the hedge again, then the next hedge, and the ditch. The wind loosened the fat braid that was pinned atop her head. How good it felt to have her hair flowing free, to feel a good horse between her legs, to smell the autumn smells, and feel the brisk, fresh air on her face.

She reined Goldie to a halt. Andrea and Prissy, who had followed behind, stopped beside her.

"Wow!" Prissy said. "Can I try it without a saddle?"

"No," Andrea said.

"Just to trot around! Please, Andrea!"

"No!" Andrea repeated urgently. "Look who's here."

Prissy and Ellen both followed Andrea's pained gaze to where three men emerged from the edge of the woods. The high rubber boots and fishing tackle explained why Lord Chesterfield was here with the duke and his son, and no doubt Ellen's performance explained the outraged look on Jordan's face.

"Uh-oh!" Prissy moaned.

Ellen felt her face grow hot as the men approached. Tindale smirked in amusement. His father the duke was politely trying to ignore her appearance and the flamboyantly improper performance he'd just witnessed. Jordan, on the other hand, looked positively furious.

"Hello, Cousin Jordan," Andrea greeted him cautiously.

Jordan nodded stiffly, his eyes never leaving Ellen where she sat on Goldie's naked back, her skirts hiked up to show an indecent length of stocking-covered leg, her hair falling about her shoulders in a riot of ebony waves, and her face decorated with freckles of mud.

He'd never seen a woman look so outrageous, at least none who laid claim to decency. But neither had he seen one so appealing. The ever-so-serious Dr. O'Connell looked like a gypsy of old, flaunting temptation with that silken cascade of windblown hair, cheeks touched with roses from the brisk wind, and green eyes alight with lively exuberence.

Jordan was angry and fascinated at the same time. "Miss O'Connell, has something happened to your saddle?" He schooled his tone to quiet steeliness. It wouldn't do to let his young cousins think he was at all amused by this sort of behavior.

Ellen's expression traveled through chagrin to annoyance and on to apprehension, then settled back on annoyance as she lightly threw a leg over Goldie's withers and slid to the ground. "I took the stupid thing off."

"I beg your pardon?"

She smiled. "No need to beg my pardon, Lord Chesterfield. I took the saddle off, just as I said. It's now riding atop that hedge over there. Any woman who can stay on such a contraption has my hearty respect for her equestrian skills. A horse's bare back is much easier to sit upon."

Behind Jordan, Tindale chuckled. "Miss O'Connell, you're quite delightfully astounding."

"Do I take it you were demonstrating to my cousins how to ride bareback—and astride."

"Yes, sir," Ellen admitted. "Right after I demonstrated how not to ride a sidesaddle." She looked ruefully back toward the hedges, and Jordan noted that a leaf or two decorated her glossy hair. Keeping a smile from his lips suddenly became an effort.

"Wild Indians ride without saddles," Prissy informed

them knowledgeably. "Miss O'Connell's mama is a wild Indian."

"Perhaps that is why she is so talented a horsewoman," Tindale said with an oily smile.

Jordan sent him a silent but unmistakable warning.

"It takes more talent to ride sidesaddle than to ride astride, saddle or no," Ellen challenged half seriously. "Anyone who stays on one of those awkward things has to be twice the equestrian of someone who rides astride."

"A novel notion," the duke agreed equably.

"A very original idea," the earl noted with a chuckle.

Jordan was not entertained. The more amusing the others found the novel Miss O'Connell, the more irritated he became—both at their condescending remarks and her ridiculous behavior. "Miss O'Connell," he hissed. "Will you walk with me a moment?"

A perverse light sparkled in her eye as he offered his arm and drew her away from the others.

"You were not hurt in your fall, I trust."

"Only my pride. My sister Katy once said: 'O'Connells don't fall from horses. The horses fall first.'"

He squelched a smile. "You come from a very . . . interesting background."

"You don't know the half of it," Ellen said.

"But surely you realize that you can't tempt impressionable young girls to experiment with such unorthodox behavior."

"I didn't tempt them to experiment with anything," she denied, then glanced down at her exposed calves— temptation if Jordan had ever seen it—and flushed. With a sigh she arranged her skirt into a more proper configuration. "Besides, Lord Chesterfield, some of your precious orthodox behavior makes no sense."

"Rules and traditions exist for a reason."

"And I suppose you always follow all the rules."

She was much too perceptive for her own good, Jordan thought. Outrageous, perceptive, intelligent, and beautiful. A dangerous woman indeed.

"Even in this modern day and age, Miss O'Connell, it's more important for women to limit their behavior than for men. Perhaps it seems unfair, but that is simply how the world works."

She gave him a long, measuring look with glinting emerald eyes. "Do you know, Lord Chesterfield, no offense meant, but you are every bit as stuffy and hidebound as your mother."

"I'm flattered that you think so." It was a lie, of course; he wasn't flattered at all. In fact, he was angry and disgusted. At himself for wanting to impress the damned difficult minx. At Ellen for casting a woman's spell when she looked like a hoyden.

His usually admirable control was slipping, and Jordan didn't like the feeling one bit. He stiffened his posture, vowing not to fall prey to the web she unwittingly cast. "May I trust that you will refrain from encouraging my cousins to bounce along bareback on their mounts or lecturing them on the advantages of turning their skirts into trousers?"

"I wouldn't dream of it." Her jaw was stiff with her contempt for his antiquated ideas, and probably for him.

Just as well, Jordan mused. If Ellen O'Connell liked him, she wouldn't be just dangerous to his equanimity. She'd be lethal.

Ellen fumed as Lord Chesterfield led her back to Goldie, but in a way she was glad of the reminder that Jordan Chesterfield was a stuffy scion of a regimented society that she'd learned—the hard way—to despise.

She didn't want to like him, his roguishly charming brother, his cousins, his dogs, or his horses.

She just wanted to go home.

Ellen was still in a contrary mood that evening when George joined the after-dinner socialization for the first time since his accident. He entered the salon with a diffident Jane in tow. Ellen could sense that, for all her friend's talk about mingling with Society, Jane was uncomfortable intruding upon the lofty personages gathered for genteel conversation and entertainment. On the excuse of being concerned for her patient, Ellen joined them.

She wasn't alone, however, for the entire room wanted to greet the returning invalid. Ellen scarcely had time to say hello before she was upstaged by Lord Tindale, Mr. and Misses Henley, Sir Nigel, and Lord Clifton, all crowding around George and congratulating him on his escape from the jaws of death. As befitted his rank, the duke remained seated beside Lady Chesterfield, who did not deign to rise. Jordan observed his brother's mobbing from his seat on the divan, where he was reading—of all things—Mark Twain. And Hillary Moorsmythe couldn't have been pried from Jordan's side by a crowbar.

Ellen did manage to separate Jane from the crowd, and Jane breathed a sigh of gratitude, though her eyes kept darting back to George, who was soaking up his friends' attention like a sponge absorbing water.

"How is our patient doing, now that I've let him up from his bed?" Ellen asked.

"As you can see, he's fine. We took a stroll in the maze—that is really the most amusing place! And George . . . I mean, Mr. Chesterfield . . . told me stories about how he and his brother used to lure people into the maze to get lost during their mother's garden parties."

"I can picture George Chesterfield getting into that sort of mischief," Ellen said, "but not his brother."

Ellen was surprised when George broke away from his friends to rejoin Jane. He greeted Ellen with a friendly smile. "Dr. O'Connell. As you can see, I'm all the better for a bit of exercise. Hale and hearty."

"So I see. You're a fast healer, Mr. Chesterfield."

He took Jane's hand and squeezed lightly. "I had good care." He pulled his eyes off Jane long enough to give Ellen a distracted smile. "And, of course, I owe much to your medical skill, my good lady."

Ellen felt more than saw Lady Chesterfield's scowl as the mistress of Endsfield rose and proceeded majestically toward her younger son. The dowager baroness would never dream of revealing her feelings in a straightforward manner. A slight wrinkle of the brow, a tightening around the mouth, a lift of the chin—all subtle signs that George's intimacy with Jane did not go unnoted. Hillary, also, watched them with a slight curl to her lips that would never be described as a smile.

"Good evening, Miss Browne," Lady Chesterfield condescended to greet Jane. "We are all very grateful for your attentive care to dear George. How fortunate we are to have not only a physician among us, but a surgeon's daughter as well."

If Lady Chesterfield had identified Jane as an ironmonger's daughter or a butcher's daughter, her tone could have carried no more disdain. Under the guise of thanking Jane, she was making it clear to her guests—and passing a sharp reminder to George—that Jane's pedigree was not up to their social standards. Ellen saw

Jane blanch at the contemptuous regard of the others in the room.

George stiffened, and his fingers wrapped more tightly around Jane's hand, but it was Jordan who came to the girl's defense.

"Miss Browne is welcome at Endsfield Park anytime," he said clearly. His gaze locked momentarily with his mother's, then surveyed the room for anyone else who might dare to belittle Jane. "Dr. O'Connell also. Their service to this family has earned them a permanent place in our regard. Is that not so, Mother?"

"Yes," Lady Chesterfield said curtly. "Of course."

The tension in the room relaxed somewhat. Glances slid self-consciously away from Jane and Ellen, and everyone suddenly seemed very busy at whatever it was they were doing.

As had happened before, just as Ellen had worked up a good, solid dislike of the baron, he did something to make her like him again. Her opinion of his guests, however, was nowhere near as charitable. They were so eager to convince themselves of their own superiority that they couldn't bother to concern themselves with someone else's feelings.

How much of her anger stemmed from Lady Chesterfield and her guests and how much from Henri Chretiens and his ambitions? Ellen wondered suddenly. She didn't much care. They were all cut from the same cloth, it seemed.

"Miss O'Connell, would you join us for a foursome of bridge?" Tindale asked with an ingratiating smile. He waved her toward a table where Sir Nigel and the elder Miss Henley sat with their sherry and cards.

"Thank you," she said in a cool voice, "but I don't play bridge."

"What do you play then? I'm sure we could use some variety in our entertainment."

That was an understatement, Ellen thought. Then a wicked notion made her smile. "Do you know poker, sir?"

"Poker?" His brows arched upward. "I've seen it played a time or two. I don't believe it is considered a game for mixed company."

"Certainly it is," Ellen said. "Poker's all the rage at home in Montana."

"So is galloping over the countryside bareback like a—as Prissy would no doubt say—a wild Indian." The warm masculine voice came unexpectedly from close behind her. Jordan Chesterfield seemed to have recovered his humor since that afternoon.

"That's true." Ellen refused to be embarrassed. She met the challenge in his eyes with a firm smile. "In America we prefer our games and sports to be somewhat less sedate than those the English find entertaining."

Tindale interjected himself into the conversation. "Some English activities are not as staid as you might think, Miss O'Connell. And never let it be said that we're not a sporting lot. Perhaps you would show us the intricacies of this game Americans like so much."

The jackass was asking for it, Ellen thought.

"Yes," Jordan agreed with a lazy smile. "Perhaps you should."

Miss Henley excused herself from the table, leaving Ellen with Tindale, Sir Nigel, and Jordan. Ellen was in no mood to be charitable. Tindale obviously thought he was merely indulging a female whim. Sir Nigel Higgenbotham, a middle-aged, stout fellow, paid more attention to his port than his cards, and Jordan Chesterfield was no doubt hoping to see her prove herself a barbarian once again. At the end of an hour's instruction in seven card stud, five card draw, and several more exotic varieties of poker, Ellen held markers from all three players that would have paid her way across the Atlantic two or three times over. Apparently the English thought betting small amounts was for the common masses. They were above such thrift.

Money was not what she wanted from these people, however. She didn't know exactly what she wanted, but the flush of embarrassment on her opponents' faces when she handed them back their markers gave her a small amount of satisfaction. Only Jordan accepted the return of his IOU with equanimity. Did nothing ever ruffle the man's composure?

Jordan Chesterfield's composure, if the truth be known, was enduring more strain that it had in years. When Ellen excused herself from the table to seek fresh air in the garden, the room seemed to dim without her presence. He resented that. He resented the feelings her smile gave him, and he resented the urge to laugh at her unpredictable, sometimes annoying, but always interesting behavior. He resented the way his pulse quickened at the sound of her voice, the way he looked forward to seeing her at the beginning of each day.

Since the death of his wife, Jordan had sustained little interest in any woman past the inevitable needs of a healthy man. He was satisfied with that situation. He had not been able to give Mary Catherine his heart and soul as she had expected and no doubt deserved, but at least he could give her his loyalty. His foolish attraction to this unconventional American made him feel disloyal to the wife who had died trying to bear his child.

Jordan resented that disloyalty. He resented Ellen for making him feel disloyal. He resented being lured from his dispassionate cocoon. But, as the earl of Tindale made toward the door with the obvious intent of following Ellen into the garden, Jordan discovered he resented that more than all the rest.

With a flinty look in his eye, he decided that three in the garden might be more comfortable than two.

CHAPTER 6

"**B**eautiful evening, isn't it?"

At Tindale's unexpected comment, Ellen spun around, startled that she wasn't alone on the little path that wound through the moonlit flower beds. Solitude had been her intent in fleeing the gathering in the house, for she was in a dangerous mood tonight, and had been for most of the day—easily annoyed and all too ready to express her annoyance in some untoward remark or behavior. She'd already been cross and discourteous to the Chesterfields' guests. Right now, she was better company for flowers and bushes than for human beings. Plants were less annoying.

"Don't you agree?" Tindale prompted. "Considering the season, I mean. The air's a bit brisk, but it is late in the year, after all."

Ellen sighed. Speaking of annoying. . . . "Lord Tindale, please don't feel the need to keep me company. I came out simply for a breath of fresh air."

"Ah, you Americans," the earl chuckled. "Like the

wild savages of your land—can't be closed in for long, eh?"

Ellen sighed. The man was a lout. "There are no wild savages in Montana, sir."

"No need to be so formal." He stepped closer. She moved away, but he seemed oblivious to the message. "I know how Americans despise such ceremony. Call me Wesley."

Ellen didn't like the direction this conversation was headed. She started back toward the house, but he caught her arm, gently enough, but effective in stopping her unless she wanted to make a spectacle of herself by struggling.

"Don't be standoffish, Ellen. You needn't worry that your lack of polish offends me. I like women who are unconventional and a little rebellious. They make interesting companions."

"Lord Tindale, I don't give a rat's ass if I offend you or not." Ellen was beyond patience. "Your opinion and what you like is a matter of total unconcern to me. Now, if you don't mind, I intend to return to the house."

"You want to play coy?" he asked with a condescending smile. "I thought you would have the audacity to be forthright, but I can see that you enjoy these little feminine games as much as any debutante, eh? Very well, I can play the role of seducer with the best of them."

"Let me go, you conceited idiot!" She tried to jerk free of his grasp, but his fingers only tightened. With a low chuckle, he pulled her against him.

"Very convincing," he whispered as his hand twisted in her hair, pulling it out of its pins and holding her head immobile. His mouth fastened upon hers in a wet, disgusting assault. She pummeled him ineffectually with her free hand and tried to twist into a position where she could land a kick to the overactive piece of male ego between his legs. Before she had time to do much more than groan out a protest, however, Tindale was yanked away with a violent jerk.

"I would pay more attention to the lady's protest if I were you, Tindale." Jordan Chesterfield held the earl by his back collar much as a huntsman might take an unruly hound by the scruff. Tindale looked ridiculous hanging there with his toes not quite touching the ground, but the baron's voice hadn't an ounce of humor in it. "I will not tolerate such behavior from anyone on this estate. Not servant, nor family, nor guest. You will apologize to the lady."

Set abruptly upon his feet, Tindale hastily stammered out an apology. Hair hanging loose, dress askew, Ellen's face heated with mortification. With a shaking hand she wiped the moisture of Tindale's kiss from her face.

"Please accept my heartfelt apology." Tindale pleaded as if his very life depended on it. Lord Chesterfield looked as though at any moment he might shake him like a dog until he couldn't tell up from down. "Please!" he whimpered.

"Miss O'Connell?" Lord Chesterfield fixed her with a stern demand for response.

"Touch me again, Tindale, and Lord Chesterfield won't be rescuing me; he'll be rescuing you," she promised. "Understand?"

"I understand!"

Tindale beat a hasty retreat toward the safety of the house. The baron stayed, staring at her in a manner that made Ellen burn with both humiliation and anger—and something else she didn't want to think about.

As he stiffly offered his arm to escort her back inside, Ellen backed away. "Just leave me alone." She dismissed him with a sweep of her arm as she turned and marched toward the solitude of the maze. Before she'd gone ten steps, Lord Chesterfield stopped her with a curt command.

"Miss O'Connell. The maze is not a good place to be at night." He caught up to her and laid a hand firmly on her shoulder.

Ellen looked coldly at the restraining hand. Why did all Englishmen think their 'suggestions' should be enforced with a grip upon some part of her anatomy? "It seems to me that an open path in this garden is not a good place to be either, Lord Chesterfield."

"Tindale's behavior was unforgiveable," Jordan agreed. "But you can't assign him all the blame."

"Just what is that supposed to mean?"

"That means that you can cite modern times and liberal philosophy all you please, but if a woman steps out of the role in which she is traditionally respected and protected, many men will take that as tacit permission to deviate from the rules regarding proper behavior. Surely this is not the first time you've met such an attitude."

Ellen's heart skipped a beat. Did he know? Had Jane told him, perhaps? Or maybe it showed. No. Not possible. She shrugged his hand off her shoulder. "There is no excuse for a man to be a boor and a debaucher."

He smiled wryly. "All men at heart are boors and debauchers, Miss O'Connell. It is only the rules that you so despise that makes them pretend to be otherwise."

"Then perhaps they should all be put in cages along with the apes in a zoo."

He had the audacity to laugh. "You are the very devil of a woman, Miss O'Connell. You run rampant through a man's sensibilities—dashing about the countryside flashing your legs like a gypsy, then trouncing a fellow's self-regard by humiliating him at cards—not a friendly social game, mind you, but a bloodletting session of poker. You bait the wolves, then when they come after you, you indignantly declare they should be locked into cages."

"You exaggerate."

"Only you would say so. You invite more trouble upon yourself than you know."

"I invite nothing."

"Not true. You invite this."

He caught her hand as she started to walk away. Before Ellen knew it, she was drawn toward him, surrounded by strong arms and a spicy masculine aroma. Caught unaware, she responded out of instinct, not intention, melting against him, letting her curves mold softly to the hard planes and muscular swells of his body. His sharp intake of breath signaled his surprise. He would have let her go, Ellen sensed, if she'd just had the strength to step back. But she stood frozen in his embrace, like a helpless mouse staring into the eyes of the eagle.

His mouth descended upon hers gently but firmly. The kiss was nothing like Tindale's. Nothing at all. At the same time he stole her breath, he stole her last will to resist. Every muscle in her body became loose and warm, every nerve alive. His lips coaxed, demanded, played, commanded, and she hadn't the iron in her soul to contest him.

Suddenly she was free. The eyes that looked down at her glittered in the moonlight—with desire and a fair amount of "I told you so." Anger and embarrassment corralled Ellen's stampeding senses. The bitter taste of betrayal and her own ludicrous foolishness rose in her throat. Before she was aware of moving, her hand lashed out and dealt a stinging slap to his aristocratically chiseled cheek.

For a moment Ellen was stunned and frightened by the violence of her reaction. The desire in Jordan's eyes froze to a dangerous glint of steel. Indignation came to her rescue.

"How is *that* for conventional feminine behavior?" she taunted. "Isn't such the acceptable reaction for a well-bred lady when a gentleman forgets he's a gentleman?"

For a wild moment she feared he would hit her back. He didn't. There was violence in his stance, with his glittering eyes and hard slash of a mouth that had only moments before been gentle and coaxing. But he didn't move.

Ellen doubled her fists so tightly that her nails bit into her own flesh. Summoning her strength, she turned and marched toward the house, then, at a safe distance, stopped in midretreat to deliver her parting shot. "Lord Chesterfield, sir! If you think I find your advances any more appealing than those of that moron Lord Tindale, then you are so sunk in your own masculine ego that you can't see straight."

It was a lie, and she knew it. Lord Chesterfield knew it also. The cynical smile that slanted across his face left no doubt. Face flaming, Ellen ran the rest of the way to the house like the gypsy he'd accused her of emulating.

Hidden from the moonlight in the shadows of the maze, Andrea and Prissy had scarcely been able to contain their glee when their lordly cousin had kissed Ellen, and then their groans when Miss O'Connell, whom they had expected to swoon from the passion of the moment—or at least melt from the heat of Jordan's attention—

flattened his face with a blow that practically spun his head around on his neck. The girls managed to keep their hands clamped over their mouths until Jordan had left—heading not for the house, but the kennels—where he often retreated when he was in high dudgeon.

"Oh no!" Andrea moaned softly when he was out of sight. "Cripes! Why can't she just cooperate?"

"Maybe she doesn't like him," Prissy offered with a sigh.

"Of course she likes him! He's handsome! He's rich! He's clever!"

"He's cranky," Prissy added.

"Well! She's cranky, too." Andrea sighed morosely. "It's fate. We go to all that trouble to try to lead her to the river, where they can get cozy, and what's she do? She falls off poor Goldie, then gets wild as a circus performer while Jordan is looking on from the woods. Now she gets her big chance out in the garden."

"Yes!" Prissy agreed indignantly. "Cousin Jordan was in a mushy mood, too. I could tell from the look on his face."

"And she botches it!"

"She did!"

"Maybe it's hopeless," Andrea groaned.

They sat in silence for a moment, sitting back against the branches of the hedge and shivering a bit from the night chill. Miss Todestan would lecture them for an hour if she caught them out this time of evening, but when they'd looked from their window and seen the confrontation between Jordan and Tindale, they couldn't help but rush down the back servants' stairway and scramble unseen to the cover of the maze.

"You think we should give up?" Andrea asked her younger sister.

Prissy grimaced. "Jordan kissed her, and Hillary didn't even see him."

Together they sighed a heavy gust of woe.

"We can't give up," Prissy finally said. "We took a vow."

"You're right. We won't give up." Andrea looked up toward the window of Ellen's room, where lamplight had just illuminated the window. "This would certainly be easier if they weren't both such blockheads, though."

"I refuse to show my face in the breakfast room," Ellen said gloomily. She sat cross-legged upon Jane's bed, elbows upon her knees, chin propped upon one hand.

Sitting at the dressing table brushing her hair, Jane met Ellen's eyes in the mirror. "It wasn't your fault," she said for the tenth time.

"I should never have gone out there."

"You didn't know Lord Tindale would follow, nor Lord Chesterfield. I can't say I'm surprised at the earl's behavior, but Lord Chesterfield . . . Goodness!" She shivered dramatically. "Who would have guessed a fire burned beneath that stone cold exterior?"

"I am such a fool!" Ellen moaned. "All but asking him to kiss me! I shouldn't have slapped him. He should have slapped me."

"Pooh! Don't bother yourself about it." Jane twisted her hair into an elegant topknot and regarded herself critically. "Do you think this makes me look too pretentious?"

"Jane! You're not taking this at all seriously!"

Jane laughed softly. Ellen couldn't remember ever seeing such a glow on her friend's face. Or maybe her own misery was simply making Jane shine in comparison.

"Ellen, Ellen!" Jane said with a chuckle. "Don't worry about Lord Chesterfield. Any man who takes such liberties expects to get a hand across his face. A slap is rather like a boundary line in cricket or polo; it establishes where a player can go and where he can't go. It's part of the game."

"We weren't playing a game!"

"That's where you're mistaken. Romance is a very intricate game of feint, advance, retreat, and surrender."

"It isn't a romance!" Ellen exploded off the bed in a burst of frustration. "You of all people should understand I'm not in a position to indulge in romance of any kind, with any one, at anytime."

Jane turned on the dressing table stool to face her. "Ellen, dear, calm yourself. We have only ten days more. What harm is there in letting Lord Chesterfield dance around you like a bee buzzing around a sweet blossom?"

"I'm *not* a sweet blossom," Ellen reminded her darkly.

Jane gave her a bright smile. "Pretend that you are. Someday you can tell your great grandchildren that a wealthy and powerful English baron once paid court to you."

"He's not paying court, Jane, for mercy's sake! We'll be lucky if he doesn't throw us both out on our bustles, refuse to refund the passage that we missed, and leave us high and dry to find another way to New York."

"Oh, he won't do that. He's a gentleman."

Ellen snorted inelegantly. "Lord Chesterfield is no more a gentleman than I am a lady."

They had no time left to discuss the matter, for at that moment a knock on the door heralded a message—or rather a command—from Lord Chesterfield that Ellen wait upon him in his study immediately.

"Right now?" Ellen asked incredulously of the house-keeper who stood in the doorway.

"If you please, Miss. I shall tell his lordship that you'll be right down."

"You do that," Ellen mumbled under her breath as Mrs. Hawkins marched martially down the hall.

Waiting with Lord Chesterfield in his study was the duke of Marlowe. Though he greeted her courteously, the duke's manner was stiff with embarrassment. "I begged Lord Chesterfield to grant me an audience with you, Miss O'Connell."

Ellen regarded Jordan coolly. As if he had any say about who could and could not speak to her! His face could have been cast in iron. He didn't even have the grace to look ashamed.

"I wish most sincerely to apologize for my son's be-havior last evening," the duke continued.

"Your son already apologized, sir."

Marlowe smiled crookedly and glanced toward Ches-terfield. "Under duress, no doubt. It is not enough. Wes-ley has little judgment and less restraint. I'm deeply distressed that he had the poor taste to offend such an accomplished and intelligent lady as yourself, Miss O'Connell. It's bad enough when he steps over the line with the empty-headed nitwits who flutter around him because of his wealth and connections, but to mistake a woman of your stature for a person of loose virtue is reprehensible."

The duke was sincere, Ellen realized in surprise. She felt sorry for him. He was ten times the man his son was.

"I accepted Lord Tindale's apology, sir, and I accept yours as well. But you had no need to offer it. There was no real harm done."

"You are generous," Marlowe said, his face grim.

With a stiff nod, he departed, leaving her alone with Lord Chesterfield.

Ellen sighed. Wasn't this just the way she wanted to start the day?

If this was not a happy beginning to Ellen's day, it was an equally dismal morning for Jordan. He had asked himself all night long what had prompted him to make a nincompoop out of himself with Ellen O'Connell the evening before. He'd been upright and stoic as a brick wall for three years—ever since Mary Catherine had died. Then in one evening he had broken every rule of decency, manners, good taste, hospitality, and good sense. After the debacle in the garden, he had resorted to downing half a bottle of good Scotch whiskey—something else he hadn't indulged in for a long time. But the whiskey hadn't made him feel any less the fool. Nor had it answered the question of what was turning his brain to porridge.

Now, looking at Ellen, he knew what was softening his brain. It was not evil fate, the phase of the moon, the path of the stars, nor any other agency that men sought to blame for their ills. It was this woman. Her alone. Of all the women he had known in his life, Ellen O'Connell was unique. She had a vulnerability that softened her stubbornness and a quiet sadness about her that made her seem sometimes older, sometimes younger, than her actual years. As a physician, she had seen things and done things that would make most women cringe, yet she retained an aura of innocence and artlessness that seemed to be an essential facet of her character.

She was hard, yet beautifully soft. She was aggressive, yet yielded at the most unexpected times. She had the serious mien of a bluestocking, yet cavorted like a child given an opportunity. She was maddening and enchanting at the same time—a lethal combination. She was also sorely out of charity with him. Understandably so.

"Are we finished?" she asked coolly.

"Not quite."

"It was unnecessay to put the duke through that," she chided.

The frown she gave him, though Jordan was sure it was intended to look ferocious, simply made him want to kiss her. Lord but he was farther gone than he'd thought. There would be no more of that!

"It was necessary because Lord Marlowe requested it. Tindale won't bother you again. He left for London early this morning upon the request of myself and his father. However, one more apology is required."

Ellen rolled her eyes. "Such a big production you Englishmen make of this. Last time someone grabbed me and kissed me against my wishes, my sister Katy simply took him behind the nearest barn and beat the stuffings out of him."

His mouth twitched in the beginnings of a smile. "Then it's a shame your sister isn't here now to take care of these matters. I no doubt deserve a few blows, but a sincere apology will have to suffice. Since I am master of this house, I can't very well banish myself. You will have to be satisfied with my admission that I was both a cad and a fool."

She regarded him solemnly for a moment. Her eyes burned a vivid green from the shadows surrounding them. Probably she had lost sleep over the events of last night as well. Suddenly Jordan wanted to see her smile.

"We don't have a barn, as such, but the stable would probably do. You could drag me behind it and beat the—what was it you said?—the stuffings out of me."

Her mouth slanted upward. "I could try, but I'm afraid

I'm not as talented as my sister in that regard. You'd end up laughing instead of groaning."

"Then by all means, let us proceed. I could use a bit of a laugh right about now."

The slant of her lips softened to a reluctant smile. "I'd say we both got carried away last evening, Lord Chesterfield. If beatings are to be doled out, certainly I am in line for one as well."

"You were perfectly within your rights to slap me, Miss O'Connell. You could have knocked me senseless and still been within your rights."

A sparkle lit her eyes. "Seems as if that's what I tried. I'm surprised you have a face left. My hand feels like I openhanded a marble pillar."

Unable to resist, he reached out and took the injured member, too late realizing that any physical contact with this woman was a discomfiting temptation. Jordan was gratified that Ellen seemed unnerved as well. She looked ready to bolt, but he disarmed her with a rueful grin. His thumb massaged the sore fingers as he raised her knuckles to his lips. "Apology accepted?"

She bit her lip.

"Without a beating," he specified.

"If you insist."

"I promise to be on my best gentlemanly behavior for the rest of your visit."

"And I will try to behave as well."

Her smile was beautiful as a sunrise, the skin of her hand soft as silk. It was going to be bloody damned hard to keep his promise, Jordan told himself.

After Ellen had gone, Jordan sat silently at his desk for a full ten minutes. The glow of her smile lingered in the room—or perhaps it was in his heart, for it clung to him when he left to go about the day's business. He could have easily nurtured that warmth for the rest of the day had not the chill wind of his mother's voice gusted from her boudoir door as he passed it.

"Jordan! Young man, I must speak with you."

Jordan hadn't thought of himself as young since Mary Catherine had died and left him with a burden of uneasy guilt, but to his mother he would always be in knickers. Reluctantly, he entered Lady Chesterfield's boudoir, the strictly female domain from which Endsfield's mistress ran the household.

"Marlowe has left," his mother said without preamble. She sat on a love seat in a dressing robe of silk and feathers. A cup of hot chocolate steamed on the table beside her. "I doubt he has plans to return even for the first hunt of the season. His leave-taking was only minimally courteous, and he looked quite unhappy."

"The duke is understandably upset," Jordan told her.

"He'll never forgive you for embarrassing him and treating his son as though he were some misbehaving stable boy."

"I treated his son as he deserved, Mother."

"Piffle! How could you give such insult to Marlowe when his good influence is essential for your political advancement? I invited him here for your benefit, and yours alone, Jordan! Do you think I enjoy his company? The man is a bore, to say the least, and his son is a useless libertine."

"Marlowe is a good man," Jordan countered. "I did not insult him; I merely manhandled his son a bit, and the duke himself admitted the need of it."

"Wait and see," she warned. "You will be out of his circle, and that appointment as undersecretary in the Foreign Office will go to someone more circumspect than you. Marlowe is insufferably proud. He'll never forget that you've witnessed his weakness."

Jordan sighed impatiently. "You needn't concern yourself with it, Mother. If the price of the appointment is becoming Marlowe's sycophant, then the Foreign Office will have to do without me. I am no man's toady."

She ignored the warning in his voice. "All for the sake of a drab nobody who's no better than she ought to be!"

"Mother, that is quite enough."

"No, it is not. And don't you take that tone with me, Jordan Chesterfield. I'm simply giving voice to what everyone knows. No decent woman learns and does the sorts of things required of surgeons and physicians. And even aside from that, the woman has no notion of correct behavior. She's a bad influence on Andrea and Priscilla, disrupting to our guests, an object of scorn to the servants, an embarrassment to the ladies here, and a temptation to the men." She gave Jordan a stern, knowing look. "And that friend of hers is trying to get her claws into George. I can tell."

"Dr. O'Connell and Miss Browne saved George's life," Jordan reminded his mother. "Even Dr. Martin admits it."

"Then pay the woman a fee and send her on her way. Really, Jordan . . ."

Jordan folded his arms, leaned back against the door frame, and resigned himself to letting his mother vent her vexation. The storm would have been more easily weathered with breakfast in his stomach, but perhaps not. His mother's tirade would have soured Cook's good food in an instant.

Ellen stood frozen in the deserted hallway, a guilty expression on her face. She'd been headed downstairs for breakfast when the voices from Lady Chesterfield's boudoir caught her like a lariat tossed over the head of a cow. She might have been able to pass on by but for the sound of her name spoken so scornfully.

Eavesdropping was terribly rude, especially when the conversation was obviously not intended for the ears of the eavesdropper. But Ellen couldn't help herself. She stood glued to the hallway carpet to hear herself and Jane defamed and Jordan berated. Her appetite for breakfast disappeared. She felt like crawling beneath the house and moving in with the worms, who apparently were her equals in worth.

Before she could become truly crestfallen, however, outrage came to her rescue. Each step back toward her room was propelled by a higher head of steam. By the time she reached Jane's door, an explosion was inevitable. She flung open the door without knocking.

"That witch could inspire a hundred Halloween stories!" Ellen declared.

Wide-eyed, Jane retreated.

"I wouldn't eat at the same table with her if she was serving the Last Supper."

Jane sighed and sat down on the bed. "I'll send for a tray."

George was in an extraordinarily good humor this morning as he went down the stairs to breakfast—extraordinary indeed, considering a pounding headache was the price he was paying for spending so many hours upright the day before. The usually dull after-dinner gathering presided over by his mother had been considerably enlivened by Jane's gentle presence. His family and friends were terrible snobs—with the possible exception of Jordan, and Jane had looked charmingly vulnerable to their disapproval. George had felt like his namesake saint defending a damsel from dragons, the queen dragon, of course, being his lady mother, with the formidable Mrs. Moorsmythe being the foremost reptile-in-waiting.

That notion alone had been enough to make the evening a success as far as he was concerned. But dear Miss O'Connell, the esteemed physician, had managed to stage an absolute coup of amusement by challenging dim old Sir Nigel and the insufferable Tindale to a game of poker. Not to mention Jordan. George had almost laughed out loud when she'd aced the lot of them. Sir Nigel had looked like he'd swallowed a plum pit; Tindale had become quiet for the first time since he'd come to Endsfield, and Jordan—Jordan had been piqued, which required more animation than he'd shown since Mary Catherine had died.

Jordan and Miss O'Connell. George smiled at the thought. Life was improving by the day. He felt so buoyant that he slapped playfully at Pauline's backside when he met the plump kitchen girl on the stairway.

" 'Ere now, Mr. Chesterfield! Be'ave yerself, sir. Ye'll make me drop me tray."

"And who is that for, my girl? Is someone ill?"

"No, sir. The doctor lady and 'er friend are takin' breakfast upstairs this mornin'."

"Ah! That's what they think. I will deliver the tray."

"Now, sir! Ye'll be gettin' me in trouble, ye will!"

"I never would, you pretty thing!" He deftly lifted the tray from her hands. "Run along and be a good girl now."

"Be careful with that tea, sir! It's 'ot!"

"Never fear." He cockily balanced the tray on one

hand and headed back up the stairs. Pauline shook her head and left him to it.

Miss O'Connell did not look overwhelmingly pleased to see him when she opened the door to his knock. Jane, however, greeted his entrance with a gratifying smile.

"It's a beautiful morning," he announced. "How can you lovely ladies contemplate hiding yourselves in this dreary room when good company, good food, and sunshine await in the breakfast room?"

"Is that our tray?" Ellen eyed him suspiciously.

"It is," he admitted, "but you can't have it. I'm determined to have your company at the morning meal."

"Ellen would rather we eat up here," Jane said unhappily.

"I can well understand why," George said. "After the brouhaha last night, many ladies would be cringing in their rooms. But you!" An expansive gesture with his free hand included both women. "You are made of sterner stuff, I know."

"We would really rather eat up here." Ellen was obviously unimpressed with his wit. Jane, on the other hand, positively twinkled at him. He twinkled back at her, then turned all his charm on the skeptic.

"Now, Miss O'Connell. A woman of your intelligence knows that when one is in a row, the only thing to do is brazen it out and keep a stiff upper lip—particularly with my lady mother, God bless the old bat."

Jane's sharp intake of breath made him smile. "An old bat much beloved of her sons, but an old bat all the same. Give her an inch and she'll take a mile. I've not even been down to breakfast and I've already heard the servants talking about the bellows she was letting loose this morning—and it was Miss O'Connell's name on her lips, I understand. Annoying, I realize, but let my mother know she's cut you and she'll not stop till your very guts are hanging out."

Ellen was fighting a smile, he could tell.

"My brother also. Stand up to him and show him you're not at all intimidated by his bluster, or he'll eat you alive. The only way to deal with Jordan is to be more imperious than he is."

"You don't understand," Ellen protested.

"I understand enough," George said with a suddenly gentle smile. "Now come down with me to breakfast, you two. Hiding only makes the circling wolves more eager."

CHAPTER 7

Breakfast was every bit as bad as Ellen had feared it would be—not the food, the company. Lady Chesterfield gave her and Jane a greeting that could have frozen the water steaming in the teapot, then treated them to icy silence. Hillary looked right through them both as if they didn't exist. Lady Clifton nodded curtly, and her husband regarded Ellen with a bit more interest than Ellen was comfortable with. Jordan's spot at the table was glaringly empty.

The only people who seemed oblivious to the tense undercurrents were Sir Nigel, who cheerfully urged Ellen to confide the secrets of winning at poker, and George, who chatted cheerfully about the fine weather, the Kipling stories he'd been reading, the flakiness of Cook's pastries. When he detoured to the subject of the latest British setbacks with the Boers in South Africa, his mother silenced him with a brusque reprimand.

"That is hardly an appropriate subject for breakfast, George."

"What? Oh. Of course, Mother. You're right, as usual.

Sorry." He smiled innocently. "I suppose a better subject of conversation would be tonight's Hunt Ball. I'm sure all the ladies will be busy today resting up for the night's festivities." He winked at Sir Nigel and Lord Clifton. "Best thing for the gentlemen to do is stay out of their way, eh?"

"Hunt Ball?" Jane asked shyly.

"Yes, well, it isn't really a ball, is it, Mother? Though it's always called so. Merely a country dance to celebrate the opening of fox season and the first hunt, which is Monday. Tch! With this fine weather upon us, it's hard to believe that today is the first day of November. Everyone who's anyone in the county will be here, and some come up from London as well. They'll most of them be staying for Monday's hunt, of course."

"My!" Jane breathed. "It sounds thrilling."

George grinned. "You, my dear Miss Browne, will be a great success at the ball, I'm sure. You must promise to save at least one waltz for me."

Jane's face pinkened. "I . . . I—"

"Of course you and Miss O'Connell will attend. I would be devastated if you weren't there."

Lady Chesterfield choked on her mouthful of tarts. Hillary's eyes snapped in alarm, and Lady Clifton's teacup halted halfway to her lips. The buttery sunshine that streamed through the breakfast-room windows couldn't dispel the sudden chill.

Jane stuttered. Ellen opened her mouth to deny that they had any intention of attending, but she hesitated. There were at least a thousand things she would rather do than go to some insipid English ball. Yet Lady Chesterfield's horror at George's invitation inspired a perverse delight.

Jane began their excuses. "We really have nothing to wear."

"With all the closets full of clothing in this house, I'm sure something can be found," George assured her.

"Of course we'll be there," Ellen declared. "We wouldn't miss it, would we, Jane?"

Jane's wistful look brightened to delight, and George gave Ellen a knowing wink. But best of all, the expression on Lady Chesterfield's face made the prospect of a terrible evening almost worthwhile.

"This will be perfect!" Andrea said around the pins in her mouth. "Don't move, Ellen! Just one more little tuck."

Sometime during the fitting session Andrea and Prissy had both dispensed with all formality of address. Miss O'Connell and Miss Browne had become Ellen and Jane, and they all giggled together like school friends as Andrea fit one of her mother's gowns to Ellen's slighter frame. At least, Jane and Andrea and Prissy giggled together. Ellen was not allowed to laugh, or move, or even inspect the results as she stood like a statue in front of the mirror in her bedroom while being stuck with pins and listening while necklines, sleeve length, and lace trim were debated.

"This is an incredible amount of trouble to go to for just one dance," Ellen complained.

"You have to go so you can keep me company," Andrea declared. "I can't believe Aunt Elizabeth said I could come. I'm not allowed to dance, of course, because I haven't yet come out, and no one will talk to me, I'm sure. They'll think I'm just a child. The ladies will be busy flirting with the gentlemen, and no gentleman is going to be seen with a girl only fifteen years old. But you'll talk to me, won't you Ellen?"

"Ouch! Not if you keep sticking me with pins I won't."

"Hmm." Andrea cocked her head curiously as she cinched the waistline. "Do you have a corset?"

"No," Ellen replied. "And I'm not wearing one to the dance."

"You're not as skinny as you look. I can't get this to button."

"Just let it out," Jane said quickly. "You're altering everything else."

"Well, then," Andrea declared, "you're done." She carefully unpinned just enough to let Ellen slip out of the dress. "I'll have it finished in no time."

"You should let me do it," Ellen said. "I am able to stitch things other than incisions, you know."

"Or me," Jane offered. "Just because we found a gown that fits me exactly doesn't mean I shouldn't help."

Andrea gave them an indignant glare. "No you don't! I like to sew. Besides, Chelsea Burnham down in Merwyk has a new electric sewing machine. Her father's an inventor, you know, and they have a generator for electric power. Anyway, Chelsea's going to teach me how to use the machine. Isn't that exciting?"

"If you say so," Ellen admitted. "Are you sure you want to alter your mother's dress?"

"Of course. I'll never wear it. It's too old-fashioned. Cousin Jordan has promised me a whole new wardrobe next year for my coming out."

Prissy, sitting cross-legged on Ellen's bed, puckered her face. "Only if we don't get sent away to some school! If that happens, we'll march around in dull gray pinafores all day long and you won't ever get a coming-out ball. Me either."

Jane sat beside Prissy. "Are you girls going away to school?"

"If Jordan marries old Bore-smythe, she'll send us away."

"I'm sure your cousin wouldn't permit that!" Ellen told them. "Not if you don't want to go."

Andrea shrugged. "No one would blame him. Everyone said Jordan should have sent us off to school when our parents died. Aunt Elizabeth thought it would be good for us. But Jordan brought us here to live. He treats us like we were his sisters instead of just cousins, but he doesn't have to."

"Of course he does," Ellen replied. "You're his family. He's too fine a man to not share with you. Besides, he loves you. I can tell."

"Cousin Jordan's the best!" Prissy declared.

The sisters exchanged a look that Ellen couldn't interpret. No doubt they were up to some kind of mischief, but as she and Jane seemed to be on the girls' good side, she doubted they had to worry about whatever plot those creative little minds were hatching.

Not until she was dressing for the ball that night did she discover how wrong she was. The dress Andrea had altered for her fit perfectly. In fact, it fit much too well. Appalled, she marched down the hall to Jane's room.

"Jane! Look at this!" Ellen pirouetted so Jane could get the full effect of the plunging neckline, the off-the-shoulder lace sleeves, the form-fitting bodice.

"Oh, Ellen! You look stunning!"

"I look like a . . . like somebody's high-class mistress!"

"No you don't! I mean . . . well, you certainly look

pretty enough to be such a thing, but not tawdry at all. Goodness, but Andrea is a very talented seamstress. That gown didn't look anything like that this afternoon."

Ellen scowled at herself in the mirror. "Look at that neckline! Whatever was she thinking?"

"But it's all the fashion now," Jane told her.

"It's indecent!"

"You exaggerate. It doesn't reveal anything that shouldn't be seen, after all. You have a lovely figure, and you should show it off."

"Can't we find a scarf or something to pin over . . . over . . ." She gestured helplessly to the expanse of flesh above the deeply scooped bodice. Only a covering of wispy lace above the neckline gave the gown any pretense of being decently modest, and the lace merely attracted the eye to the décolletage.

"It would spoil the effect."

"That's the idea!"

"Now, Ellen. It is no longer necessary to be draped in armor from your toes to your chin every time you appear in public. Our good queen might still favor it, but in these last years Prince Edward's influence has made standards much more lax."

Ellen's eyes narrowed. "I don't notice you wearing something cut down to the base of your sternum."

"If I did, no one would notice. Now, hold your head up and be proud," Jane advised. "If I were as beautiful as you are, I'd march into that ballroom and take wicked delight at all the men tripping over their tongues at the sight of me."

Ellen stared in the mirror and bit her lip.

"It's too late to do anything about it now," Jane told her.

"No it's not. I could stay up here."

Jane's smile faltered, and when it returned, it was more dutiful than happy. Ellen realized then that if she didn't go to the cursed ball, Jane wouldn't either. Even though Jane wanted more than anything to experience such a high society affair, she would never walk alone into that pride of social lions.

"Very well." Ellen sighed. "We'll go down. But when I find Andrea, I'm going to wring her conniving little neck."

The dancing had already begun by the time Ellen and Jane made their entrance. The ballroom which had seemed so cavernous now seemed too small to hold the crowd of elite personages from Staffordshire and London who conversed, gossiped, laughed, drank, and devoured the hors d'oeuvres created by Cook and the legion of special kitchen help that Lady Chesterfield had hired. A late dinner would be served toward midnight, but no one was saving either appetite or energy for the meal.

George immediately claimed Jane and signed every dance on her card. Ellen gave Jane a cautionary frown, but Jane smiled radiantly and let George tow her onto the dance floor. Ellen hoped her friend wasn't getting in over her head with the man, though Ellen was scarcely in a postion to be judgmental in that regard.

Ellen, also, was not left unclaimed for long, though it wasn't a handsome swain who came to fetch her, but a demure-looking Andrea.

"Oh, Ellen! You look so beautiful! I knew that dress would set off your eyes and hair."

"That's not all it sets off," Ellen complained in a soft hiss. "The bodice was not cut like this when I tried it on."

Andrea's wide blue eyes were all innocence. "But, Ellen, I told you I had to alter it."

"A tuck here, a dart there, you said."

"A snip here, a snip there." The girl's cheeks dimpled in a winning smile. "I didn't want you to look drab."

"No chance of that."

"Wouldn't it be romantic if you caught some rich nobleman's eye?" Andrea said dreamily. "You could marry and make all the local ladies green with envy because you'd made such a fine catch—and you a nobody from America. Then you could stay here and we could be friends."

Ellen rolled her eyes. "No, Andrea. It would not be romantic, because it is not going to happen."

"It could!"

"No, it couldn't. Believe me, it couldn't."

Just then they caught Lady Chesterfield's eye, and the grand dragon gestured them over to where she sat on a thronelike chair overlooking the dance floor. "Andrea, quit hanging onto Miss O'Connell. How can she get acquainted with you monopolizing her so? Run along and stay out of mischief, or I'll change my mind about letting you stay up for dinner."

It was a diplomatic way to separate them, Ellen mused as Andrea obediently excused herself. Her ladyship didn't want her niece tainted with Ellen's working-class crudeness and unconventional American ideas.

"Well, Miss O'Connell, what do you think of our little gathering?"

"Very grand, your ladyship."

"Oh, this is not at all grand. You should be in London during the Season to see the really grand fetes."

"I can imagine."

It was a strain to be polite, but Ellen tried. Her effort

was no more convincing than Lady Chesterfield's, however. They both heard the gnash of teeth behind the sham
courtesies.

"I trust you will stay out of the garden this evening,"
Lady Chesterfield finally said. "My son cannot afford to
offend any more acquaintances on your behalf."

Ellen flushed a fiery red. She had to bite her lip to
hold back a cutting reply.

"Do I make myself clear?" Lady Chesterfield inquired.

"Very clear, ma'am."

"Good. Then be off and have a good time, Miss
O'Connell," she said with a dismissive gesture. Her at-
tention turned to another victim as she spied George and
Jane dancing together. Ellen wasted no time in escaping.

Andrea knew she had to do something, and do it now,
or the evening was going to be a total disaster. She'd
spent all afternoon at Chelsea Burnham's working on
that machine from hell to finish Ellen's dress in time.
Her fingers were stiff, her shoulders ached, and her patience was frayed, but it had been worth the trouble
when she'd seen Ellen in her creation. She was a vision.
The green of the dress made her eyes look like emeralds
in her pale oval face. Her hair was black as night, and
the lights of the chandeliers caught its sheen and set stars
to glittering in every curl and wave. She'd abandonned
her usual drab braided bun for a soft style of loose curls
caught at the crown and bouncing with every move she
made.

The dress, though, made her shine, Andrea thought
with a mental pat on her own back. It might not be the
height of fashion, but no one could say it wasn't eye-
catching. It was a siren's garment made demure by a few

frills of strategically positioned lace. Ellen's figure did the dress justice, and in return, the dress made Ellen a vision no man could resist. Or at least, Andrea couldn't imagine any man resisting. Even her dour, stiff-upper-lip cousin.

The trouble was, Jordan seemed to be resisting very well. He was huddled in a corner with several other gentlemen, and from the intent look on their faces they were no doubt indulging in an unentertaining discussion of politics, foreign relations, or some other dull topic. Not only did Jordan take no notice of Ellen, but he seemed to be deliberately avoiding looking her way. Andrea's afternoon of grueling labor and inventive planning were going to waste.

Not if she could prevent it, Andrea told herself. She put a smile on her face and marched toward her cousin.

"Hello, Cousin Jordan."

"Hello, Andrea. You're looking very lovely this evening." He gave her the smile that he reserved for her and Prissy, and she felt her heart expand a bit. This man had taken them in when everyone else had sought only to push them off onto a dreary school or another relative. She had to save him from Hillary, not only for the sake of herself and her sister, but for his own sake. The other gentlemen mumbled polite greetings and drifted away, as Andrea had known they would. Adults seemed to think that adolescence was a contagious disease. That worked to her advantage in this instance, for now she had Jordan all to herself.

"I feel very grown up," she confided to him. "It's a shame I'm not allowed to dance."

"You'll have plenty of time for that after next year."

"I know. But sometimes that seems a long time away."

"Don't wish the time gone, Sprite. Once the day is past you can never get it back."

"Well, when I'm old, I certainly hope I don't end up like Miss O'Connell."

That got his interest, Andrea could tell.

"What's wrong with Miss O'Connell?"

Andrea drew closer to him and whispered, "Absolutely no one will dance with her. Everyone knows she was cavorting with Tindale in the garden. I heard Lady Clifton tell Mrs. Afton-James that you were looking for an excuse to toss her out on her bustle."

Jordan cocked a brow in a manner that made Andrea wonder if she was being all that convincing. She directed a pitying gaze to where Ellen stood by the canapés, in the crowd and yet alone, surrounded by a small space of privacy that no one seemed inclined to penetrate.

"I also heard Hillary tell Miss Henley and Lady Cherbourg that Ellen is nothing more than a working-class trollop, and any man who took her out on the floor would bring his taste into question."

"Is that so? You and your ears certainly seem to have made a thorough circuit of the room."

Andrea felt her face heat. "People don't guard what they say around someone they consider a mere child."

"Well, I suppose the only thing for me to do is to dance with the lady." He gave Andrea a shrewd smile. "Do you suppose that would help the problem?"

"Oh yes!" Andrea tried not to sound too eager. Just to clinch the deal, she added, "But maybe you shouldn't, Jordan. Aunt Elizabeth won't speak to you for a week if you show partiality to Ellen in front of all these important people."

Jordan chuckled. "Even more reason to rush to the lady's rescue. By the way, Sprite. Where did Ellen get that dress? Do you have that among the nuggets of information you've been gathering?"

"I made it for her," Andrea boasted. "Or at least, I altered it. It was my mother's. Isn't it spectacular?"

"That's an apt description." Jordan smiled in a most peculiar fashion as his eyes lingered on her handiwork. "Absolutely spectacular."

Hillary Moorsmythe had been friends with Cynthia Kelley since they were both five, and through the years Cynthia had never failed to call her attention to any little incident or event that might prove embarrassing or humiliating to her. This evening she was true to form.

"Hillary, who is that woman Jordan is dancing with? I thought you said he detested dancing?"

Hillary felt her jaw tighten. She was going to have a raging headache before this evening was over. "She's nobody, believe me. I'm sure Jordan feels obligated to ensure she dances at least once. She's the American woman doctor who supposedly saved George's life, and you know how fond Jordan is of George."

"From the way he's holding her, I'd say George isn't the only one Jordan's fond of."

"Don't be ridiculous," Hillary said in a tight voice. Her head was truly beginning to pound. "She's an American, and common as dirt. She has no manners to speak of, and absolutely no notion of propriety. If Jordan didn't feel the family was in debt to her, he wouldn't give her a second look."

Cynthia gave her a sly smile. "Second looks are seldom necessary when a man can't pull his eyes away from the first one."

Wonderful! Hillary thought. Just wonderful! There was nothing Cynthia loved more than gossip. She was just the person to have the whole county, and all of London as well, believing that Jordan was positively drooling over Ellen O'Connell. Everyone knew that Jordan and Hillary were about to become engaged, and this would make it appear as though Hillary had been thrown over. Cynthia had always been jealous of Hillary's prospects of becoming the next Lady Chesterfield, and to have Hillary embarrassed would suit her very well.

As if her evening wasn't going badly enough, Andrea Chesterfield walked up with a Cheshire cat smile on her face. "Hello, Miss Moorsmythe. Do you believe Jordan actually allowed himself to be lured onto the dance floor? Doesn't Miss O'Connell look beautiful in that dress?"

Hillary scowled, but the little minx wouldn't be discouraged.

"I don't think I've ever seen Jordan look so animated!" Andrea gushed.

Cynthia and Andrea exchanged smirks. Jordan was going to regret this, Hillary vowed. She was going to make sure he did—after they were married.

No one had been more surprised than Ellen when Jordan claimed her for a dance. The situation was awkward to say the least. They'd parted on cautiously good terms from his study that morning, but their encounter in the garden was still a brilliant image in her mind—his face turning red from the force of her slap, and her lips burning from the heat of his kiss. Now, as his arms circled her for the waltz, she was too aware of how those arms had felt pulling her toward him for that kiss. The spicy, masculine scent of him brought on the same dizzying confusion she'd felt then. His hair still curled at his neckline in the same soft whorls that had slipped so silkily through her fingers. Then and now, they were so close she could see the very slight shadowing of his cheeks by a beard that refused to be completely civilized. It had felt rough against her skin when he had kissed her—rough, and erotic, and impossibly good.

Damnation! Ellen cursed silently. What kind of casual social conversation was appropriate for two people under these circumstances?

"You look absolutely lovely tonight," Jordan said. He seemed to have no trouble making small talk. Perhaps he assaulted his female guests frequently enough that this sort of thing was old hat. She smiled at the notion of the forbidding and very proper Lord Chesterfield leading a secret life as a libertine.

"Especially when you smile," he added, looking down at her face as he guided them gracefully around the other dancers.

His tone was warm—warm enough to make her insides go soft. She groped for an impersonal subject. "Your cousin Andrea altered one of her mother's dresses for me."

"So she informed me with great pride. She seems to be very desirous of us dancing together."

That explained it, Ellen thought. This hadn't been Jordan's idea at all. Suddenly, Andrea's motive for decking her out like a courtesan became obvious.

"I'm afraid the dress is a bit . . . overstated," Ellen admitted.

"I wouldn't say that," Jordan said, looking down at her with an appreciative smile. "I rather like the statement it's making."

"You and every other man in the room who catches sight of me. You know this is a plot, don't you?"

"I'm beginning to realize that. Andrea did try to be

subtle about prodding me to dance with you, but she's more talented at straightforward mischief than deception. It's one of the things I like most about her. I'm sorry if my impish little cousins have embarrassed you."

"I'm hard to embarrass," Ellen said with a sudden grin. "You should have learned that by now. Besides, I like Andrea and Prissy very much. They remind me of my sister and me not too many years ago."

As they whirled around the room, Ellen wondered if she should tell Jordan about the girls' fears of being sent away. Andrea and Prissy were most likely imagining things, and Jordan wasn't the sort of man who would readily be manipulated by a woman. Moreover, if he really did intend to marry Hillary Moorsmythe, he wouldn't appreciate the sisters' uncomplimentary tales.

She had nearly convinced herself to keep her nose out of Jordan's business when she caught Hillary's glance from across the room. The venom in the other woman's glare made Ellen miss a step. Jordan's strong grip kept her from tripping and making a complete fool of herself.

"Did I step on your foot?" he asked.

"No. Of course not. I'm just being clumsy."

Jordan's intended or not, Hillary was a witch. Ellen didn't need her medical diploma to diagnose an evil-humored spirit when she saw one.

The dance ended. Jordan whirled them to a graceful finish. With his hand firmly on the small of her back, he propelled her through the crowd toward the table that held the hors d'oeurves. Ellen saw Andrea at the end of the table, munching canapés and beaming at them like a fairy godmother who'd just matched up Cinderella and the Prince. Suddenly Ellen decided to tell Jordan about the girls' fear. If he didn't like the implication about his lady love, that was just too bad.

Before she could open her mouth to say anything, however, a footman intruded.

"Pardon, sir, but Mr. Tarahill in the kennel sent a boy to say that Maisy is whelping."

"Thank you, Loftus. Tell Mr. Tarahill that I'll be there directly." His face instantly transformed from the composed aristocrat to an expression Ellen saw on the countenance of almost every expectant father—elation, worry, dread, anticipation.

"May I come with you?" she asked. "I've had almost as much experience delivering foals and puppies as human babies."

"I shouldn't ask you to leave the party."

Ellen smiled. "I suspect the real party is going to be in the kennel."

In his answering grin, Ellen thought she saw the boy Jordan once was—the boy who still lurked beneath the stern exterior of the man.

It had already been a long day for Jordan, and the night promised to be even longer. The exhilaration of Maisy's whelping, however, buoyed him during the first hours they spent in the kennel. Two pups had been born—fat, healthy, wriggling, and diving for the nearest nipple as soon as they gasped in their first breath. Nothing had been required of him and Ellen other than to sit on the clean blankets spread in Maisy's kennel and marvel at the miracle of birth.

Jordan also found himself marveling at the miracle of Ellen O'Connell. She had changed into a plain gray dress and white apron before they had come to the kennel—almost as if she were treating a human patient. Yet in that plain attire, sitting on the floor of a kennel with Maisy's head pillowed on her lap, she looked more feminine and more beautiful than any society belle dressed in silk and sitting on velvet. She'd looked the part of a temptress in the dress Andrea had gotten her to wear, but here, speaking soft words of comfort to the panting, laboring dog, she was an angel.

"You've got the gift with animals," Jordan noted.

She looked up, her hand still stroking Maisy's head. "Many of my human patients like me as well. You'd be surprised." Her smile was a gentle tease.

Here she was at home. It was obvious. Here she was certain. She was unlike any woman Jordan had ever known.

"You're very fond of Maisy, aren't you?" she commented.

"She's one of my best friends," he admitted. "If it weren't for my mother's objections, she'd live in the house and probably sleep on my bed."

"Maisy's no doubt a more pleasant companion than some who sleep in your house."

Jordan laughed. "I'll have to admit that's true."

They sat there another half hour, and Ellen told him of the wolf that shared the O'Connell home in Montana, and how he came to be there. She told anecdotes about foalings and whelpings her stepmother Olivia had attended. "In Montana, a doctor has to be a horse doctor, a dog doctor, a pig and cow doctor as well as a human doctor. I remember Olivia telling me once that her animal patients were far more appreciative of her efforts than most of the people she treated."

"That doesn't surprise me," Jordan replied. "Animals are often more honest than human beings."

"Sometimes that's not saying much."

Jordan wondered what experience in Ellen's life prompted the sad quirk of her lips. Suddenly he wanted to meet the man—he assumed it was a man—who had caused the pain he saw in that half smile. He'd like to meet him and show him a thing or two about pain.

They waited another fifteen minutes before Ellen started to worry about Maisy's failure to produce another puppy. The dog had been in hard labor for almost an hour without anything to show for it.

"Does your Mr. Tarahill have much experience in helping difficult deliveries?" Ellen asked Jordan.

He felt a pang of alarm. "Some. Are we going to need help?"

"I think so." Her gentle hand caressed the pointer's silky head. "Poor Maisy. It happens every time, doesn't it, sweetie? A girl falls for some handsome charmer, then he gallops away and leaves you with all the dirty work."

CHAPTER 8

By midmorning, Maisy was the tired but proud mother of seven pups, after hours of hard labor in which Ellen had knelt beside her applying pressure to the dog's abdomen to encourage the contractions. Jordan had knelt at Maisy's nether end to receive the emerging pup, and Mr. Tarahill had taken the newborns, cleared the little nostrils of mucus, and coaxed the pups to breathe. The third puppy to be born—a whopping big boy—had gotten stuck in the birth canal and required a long, grueling labor to deliver. Consequently, the pups in line behind that one had been jammed into a fetal traffic jam that had caused them considerable distress.

Finally, though, all the newborns were dry, clean, and discovering the joys of their mother's warm milk. Having licked and carefully inspected each one, Maisy seemed enormously proud of herself. Jordan and Mr. Tarahill, smeared in blood and greenish slime, both beamed like new fathers. Ellen was exhilarated as she always was after witnessing the wonder of birth. Canine, equine, or human—it didn't matter. The effect on her spirit was the same.

"Do you think they'll be all right now?" Jordan asked after the kennel master had left to get some much needed sleep.

"I expect so. But all the same, I'd like to stay with them a little while."

"I'll stay as well."

Ellen marveled at yet another facet of Jordan Chesterfield. She had difficulty believing the man who had cheerfully helped blow the slime from puppy nostrils was the same haughty aristocrat who had been so cantankerous over a bit of bareback bravado, the same intimidating lothario she had walloped in the garden, or the same cool sophisticate she had danced with just the night before. Was there no end of different men hiding behind the starched facade he presented to the world?

"I'm in your debt once again," he observed. "Without you, Maisy might have died trying to deliver this litter."

"Yes, well, you probably owe me yet another passage across the Atlantic then."

"Done," he said.

"I was joking." She laughed.

"I wasn't. Perhaps I'll just give you *carte blanche* on the Atlantic and Mediterranean Steamship Line. Then I could send for you whenever a family member needs a hole drilled in their head or a puppy decides to delay his entrance into the world."

She cocked a brow. "Or whenever you need to have a brawl with another member of the peerage, or someone to demonstrate the fine art of galloping across the countryside like a gypsy?"

He grinned. "That, too."

Suddenly Ellen was impossibly tired. "I don't think

I can get up from this floor. I've been down here too long."

Jordan managed to rise, though not with his usual athletic grace. He extended a hand to help her up. His grasp was firm and warm, and somehow it drove some of the cold ache from Ellen's bones. She didn't want to let it go.

They'd crossed a line sometime in the night or early morning, Ellen knew. The two people who had rushed to the kennel the night before had been mostly strangers, sometimes allies, but always dancing on the edge of antagonism. The two people who trudged out, weary, disheveled, and dirty, were friends. More than friends, Ellen admitted to herself. Her hand still felt the heat of his touch, and that heat was more than just the warmth of flesh pressed to flesh. It came from inside—a glow, an awareness, a tingle of desire. Was it her imagination, or was desire also there in Jordan's eyes when he looked at her? In the polite offer of a hand or support of a strong arm? In the slow curve of his smile?

What a concept, desire. It encompassed both joy and shame, at once delightful and forbidden. It could no longer be a part of Ellen's life. Not now, at least. Yet there it was a building warmth inside her heart and a bright glint in Jordan Chesterfield's eyes. She would ignore it, of course. And Jordan would no doubt forget her as soon as she left England. She would forget him, also, Ellen told herself.

Meanwhile, it felt good to know they were friends.

Before the day was over, Ellen convinced Jordan to move Maisy and her puppies into the house. November was upon them, and though the last few days had been bright, the nights were cold. The newborns were vulnerable to the fall in temperature, she explained, because they couldn't maintain their own body temperature until they were two weeks old. Jordan promptly moved mother and pups to a cozy, blanket-lined box in front of the fireplace of his private sitting room, despite his mother's sharp objections. For the next few days, anyone looking for Jordan or Ellen had merely to go there, where the two of them watched with fascination while Maisy's puppies tightened their grasp on life.

The two last born pups were weak from spending so much time being battered by Maisy's labor. One stubbornly clung to life. The other died, and Jordan and Ellen together buried the little body beneath a huge, spreading tree at the edge of the woods. They sat by the little grave for the better part of an hour, mostly silent, each with their own thoughts inspired by even so insignificant a death. Walking together back to the house, Jordan reached for Ellen's hand as if it were simply the natural thing to do. She didn't pull it away. Her hand resting in his felt too comfortable, and the warmth that radiated from his touch was too seductive in a friendly, nonthreatening way. She was a fool, Ellen told herself. The worst kind of fool. But she still didn't pull her hand away.

While her surviving six babies thrived, crawling blindly over one another and her, falling into milk-sated sleep in warm puppy piles, Maisy calmly welcomed a small parade of visitors. George and Jane came together. While Jane and Ellen cuddled the little furry bodies, Jordan and George predicted their glorious careers as field dogs. Andrea and Prissy were in Jordan's sitting room every time Miss Todestan turned her back. Prissy was anxious to pick out the puppy Jordan had promised her. She didn't have the patience to wait a couple of months as her cousin advised. It was a difficult decision for a ten-year-old who melted every time a puppy tongue reached out to touch her skin or a milk-laden puppy sigh caressed her cheek. She hugged them all, kissed them all, held one-sided conversations with each of them, and finally settled on the smallest—the last born female who had survived the first day by the skin of her teeth.

"Her name is Anna, after my mama," Prissy told them, giving Jordan a cautious sideways look.

"Prissy!" Andrea objected.

Jordan smiled, however. "Your mother would be proud to have such a beautiful pup named after her. Don't you think so, Andrea?"

Andrea rolled her eyes, but Prissy rewarded Jordan with a glowing smile and an enthusiastic hug. Ellen thought she might hug the man herself unless she got control of herself.

When Jordan looked at her, she couldn't keep back the flush, but if he noticed, he politely ignored it. "You should pick out a puppy as well, Miss O'Connell."

She laughed shakily. "Not me. Much as I'd love to have one, I'm headed back to America. Remember? And these little ones won't be old enough to travel when I leave."

"You've got *carte blanche* on my ships. You can come back to England and pick it up."

"And visit!" Prissy declared.

Andrea gave Ellen a pleading look, but Ellen declined. "I don't think so. But thank you."

"I'll save you a pup anyway," Jordan said, "so you'd better think of a name."

"Name it Daisy!" Prissy demanded.

"Too close to Maisy," Andrea objected.

"How about Clover!"

"That's dumb!"

"Brownie!"

"Dumber!"

While the sisters loudly debated a proper name, Maisy curled contentedly in one corner of her box. The puppies piled into a heap and fell asleep. Jordan drew close to Ellen and leaned down to whisper in her ear. His warm breath sent a delicious shiver traveling down her spine. "I think the fat one with the short tail likes you."

"Don't tempt me."

Suddenly Ellen wondered if she was talking about puppies or a temptation entirely more serious. The wicked smile Jordan sent her left no doubt that he was speculating about the same thing.

"Well!" A melodious exclamation interrupted the exchange and the ongoing argument over names. "Isn't this . . . homey!"

Hillary strolled into the sitting room. Or perhaps, Ellen thought with sudden waspishness, strolled was too flattering a term. Undulate was more descriptive. Her stride combined the upright dignity taught by ladies' finishing schools with the enticing motion of a woman confident of her own allure. For the first time in her life, Ellen almost wished she could learn to walk with that feminine swagger, but it was far too late now.

"Aren't they cute!" Hillary exclaimed, bending over Maisy's box. Her smile was determined, though her voice didn't carry much conviction. "Puppy, puppy, puppy!"

Behind Hillary's back, Andrea rolled her eyes. Prissy bit her lip to keep from giggling. Maisy gave Hillary the look that dogs reserve for people who prefer cats.

"Can I pick one up?" Hillary asked Jordan.

Ellen was tempted to join Andrea in rolling her eyes. Any fool could see that Hillary would pick up a live coal if the feat would get Jordan's attention. When she plucked a sleeping puppy from the pile, she handled it in much the same manner as she might have handled that hot coal.

"Rub its little tummy," Prissy invited. "Puppies like that."

Ellen bit her lip as Hillary followed Prissy's instructions. The puppy did indeed like the tummy rub. True to puppy instincts, it reacted to the stimulus and let loose its bladder into Hillary's hand.

"Oh my! Oh my God!" Hillary cried.

Jordan dashed in and took the little bundle of fur before she dropped it.

"It's only puppy pee," Prissy said with a smirk, and was rewarded with Hillary's poisonous glare.

"You did that on purpose."

"I didn't!" Prissy lied.

"Now, Hillary," Jordan soothed. "It's not going to hurt you. Just wash your hands."

Hillary made a visible effort to wipe the venom from her expression as she marched to the washstand and poured water over her hands. Ellen wondered how a man of Jordan's intelligence could be taken in by such an act.

"Really, Jordan. Turning your sitting room into a kennel is going a bit far, don't you think? Your mother's fit to be tied."

"My mother will get used to it."

Hillary clucked with fastidious distaste, but dropped the subject as a losing proposition. Instead, she tried to persuade Jordan to come down to tea. After a few moments of unsuccessful cajoling, she attacked from another flank. "I hope you're not going to use baby-sitting these dogs as an excuse to miss the hunt tomorrow. You promised to show me that new hunter of yours, if you remember, Jordan."

"Couldn't it wait until next week, Hil?"

"Next week Mother and I are going down to London with your mother. Come now, Jordan. You've been boasting about this horse for weeks. And you promised. You wouldn't break your promise, would you?"

The pleading pout of the mouth and wheedling tone were laying it on a bit thick, Ellen thought, but the ploy was successful all the same. Jordan assured Hillary that he would ride with her in the hunt the following morning.

"What of you, Miss O'Connell?" Hillary sent her a tart smile. "Do you hunt?"

"Hunt what, Miss Moorsmythe?"

"Hunt foxes, of course."

"No," Ellen stated flatly. "I've hunted bear, squirrels, rabbits, and once a pesky mountain lion that kept taking calves from my father's herd, but I've never hunted a fox. Why do you hunt them?"

"Because it's good sport. And foxes are vermin."

Hillary's sour tone left no doubt that she considered Ellen in the same class.

Ellen merely smiled. "In Montana there are bigger vermin to hunt than foxes. Many of them carry guns— just to make the event really sporting."

"Colloquial humor. How amusing. Of course, I can understand that you might think the hunt a bit too much for you. I heard about your flying off Goldie into a hedge a few days ago. You're probably still sore."

Ellen refused to be goaded. "I'm not so sore, nor so embarrassed, that I feel I have to prove myself by chasing a harmless animal through the woods. You and Jordan ride out on your hunt, Miss Moorsmythe. I don't feel the least urge to join you."

Hillary was not the only one with foxes on the mind, however. All the guests at Endsfield were looking forward to the next day's hunt. The first hunt of the season had ridden out the day after the hunt ball, and it had been a dismal failure. Despite the best effort of huntsmen and hounds, no foxes had been found to give the local gentry their sport. Everyone was in high hopes that the second hunt of the season would prove more exciting.

That evening, after an interminable dinner enduring Lady Chesterfield's complaints about the house being turned into a kennel, watching George and Jane exchange glances they apparently thought were subtle, and listening to Hillary, in her place next to Jordan, chatter about wanting one of Maisy's puppies, Ellen found herself cornered by Sir Nigel Higgenbotham in the salon. If riding to the hounds was Sir Nigel's favorite pastime, then talking about it was a close second, and in Ellen he found virgin territory—a person who knew nothing about the sport, therefore was in great need of enlightenment.

"The hunt is a true gentleman's sport," he told her. Not that she'd asked, but he assumed her interest. "Ladies, too, of course. No one can follow the hounds like a true English lady, to be sure."

Ellen tried not to look bored.

"The field will be a fine one tomorrow," Sir Nigel predicted, "for everyone in the county has their blood up, and the last hunt simply got it up higher. If we have thirty people mounted, I'd not be surprised."

"Thirty hunters after one little fox," Ellen commented. "Indeed, that does sound sporting."

Sir Nigel missed her sarcasm. "Good sport indeed!

We'll be using Harvey Munn's pack of hounds. Bred in Leicester, they were, and they're a sharp, fast lot. Harvey's good with them, too. Sleeps with them, like as not, he knows them so well."

"What if the fox doesn't want to come out and play?"

Sir Nigel laughed tolerantly at her ignorance. "The boys'll see to it that he does. The huntsman's crew goes out to stop up all the fox holes very early in the morning so when the little beasts come in from their nightly wanders, they find their front doors closed and locked, eh?" He laughed at his own feeble joke. "Then, after the field is mounted and the hounds gathered, the dogs are sent in to flush the fox from whatever thicket he's taken to hiding in. The drawing, this is called. The fox breaks his cover, the hounds take voice, and the chase is on—a rousing gallop over the countryside, in good company, with a good horse beneath you, with the baying of the hounds to lead you on. Ah! I tell you, Miss O'Connell, life doesn't have much better to offer than a good fox hunt."

"And what happens to the fox? Do you shoot him when he's finally cornered?"

"Oh no! That wouldn't be sporting, would it?"

"I doubt the fox would think so."

"Yes, well . . . ah . . . the hounds eat the little beast, usually. We save the brush and the head, of course, and sometimes the feet, to award as trophies. And any youngster who's riding to the hounds for the first time gets a mark of blood. Got mine when I was fourteen. One of the best days of my life."

Ellen kept the disgust from her face, but not from her thoughts. These English had no right to call other people savage. At least when Ellen's Blackfoot relatives hunted, they did so out of need, not a simple desire to kill a helpless creature.

Next morning, she didn't have to rise particularly early to be on hand for the gathering of the intrepid hunters. At ten o'clock they were still devouring the sumptuous brunch that the mistress of Endsfield had provided—not only for her own house party, but for everyone who'd come—representatives of the upper crust from all over the country. Jordan played the host, and Hillary kept herself glued to his side as he greeted his neighbors and acquaintances.

"She looks as though she's already mistress here," Ellen observed tartly to Jane as they sipped hot chocolate and shared a plate of ham and spiced muffins. The morning was too brisk to eat on the front lawn, as had been planned. The entire hunt was crowded into the drawing room, with the overflow finding seats in two of the smaller salons. Dressed in their scarlet coats—called pinks, for some reason Ellen didn't understand—and stuffing themselves with Cook's ham, kippers, eggs, pastries, and cold meats, they seemed in no hurry to get to the business of the day.

"I believe that's a *fait accompli,* for all intents and purposes," Jane said. "Everyone in Staffordshire's been assuming for simply ages that they'll marry. Certainly Lady Chesterfield and Mrs. Moorsmythe are in favor of it."

"And I'm sure Hillary will make just as charming a Lady Chesterfield as her predecessor."

Jane blinked at Ellen's tone. "Goodness, aren't we snippy this morning!"

"Sorry." Ellen grimaced. "I am out of sorts, aren't I?"

"It's all right," Jane said immediately. "You're entitled. If you're not feeling well, why don't you go up-stairs and lie down? Look, they're all getting ready to leave. The house will be peaceful, finally."

"Hello, Miss O'Connell, Miss Browne." Prissy plopped herself down in a chair beside them. Andrea wasn't far behind her. "Aren't you going to ride out with the hunt?"

"Oh no," Jane told them. "I don't ride."

"Ellen does," Prissy said with a giggle.

Ellen gave her a quelling look, which had absolutely no effect on her impish smile. "Don't you have lessons with Miss Todestan?"

"It's Saturday," Andrea reminded her.

"We're going to—"

Andrea hastily shushed Prissy as the last of the guests filed past them. "We're going to follow," she whispered when it was safe. "We're not allowed to ride with the field, but no one forbade us to go out riding on our own this morning. Do you want to come?"

Ellen was seized by the urge to say yes. She wanted to be in on the chase to cheer on the poor fox. "I think I will."

"Ellen!" Jane remonstrated. "You just said you weren't feeling well! Besides, you should be more care-ful. You've already taken one fall from gallivanting about on the back of a horse."

"I'll be careful," she promised, and winked at Prissy. "I just won't use a sidesaddle."

They were indeed careful, she and Andrea and Prissy, as they followed the field of hunters to the covert, pro-nounced "cover," Andrea explained, where the hunts-man believed a fox had taken refuge. Their care, however, was aimed at not being discovered by the host of scarlet-clad riders ahead of them. Not that there was much chance of that. The pack of hounds was excited. The yipping and barking bounced off the thickets and rolled around the meadows in a constant tide of sound. The riders themselves engaged in lively chatter from atop their long-legged, glossy hunters. The horses were painstakingly groomed from the tips of their alert ears down to their polished hooves. The riders were equally well turned out. Not a wrinkle marred their scarlet coats. The ladies' hats perched just so upon their flawless coiffures, and the gentlemen's cocked jauntily to one side.

"Lord help us if any one of them gets a speck of mud on their fine pinks," Ellen observed tartly as she peered at the gathered field through a screen of scraggly hedges. The hunters milled and chatted as Harvey Munn sent the dogs into the covert—a thicket of vegetation so dense that a man would have trouble making his way through. Not so the agile fox, however, nor the eager, yipping dogs. Only a moment passed before a streak of red lightning shot into the open field.

"Tally ho!" came a cry in Nigel Higgenbotham's high-pitched voice. The cry was repeated by other voices, and with a blast of a horn, the huntsman and his hounds were off after their prey.

"There they go!" Andrea exclaimed.

"Not very quickly," Ellen noted. The field was still milling, some having to sharply rein in their horses to keep them from bolting off to the chase.

"They don't want to follow too quickly," Andrea explained. "One doesn't want to take a tumble in the confusion, after all, or overrun the fox."

"I don't think there's much danger of that," Ellen noted.

With typical English orderliness, the field set off at a discreet distance behind the huntsman and hounds. Ellen and the girls followed, keeping to the cover, which made the going all the more difficult. Ellen was very glad she'd insisted that the scandalized groom put a man's saddle on Goldie, and gladder still that she wore a pair of sturdy trousers beneath her skirt—it was really a miracle what items Prissy could produce when required. Ellen had been afraid to ask her just where the trousers had come from.

The saddle wasn't like the stock saddles she had ridden in Montana. It had no horn and no high pommel to keep her in her seat. Instead of heavy stirrup leathers, a mere strap held the irons. Riding the English hunt saddle was almost like riding bareback—something at which Ellen excelled. She had no difficulty staying on Goldie's back as the mare jumped hedges, vaulted ditches, and flew over fences.

Ahead of them, the field stopped. The fox had taken cover in the gorse, and the hounds were trying to rout it. Andrea and Prissy, breathless and perspiring, reined in gratefully. Ellen felt as though she could go on forever, except that she wanted the sky to be the brilliant Montana blue, the wind to smell of prairie grass and cattle, and the mountains to rise in front of her in a jagged wall of purple and green and brown.

"Oops! There he goes again!" Prissy cried.

The fox was a clever little beast. He led them through ditches and woods, over culverts and across planted fields. Heedless of the damage to crops, hedges, or gardens, the hunt followed, looking as though they were having a rollicking good time. After three solid hours of chase and stop, chase and stop, chase and stop, the hounds managed to corner their prey in a windfall that proved a trap for the wily little fellow rather than a refuge. Their baying was dark with bloodlust as the field gathered around for the finish.

"Good work, Munn," Master of Hounds Willard Digby congratulated the huntsman. The Master, a local squire who bred exceptionally fine horses, was nominally in charge of the hunt, while the huntsman had actual charge of the hounds and did most of the work. "Let them have at him, eh?"

Jordan Chesterfield trotted up beside the Master. As always, Hillary was at his side. She looked cool and fresh, every hair still in place. If a sweat had broken out upon her milk and roses skin, it only gave her a wholesome glow.

"It was a good run, Digby," Jordan commented. "Give the fox his due and let him go."

Such a thing wasn't unheard of after a particularly good effort by the fox, but murmurs from the field proved that more than one of the 'hunters' were hoping for a trophy to boast about.

"They're going to let it go," Prissy whispered. The three of them watched anxiously from the cover of tangled thickets and trees.

"No they're not," said Andrea. "They didn't get a fox last week, so they'll take this one."

"Jordan told them to let it go." Ellen parted the branches for a better view. "Won't they do what he says?"

"Maybe not," Andrea answered.

"He's the grandest lord out there, isn't he?"

"Not really. There's an earl and a couple of viscounts in the field. Rank doesn't matter much on the hunt, though. The Master of Hounds is in charge. He makes the decisions."

"Well, he should let the little fella go."

"Not likely."

Andrea was right. The field had been denied a kill in the last hunt, and they were hungry for blood now. Ellen didn't understand it. She realized why ranchers hunted down the occasional mountain lion, bear, or wolves who preyed on their herds, but the most a fox might do was take a few chickens or an egg or two, and a good farm dog could keep it from doing that.

"Poor little fox. He doesn't stand a chance." The vicious baying of the hounds seemed to swell until it filled Ellen's head, and something snapped inside her. It was Ellen O'Connell cowering in the windfall instead of the fox, hounded by the mistakes she'd made out of ignorance, innocence, and too bold a confidence, about to face a merciless end to—not her life—but to freedom, love, the regard of everyone she held dear. The hounds snarled, barked, and howled. Her heart pounded, pounded, pounded until her chest hurt.

"No," she breathed desperately. "I won't let them do it." Scarcely aware of what she did, Ellen slid from the saddle and crouched low to the ground—the hunting stance taught to her long ago by Crooked Stick, her mother's brother. Her fingers curled around a stick the size of her arm. Andrea hissed for her to get back, but the girl's pleas fell on ears that heard only the baying of the hounds, both the pack around the windfall and her own personal pack of demons. Stick held high, she broke into the clearing where hunters, dogs, and fox were playing out their drama.

"Git there!" she shouted at the hounds. "Git you! Git!"

Confused, the dogs scattered as she swung the stick in an arc to force them back. Concentration broken, they snarled among themselves, turning their lust for violence upon one another. Harvey Munn shouted a string of commands at them, while the Master of Hounds and the alarmed field of riders gasped and cried indignant orders for her to desist.

The fox saw his chance to bolt. Intent on escape, his focus was behind him, not in front. Driving the hounds back and causing general chaos, Ellen didn't look where she was going any more than the fox did. Which of them was more astonished when they collided was anybody's guess. Ellen toppled more from surprise than the sudden compact weight that tackled her at full run. The fox's speed took him almost up to Ellen's shoulders before he realized his mistake. For a moment of suspended time they regarded each other, Ellen flat on her back and the fox frozen on her chest. Ellen held her breath, staring wide-eyed at the pointed red face with its tufted ears and alert black eyes. Just as wide-eyed, the fox stared back. Then the moment was over. Time started up again. The fox fled in a red blur. The only thing left of him were the muddy little paw prints on Ellen's chest.

Chaos reigned—cries of indignation and amazement from the genteel hunters, shouts from the huntsman and his helpers, yelps and snarls from the fractious hounds, who were dividing their attention between chewing on one another and trying to get to Ellen. A prone woman with fox prints running up her body must have seemed almost as good prey as the fox.

Then Ellen's world came to a standstill again when a hand reached down to help her up, and above her, out of the confusion, one face came into focus. Eyes glittering like polished steel, mouth a tight line of silence. Jordan Chesterfield's face—dark, saturnine, and ominously calm.

CHAPTER 9

Jordan had never seen anything more absurd, or more infuriating. When Ellen had shot out of the shrubbery and started forcing the hounds back, he'd thought the scene was part of a particularly ridiculous nightmare. It wouldn't have been the first time that Ellen had invaded his dreams.

The chaos that erupted as the fox made good his escape was more appropriate to a two-penny opera than a dream, however. The older Miss Henley threatened to faint. Sir Nigel was as scarlet as his coat—so red in the face he appeared in danger of being strangled by his collar. Digby's mouth kept opening and closing, but nothing came out. Hillary had as much bloodlust in her eyes as the dogs. Lady Chesterfield was sputtering frenetic commands, to which absolutely no one listened, and above it all was the frantic yelping, howling, yipping, and baying of the hounds, along with Munn's wrathful shouts to keep them in line.

Jordan didn't know whether to laugh at the macabre confusion or to march over to Ellen and strangle her for staging such a dangerous, ludicrous, and utterly insane stunt. The certain thing was that he had to get her out of the clearing before the hunters joined with the dogs in ripping her limb from limb.

So he had done just that, and now she stood uneasily in his study, dry leaves adorning her hair, braided top-knot listing to one side, smears of mud and grass staining her backside. She looked younger than Prissy, wilder than a gypsy, and not a bit contrite. And then there were those muddy little fox prints traveling from the hem of her skirt to the starched collar of her shirtwaist. The sight of them made him want to sink into his chair and indulge in a knee-slapping fit of laughter, but he hadn't been drilled in aristocratic restraint for nothing. Not so much as a chuckle escaped him.

After all, he reminded himself, this was no laughing matter.

Forcing Ellen to stand before him like a misbehaving schoolgirl awaiting a reprimand was not having the desired effect, however, for the culprit didn't look intimidated in the least. Her flushed cheeks and muddy dissarray might make her look like a ten-year-old hoyden, but the firmly clenched jaw, uptilted chin, and glittering eyes belonged to a determined woman. A woman, indeed! Jordan wanted to shake some sense into her, then he wanted to kiss her out of sheer relief that she'd come through the escapade in one piece. He could do neither, though, for while she was definitely a woman in need of a shaking, and perhaps a kissing, she wasn't *his* woman.

When Ellen spoke, there wasn't a hint of apology in her voice. "If you intend to simply stand there and stare at me, I'll excuse myself and go to my chamber to clean up." The glitter in her eyes was defiant and a bit apprehensive, but not in the least penitent.

"You stay where you are," he said firmly. "Be grateful that you're a guest here, and not in my charge, for if you were, you'd be marking time standing in a corner of the schoolroom with Andrea and Prissy. Childish behavior merits a child's punishment."

"I'm not in your charge."

"Well, you should be in someone's charge! Obviously, you can't govern yourself as an adult should. What in heaven's name possessed you to do such a thing?" His voice climbed in volume as the morning's fear turned into anger. He wondered at the intensity of his feelings. Lord take him for a fool, but this woman had certainly gotten under his skin. "Do you realize what those hounds could have done to you? Or the damned fox? What if it had bitten you?"

"I merely wanted to let the fox escape. Why was it so damned important for the dogs to tear the poor beast limb from limb? Is it so entertaining to see a creature suffer?"

"That is beside the point!"

"That is the entire point!"

"You behaved like an absolute idiot!"

"I have a right to be an idiot if I want to be one!"

"Now, now, you two!" George's voice intervened between them like a referee separating two boxers. He sauntered into the room as though he had a right to be there, which he didn't. But then, George seldom let that get in his way. "Let's show a little decorum here."

Jordan and Ellen replied at the same time.

"She doesn't know decorum from a—!"

"You can take your decorum and—!"

George cut them off in mid insult. "Temper, temper! Jordan, don't be such an old woman! And Miss O'Connell, don't forget you're addressing the Lord High Arbiter of what's Good, Right, and Proper."

"George, shut up!" Jordan said. "And get out of here."

"What? And leave poor Ellen—you don't mind if I call you Ellen, do you, Miss O'Connell? Leave poor Ellen to your dubious mercy? The whole household believes you are in here strangling her, or perhaps dangling her out the window with thoughts of dropping her to the paving stones below."

"That's ridiculous!"

"So I told them. 'My brother's a reasonable fellow,' I said, 'for all that he's a bit stiff and testy.' But poor Jane petitioned me to storm your study and rescue the fair lady from your retribution." He turned to Ellen with an impish smile. "Consider yourself rescued, fair lady."

Jordan raked his fingers through his hair and glared at the two of them. Once his life had been sedate and under control. Then Ellen O'Connell had come into his life.

"That was quite a ride you made this morning," George continued admiringly. "I've never seen Goldie jump so well. You have a way with horses, don't you?"

"How do you know how well Goldie jumped?" Jordan demanded. "You were here."

"Well, actually, I was following right behind Ellen and the girls."

"What?" Ellen cried.

Jordan didn't know that his patience could stretch so thin without snapping. "You were following behind them?" he asked with deceptive softness.

"Yes."

"On a horse?"

"Of course."

"Riding fast enough to keep them and the field in sight."

"Certainly."

"Christ! Is this whole household full of idiots?"

Ellen was equally angry. "Is that what you call limiting your activities? Do you realize what could have happened had you taken a fall? Let me tell you . . ."

Jordan willingly deferred to Ellen's Hippocratical indignation. The fool was her patient, after all. He was only Jordan's brother. Besides which, Ellen was vastly entertaining to watch when she was in high dudgeon. Indeed, her anger gave her a look of passion that was well nigh irresistible. Jordan's own anger, however, threatened to slip away as he let himself enjoy the sight of Ellen upbraiding her patient.

George took her tongue-lashing with good-natured equanimity, then returned to his original topic.

"All you say is true, dear lady. But, as you see, I was not hurt. And as Jordan can see, neither were you. But I must say, you are a corker on horseback! I wish Jordan could have seen you ride."

"I've seen her," Jordan said darkly. He remembered all too well how she had looked, barelegged and windblown, astride Goldie's naked back.

George mercifully interrupted the image. "With you on his back, my King could outrace Jordan's Romeo on any course that Jordan might choose. I'd wager half my fortune on it."

Jordan sensed trouble ahead as the mad idea took hold and lit his brother's eyes.

"I'm not the horseman to ride against Jordan, but you are, my dear. What a unique race that would be!" George grinned hugely. "The proven, experienced hunter against an upstart colt. The lord of the manor against an upstart woman."

"George! Get out!" Jordan commanded.

As usual, George ignored him. "We could offer a purse, just to make it more exciting. The scandalmongers in London would love it. Jordan Chesterfield outraced by a slip of a woman—an American, of all things. Tindale and deClare would have to eat their words about my not knowing a good piece of horseflesh if it kicked me in the backside. Everyone in the county with a good horse would fall in line to see if he could beat my King. It could make my season. Yes indeed!"

The madness was contagious, for now Ellen's eyes had caught the gleam. "Could I put a wager on the race?"

"Of course!" George said expansively. "That's the spirit! What a lark this is going to be."

"It's going to be no such thing!" Jordan bellowed. "George, get out of here!"

"But, Jordan, *mon frère,* think of it as a chance to defend England's honor, prove the natural superiority of men, and have a rollicking good time!"

Jordan advanced upon his brother with quiet, menacing intensity until the interfering nitwit was backed up against the wall. "There is no chance that I am going to ride in a race against a woman," he told George with unmistakable conviction. "Particularly this woman. Never will it happen. Never."

George gave him the look of puppy dog charm that he'd perfected to an art. "You're absolutely sure?"

"I'm sure."

"Not ever?"

"Never!"

* * *

So how, Jordan wondered early the next morning, did he find himself in the stable tightening the cinch on Romeo's saddle while George gave a bright-eyed Ellen instructions on how to ride King to certain victory? He should know better than to use the word "never." Whenever he did, it got him into trouble. Never say never, especially when there was a woman involved.

Of course, the how was merely a rhetorical question, for he knew very well why he found himself saddling his new hunter before the sun had crested the horizon. Ellen O'Connell. Again. He pitied the men of America if all American women were as confounding as she was. Pitied them, and perhaps envied them a bit, too. Life with Ellen around would never be dull, and a man would be hard put to be bored if he woke up every morning to that face, those green eyes, that slow-burning smile.

It was the last that had done him in. Her smile was all innocence at the same time it promised anything but innocence. She used it unconsciously, Jordan was sure, and it was all the more effective for its artless spontaneity.

George's intrusion into Jordan's study, annoying as it had been, at least had broken the tension between them and returned them to a footing that resembled friendship. Ellen had wheedled an admission from him that he had been happy to see the fox escape, and he had made her understand what an extremely foolish chance she had taken. Then she had started a good-natured teasing about his refusal to race her. He was afraid to lose to a woman, she accused. He was reluctant to have his vaunted Romeo bested by George's King—and a half-dozen other silly reasons she laughed at and flung in his face.

He'd tried to reason with her. Why did she want to race? She answered only half flippantly: she was in the mood to dish out some humiliation after having endured a wagon-load of it herself. She was of a mind to make him eat his words about her horsemanship. Or she was simply feeling ornery. He could take his choice. Then she'd turned that smile upon him and reminded him that he owed her. What harm would it do to take an early-morning ride and turn it into a friendly race?

Was there a man between thirteen and ninety-five who could resist that smile? Jordan wondered. If so, it wasn't him. He'd wanted to kiss her as she'd stood there, all challenge and sass—and to continue kissing her until the freshness of her spirit invaded and brightened his soul. But he hadn't kissed her, of course. He'd given in, wrangling a compromise that had done little but save him a bit of face. The competition was to be a private, friendly race. No chances were to be taken, and all gloating was to be done in private.

And only one wager was allowed. If Ellen won, he agreed to forbid the killing of foxes at the end of any hunt on Chesterfield land for the entire season, and if Jordan won, she would convince Andrea and Prissy to quit pestering him to let them ride astride.

Jordan gave Romeo's muscular shoulder a friendly slap. "Well, old boy, I hope you're prepared to strike a blow in the battle of the sexes this morning."

Romeo snorted twin puffs of vapor into the cold air.

"That's the spirit! Just remember when King is breathing up your tail that he has only an insignificant woman on his back. An American at that. We should win this one easily, right?"

"Don't listen to him, King!" George grinned as he led King out into the aisle and tested the saddle's cinch. "He's an overconfident blowhard, and he doesn't stand a chance."

The race turned out to be not quite as private as Jordan and Ellen had agreed. Inevitably, George had learned the gauntlet he'd thrown down had been picked up, and he had told Jane. Who had leaked the news to Andrea and Prissy was anybody's guess, but Jordan was resigned to the fact that if there was trouble or excitement anywhere in the vicinity of Endsfield Park, his cousins would be in the thick of it.

"Are we ready?" Jordan asked impatiently. "If so, then let's get this over with."

Jane, a thunderous look on her face, had dragged Ellen into the tack room five minutes earlier. Andrea and Prissy had followed, but they'd been summarily booted out and the door slammed behind them. Jordan assumed Jane was giving Ellen a piece of her mind. He could only hope it was a piece that included some good sense.

"Cousin Jordan?" Prissy asked winningly. "May we ride down to the Collins's cow pasture where we can see the race better?"

"No," he said tersely. "You're lucky I don't send you back to your rooms where you belong."

Prissy's lower lip slipped outward in a pout, but this morning Jordan was immune. This morning Ellen was all the female he could deal with.

"Don't worry about Miss O'Connell," Andrea advised him with uncanny intuition. "She rides like a champion unless you make her use a sidesaddle."

"Then perhaps that's what I should do."

Andrea gave him a face that warned him he'd best be teasing, then babbled on. "Did you know her father has a silver mine and a huge big ranch that's ten times bigger than Endsfield Park, and her sister has a gold mine in Alaska? Ellen must be really rich, and her family very important."

"I'll remember that if I break my neck in this fool race," Jordan said caustically. "Maybe I can bring a suit for damages."

"Oh, Jordan! Be serious!"

"I am serious."

Just then, Ellen emerged from the tack room with an unhappy-looking Jane in her wake. Ellen was a sight in loose-fitting woolen trousers—God only knew where she had found those!—and a bulky knit pullover that fell to her hips. It was not quite bulky enough to disguise the neat shape of her rounded backside nor long enough to hide the enticing length of her legs. As if he did not have enough distractions already!

She greeted him with a twinkle in her eyes. "Did you expect me to wear a skirt?"

"I believe that is still considered proper female attire."

George laughed. "You should know better than to expect our Ellen to be constrained by dull propriety."

"Skirts flap in the wind and catch on the shrubbery," she explained.

"There is no wind this morning," Jordan said.

She lofted a taunting brow. "There will be at the speed I'll be riding."

"Likely most of that wind will come in the wake of me passing you."

"We'll see if you ride as good a race as you talk."

"Maybe you'll see and maybe you won't," he taunted. "I'm likely to be out of sight ahead of you."

"Or behind me."

Jordan was beginning to enjoy the exchange when George called them back to business. "You both know the course?"

"Yes," they both answered.

George elaborated anyway. "Down the drive, left on the road to the big curve, over the fence to the pasture, over the hedges, cross the river, over the Collins's gate, around that spot of woods, and back the way you came. It's five miles, or thereabouts."

"Got it," Ellen said confidently.

"May the best man win." Jordan gave her a daunting smile.

"Or the best horse," George amended.

"Or the best woman," Andrea said.

Without further verbal fencing they mounted up and let the horses prance out some of their early-morning nervousness. Then George gave the signal—a dropped handkerchief—and they were off in a spray of gravel and clatter of hooves.

Jordan let Ellen lead off, giving her the chance to make the mistake of tiring her horse early. Besides, the view of her trouser-clad backside riding a man's saddle was entertaining, to say the least. Not a very gentlemanly observation, but true. His own mount had no trouble keeping a constant distance behind King as they galloped down the drive and turned onto the road. Jordan had acquired Romeo only six weeks ago. The young horse was fast, spirited, and a bit skittish, but Jordan was confident that once he had some age and experience behind him, he would be a champion hunter. He was also confident that Romeo could leave King in the dust if he let him run full out. Not that King was a plug. George was an indifferent rider, but he had an eye for good horseflesh. King was a fine hunter. But Romeo was better.

Ellen still led as they left the road and galloped toward the first pasture. King took a four-foot fence with grace and confidence. Romeo jumped almost right beside him.

Ellen did have a natural seat on a horse, Jordan noted, and King responded to her steady and confident hand. As they galloped toward a series of hedges, King and Romeo were dead even, both running easily with scarcely a streak of sweat. They took three hedges side by side, with Jordan and Ellen knee to knee. Ellen flashed a grin at him. Her face was flushed, her eyes alight. Her hair had bounced free of its pins and blew back from her face in ebony glory. The sight of her was so riveting, and Jordan so engrossed, that he didn't see the ditch in front of them.

Jordan was caught off balance, therefore, when Romeo left the ground. The rider's lack of balance threw the horse off stride. The landing was bad, with Romeo careening one way and Jordan tottering the other way. An older, more experienced horse might have recovered. Romeo didn't. He went down on his knees. Jordan flew over his head and slid through the grass, finally coming to rest against a hummock of damp weeds.

Before Jordan knew quite what had hit him, Ellen was kneeling beside him, looking anxiously into his eyes and running deft fingers over ribs, arms, and legs to discover broken bones. If he'd had injuries, the pain would have been masked by the swell of response her innocent touch inspired.

"I'm all right," he growled.

"You're sure? God, Jordan, you hit the ground like a ton of bricks."

A smile twitched his lips. "A graceful fall, you say?"

She laughed. "I've seen worse. To tell the truth, I've taken worse."

"How's Romeo?"

Ellen pointed, and when Jordan turned his head—painfully—he saw the horse standing nearby, regarding him with equine disgust. He looked back at Ellen and grimaced. "Beaten by a woman. Plowing a furrow in the meadow with my backside. And I suppose you'll make a full report."

"Of course." Ellen grinned. "I won, didn't I?" She seemed absolutely delighted with the notion. Her smile was bright with mischief, her face a study in wicked joy. Somewhere inside her was the sober physician, the proud feminist, the gentle healer who labored over puppies as well as people; but at this moment she was pure imp. Sprite and woman in one, was Ellen, and a man would never know for certain which to expect.

She was too much to resist, and Jordan was beyond resisting. He reached up and pulled her down in the grass beside him. "I'm not going to be the only one sporting grass stains."

"Lord Chesterfield!"

"I think you can call me Jordan."

Her eyes widened when she read his intention, but she didn't pull away. Both of them, it seemed, were being manipulated by some force that brooked no opposition. For a tantalizing moment he merely looked, enjoying the sight of her sweetly bowed lips, impish green eyes, and wind-tangled hair. Ellen met his warm perusal with one of her own. He could feel the caress of her gaze as if it was a physical touch on his mouth, his mud-smeared cheeks, his grass-adorned hair, then finally locking onto his eyes. Something that she saw there made her give him an uncertain smile. He reached out and touched her mouth with one finger, fascinated beyond words with the soft curve of her lips.

Voices in the back of Jordan's mind clamored for his attention, shouting that he shouldn't think what he was thinking or feel what he was feeling. He paid them no mind. Ellen made no resistance as he urged her to lie back in the grass. Savoring every moment, he lowered his mouth to hers. Her taste was achingly sweet. He wanted to devour her. A flood of desire washed through him, hardening his groin and turning his mind to mush. Her lips parted, and he wooed her with his tongue, pushed up the ugly knit pullover and explored the beauty beneath. Only the thin lace and satin of her chemise kept him from the full joy of her naked breasts.

Ellen's quiet groan of passion nourished Jordan's desire. Her arms pulled him closer. Her mouth met his assault with one of her own. Lust and longing combined to explode in a white-hot fire that burned away everything except need. Her ridiculous trousers made it easy for him to part her legs and caress her through the barrier of wool. She strained toward his seeking hand. Tangled hopelessly in desire, he knew they were lost. Only his fumbling incompetence with the stubborn buttons kept them from the precipice.

He cursed and released her, determined to rip through the damned buttons if he had to. She lay back and let him do battle with her clothing. Her hair was a riot of ebony curls woven through with grass. Her face was flushed, her mouth dewy and swollen from his kiss. Jordan couldn't resist the need to claim that mouth again, to kiss her brow, her eyes with their thick, spiky lashes, the pointed chin, the smooth, silken column of her throat. Finally, the buttons surrendered to his urgency, giving him access to her sweetest, most intimate flesh. She was warm and moist, velvety soft.

Suddenly Ellen jerked away as if he'd touched her with a hot iron instead of a gentle hand. Scooting frantically to a sitting position, she held out a hand to ward him off. "What am I doing?"

The question wavered uncertainly, turned inward toward herself rather than flung as a challenge toward him.

"Ellen, it's all right. Listen to me. I'm—"

A sharp denial sliced through his declaration. "No! No, no, no!"

Before he could stop her she staggered to her feet and ran for King, who grazed fifteen feet away. He called after her, but she paid no heed. He was left with the rapid drum of King's fading hoofbeats echoing in his head along with the pounding of his own heart.

Hillary Moorsmythe was an early riser by habit. She enjoyed the tranquillity of the early hours, when she could read, take a peaceful walk, or simply sit in solitude and think without her mother—who never rose before ten—watching every move and listening to each word. The servants at Endsfield had learned that she wanted her hot chocolate by six each morning, not in her room, but in the family salon where the rising sun sent rosy streamers through the windows and one could look out upon the pastures that rolled down to the river.

So it was this morning that she was sitting by the window with her cup of steaming chocolate, a book of poems in her lap, when the rising sun silhouetted a strange parade filing up the path from the stable, Ellen O'Connell in the lead, Jordan following a few yards behind. Far to the rear, Jane Browne had attached herself to George, who appeared to be restraining his two young cousins from running ahead. The O'Connell woman was dressed in outlandish trousers and hurried across the ground as if the devil were in pursuit. In truth, Jordan himself might have passed for the devil with his doubled fists and determined stride. They both looked ill used.

The American woman's hair was a tangled mess. Her clothing, such as it was, looked damp, and when Ellen turned to face her pursuer, Hillary could see the grass stains on her back and seat. When Jordan gesticulated impatiently, Hillary felt rather than saw his frown. His displeasure seemed to darken the air around him like a cloud. The O'Connell woman plainly was in a huff also, and when Jordan took her by the shoulders in a disturbingly intimate gesture, she shrugged him off. Before she marched away, though, she darted a covert glance toward the four who followed and surreptitiously hiked up her pullover to button her trousers.

Standing at the window, Hillary closed her eyes and bit her lip. The slut! The common, hoydenish, crude, stupid slut! It was obvious as the nose on her face that the American had lured Jordan into an early-morning assignation. They'd rolled in the grass like a couple of lusty peasants, both of them, no doubt, with their trousers down around their ankles and their backsides bare to the morning dew. The very thought of it made Hillary want to vomit.

What were they fighting about? she wondered sourly. Had the American demanded money, or marriage, or both? Had the trollop led Jordan to the brink, then shut him down in hopes of getting whatever it was she wanted? Hillary knew more than one girl who'd gotten a rich husband that way. Men were easily manipulated, she'd been told, if one could get them to think with their loins instead of their brains.

She wouldn't know. Hillary had always believed such tactics beneath her. She'd guarded her virtue zealously like the precious thing that it was—a prize to be awarded to the man who could offer her wealth, position, and a lifetime of security. She was a woman of old-fashioned

standards, believing that grace, beauty, coy flattery, and
a touch of feminine scheming should be able to win a
lady the man of her choice. A proper maiden did not
allow her potential husband physical liberties. Passion
was for crude animals, and groping in the grass, as Ellen
O'Connell plainly favored, was for pigs.

Yet the look on Jordan's face as Ellen marched toward
the house struck a bolt of fear deep into Hillary's soul.
He was clearly infatuated with the slut. Might he surrender good sense and ask Ellen O'Connell—an American
nobody, a mannerless strumpet with no sense of delicacy
or class—to be his wife?

Hillary would be the laughingstock of London. She
wouldn't even be able to hide away at the Moorsmythe
country home, for all of Staffordshire would know she'd
been jilted. It didn't matter that she and Jordan were not
formally engaged. She and her mother had made sure
that the whole world believed their marriage was a certainty.

The copper taste of blood polluted Hillary's mouth as
she bit down too hard on her lip. Damn Jordan Chesterfield for having the taste of a boar and the sense of a
horse's butt! She was determined to have him, though,
and no working-class floozy was going to steal him
away. If Jordan liked his women pushy and modern with
the morals of a bitch in heat, then that's what Hillary
would be.

CHAPTER 10

Ellen yanked off her trousers and hurled them across the room, narrowly missing Jane. "I can't believe what I just did! What a moronic, adolescent, irresponsible, downright stupid stunt to pull. I ought to be locked up in Bedlam with the key thrown away."

When Jane had come to investigate the stomping, slamming, and muttering going on in Ellen's room, Ellen had told her a somewhat sanitized version of what had happened in the meadow, sparing not her own dignity but Jane's innocent sensibilities. The more she thought about what had happened, the more embarrassed and angry she became. The race itself had been a stupid, childish prank, but rolling in the grass with Jordan Chesterfield . . . lord! She didn't even want to think about it. A haze of leftover passion had cushioned her ride back to the house, but now that had dissipated, leaving her with the stark, unvarnished truth of her own stupidity.

"What on God's green earth did I think I was doing?" she moaned. "What was I thinking?"

Jane picked a blade of grass from Ellen's hair and shook her head. "I'm told that men and women seldom think when it comes to affairs of the heart."

"Hmmph!" Ellen grunted as she tugged off her pullover. "The heart was not one of the body parts involved."

Jane's fiery blush made Ellen regret her candidness. "I'm sorry, Jane." She flopped down on the bed and pulled the coverlet up to her chin. "I just feel like such an idiot. And a tramp. I feel like a tramp."

Jane sat on the bed beside her and fondly brushed a wisp of hair from her face. "Ellen, dear, you are much too hard on yourself. This is all my fault, you know."

"Your fault? How is that?"

"I was the one who made you stay. I was the one who urged you to let go of reality for a few weeks and indulge in fantasy. This is what has come of my bad advice."

"No." Ellen covered her face with her hands, wishing that she could shut out the world so easily. "This is in no way your fault. It's me. Just me. Since I left America I've made nothing but mistakes. Mistake after mistake after mistake. He must think I'm a veritable slut."

"Lord Chesterfield?"

"Yes. Lord Chesterfield." Ellen sighed. "Jordan."

The name swelled in the silence that followed, and the image of the man dominated Ellen's mind. So many images. Who would have thought the stiffly correct aristocrat would have spent all night in a kennel—in his evening clothes, no less—helping to birth puppies? Who would have pictured the coolly composed lord of the manor dangling the earl of Tindale by his scruff because the pipsqueak had dared to steal a kiss from her? Less likely still, who would have believed Jordan would attempt much more than a kiss, with Ellen's enthusiastic cooperation?

What a mess! She was totally confused. Jordan was angry and huffing about like a wounded bear. He'd caught up with her on the path to the house and demanded that they talk. They had nothing to talk about, at least nothing he would want to hear. Whatever part of her he wanted she couldn't give him. She should never have kissed him, never have let him see the longing in her eyes. If there was anything worse than a fool, it was a liar.

"Ellen." Jane's gentle touch on her shoulder interrupted her recriminations. "Do you want me to ring for some hot chocolate? It might make you feel better."

"Only living the last year over again would make me feel better."

"Perhaps you should just avoid Lord Chesterfield for the rest of our stay."

"Avoid him. Lord! Wouldn't that be nice! But I could hide under the bed for the rest of our stay and not avoid him. He's stuck in here." She put a finger to her head as though it were the barrel of a pistol. "When he's in the same room with me, I can't look at anything or anyone else. I can't concentrate on anything else. When he's gone, I still see him in my mind. I imagine things he would be saying to me. I see the look on his face and the way his eyes crinkle when he smiles. Not when he's just giving one of those polite society smiles, but when he really smiles—with his whole face."

Jane's eyes had gotten wider as Ellen's lament had progressed, her lips rounded into an 'o' of surprise. "Oh, Ellen! Poor, dear Ellen. You've fallen in love with Lord Chesterfield."

"Bite your tongue! I have not!"

"Listen to yourself! You have!"

"I love Henri Chretiens."

Jane made a rude sound.

"I do, Jane! I must love Henri. If I didn't love Henri with all my heart and soul, then I would truly be a slut, wouldn't I? This thing I have for Jordan Chesterfield is simply . . . well, some strange deviation of my female system. Much as I hate to admit it, men do have a point when they claim that women suffer from strange humors."

"Oh piffle! You're in love. Tragic, but true. And it's all my fault."

Ellen was reaching the end of her patience. "Nothing is your fault!" she cried, gritting her teeth. "And I am not, not, not in love with Lord High-And-Mighty, any more than you are enamored of the Honorable George Chesterfield."

Jane blanched, and Ellen immediately regretted her mean-spirited thrust.

"I am certainly not in love with George Chesterfield. I have entirely too much sense to let my heart be engaged by a man so inaccessible to me."

"And I am certainly not in love with his Baronship Lord Chesterfield," Ellen echoed. "I have entirely too much sense—well, maybe I don't, but I should have—to let my heart be engaged where it can't be given."

Ellen regarded Jane somberly, and Jane returned the look full measure.

"We need to leave this place," Ellen said quietly.

"Yes, we do."

"We could lodge in London for the few days until the *Mary Catherine* sails. I should tell Jordan that we want to leave by tomorrow morning at the latest."

"That would really be for the best."

"It would be for the best," Ellen agreed with sober gravity.

Ellen bit her lip. Jane lowered her gaze. Both knew it wouldn't happen.

Jordan fumed the day away, unable to work, to read, even to play with Maisy's puppies without fretting about the morning's debacle. Unwilling to let a woman so destroy his balance, he gathered together his fishing tackle and set off for the river. The hook went unbaited, though, and the line never got wet. He ended up sitting by the river and staring out over the gray, misty water in an unfocused gaze that saw nothing but that woman, that witch, that siren who had invaded his life and banished all sensible, productive, ordinary thoughts from his brain. What had happened that morning had been unforgivable and completely foreign to his character. When Ellen O'Connell was near, he lost all discipline and control. When she was near, he wasn't himself. He wanted to smile, to laugh, to abandon serious pursuits and play with puppies, talk with her, and dally in ways that were not so innocent.

When he finally went back to the house, George twigged him about the empty fishing basket. Jordan gave him a scowl rather than an explanation, but his brother only grinned. That piece of insolence only worsened Jordan's humor. Intuition, not intellect, was George's strong suit. No doubt he'd guessed something about what had caused Ellen to gallop back to the stable that morning, hand over King without a word, and storm up the path toward the house with Jordan chasing after her like some lovestruck adolescent.

For the rest of the afternoon, Jordan stared at the correspondence sent him by his business partner in New

York. At the end of an hour he didn't know what he'd read, and he cursed himself for his lack of concentration. This had to end. He and Ellen O'Connell had to have a serious talk. Perhaps he was infatuated, or suffering from a mere passing fascination. Her response to him that morning no doubt had been rooted in the same fleeting causes. Yet what if it was more? What if their feelings were the beginning of something that could last a lifetime?

They owed it to themselves to explore the possibility instead of running from the mere thought like cowards. Running was certainly Jordan's first instinct, and judging from Ellen's panicked retreat that morning, it was hers as well. He had his reasons, and no doubt she had hers. But real passion was so rare, didn't they need to pause long enough to consider their feelings rationally?

Jordan crumpled the page of the letter he was trying to read and threw it against the wall. Rational was the last word that described his state of mind about Ellen. He should be anxious to have her gone, so he could return to his normal, calm, predictable routine. But strangely enough, he didn't want to see her go. He hadn't realized there was a void in his life until she had filled it. He had to convince her to stay longer, until he could convince himself he didn't need her, or convince her that she needed him.

Ellen and Jane did not come down for dinner that night. Jordan was disappointed, and a bit relieved as well. In the morning both he and Ellen would be fresh. Today's mistakes would be one day removed, and facing each other would be that much easier. Rather than endure a dull evening playing cards with Sir Nigel or discussing politics with Lord Clifton, Jordan made excuses to retreat to his study, where he indulged in reading an

Oscar Wilde novel. He retired late. As he passed his mother's suite of rooms, Lady Chesterfield called out a good night that was sour with the reminder that he'd neglected his duties as a host that evening. Jordan paid the barb no heed. He had other things on his mind.

In his sitting room, Maisy greeted him with a happy whine and a thump of her tail. Her pups were in a neat row, each fastened to a teat for a midnight snack, their little tails vibrating in glorious joy. In a day or two, their eyes would open. Then they would start getting up on their feet to jump about and play. Ellen should be at Endsfield to see that. After all, they were hers as much as his and Maisy's.

The maid had forgotten to light the lamp in his bedroom, but Jordan didn't need light to undress and throw his clothes over a chair. His one uncivilized habit was sleeping in the nude. Well, perhaps it wasn't his only uncivilized habit. With Ellen in the house, he seemed to be shedding civilized manners at the rate of several each day.

With his mind full of Ellen, Jordan thought he was dreaming when warm arms reached for him as he climbed between the sheets. "Hello, my love," said a throaty feminine voice. "I've been waiting a very long time."

"Jesus Christ!" Jordan shot out of the bed. "Hillary? What the hell . . . ?"

He lit the lamp and was treated to the sight of Hillary Moorsmythe lying in his bed, blond hair enticingly tousled, the sheets artfully draped to reveal just enough of her tempting body.

"Hello, Jordan." A slow, seductive smile curved her full lips. "I've kept the bed warm for you."

"What the hell do you think you're doing?"

In answer, her eyes flicked to his groin, where a predictably male response was in progress. Her smile grew wider, and Jordan remembered suddenly that he was standing there bare-butt naked. Muttering an oath, he grabbed for an edge of the sheet to cover himself, with devastating effects on Hillary's artful drape. She didn't seem to mind the loss of covering, but shifted to reveal herself even more fully.

"I'm ready for you, Jordan. And you're ready for me, aren't you?" She reached out a hand in an invitation to join her in the bed.

"Hillary, are you crazy? I never . . . ! I'm not . . . !"

"Stop sputtering, my love. Come keep me warm." She rolled over on her back, folded her arms behind her head, and shot him a glance at once amused and sultry. "Better yet, come make me hot."

"You are crazy. Get up this instant!"

"There's no need to pretend you're virtuous and horrified, Jordan."

"Get up, dammit! And get out. Hillary, I have no intention of doing anything but sleeping in this bed, and I want to sleep alone."

She rolled over, bringing a trimly cushioned backside into view. Propped on her elbows, her generous breasts dangling seductively, she winked. "I could make you forget sleeping."

"Get . . . out!" He made the words into separate curt commands that could not be mistaken for anything but a final dismissal.

Hillary's face rearranged itself into a pout. "I don't understand, Jordan. I'm offering myself to you, body and soul. Are you so cold you don't feel anything?"

"Hillary, we can discuss this in the morning, somewhere other than my bedroom."

"It's that slut American, isn't it? You think she knows tricks that I can't learn?" She sat up and leaned back on braced arms, thrusting her breasts forward and upward. "She's not half as pretty as I am, and I'll bet she falls into bed with every man who gives her the eye."

"Leave Ellen out of this."

"Just kiss me, Jordan." Her smile was wet and inviting. "Let me show you how good I can be."

Jordan reached down impatiently to pull her from the bed, and she leaped desperately at him, plastering her naked body against him, her arms circling his neck like a noose, her mouth latching onto his with the force of a leech. Gently, but firmly, he pushed her away. "Get dressed, Hillary."

"No." She collapsed back onto the bed. "I can't believe you're doing this. How could you reject me, after all we've been to each other over the years? I've kept myself pure for you. I've studied your every like and dislike."

"Then you should know I dislike being pushed," he said ominously.

Hillary wasn't listening. She was too deeply immersed in her own self-pity. "I dress to please you. I follow all your interests—even to letting a stupid puppy pee all over me. I read what you read. I learned to paint because you like art. And what do you do but throw me over for a self-styled New Woman who probably marches with the suffragettes and traces her lineage back to some savage squatting in a tepee!"

"That's enough, Hillary. Where are your clothes?"

"In my room."

"You mean you came down here naked?"

"Of course not! I wore a robe."

Discarded at the foot of the bed was a diaphanous peignoir meant more to enhance than conceal.

"You walked down the hallway in that?"

Her chin began to tremble at his tone. "There was no one around. I didn't think about it. All I thought about was trying to please you." She whimpered, and a tear dribbled down her cheek.

"For God's sake, Hil. Stop blubbering. We both know why you came down here, and I'm having no part of your plans to push me into marriage. I thought I'd made that clear at least a dozen times in the past, but if not, let me put it in terms you can't mistake. I am not in the market for a wife. Slinking around my bedroom and luring me into sleeping with you will not earn you a wedding ring. Can I be any clearer?"

"How can you be so cruel?" she wailed, and burst into noisy tears.

"Stop it. Stop it right now." He might as well have told a river to stop running. Jordan knew from experience that once Hillary started a good cry, nothing could stop her before every last tear had been artfully shed and every last ounce of pity wrung from her audience. And if she didn't stop sobbing as though some dreadful injury had been done, an audience she soon would have. He had to get her to her own room before the whole household gathered at his doorway to investigate.

"Put your robe on, Hil. I'm taking you back to your room."

She shook her head helplessly. Apparently weeping and walking at the same time was a feat beyond her capability.

Cursing women and their schemes, Jordan pulled on his own dressing robe and grabbed another one—notably more substantial than hers, to cover Hillary. He was entertaining the possibility of stuffing a gag in her mouth and hoisting her over his shoulder when disaster struck. Someone knocked on the sitting-room door.

"Is everything all right, sir?" came Codgkins's worried query.

Jordan's assurance that everything was fine was drowned out by a well-planned crescendo of hysteria and feminine weeping that could no doubt be heard in every corner of the house. The alarmed butler burst through the sitting-room door, then stopped in his tracks as he caught sight of the scene in the bedroom. "Oh my!" he breathed.

An understatement, if Jordan had ever heard one. He closed his eyes and tried to convince himself that this wasn't really happening, that he would soon wake to sunlight streaming in his bedroom window and a peaceful house with no wailing women and no curious butlers.

A book of Yeats' poetry lifted from the Endsfield library failed to lull Ellen into a peaceful state of mind. All day long she'd kept to her room, sometimes with Jane for company, sometimes with only a book. She wasn't hiding, Ellen assured herself. Merely thinking. Her sister Katy would have called it sulking. Ellen preferred the term thinking.

She was sitting in bed, the book on her lap turned to the same page it had been an hour ago, when a hint of sound that didn't belong in the dead of night impinged upon her morose thoughts. The sound grew and became recognizable. Someone was sobbing in a very dramatic fashion. A calmer voice rose above the wails—Lady Chesterfield's, Ellen discerned. But the words were unclear. Then came Jordan's clear baritone.

Unable to resist, Ellen pulled on her robe and went

out into the hallway. At the other end of the wing, a crowd gathered outside Jordan's suite of rooms, and it was from there that the sobbing, hiccuping, and wailing arose.

Jane joined her in the hallway. "What is it?"

"I don't know, but it sounds catastrophic." A sick foreboding twisted Ellen's stomach into a knot. As they padded down the carpeted hallway, she reminded herself that the doings of the Chesterfield family were not her business. Jordan and his antics, whatever they were, were not her business. And while this commotion would pique anyone's curiosity, there was no reason for sick worry to clog her throat. No reason at all.

In the confusion, no one noticed when Ellen and Jane joined the crowd. In the center of a solicitous flock of females, including Lady Chesterfield, the Misses Henley, and Mrs. Moorsmythe, was a weeping Hillary. Mrs. Moorsmythe was sobbing almost as dramatically as her daughter. Hillary was incompletely dressed in an oversized man's dressing robe, her hair tangled, her face blotched and puffy with tears. Wrapped in glacial silence, Jordan stood off to one side. The robe he wore was identical to Hillary's.

In the crowd, Lady Higgenbotham and Lady Clifton were doing their best to look mortified, though their eyes gleamed with secret delight. The gaggle of noble gentlemen looked embarrassed to be witness to the misbehavior of one of their own gender, except for George, who observed the scene with a wry smile and laughing eyes. The only members of the household who weren't present were Andrea and Prissy, and they were probably plotting to escape the restraint of their governess in order to investigate the commotion.

Even in the midst of all the confusion, Ellen had little

doubt about the cause of the uproar. Jordan and Hillary had been caught in the act. *Flagrante delicto.* Playing footsie between the sheets. A lustful encounter of the most intimate kind.

Jane's hand closed around Ellen's in silent comfort. There was no comfort possible. All Ellen wanted was to be gone—from this scene, this house, this country. The sooner the better.

The next morning was dreary and wet, and the damp cold would not be banished even by fires burning in every fireplace. Guests and servants alike skulked about as if a misstep might cause the house to tumble down upon their heads. Conversation was somber, spoken in hushed tones. The ladies put their fair heads together and speculated with scarcely a pause for breath, while the gentlemen harrumphed and shook their heads over Jordan's downfall and probable sad fate.

Things were not so quiet, however, in Lady Chesterfield's boudoir, where, for the second morning in a row, the day was not starting well for Jordan Chesterfield.

"I have never been so embarrassed, so humiliated, so mortified in my entire life!" the dowager baroness proclaimed. Straight and stiff as an iron rod, she sat in the big wing-back chair by the window of her boudoir. Jordan had always regarded that chair as his mother's throne. It was the platform from which she issued all serious reprimands and admonishments to her sons—and her husband as well, when that worthy gentleman had been alive. Though Jordan had grown much larger over the years, the chair had seemed to remain just as big and imposing.

"I regret that you were embarrassed, Mother."

"Is that all you have to say?"

Jordan sighed. She wasn't going to let him off easily, but there wasn't much he could say to ease the situation. Mrs. Moorsmythe, wailing that her daughter had been seduced, had needed a healthy dose of sherry to calm her cries of indignation. Hillary had played the wounded virgin to the hilt. The servants and guests alike had gotten an eyeful and an earful.

There was going to be an unpleasant scandal, but it was not of Jordan's making, no matter what anyone thought. Likewise, the solution was not within his reach.

"The Chesterfield name," the baroness reminded him, "traces its lineage back through several centuries, and not once—not once!—has a shred of scandal tarnished our honor."

"Mother, you're exaggerating the importance of this incident. Besides, none of it was my doing."

"Indeed? Was it some other man I saw in your rooms with Hillary, both of you in a state of undress?"

It was useless to protest that nothing had happened. The appearance of something having happened was every bit as damning as the act itself.

"At least you had the good sense to seduce someone suitable to our line," Lady Chesterfield conceded with a sniff. "I suppose all is not lost, but the announcement of your engagement must be immediate, and you must marry as soon as a proper wedding can be planned. We will brazen this out, and if anyone dares to raise an eyebrow or whisper a slur, I will make them sorry. I will send the *Times* an announcement this very morning."

"You will do nothing of the kind, Mother."

Her face grew sharp at his tone. "And why won't I?"

"Because I have not asked Hillary Moorsmythe to be my wife, and I have no intention of doing so."

"Luring a gently bred virgin into your bed is proposal

enough, Jordan. I refuse to believe that I have given birth to a man so insensitive to honor."

"I didn't lure Hillary into my bed. She went there of her own choice, and without my invitation or consent."

The baroness made a rude sound. "You expect me to believe that Hillary—?"

"It doesn't matter what you believe. I will not marry the girl."

He could see his mother considering what tactic to use. Her sharp-eyed disapproval made him feel like a little boy called on the carpet for some misdeed, as it was intended to. Suddenly, he felt a great impatience with his mother's manipulations and Society's expectations for his life. He returned her look with one just as sharp. Lady Chesterfield managed to look hurt.

"I cannot imagine why you are so determined to rip this family's good name to tatters, Jordan. You have always been a good and responsible boy."

"I am not a boy, Mother. I am thirty years old."

"All the more reason why you should be married."

"I was married. I have no desire to marry again."

"Mary Catherine has been dead for three years—much more than a decent period of mourning, Jordan. You need a wife to be the mother of the next Chesterfield generation, and Hillary is eminently suitable. She's attractive, refined, well educated, and while it's true her family has no title, they are good stock. I cannot understand your stubbornness in this matter."

"You don't need to understand it. Just accept it. I have no intention of marrying anyone, much less Hillary."

"You should have thought of that before you ruined the poor girl's reputation."

"She ruined her own reputation without any help from me."

"And what of your reputation?"

"My reputation be damned, madam! I think I can survive a few snickers."

Lady Chesterfield rose from her throne, stiff with imperious anger. "I thought I would never see the day when I was ashamed of my eldest son! You have always been rather casual about your obligations to Society, but I attributed it to the arrogance you inherited from your father and told myself it could be tolerated. But this! I will not let you subject our family to the sneers and lurid speculations of people not fit to wipe our shoes. If necessary, I will announce your engagement myself. You will come to realize that I have only your good in mind."

"You have only your own schemes in mind, Mother. Yours and Mrs. Moorsmythe's." Jordan pointed a warning finger in her face. "Do not announce an engagement, because neither an engagement nor a marriage will take place. The queen herself could announce my nuptials, and I would still refuse. I will not be manipulated by a flock of scheming hens!"

On that sour note, he turned on his heel and marched out, ignoring his mother's protests. Women, he reflected as he stalked down the hallway, should not be allowed to run loose in the world to make life miserable for unsuspecting, bumbling men like himself. His life was careening out of control because of women: his mother, who wouldn't be discouraged from having her way by a round of mortar shells landing on her head; Ellen, whom he had not seen, much less talked with, since their highly charged encounter the morning before; and Hillary, whom he had seen entirely too much of.

That state of affairs was going to end right this moment, Jordan vowed. He strode into his study and rang for Codgkins. The butler appeared a brief moment later.

"Has Miss O'Connell come down yet this morning?" Jordan asked.

Codgkins regarded him blandly, but behind the butlerish detachment Jordan detected a smirk. Or perhaps he was simply developing a case of paranoia.

"I don't believe so, sir."

"I wish to see her in my study as soon as possible. Please inform her."

"Yes, sir."

So that was that! Jordan thought with satisfaction. He wouldn't let Ellen hide from him any longer. He would insist that they talk about their relationship like two intelligent adults. And then he would deal with Hillary, firmly, frankly, and with dignity—the way men should deal with women.

Codgkins appeared a moment later and, with a grave demeanor, handed him an envelope. "This was on Miss O'Connell's dressing table, sir."

With a sinking heart, Jordan ripped open the envelope, read the note inside, and cursed. So much for taking control of the women in his life. One of them, at least, was gone.

CHAPTER 11

Ellen stood at the deck rail and stared out over the Thames as the *Mary Catherine* steamed its way down the river toward the open Atlantic. There wasn't much to see—fog, fog, and more fog, gray and damp, matching her spirits. She wondered if England ever saw a bright, sunny morning. While there was a certain quiet beauty to the misty river and the muted shapes of London slipping slowly past, Ellen longed for the crystal clarity of a Montana dawn, the crimson gaudiness of a western sunrise. The constantly gray weather here was what had her feeling so low. That and her foolishness in Paris, a mistake that she would pay for the rest of her life. Jordan Chesterfield had nothing to do with her mood, Ellen told herself. She did not miss him. She was not angry with him, merely grateful that he'd reminded her so graphically that men were nothing more than walking, talking invitations to trouble.

Beside her, huddled deep in the woolen folds of her redingote, Jane was not much help in the matter of raising spirits. She'd said little since they left Endsfield

Park, though she'd made a valiant effort to act her old self. Jane's irrepressible good humor had successfully been repressed. It was not difficult to guess the cause. Despite her claims to the contrary, she was pining for the merry, mischievous George.

What a pair they were.

"Here we are at last," Ellen said in an attempt at conversation. "It's fortunate that Lord Chesterfield had already sent word that we were to be allowed free passage. I feared we might have to apply to your father for a loan to pay our passage."

"Yes." Jane sighed. "It's fortunate."

"I'm glad we had those two days to shop in London. My stepmother will love that fine woolen shawl."

"It's a lovely shawl."

"My father will protest my buying those chess pieces, but he'll like them all the same. He taught me and my sister to play chess when we were children. We trounced him regularly, and he would pretend to be mad, but he loved it."

"I'm anxious to meet your father."

Jane's smile was forced, and the conversation lame. Ellen sighed and propped her elbows on the damp railing.

"I shouldn't have taken you away from George."

"What?" Jane gave her a look of genuine surprise. "Ellen, dear, you didn't take me away from George. George Chesterfield and I were not an item. There was nothing to take me away from."

"Then why are you in such dreary spirits?"

Jane stared at the fog for a moment, then shrugged. "I suppose I must admit an attachment to the man. I do miss him. We truly have no future together, but I hadn't prepared myself to leave so abruptly—without even a good-bye. It's of no importance, really. I'll recover quite nicely, I assure you."

"Recover from what?" came a masculine question from behind them.

Both women spun about. Ellen's eyes grew wide with surprise, Jane's with joy.

"George!" they exclaimed in one voice.

"In the flesh, fair ladies."

"What are you doing here?" Jane demanded. Suddenly her voice was full of vitality and light. So much for obdurate English good sense, Ellen noted with a trace of amusement.

"An Atlantic crossing is always diverting, and I found Endsfield Park deadly dull without you lovely ladies. London would be much the same, I fear. So I thought I would offer you the benefit of my company. Be warned, though, that I intend to require serious amends for your leaving without saying good-bye."

Jane's smile was so bright it could have dispersed the fog.

"I believe breakfast is being served in the dining room, ladies, if you would care to join me."

In this situation, Ellen knew, three was definitely going to be a crowd. "You two go ahead," she said. "I believe I will lie down for a bit."

George curled Jane's arm around his. "If you change your mind, Miss O'Connell, the dining salon is forward on deck three."

"I'll remember."

"Oh, yes." A dangerous twinkle appeared in George's eye. "I should warn you that the Ogre is on board."

"I beg your pardon?"

"My estimable brother. The Ogre. I think it was Prissy who conferred the additional title upon him. He has been rather surly these last few days, or—what is that American term I once heard you use in reference to one of your father's bulls?—ornery." He pronounced the word with an Old West flavor that made Ellen laugh. But she sobered instantly as an appalling thought occurred.

"Is Miss Moorsmythe on board as well?"

"Hillary?" George made a rude sound. "I should say not. Beware the Ogre if you should encounter him, Miss O'Connell. My brother has not had a good week."

Ellen gusted out a hearty sigh as she watched George and Jane walk away. She wanted to run after them and ask George at least a dozen questions. Had Jordan been upset at their departure? What had happened with Hillary? Why was Jordan on board the *Mary Catherine*? And more. Inexplicably, her heart felt as though a lead weight had been lifted from it. She wanted to laugh, to smile, to do a little jig right where she stood.

Yet all that was nonsense. Jordan was nothing to her. Most probably he was engaged to Hillary by now, whether or not she was on board. Even if he wasn't, Ellen was certainly not in a position to encourage a man's attentions. What had happened at Endsfield had been a serious lapse of judgment.

When she got to the tiny cabin that she and Jane shared, she found a steward gathering their luggage.

"What is this?" she demanded.

The steward touched his cap. "Captain's orders, Miss. I'm to move you to one of the suites reserved for the Chesterfield family."

"But this cabin is fine."

"Oh no, Miss. The purser didn't know you ladies were personal friends of Lord Chesterfield, or he never would have sent you down to this deck. The captain sends his compliments and begs you to forgive the blunder, Miss."

Bemused by the steward's anxious deference, Ellen followed him to a spacious suite of rooms that boasted a sitting room with two chairs, a love seat, and table. A door from the sitting room led to a bedroom with two comfortable beds, a private bathroom, and a porthole looking out upon the fog.

"We're all glad to have the Family on board for the crossing," the steward told her as he plumped the pillows upon the love seat. "I served as Lord Chesterfield's personal steward on a crossing two years ago, and I tell everyone who asks what a pleasant and good-humored gentleman he is."

Was he talking about the Jordan Chesterfield she knew? Ellen wondered.

"If there's anything else you need, just let me know, Miss. My name is Curtis."

"Thank you, Curtis."

When he was gone, she explored their new quarters, sinking a finger into the soft cushions of a chair, bouncing experimentally on one of the beds, inspecting the fine marble fixtures in the bathroom, which included a small bathtub, of all things. Ellen imagined lying in that tub with the bath water rocking to and fro with the rhythm of the ship's motion. Pleasant as it was, the image made her slightly nauseous.

"I see you've been installed in your new rooms," came a voice from the sitting room.

Ellen's already churning stomach did a double flip. "Jordan!" She peered out of the bedroom door, to find him regarding her in a manner that indicated he had indeed been upset at her abrupt departure from Endsfield. His dark glare made her understand why Prissy had lately christened him the Ogre. She reminded herself that she had no reason to be apologetic. He was the culprit. She was merely a fool. "I wasn't aware . . . uh . . . that you were making this journey."

"I decided to confer with my business partner in New York."

"The mail or telegraph is insufficient?"

"At times," he said coldly.

"Ah."

The conversation, such as it was, faltered into silence. As she left the dubious shelter of the bedroom, he folded his arms across his chest and gave her a look he must have inherited from his arrogant mother. "You left without saying good-bye," he accused. From his tone, she might have fled with the silverware.

"I left a note."

"So you did. Do you consider that sufficient?"

Ellen straightened her spine and answered in a tone as arrogant as his own. "Under the circumstances, I considered it more than sufficient."

"It was rude."

"It was very polite."

"And you were foolish to be taking off on your own. How did you get to London? None of the coachmen drove you."

"Jane and I are perfectly capable of taking care of ourselves. Not that it is your concern, but we took the van to the railway station in Stafford."

He made a rude noise that showed what he thought of them climbing aboard the public-drawn transportation that periodically traveled the road to town. "Now I know you're a fool. Do you realize what sort of rude and downright dangerous fellows you might have encountered on the van?"

Ellen was beginning to steam. "Neither more rude nor dangerous than the ones we left behind at Endsfield Park," she snapped.

"Indeed?" The single word was enough to frost the glass of the porthole. "I am such a rude fellow because I frightened you with one little kiss?"

"You did not frighten me! And it was much more than one little kiss."

"All right, two kisses."

"If you consider the conclusion of our race a 'little kiss,' Jordan, then you need a serious lecture concerning the facts of life."

"I am well acquainted with the facts of life."

She skewered him with a pointed glare. "That was obvious from the disgusting scene with poor Hillary!"

"Poor Hillary?" His mouth flattened in distaste. "Let me tell you about poor Hillary."

Ellen folded her arms and turned away. "I don't want to hear it."

"Well, you're going to hear my explanation and a good deal more!"

"No explanation is necessary. You and Hillary are obviously well suited. Now, if you'll excuse me, I feel the need of some fresh air."

She swept past him out the door and fled to the nearest companionway. Short of bodily dragging her back into the suite, he couldn't make her stay. Once on deck, she didn't stop until the stern rail pressed against her uneasy stomach. Going any farther would require walking on water. Call her a fool, would he? Call her rude! How dare he! She had told him, the arrogant jackass. Yes she had!

Ellen gripped the deck rail until her knuckles were white and wondered why she felt so empty inside.

* * *

George and Jane walked out of the dining salon together and wandered up to the breezy deck. The fog was lifting to reveal a pale blue sky dotted with puffy clouds.

"Breakfast was delicious." Jane sighed happily.

"The Atlantic and Mediterranean Steamship Line offers nothing but the best," George told her with an expansive smile.

"It's good to once again feel satisfied after a meal. We've been on slim rations for the last few days. Our lodging was more expensive than we expected."

"Serves you right. It was very bad of you two to depart without so much as a by-your-leave or farewell."

"Ellen had her reasons," Jane said firmly.

"And you?" His voice turned soft. "Did you want to leave, Jane?"

Her heart skipped a beat, but she was not going to tell George what he obviously wanted to hear. There was no point in opening a subject that had no satisfactory conclusion. "Ellen and I are traveling together," she told him crisply. "Where she goes, I go also."

George laughed. "Then you're going the wrong direction, sweet girl."

"What?" She stopped and took her bearings. The ship was huge and confusing, but she thought their cabin was in this direction.

"Jordan had your things moved to one of the family suites. The one right next to ours, as a matter of fact."

She didn't like the implication in his tone. "Why did he do that?"

"Friends of the Chesterfield family receive only the best the ship has to offer. We have a majority holding in the line, you know." His smile grew wry. "At least, Jordan does. And though Mother abhors his connection to business and trade, it does come in handy now and again."

Arms crossed, Jane gave George a severe look. "I'm not sure it's proper for us to stay in one of your family suites. Is Lord Chesterfield pursuing poor Ellen?"

"One can never tell exactly what my brother is pursuing," George confided with a chuckle. "He doesn't tell me his plans. And why is Miss O'Connell poor Ellen, pray tell? If Jordan is pursuing her, his intentions are most assuredly honorable. My brother is nothing if not tediously upright. Is a name hundreds of years old and an English barony so insulting a gift to offer a woman?"

Jane couldn't meet his eyes. "That's not what I meant."

"Then what did you mean?"

"Nothing. Really. Except . . . well . . . you should tell Lord Chesterfield to leave Ellen alone."

George cocked his head speculatively. "I seldom tell my brother how to conduct his life, in constant hope that he will stop telling me how to conduct mine. It hasn't worked yet, but someday it might."

Jane regarded him quizzically. "You and your brother are both very peculiar men."

"Not peculiar, dear Jane. Simply English. You should be well acquainted with the condition, since you are infected with it as well."

His smile made her uneasy. "Are you going to show me where I'm to stay?"

"I'd rather take you dancing."

"Be serious, George. No one dances at this time of day. It's not even noon."

"On the Atlantic and Mediterranean Line, one can dance whenever the mood strikes. There is always an orchestra in the red salon, and I am completely at your disposal."

She laughed and tried to back away as he playfully took possession of her hand and waist and whirled her about the deck. "Stop! Someone will see us!"

"There's not a soul about. They're all still gorging themselves in the dining salon or unpacking their bags."

Jane found herself danced into a small alcove below the companionway that led to the next higher deck. Suddenly her frantically beating heart was the only thing in motion. They stood there, the two of them, Jane trapped against the bulkhead by George's chest. Why had she never before noticed how broad the man was, or how imposing he could seem when he was not laughing at himself or someone else?

Jane froze as George lowered his mouth to hers. She had never in her life been kissed. The sensation of a man's lips moving on hers was odd—and enticing. She was beginning to enjoy herself when he urged her lips to part and darted inside with the tip of his tongue. Jane gasped and cringed back. Kissing was one thing, but surely that was very wicked.

George apologized softly. "I'm sorry, Jane. I didn't mean to frighten you."

"I . . . I wasn't frightened. Let me go, please."

He complied, and Jane felt suddenly cold without his arms to warm her. She told herself to show some backbone. "I'm not that kind of woman, George Chesterfield."

"I didn't think you were." His mouth curved into the familiar roguish smile. "But I've wanted to kiss you since the first time I saw you leaning over my bed with that oh-so-serious expression on your beautiful face."

"My face is not beautiful," she denied. "And the situation at the time called for a bit of seriousness, don't you think?"

"If you say so, sweet girl. But it isn't all that grim right now, is it? Let me see you smile."

"Mr. Chesterfield! I suspect that you're a very wicked man."

"Only if being frivolous is wicked," he said with a beguiling smile. "I promise no more assaults on your virtue—if you'll only smile for me."

Jane tried to be serious and chiding. She tried to resist the twinkling eyes and the endearing dimples that dented his cheeks. But the smile that fought for control of her mouth would not be denied. She gave him what he wanted.

George had less success charming his older brother than he had beguiling the innocent Jane. Jordan looked up from his book when George walked into their suite. His shrewd gaze dissected George's smile and pounced on the reason behind it.

"What trouble have you been up to, little brother?"

"Trouble? Me?"

"Trouble is your patron saint."

George did his best to look put upon. "I'm hurt, *mon frère*. I've spent the morning being of service to you, and what do I get? Accusations and abuse."

"And just how have you been of service?"

"I troubled myself to occupy Miss Browne so you could have Ellen O'Connell to yourself."

"What makes you think I wanted Miss O'Connell to myself?"

George plopped into a well-cushioned chair and regarded his surly brother with a superior air. "Oh come now, Jordan. Don't dissemble. This is your brother you're talking to, not some gullible fellow you can intimidate with that frosty glare. If Miss O'Connell isn't the reason for your sudden decision to cross the Atlantic, what is? When you learned she had left Endsfield, you were as steamed as one of the *Mary Catherine*'s boilers. A few hours later, you suddenly developed a need to talk face to face to Spencer Crabbe in New York."

Turnabout was fair play, and revenge was sweet. How many times had George been subjected to lectures about his merrimaking with the ladies? How many times had Jordan bored him to tears with admonitions to show restraint and good sense. For the first time, George had the opportunity to be on the giving end of such grief rather than the receiving end, and he was enjoying himself enormously.

Jordan slammed his book shut and tossed it onto a table. His brows pulled together to make a single dark slash over his eyes. "My relationship with Miss O'Connell is not subject to your lurid speculation."

George congratulated himself on hitting a nerve. There were many who thought Jordan Chesterfield didn't have a nerve to hit. He couldn't resist digging a bit deeper. "Jane fears you're pursuing Ellen with dishonorable intentions. I assured her that my brother never did anything that wasn't strictly honorable. She seemed to have some doubt about that. Perhaps she was thinking of the scene with Hillary."

Jordan gave him a cool stare. "George, I'm not in the mood for this. And I don't like the way you're hanging on Jane Browne's skirts like a burr on a saddle pad. She's an innocent, inexperienced girl, and she doesn't deserve some rake toying with her emotions. For some reason I don't understand, women seem to melt whenever you smile. I don't want to see Miss Browne in a puddle beneath your feet."

"I thought we were talking about you and the beautiful doctor," George said sharply. Trust Jordan to turn the conversation around to land like a ton of bricks on George's head. Well, this time, he wasn't going to get away with it. "It seems to me that Ellen O'Connell is in just as much danger as my lovely Jane. Tell you what, big brother. I propose a bargain between us that will do right by both ladies."

"And just what is that?"

George gave him his most wicked, challenging smile. "I'll stay away from Jane Browne just as long as you stay away from Ellen O'Connell."

Unless George missed his bet, he was in very little danger of being deprived of Jane's company for long.

Three days into the crossing they hit rough seas. Ellen had endured a bit of uneasiness ever since the *Mary Catherine* headed into the open Atlantic, and now the queasiness escalated to full-blown misery. She tried to hole up in her suite with her rebellious stomach, but the walls closed in on her until the cabin felt like a coffin being tossed about by a careless giant. She tried to sleep, but closing her eyes only made things worse. With their valises, shoes, books, and every other loose item in the cabin careening back and forth across the deck, having her eyes open was no treat either.

She was curled on her bed in a tight little ball of suffering when the door opened and Jane waltzed in.

"Isn't this exciting!" Jane exclaimed.

Ellen couldn't dredge up enough energy for a good glare.

"Oh, Ellen! Look at you!" Jane hurried to the bed.

"You're the color of pea soup. Goodness! I didn't know people really could turn green."

The image of pea soup didn't make Ellen any happier. Fortunately, there wasn't anything left in her stomach to throw up.

"You must come up on deck," Jane told her. "It's a well-known fact that seasickness is worse if one can't see the horizon. My cousin John is in the Royal Navy, and he told me so."

Ellen allowed herself to be pried from the bed and helped along the companionway to the upper deck, where she clung to the rail in an attempt to stop her head from spinning. The cold wind sucked the breath from her lungs and sent her hair flying about her face in annoying streamers, but it did make her feel a bit better—until she looked out upon the heaving, rolling, foaming sea.

"Oh my God." She groaned and leaned over the rail to heave up absolutely nothing, which, she discovered, was even more miserable than throwing up something. The sight of other passengers also hanging over the rail made her even sicker. Jane covered Ellen's white-knuckled hand with hers, but there was little she could do to help or comfort.

"Good Lord!" came a voice from behind her. "What are you two doing on deck in this weather?"

Ellen hadn't believed things could get any worse, but they could. Jordan had left her strictly alone since their first encounter in her suite. What a time for him to show up.

"Poor Ellen is seasick," Jane explained unnecessarily. "I don't know what to do."

"Keeping her out here in the wind and cold aren't going to do any good." Jordan took Ellen by the shoulders and turned her to face him. Her head swam with the movement, and she wondered how he felt about being thrown up on. "You do look awful," he observed.

Was that a gleam of amusement in his eyes? Ellen wondered sourly. She hoped he ended up marrying Hillary Moorsmythe and siring a houseful of children with his mother's disposition. It was the worst curse she could think of at the moment.

"Let's take her to the suite," he said to Jane, as if Ellen was a child not worthy of consulting. "I've heard soda crackers and chamomile tea are a help for seasickness. I'll try to get her some."

"I'm not going anywhere," Ellen croaked. The thought of being cooped up in that tilting, rolling coffin made her feel even sicker. "I'm staying here."

Cold sea spray showered them as the ship plowed into a large wave. They all three fought for balance as the deck beneath their feet rose, then dropped away. Ellen groaned miserably.

"You're going inside!" Jordan commanded. "The weather's getting worse."

"No. Dammit! No!"

"I'm not going to stand her and argue with you."

"Good!"

Before Ellen could raise a hand in protest, Jordan lifted her into his arms. The deck rolled precipitously beneath them, but he balanced like an acrobat as they headed toward the nearest companionway with Jane following behind. In the dizzying chaos of sea, wind, and spray, the solid bulwark of his chest and the strong grip of his arms seemed the only stable things in the world. Ellen was loath to admit it, but it would have been a comfort to stay as she was, her faced pressed against Jordan's shoulder, her arms wrapped around the muscular column of his neck, until the world became sane once again.

The security of Jordan's arms was only a fantasy, however, and it ended the moment he laid her on her bed. "You loosen her clothes," he ordered Jane. "I'll go to the galley for some crackers."

Then he was gone. The cabin had seemed steadier with Jordan in it—a foolish notion, Ellen told herself. This seasickness was affecting her mind as well as her stomach.

"Lord Chesterfield is right, you know," Jane admonished. She unbuttoned Ellen's collar and the front of her snug bodice. "It really is getting too wild on deck for us to be out, though it seemed a good idea at the time. I can't imagine why you've suddenly become so stubborn. Here, why don't you get out of that dress completely? You'll be much more comfortable in just the shift."

Jane had Ellen undressed and safely beneath the covers before Jordan returned with the crackers and a pot of tea.

"You're in good company," he told Ellen with a smile. "Almost everyone else on the ship is sick as well."

"Not you?" Ellen asked weakly.

"I don't get seasick," he announced. "Never get sick at all, in fact."

"Don't you have any weaknesses?"

"None that I'd tell you," he said with an infuriating grin.

After Jordan had gone, Jane persuaded her to try the crackers and tea. Ellen was game, but her stomach wasn't. No sooner had she swallowed than the crackers came back up again. The tea was little better.

The sea grew rougher. Ellen grew sicker, and Jane dithered and fluttered about trying to find something that would relieve the misery.

"Don't worry so much," Ellen told her after several hours of being curled into a wretched ball in her bed. "As a physician I can tell you that people very seldom die of seasickness." She had to pause for breath between phrases, so little energy did she have. "They just want to die. That's all."

Jane knelt beside the bed and took Ellen's hand. "It's not only you I'm worried about," she said gently. "How long can this last, how weak can you become, without . . . without it affecting . . . oh, my! Oh my goodness!" She launched herself toward the basin and lost the entire contents of her stomach.

So it was when Jordan politely knocked on the door an hour later, he was greeted by two miserable groans instead of just one.

"Oh, damn!" His gaze took in the green faces and his nose twitched at the odor. "Bloody damn."

Jane was actually worse off than Ellen. Even though she'd been fine for hours, once her stomach had surrendered, it made up for lost time with a vengeance. Jordan left her in the suite under the care of the purser's wife—a veteran of countless voyages and never once seasick—and took Ellen to his own suite.

"Why didn't you just leave her with Jane?" George demanded when Jordan told him they were moving into the smaller cabin next door. "Mrs. Botts could have seen to them both."

"They're just setting each other off," Jordan told him. "Every time one of them pukes, the other follows suit."

"Well, I'm going to check on Jane."

"You'll do nothing of the kind. I'm sure she wouldn't want you as an audience as she turns herself inside out."

George look pointedly at Ellen, who was half dozing in Jordan's bed.

"I'm going to call Abby Sharpe to see to her. She seldom gets seasick. And I'm going to stay in the cabin across the hall with you. And we're both going to mind our own business."

That arrangement lasted only a few hours. Mrs. Sharpe, who was head of housekeeping on the *Mary Catherine,* knocked on Jordan's door shortly after midnight to say that her patient was giving her no time to sleep and she had more than a full day's work ahead of her. Jordan released her from her nursing duties, left George sleeping in the cabin, and went to sit at Ellen's side, Propriety be damned.

Ellen was scarcely aware of the changing of the guard. She couldn't swallow her own saliva without wanting to throw up. Her sense of up and down had died hours ago, and the room lurched beneath her in a nightmarish dance. She cared not who wiped her face and dribbled water down her throat for her to throw up again and again. She simply wanted to either feel the solid earth beneath her or die, whichever might come sooner.

Despite the mind-numbing misery, however, a rational part of her brain told her that in her situation, she could not afford to be so violently ill. This stress, dehydration, and skating on the edge of shock was going to lose her much more than the contents of her stomach if she didn't somehow get herself under control. Jane had been worried for her also, and that attested that the concern was real—not some fear conjured up by her illness. Perhaps she should be glad, Ellen thought wearily. Such trauma was a solution to the whole nasty mess she'd made of her life. But that didn't wash. The burden she'd carried these past few months was more than just a burden. No matter what the circumstances, she wouldn't give it up without a fight. She had to drink, to keep water down, to insist that nourishment stay in her stomach—somehow.

She lifted her hand, and someone took it. She recognized Jordan's voice asking how he could help. What was Jordan doing here? Then a spasm of nausea gripped her, and she forgot who it was holding the basin and who it was brushing damp hair from her face and speaking words that didn't help and didn't matter. Her stomach, chest, and throat were so sore that every bout of vomiting brought on painful muscle cramps, and the pain brought on still more vomiting. She was a doctor, dammit! Why couldn't she do something for herself?

Scarcely aware of where she was, she fell back to the bed. "I've got to do something," she croaked. "Got to . . ."

Someone wiped her face with a cool cloth. "Calm down," said Jordan's voice. Ellen remembered then. Jordan was here. "You're going to be all right. The captain says these seas will last only another half day or so."

A half day. Hours and hours. An eternity. Mindless panic took her. It would be too late then. Too late.

"No!" She tried to rise, not knowing what she was going to do, but knowing she had to do something.

"Ellen, lie down."

"You don't understand."

"You'll be fine. You're a strong, healthy woman. You're going to be all right."

"My baby," she whispered. "What about my baby?"

CHAPTER 12

Jordan—wet, cold, and ignoring both—paced the stern deck. The wind, rain, and angry sea matched his mood perfectly. He wouldn't have believed it if someone else had told him. He scarcely believed it after hearing the truth from Ellen O'Connell's own lips.

She was pregnant. All the time he'd known her she'd been carrying some bastard's byblow. When she was telling him off in George's sickroom, when she was jumping bareback over hedges like some wild gypsy, when she'd been up to her elbows in the muck of Maisy's whelping, when she'd been racing like the wind beside him on King, and when he'd nearly made love to her on a carpet of damp English grass—all that time she had been with child.

Her nerve amazed him. His own stupidity astounded him—that he could have taken her for someone fresh, innocent, unspoiled by the studied sophistication of the women in his own circle. Furious was inadequate to describe his reaction.

He slammed his fist down on the rail with a curse. Why did he care so much? What did it matter if Ellen O'Connell was not what she seemed? She was nothing to him. A casual acquaintance, and a damned annoying one at that, a brief flirtation that had ended before any harm was done. Disillusionment shouldn't be this painful, but it was, and the fact that it was made Jordan even more angry. Ellen had engaged his sympathies and friendship under false pretenses. He'd thought her a virtuous woman, and she was not. He'd thought himself a discerning judge of character, and he was not. He had overestimated them both.

Jordan wiped the rain from his eyes, wishing he could stay on deck. The rain and wind were easier to face than returning to Ellen's side. He'd left on the pretense of getting her a pot of tea, but he couldn't leave her alone for long. She was sick enough to be nearly out of her head. He might find someone to tend her, but that was the coward's way out, and while a Chesterfield might be a fool, he was not permitted to be a coward.

The rest of the day was torture. In the late afternoon, the sea calmed somewhat, but the same couldn't be said of Jordan's emotions. Even with the smoother sea, Ellen continued to be disoriented and ill, weak and weepy, silent and withdrawn. Most of the time she was scarcely aware of who tended her, Jordan was sure. That was just as well. She couldn't have wanted him to be privy to her secret any more than he had wanted to hear it. He tried to turn himself to stone, to not care, or wonder, or think. But just as with everything else that concerned Ellen O'Connell, he found doing what he ought to do very difficult.

Questions clamored to be asked. Who was the father? Why had she left him? Why had a woman with her intelligence and spirit allowed herself to sink so low? Accusations and recriminations pressed for a voice. How dare she deceive him? How dare she look so innocent, so beautiful, so alluring when she was soiled?

Jordan spoke neither the questions nor the accusations. He spoke scarcely at all, in fact, merely went about the business of tending Ellen while torturing himself with visions of her making love with some faceless man who was not Jordan Chesterfield.

It shouldn't matter, Jordan told himself, but it did.

Late in the afternoon Jane came into the suite. Nothing in her fresh and pristine appearance gave a clue that she'd been turning herself inside out last time Jordan had seen her.

"What are you doing here?" he asked. His tone was more surly than he intended, for Jane's sunny smile immediately faded to perplexity.

"The sea is much calmer," she explained. "And so is my stomach."

"So I see." He ran a hand through his already ragged hair. "Then you can see to Miss O'Connell."

"Yes. Of course." Her eyes narrowed slightly as she studied him. Jordan was sure every hour of this day had put a line in his face. "You know, don't you?" Her resigned tone made the words more a conclusion than a question.

"*You* know about this travesty?"

"Yes. I know. I was her friend before it happened, and I'm still her friend." She frowned down at Ellen's pale face. "How bad is it? Is she bleeding? Did she lose the baby?"

He grimaced. "To my knowledge the baby is still where it always was."

The sharpness of his tone inspired a pugnacious tilt to

Jane's chin. "I suppose you must be seething with contempt and stiff with righteous indignation."

"I dislike being deceived, Miss Browne."

"And just how were you deceived, Lord Chesterfield? Did Ellen ever lie to you?"

His jaw tightened. "That begs the point."

"No, it doesn't. Did she?"

"By implication."

"Ellen never implied anything. You simply made assumptions."

"And why shouldn't I have? One assumes a woman who presents herself as a decent, unmarried lady has guarded her character. Should I have put the question to her? 'Oh by the way, my dear lady, do you happen to be increasing?' "

Jane gave a scornful sniff, as if it were he who had offended. "It was none of your business, was it? We hardly asked to be invited into your home. Ellen abandoned her own plans in order to save George's life. I suppose, considering her state as fallen woman, she shouldn't have imposed herself on you."

This was a Jane Browne Jordan had never seen. Usually the girl was a meek and mild little thing, but in defense of her friend, she became a veritable terrier. The hell of it was, her reasoning made a twisted kind of sense. Jordan didn't like that. He was more comfortable with betrayal and indignation than confusion.

"Let me tell you something, Lord Chesterfield." She pointed a finger at him as if it were a loaded gun. "Ellen O'Connell is the most caring, bravest, best person I've ever met. You didn't see her after three days and nights at the clinic where she worked straight through with no sleep and hardly a meal, trying to save the life of a whore suffering a miscarriage. Your stainless society females wouldn't know how to give of themselves like that. You didn't see her cry after a child had died in her arms because its parents were too poor to pay for the medication that would have saved it. You didn't see her cajole a frightened old man into having the surgery that would give him years more of a good and useful life.

"I saw all that because, while I was visiting a cousin in Paris, I was a volunteer at the clinic where Ellen worked." Her voice grew quieter, yet sharpened with uncharacteristic bitterness. "I also saw the dashing French physician who was society's darling—and everybody else's—take advantage of her good heart and innocent soul. He coaxed her into falling in love with him, enjoyed her adoration, then abandoned her in favor of an heiress who would increase his status as well as his fortune. When Ellen found out she was pregnant, he offered the services of a friend to rid her of the unwanted burden. By that time she was broken in both spirit and heart. She had just enough mettle left to defy him, and then she gave up the study she had worked so hard to achieve and fled for home." Jane's mouth twisted into a wry smile. "With a short visit to my people in England to collect her wits before facing her family."

The story ate at Jordan's soul—all the more because it wasn't unusual. The upper crust of society rarely regarded the classes below them as having feelings that could be hurt or a heart that might be broken. If the working and lower classes possessed such things, they weren't important enough to matter.

"Did she imagine he would marry her?"

"Of course she did!" Jane snapped. "Where Ellen comes from, love and marriage are one and the same thing. A seduction is tantamount to a proposal. It was he who pursued her with sweet words and declarations. She had no way of knowing it was a meaningless game."

The culprit and his friends had no doubt laughed at the American woman doctor who had entertained the absurd notion that such a man actually meant to marry her. The anger Jordan had felt at Ellen was nothing compared to the fury that choked him at the thought of some careless, self-absorbed gentleman and his circle of cronies using Ellen as a topic of amusement over drinks in some pub or gentlemen's club.

"Ellen made a foolish mistake," Jane conceded tartly. "But women in love are often fools. Her misstep resulted from having too trusting a heart, and she'll pay for that the rest of her life. I, for one, don't think that is just. But it is the way the world works."

Jordan glanced at Ellen, who had sunk into the oblivion of an uneasy, exhausted sleep. One mistake and her life had been turned upside down, dreams shattered, a future destroyed. He suffered a sudden mad urge to hold her and tell her that everything would be all right, but he couldn't, even if it had been his place. For her, everything was not going to be all right. She would wear disgrace like a brand for the rest of her life. Decent women would avoid her. Men would regard her as a whore who had surrendered all right to the courtesies customarily afforded her gender. They might seek her out, but not for purposes that were honorable.

All this because she had trusted a man who claimed to love her. A harsh punishment for the crime of innocence and naïveté. She had so much spirit, wit, courage, and heart. How could such survive the ordeal she would suffer?

"Of course," Jane continued, "Henri Chretiens will not pay for what he did to her. Society puts the entire burden of responsibility on the woman in these cases. Even though he pursued, she is at fault for succumbing. Even though he deceived, she is to blame for believing him. Men will be men and play their games, but if they sin, it is always the woman's fault—simply for being female and therefore tempting."

Limp from the vehemence of her outburst, Jane dropped into a chair. "So proceed, Lord Chesterfield. Rant on about how Ellen deceived you into believing she was a decent woman. Spout off about her putting a blot on your family's stainless purity by being a guest in your home." She gave him an uncomfortably shrewd look. "But I wonder if your intentions were any more honorable than Henri Chretiens."

Jordan clamped his jaw on an automatically sharp reply. What *had* been his intentions toward Ellen? When he'd had her pinned in the grass of that meadow, had he any thought beyond his own immediate need? He didn't want to believe he was the same sort of profligate who had cast her into this sorry situation. He didn't want to believe he would have seduced her and left her alone to face the consequences.

He would not have done that. Of that he was sure. It was the only thing he was sure of at this moment, except for the intention to seek out a French physician by the name of Henri Chretiens and make sure he paid for his offense.

That evening Jordan sat with George in the Gun Room, a drinking salon that was devoted to gentlemen only. After an unpleasant day thinking about Jane's words and Ellen's predicament, he still felt as though his world had toppled from its stable foundation.

"You've been sucking down that brandy like it was mother's milk," George observed.

Jordan glanced at the empty glasses on the table between them. "That's not tea you're drinking yourself."

"I'm known for my intemperate habits," George admitted with a sunny grin. "You, on the other hand, are known as the upright defender of Restraint and Prudence. I don't think I've ever seen you drunk."

"I am not drunk. Not even close."

"You sound as though you'd like to be. What's wrong, big brother? Is the new expensive triple-expansion engine on this tub not performing up to snuff? Did the captain discover the purser pinching profits?"

"Don't be ludicrous." He gave George a keen-eyed look. "Do I really seem that unfeeling to you?"

George lofted a brow. "Unfeeling? What do you mean?"

"The word is self-explanatory. Unfeeling. Without human emotion or concern. More interested in things than people. When you inquired what was wrong, you just naturally assumed I was troubled about business and profits. Would it enter your mind, or anyone's mind, that I might be concerned about someone rather than something?"

George chuckled. "So that's it. Worried about the ladies' scheming? Mother and Hillary will reel you in if it takes them a decade to do it." He raised his glass in mock salute. "You have to give the darlings credit for persistence."

"I'm not worried about Mother or Hillary."

"I would be, if I were you. I say prayers of thanks every day that you were born first. A younger son isn't worth all the plotting and pursuing, not when there's a title available elsewhere. I'm allowed to go on as I please and enjoy all the pleasure of wealth and position without any of the responsibility. Mothers plot to keep their daughters away from me rather than connive to have them found in my bed."

Jordan gave an ill-humored grunt.

"Of course, Jane thinks I should reform and take up some worthy pursuit such as politics or social philanthropy. She says I have more substance to me than I show to the world. Imagine that. She's a corker, isn't she?"

Jordan regarded the glint in George's eye with suspicion. His recent conversation with Jane made it natural to form the worst possible conclusion about his brother's intentions. "I've warned you once to leave her alone, George. I shouldn't have to warn you again."

George was instantly defensive. "What do you have against Jane? You think an honest surgeon's daughter isn't good enough for a Chesterfield?"

"Quite the opposite," Jordan replied calmly. "I think she's much too good for you, and I think you're much too experienced and jaded for her. I wouldn't like to see her character dishonored."

George's face registered his astonishment. "What do you think I am?"

"I know what you are, George. I've had to bear the malice of more than one cuckholded husband who carries a grudge against the Chesterfields."

"But Jane is an innocent—a trusting angel. What sort of monster would abuse the trust of such a fresh and virtuous creature? Not I, I can assure you! I'm insulted that you should even think it."

Jordan believed him. The look on George's face bore witness to his sincerity. He was both relieved and surprised—relieved that his brother, for all his licentiousness, had at least some limits, and surprised at the vehemence of George's reaction. He ordered another brandy while his brother subsided.

"I'm glad to hear that, George. Jane is an exceptional girl. She has a rare strength of character, and a saint's loyalty to those she cares for."

"She does, doesn't she?" George reached across the table to borrow Jordan's drink. "I don't think I've ever met a woman who is so sweet and yet so intelligent. She can lecture you upon poetry and politics in the same breath. And though she's a shy little thing, she can hold her own in the best of company when she tries. It's incredible that she's lived her whole life just on the other side of Darwood and I've never met her."

"She's a surgeon's daughter, George. You weren't likely to meet her among the company you keep."

"Yes, I suppose."

The distracted reflection in his brother's face inspired speculation that a month ago never would have crossed Jordan's mind. "You're truly fond of Jane, aren't you, George?"

George reddened and studied the swirl of ice in the brandy that had formerly been Jordan's. "I am. I've become more attached than . . . well, than I should have. When I can no longer see her every day, talk to her, look forward to hearing her laugh or seeing that bright smile that makes her so lovely, the world will become dull." He grinned ruefully and shook his head. "I even look forward to her little lectures on my character and deportment."

Right then, Jordan envied his brother so much, the feeling left a sour taste in his mouth. George's words replayed in his mind, as true for Jordan as they were for George. How much he would miss Ellen O'Connell when he could no longer see her every day, talk to her, hear her laugh, see her smile. How dull the world would be.

But while Ellen was irrevocably lost to Jordan, only convention held George from Jane. Jordan fixed his brother with a stern look. "If you are so fond of Jane Browne, why don't you do something about it?"

George gave him a black look. "Weren't you the one who was just now telling me to leave her alone?"

"I do occasionally make mistakes," Jordan admitted with a twisted smile. "I didn't realize you had such tender feelings for the lady. Brief flirtations are more your style. Perhaps you're ready to settle down."

George snorted. "Good idea, Jordan. I can picture Mother's reaction. There wouldn't be an intact eardrum in the whole house, and the hole in the ceiling of her boudoir would take a small fortune to repair. Mother doesn't give a damn *if* I marry, since I don't carry the title, but she certainly would care *who* I marry. She would not have a surgeon's daughter as a daughter-in-law."

Jordan shrugged. "Since when have you eschewed an opportunity to irritate our mother? I had always thought that task occupied the majority of your week's planning."

George's brows puckered in hesitant incredulity. "You mean it, don't you?"

"Jane is a rare find, George. As I said, she's too good for the likes of you, but for some peculiar reason she appears to return your affection. Perhaps a happy marriage is worth overcoming an obstacle or two."

George regarded the brandy as if it were tainted by something more dangerous than mere alcohol. "You have taken on a load, haven't you?"

"Not that much of a load, I assure you."

"I suppose you know whereof you speak. Is it because you found such happiness with Mary Catherine that you resist Mother's arguments to remarry?"

"Not exactly." Jordan sighed. He was not a man who was comfortable trading confidences, even with his brother. But it seemed today was a day for changes. "Mary Catherine was a sweet girl. She always behaved herself. Mother approved of her. Society approved of her." He shook his head in wonder. "Even the servants loved her."

"The perfect wife," George observed.

"Yes. The perfect wife. I was incredibly bored the whole time we were married. Mary Catherine deserved to be loved, but that was something I couldn't give her. I don't think she ever forgave me for that."

"You gave her everything any woman could wish for," George insisted.

"She wanted my heart. That's what every wife wants. That's what any woman who marries expects from a husband. I'm afraid that in spite of Mother's ambitions for me and the dreams of many of the single ladies in our set, particularly Hillary, I am not good husband material. I have little patience with female sensibilities, little love for the social inanities that women adore, and no desire to give the institution of marriage another try. Any woman who is suitable to be Baroness Chesterfield has of necessity had any interesting spirit, independence, and originality drilled out of her in favor of social correctness. Otherwise she would not be considered suitable."

"So marry someone unsuitable," George advised with a twinkle. "If you're fortunate, Mother will be so annoyed she'll move permanently to London. Either that or huff off to the dower house and stay there."

"There's a thought."

George's grin faded. "You're right, you know. Jane Browne is much too good for me."

They exchanged a look of mutual understanding.

"You know, Jordan, you are quite human after all. Few people realize it, but you really are."

A little too human, Jordan reflected when George had gone. There were two empty glasses in front of him, and he was beginning to feel the effects of the brandy. He was also feeling the effects of a long, tiring, and entirely too provoking day. His mind was beginning to conjure up ideas that were patently ridiculous.

Not that George marrying Jane was ridiculous. He'd meant what he said to his brother. Happiness was a rare thing, and no chance at it should be allowed to pass by. Jane Browne could do nothing but brighten George's future.

But what of Ellen's future? That was the question that was inspiring a rush of nonsense in his head—that and George's facetious advice.

Ellen O'Connell—such an intriguing bundle of contradictions. On one hand, she was a living illustration that women needed a man's protection to survive the pitfalls of this harsh world. On the other, she was proof that a woman of independent spirit and intellect could excel in even the most challenging profession. She was tragedy and victory in one woman. Naive child and tempting female rolled into one. He hadn't been able to stop thinking about her all day. Hell, he hadn't stopped thinking about her since the day she'd told him she was going to drill a bloody damned hole in his brother's head.

Maybe George had a point after all, and maybe the

nonsense in Jordan's head wasn't nonsense, but an out-landish solution to both his problems and hers.

Jordan tilted his head back, closed his eyes, and re-sisted the temptation to call for yet another brandy. No amount of liquor was going to help him sleep tonight.

The next morning, a much improved Ellen was tidying the bed, cleaning the washstand, and making sure no evi-dence of her presence remained in Jordan's suite as she prepared to move back to her own rooms next door. She was almost ready to leave when Jordan came in. Without preamble or so much as a "good morning," he folded his arms across his broad chest and leaned against the door frame, conveniently blocking her exit should she make a bolt for freedom. From that vantage point he regarded her with a disconcertingly possessive expres-sion.

"Marry me, Ellen."

Ellen's breath froze in her lungs. A moment of tense silence passed before she could get a word out. "What did you say?" Her hearing must have been affected by her illness. Or perhaps she hadn't recovered at all, and she was simply caught in a delirium.

Very calmly he repeated himself. "Marry me."

Suddenly weak in the knees, Ellen sank into an or-nately carved wing-back chair.

"I suppose I should have put it more gracefully," Jor-dan conceded. One corner of his mouth lifted in a smile that made him look marginally less forbidding. "No doubt I should have led up to the subject with some meaningless chitchat, progressed to flowery compli-ments, and then broached the real subject. But under the circumstances, I thought a more forthright approach was appropriate."

"You just asked me to marry you." Ellen felt foolish even saying it.

"That's correct."

"You must be insane."

He didn't exactly look insane as he stood there and surveyed her with unnerving speculation. His hair was rumpled into unruly black curls. His suit coat was wrinkled. His cheeks were shadowed with a stubble that made him resemble a ruffian more than a pedigreed peer of the realm, and the unmistakable odor of liquor added to the illusion. He looked weary, disheveled, and disreputable. But he didn't really look insane.

"I can see where you might think that I've taken leave of my senses, but I assure you that I haven't. It seems to me that a marriage would be an admirable solution to the problems facing both of us."

"Really." Ellen looked down at her hands, then forced herself to meet the challenge of those unrelenting gray eyes. She had vowed that she wouldn't go through life abasing herself because of her mistake, and now was the time to start. "I assume the problem you refer to on my part is the fact that I carry a child. I don't remember much about what I said and did when I was sick, but I do remember your reaction when I made that unthinking confession. It was an understandable response, but not one that convinced me you were so entranced by my condition that you would want to wed me."

His steady gaze didn't flinch at her cool tone. Neither did he say anything. His proposal hung in the silence between them, charging the air with a sizzle of tension.

Finally, Ellen looked away. "Why on earth would you want to marry a woman who is carrying another man's bastard child?"

"Because your having a husband would save your respectability and give your child a legitimate name." He abandoned his guarded stance at the door and sat in the chair opposite Ellen, perching on the edge and leaning toward her. "Because my having a wife will rid me of the machinations of my sainted mother and a bevy of marriageable Society females."

"What of Hillary?"

"Hillary and I have been acquainted since we were children, and for all those years I have found her exceedingly dull. I assure you, the unfortunate scene you witnessed was not of my making. I have no desire to marry Hillary. In fact, I have no desire to marry any woman who would make a suitable Baroness Chesterfield."

"So you saddle yourself with a wife no sane man would want—when you have no desire to take a wife at all. Your reasoning defies logic, Lord Chesterfield."

"Not at all. I proposed marriage, Miss O'Connell. I did not propose that we live in each other's pockets for the rest of our lives."

"So this would be a cold-blooded business arrangement. Is that it?" Ellen's usual clarity of thought was swamped in a morass of churning sentiment. The past day and a half of sickness had weakened both her physical and emotion fiber. As she'd recovered, she had been horrified to remember her slip in Jordan's presence— and somewhat relieved, as well, to finally put the burden of pretense behind her. Ellen's emotions were very close to the surface. Feelings that had been hidden and ignored too long now showed her no mercy, and she felt as though she might shatter if one more ounce was added to the burden she already carried.

Now this . . . this cold-blooded proposal. For some reason she wanted to break down in tears, while another part of her wanted to scream at Jordan to leave her alone.

She neither wept nor screamed, however, as she answered him in a tightly controlled voice.

"Thank you for being concerned for my reputation and respectability, Lord Chesterfield. But I have no intention of living a lie—or of keeping the truth from my family."

His steady gaze didn't waver. "What of your friends?"

"Friends do not desert a person because they've made a mistake. At least true friends don't."

"And your patients?"

"My patients? What do you mean?"

"Surely you don't mean to waste your talent and medical education by giving up your profession."

"No. Of course not."

"How many men would let their wives be treated by a doctor who has given birth to an illegitimate child? How many mothers will bring their children to you? If you join in practice with your stepmother, are you willing to let her reputation suffer because of your disgrace?"

Ellen didn't like the thread of his reasoning. She had thought only of fleeing home to the comforting bosom of her family. Truthfully, she hadn't thought much beyond the pain of telling them what she had done. She got up and started to pace. Frustration swelled in her chest. Jordan's intense regard followed her every step, as did his words. She couldn't escape his merciless arguments.

"Do you expect to find a husband in this Montana of yours?" he asked finally. "Surely not."

She stared morosely out the porthole. "I have no more desire for a husband than you have for a wife. I've had enough of men to last me a lifetime."

He didn't relent. "What of your child? Will you punish it for your mistake?"

Her temper flared, and she spun around to face him. "My child will be dearly loved in every way!"

"And raised without a father."

"You are not offering fatherhood, unless I understand you incorrectly."

"A father's name and support doesn't necessarily have to come from someone who is there all the time."

He was wearing her down, and she was running out of defenses. This man was going to make a good politician.

"Your instinct to be honest is admirable, Ellen." His tone softened from relentless to persuasive. "But your child and family will both suffer humiliation if your situation is known. Your Montanans may be more liberal than us English snobs, but I doubt very much they are that liberal."

Ellen sat down again, leaned back into the chair, and closed her eyes in resignation. "Actually, they are not liberal at all."

When she opened her eyes, Jordan was kneeling on one knee in front of her. He folded her cold hands in his infinitely larger, comfortingly warmer ones. "Marry me, Ellen, and we can help each other. We are friends, are we not?" A roguish twinkle matched his sudden smile. "Surely you don't want to condemn me to a life fending off my mother and Hillary, and yourself to a life weighed down by disgrace."

"This is insane.

He merely smiled.

The future before Ellen loomed dreary and difficult, not only for herself, but for everyone who loved her. She had fled Paris hoping for safety, but safety didn't exist. That was what Jordan was telling her, and he was right.

She hated to admit it, but he was right. There were no sane solutions, so why not take an insane one? The idea made as much sense as the rest of her life had over the past few months. Yet . . . to marry Jordan Chesterfield, of all people?

Ellen didn't know what to say. So she said yes.

CHAPTER 13

The ceremony was to be performed that very night by the ship's captain. Ellen was not overly surprised when she learned it would be a double ceremony. Since leaving America behind, the events of her life had been bizarre enough to leave her beyond surprise. Jane marrying George Chesterfield seemed much less extraordinary than her marrying Jordan.

Now, sitting in front of her mirror and looking at her own wan face, Ellen still couldn't imagine how she had said yes to Jordan's proposal, or what had prompted him to so eccentric an action. Surely there was a less drastic way for him to win peace from the plotting females in his life.

Jane appeared in the mirror behind her. "You look beautiful."

"If you see someone beautiful in that mirror," Ellen said wryly, "then it's you."

It was true. Jane glowed. Ellen had always known her to be a quietly happy person. Now, however, she radi-

ated joy. Ellen was glad for her friend. For herself she
was only numb.

"I still can't believe it!" Jane bubbled. "I was so
stunned when George proposed, you could have
knocked me over with a feather. It was just so romantic.
I won't ever forget a moment of it."

Ellen had heard the story at least five times already,
but she let Jane gush on. They were dressing for their
weddings, after all, and one of them at least should play
the role of the ecstatic bride.

"I was standing at the rail, looking at the dolphins
playing in the ship's wake. He came up beside me and
just stood for the longest time. I wondered what he was
thinking, but I didn't ask, because there was this look on
his face. You know the look people get before diving off
a high bank into a swimming hole, or before getting
back on a horse that's just tossed them into a hedge?
That was the look he had on his face, the poor dear."

Ellen couldn't help but smile. "The poor dear," she
echoed teasingly.

Jane slapped at Ellen playfully for her lack of proper
reverence. "George was very brave," she insisted with
an upward twitch of her lips. "He must have been very
nervous. Lady Chesterfield will want to hang him by his
heels, for I'm a most unsuitable match, you know."

"I know no such thing. He's lucky you didn't turn
him down flat, for he's not nearly good enough for you."

"Oh piffle! He's much too good. His proposal was so
ardent. He said I was the sun of his days, and if I refused
him, the rest of his life would be gloomy as a winter in
Scotland."

"Oh, that is poetic," Ellen said with a snicker.

"And he's so thoughtful of my feelings. If Lady Chesterfield is rude about this, we're going to move some-

where so we needn't deal with her. George has an independent fortune from his grandfather, so he's not at all dependent on Lord Chesterfield or the dowager baroness." She sighed. "Not that I wouldn't marry him if he had empty pockets. My only regret is that now I won't be able to see Montana." Jane blinked. "But what am I saying? You won't be needing me in Montana now, will you? And I'm sure that as soon as Jordan has met your family, you'll be coming back to Endsfield Park where you and I can visit whenever we like. Oh, I'm so happy!"

Ellen rose abruptly, not wanting Jane to pursue that line of conversation. She diverted her with a show of feminine frustration. "I wish I had something to wear more suited to a wedding."

She had dressed in her very best, which was a dress she'd bought in Paris when she'd still felt she had the world by the tail. The bodice was draped green satin, the trim skirt a lighter green with inverted pleats revealing the same darker shade of the bodice. The sleeves were long and tightly fitted with only a hint of a puff at the shoulder. A velvet vee-shaped belt was intended to complement a fashionable wasp waist—Ellen had needed to expand it a notch or two. A poufy bow at the neck and a stylish felt hat completed the rather plain ensemble. It looked more like something a woman would wear to the smart London shops than to her wedding.

Not that it mattered what she wore. This wasn't a real wedding, Ellen reminded herself. It was a business arrangement. The thought made her sad. She envisioned her father and stepmother, who were so much in love and showed it every time they looked at each other. Even her sister Katy had found a man to love, and Katy, with her wild, boyish ways, was probably Montana's least

likely candidate for romance. And here was Ellen, about
to marry for convenience and protection, marry a man
who wanted her primarily as an excuse to keep other
women from hounding him.

Some marriage. Some life. But it was better than the
prospect she had faced only hours ago. She might as
well surrender to the realization that her life was not
going to be what she once had hoped. She needed to be
grateful for what she had and forget what she had lost.
After all, she had no one to blame for her misfortunes
but herself.

Ellen looked at herself in the mirror and saw a woman
she didn't really know. She wasn't sure she wanted to
know a creature who looked so depressed and spiritless.
Perhaps she felt so low simply because she wished this
marriage was real, that Jordan Chesterfield's proposal
had been one of romance and passion rather than painful
realities. What did she actually feel for Jordan? What
happened to her love for Henri Chretiens, the man she'd
once thought she couldn't live without? How much of
this was she doing for her child, and how much for herself?

She closed her eyes, not wanting to think about such
things, but when she opened them once again, her reflection in the mirror stared at her uncertainly. Eyes that
were usually a sharp, crystal green were clouded and
doubting.

Jane squeezed her shoulder. "Ellen, you look positively ill. You're not seasick again, are you?"

Ellen reached up and patted Jane's hand. "No. Not
seasick. I'm just a little nervous."

"Well of course you are, with such an unexpected turn
in your fortune! And about to be married to such a . . .
such an imposing man. Who would have expected this

to happen? Especially given the circumstances. Jordan Chesterfield must love you very much. Though I could tell from the first he was taken with you."

Ellen smiled wanly. "You could, could you?"

"And you with him." Jane nodded knowingly. "All that squabbling between you—his stiff manner, your huffy resentment—all that was just dressing for the romance brewing in your hearts. Wasn't it?"

"If you say so." Ellen gave her reflection a contemptuous glare in the mirror and got up. "Let's go get married."

The wedding was a quiet one, with only the pursuer and his wife as witnesses. Ellen didn't know how Jordan had contrived to obtain the licenses, but she supposed being a peer of the realm had its advantages, not to mention being owner of the ship upon which they stood. The captain was a somber man who conducted the ceremony in a manner more fitting to a graveside than a wedding, but his funereal tones seemed all too appropriate to Ellen. She was wedged between George on her left and Jordan on her right, feeling dwarfed and hemmed in. Jordan stood beside her like a granite tower. When she risked a glance at his face, he was calm, dignified, and in control. On her left, George made up for Jordan's ungroomlike composure by looking like a man who was about to step off a cliff. Sweat glistened on his brow, and his face was so pale that Ellen feared her medical skills would be needed before the ceremony was over. But his jaw was clamped in determination, and he held on to Jane's hand like a drowning man might cling to a buoy.

Through the blur of her own thoughts, Ellen heard Jane taking her vows. Sickness and health, better or worse, till death us do part. Jane was making a promise from her very heart, but Ellen was about to speak a lie, before God and everyone else. For her and Jordan, there would be no "till death us do part," for Jordan didn't want a real wife, and Ellen didn't want a husband—at least not this husband, she told herself.

What was she getting herself into? She'd scarcely seen Jordan since his proposal. So many questions remained unanswered. Just what did he mean by not living in each other's pockets? How businesslike was this arrangement to be? If they lived apart, how would they explain that to George and Jane, to Ellen's family, to Jordan's family and friends? If her child was a boy, surely Jordan couldn't mean for him to be his heir. And what if, somewhere down the road, Jordan did find a woman he truly wanted as wife?

Ellen suffered a sudden urge to turn and flee, but she didn't.

Coward! she chided herself.

Realist, her logic replied—but perhaps realist was just another word for coward.

For his part, Jordan was not quite as composed as he appeared. Generations of breeding and years of training enabled him to face almost any situation with aplomb, but a wedding was enough to shake any man loose from his moorings. When the time came, he spoke his vows in a firm voice, but his own words echoed in his head with a ring of falsehood.

What did he really intend for this marriage? The reasons they should marry had seemed logical enough when he'd talked himself into proposing, and with a little work, he'd convinced Ellen of their soundness. Jordan had never been good at lying to himself, however. He didn't want to probe very deeply into his true motivation for this marriage for fear he would find some fool-

ishness that would only lead to hurt in the end. Ellen
might be legally his after this ceremony was concluded,
but in truth she belonged to another man. The dark feelings that thought engendered were frightening in themselves.

Ellen made her vows in a quiet voice, not meeting his
eyes as she spoke. When he took her hand to slip a ring
on her finger, her flesh was cold as ice. Her eyes darted
up to his, and he gave her what he hoped was a reassur-
ing smile. She answered with a wry twitch of her lips.

The captain pronounced the two couples men and
wives. George promptly kissed his bride in a most thorough fashion.

"Shall we?" Jordan asked Ellen.

Before she could say yea or nay, he kissed her. He'd
meant it to be only a formal peck, but her lips tempted
him from his good intentions. Soft, sweet—they were
every man's dream of a woman's mouth. He made a
very thorough job of sealing their bargain. By the time
he released her, even the dour captain looked a bit
amused.

Ellen appeared dazed by it all, and Jordan found himself missing her usual sharp-tongued brass. She would
be back to herself soon enough, he figured. Ellen wasn't
a woman that anything could knock down for long.

Strange that he could like a woman who gave him so
much back talk at times. But he did like her, dammit!
He liked her too much.

Though the wedding ceremony had been quiet and private, the wedding supper was not. The ship's cook,
learning that Lord Chesterfield and his brother had both
taken brides that very evening, prepared a feast worthy
of the auspicious occasion. Not all three thousand pas-

sengers attended, fortunately, but enough of them did to make the celebration very raucous and very long.

Ellen excused herself early, abandoning her new husband to the dubious influences of his brother. Jane offered to accompany her, but Ellen urged her to stay.

"Enjoy yourself," she told her friend. "You have only one wedding celebration in your life. Besides, who will make George behave if you come with me?"

"But you look pale."

"I'm fine. Just tired, really."

"Ellen, are you all right?" Jordan broke in.

He looked genuinely concerned, so she gave him her best smile. "I'm fine. Stay."

She was fine, Ellen told herself. Nevertheless, the fresh breeze outside made her a good deal better. If she'd had to listen to one more round of hearty congratulations, she would have been sick. Now, however, with the cold wind in her face and the quiet hum of the engines the only sound in her ears, she felt her mood lift. The moon was low in the west, almost directly ahead of the ship, and the *Mary Catherine* followed a glistening silver path through the sea. Stars banded the sky in crystal pinpricks of light. The world was a beautiful place, and certainly a friendlier place than it had been only a day past. She was safe. Her unborn child was safe. Everything was going to be all right.

Then why did she feel as though she was standing at the edge of a cliff, looking out over empty space as the earth crumbled beneath her feet?

Ellen went to her suite without thinking, but George's clothing hung where hers had hung a few hours earlier, and a man's hairbrush instead of hers lay on the dressing table beside Jane's. Ellen's clothing and toilet articles had been moved. She shouldn't have been surprised.

Married people shared the same room—and the same bed.

In the suite next door, she found her clothes hung neatly in the closet beside Jordan's and her toilet articles laid out upon his dressing table. The bedroom had two large beds. That was some comfort, at least. Already this marriage was getting more awkward than she had anticipated.

Ellen was behind the privacy screen changing into her nightgown when Jordan came into the room. The sound of his voice gave her a start. She certainly was not accustomed to having a man in the same room where she was dressing—or rather, undressing.

"Are you all right?" he asked from the other side of the screen.

"Yes." Her voice shook, and she hated it. "I'm fine. I thought you were going to stay at the dinner for a while longer."

"I did stay. It's nearly midnight."

"Oh." Had she lingered on deck so long? So much for her plan to be fast asleep when Jordan came in. She was glad she'd taken her heavy dressing robe from the closet. Wrapping herself in its concealing folds, she peered cautiously around the screen. Jordan's black felt top hat lay on one of the beds along with his discarded ascot. His black Prince Albert coat hung from the back of one chair, and he lounged in the other, looking distressingly undone. Much of his clothing was undone, that is, his waistcoat hung open, and his linen shirt was unbuttoned halfway to his waist, revealing a dark mat of chest hair beneath. The elegantly tailored gray and black striped trousers were still intact, thank heaven! His head was tilted back against the chair, and his eyes were closed.

"You've been drinking, haven't you?" Ellen sniffed cautiously at the faint aroma of liquor in the air.

"All grooms imbibe on their wedding night. It's tradition."

Ellen remembered the night her father had wed her stepmother. If her memory was correct, Gabriel O'Connell hadn't drunk a drop that evening, but then, he'd had something else very much on his mind. That had been obvious even to his twelve-year-old daughters. That was a tradition as well, she thought uneasily. How she wished they'd talked about this arrangement in much greater detail.

"Maybe you should drink some tea," she suggested tentatively.

"Maybe I should." His eyes opened. "Good lord! What is that you have on?"

"My dressing gown."

"You don't sleep in that, do you?"

"Of course not. I sleep in a nightgown, like any normal person."

"Is it as much a piece of armor as that thing?"

"It's not a piece of armor. It is simply sensible."

"Is it indeed?" His eyes glittered in a way that made Ellen's heart start to speed. "Is it made from steel plates?" His slow smile matched the threat—or promise—of his eyes.

Ellen stiffened her spine. "Don't be ridiculous."

"Let me see it."

"Certainly not!" She clutched the robe more tightly about her body.

"Don't be silly, Ellen. Do you think we can sleep in the same room and not have me see your bloody nightgown?"

She'd never heard him curse before. Now she knew he'd had too much to drink.

"I think we should just turn out the lamps and get a good night's sleep," she said. "I can't remember when I've been so tired."

"At least let me get undressed before you bring down the dark."

That wouldn't have been Ellen's choice. As Jordan rose and pulled his shirt from the waistband of his trousers, she looked resolutely out the porthole. "There is a privacy screen," she suggested. Her voice was more tart than she had intended, but when her nerves were on edge, as they were now, everything else about her seemed to become sharp as well—her voice, her temper, the fingernails that were digging into her palms.

A long silence greeted her suggestion, followed by a sigh. "Ellen, we are husband and wife, and we're going to be living together in this suite for the next four days. I don't see any need to play hide-and-seek with each other all that time."

"I'm not suggesting—"

His hand landed unexpectedly on her shoulder, making her jump nearly out of that armored robe he so despised.

"Ellen, we are neither one of us possessed of innocent sensibilities. You're a physician, for heaven's sake. And you're a woman of experience."

He turned her away from the porthole, and she was forced to either face him or make a production out of resistance. His chest was bare, revealing sculpted muscle and a thick mat of curling black hair. Ellen took a steadying breath and willed herself not to look at the alluring expanse of masculinity before her. "You're not my patient," she reminded him. Though the odor of liquor clung to him, the gray eyes that looked down at her were clear. "And why is it that when a woman isn't a virgin, a man simply assumes she has no sensibilities left to offend?"

The eyes darkened to steel. "All I'm saying is . . . is . . ." He seemed to lose the train of his thought as his eyes bored into hers. "God, your eyes are beautiful."

Jordan was definitely not his usual disciplined self. Ellen told herself to move away before it was too late, but for some reason her body chose to stay, and when he moved to capture her mouth with his, her head merely tilted back to meet him.

For a moment Ellen's mind went blank, and her resistance was as weak as her watery knees. Jordan's touch was intoxicating, his mouth irresistible, and the barriers inside her soul tottered on the brink of collapse. She hadn't enjoyed kissing Henri half so much.

The thought of Henri dashed an icy flood of good sense on Ellen's rising passion. Desperately she pushed away. "What am I doing?" she gasped.

For a moment Jordan looked bemused. Then he reached for her. She fended him off with both hands.

"We aren't supposed to do this! I'm pregnant, for mercy's sake! This is a business arrangement, isn't it?"

His eyes froze to slivers of cold steel. The transformation was immediate and thorough, leaving the cool aristocrat in place of the all too human, slightly intoxicated groom. "If that is what you want it to be, certainly."

"Isn't that what you intended it to be?"

The slight wavering of his gaze was an echo of the uncertainty in her voice. Ellen wondered just how much thought he had given the details of their marriage before making his proposal.

"Isn't it?" she prompted.

"That certainly would seem the wisest course." He sighed. "You're right, and I apologize for getting carried away."

His tone put an ache in Ellen's throat. At Endsfield, she had learned there was much more to this man than the pedigreed tyrant she'd first thought him. She had come to value his friendship, and perhaps, she admitted to herself, she had valued him as more than a friend. But what were they now? Friends? Partners? Husband and wife? Surely they could not be lovers.

"Anything else would be a mistake." She put the chair between them, more to give herself an anchor than to fend him off.

He ran fingers through his hair and looked away. "A mistake. Yes. It would be a mistake."

"After all, ours is an arrangement for mutual benefit, isn't it? And even though pregnancy doesn't preclude . . . well . . . you know . . ."

The rigidity of his stance softened and his eyes acquired a small gleam of amusement as she dug herself in even deeper. "I know," he assured her.

She clung more tightly to the chair. "Physical entanglement . . . uh . . ."

"Physical entanglement . . . ?"

"Yes, entanglement. Physical entanglement leads to high emotions, one way or another . . . and . . . well . . . this is not an emotional relationship we have, is it? This is a business arrangement. No feelings are involved."

"No feelings."

"None at all."

They stared at each other for a moment. She could sense he was fighting a smile, and she herself felt a bit of softening inside.

"Maybe a bit of feeling," he finally admitted. The smile won. It warmed his eyes and lifted his mouth.

"Well . . ." she ventured hesitantly. "Maybe just a bit."

"Such as respect. I have a good deal of respect for you, Ellen."

"You do?"

"Yes. You're an extraordinary woman, and you should never let anyone or anything make you feel otherwise."

"I'm having a child out of wedlock," she reminded him tartly.

"That doesn't change who you are." His smile turned wry. "Besides, it's not exactly out of wedlock any longer."

Ellen bit her lip. If he could admit to a little partiality, then so could she. "I have a lot of respect for you also, Jordan. Beneath that stuffy manner you're quite an unusual man."

"Thank you." He picked his shirt up from the floor and shrugged it on. "Is there a reason you're trying to squeeze the life out of that poor chair back?"

Ellen looked down at her white knuckles and laughed uneasily. "No. Of course not." Cautiously, as though there were a predator in the room who might notice her if she moved too fast, she stepped around the chair and sat down.

"A bit of affection, also," Jordan said thoughtfully. He hung his jacket in the closet, and Ellen couldn't see his face.

"I beg your pardon?"

"Affection." He closed the closet door and sat down in the chair opposite her. "As long as we're laying open our feelings, I'll admit that you've softened a place in my otherwise hard heart."

"Your heart isn't hard, Jordan."

"What makes you think it's not?"

"I've seen you with your brother. I've seen you with Andrea and Prissy, with Maisy. And . . . well . . . with me. You're loyal and quick to defend. And you're kind. Andrea and Prissy adore you, and in spite of his casual manner, George adores you also."

"I'm that wonderful, am I?"

Her face heated. "I didn't say you were wonderful. But I'd guess you guard your feelings so carefully merely because they run so deep."

He smiled. "You know me quite well for a mere business partner."

"I've thought about you a lot," she admitted. "I suppose I must admit to some affection, also."

He reached out and took her hand. "Since we are to maintain some connection for the rest of our lives, I would say some affection is a good thing."

"As long as we don't let it get out of hand," she said cautiously. Her eyes couldn't seem to leave his, and the softening she had felt inside was turning to heat.

He raised her hand to his lips. Startled, she stood. He stood also.

"I suppose we should say good night, then," he said quietly.

"Yes."

His smile twisted with a hint of irony. "As friends. With respect, and just a bit of affection."

She held her breath as he pressed a chaste kiss to her brow. She could sense the beat of his heart, feel the quiet rush of his warm breath. His hand tightened on hers.

"Damn!" His curse was a quiet one, but vehement all the same. "What kind of game am I playing?" He pulled himself away from her, grabbed for his waistcoat, and headed for the door.

"Where are you going?"

"Across the hallway. There's an empty cabin."

"Don't," Ellen pleaded. "Please, Jordan. I'll not have us embarrassed. The whole ship will know you spent your wedding night sleeping apart from your bride."

"No one will know."

"The steward and housekeepers will know," she insisted. "And if they know, then the whole ship will know. It will embarrass us both."

He flung his waistcoat down upon the bed. "Ellen, don't tempt me."

"I don't mean to tempt you, Jordan. We're both mature adults. Surely we can sleep together in the same room without . . . without indulging in . . . intimate behavior."

He chuckled cynically. "One would think."

"It's not as if we are required to sleep in the same bed."

He sent the two separate beds a narrow look she couldn't interpret.

"And I assure you that you're not missing much of anything, Jordan. Truthfully. I've been told that I'm not . . . well . . . a very entertaining bedmate."

Jordan groaned, then laughed. "Lord, Ellen, quit trying to convince me. Just turn out the lamps so we can each climb into our separate bed and get some sleep."

She complied. Lying in her bed, she listened to the sound of Jordan undressing. The darkness seemed to intensify every sound. She heard his shirt slither against the velveteen upholstery of the chair, his black patent leather shoes and gray spats hit the floor, and his trousers slide down his long legs. At least she imagined the last.

"If you want to turn up a lamp to hang your clothes, I'll hide my eyes," she generously offered.

"A night on the chair won't hurt my clothes," was the answer.

"Can you find your nightshirt in the dark?"

"I don't wear a nightshirt."

Ellen reached the obvious conclusion, and her imagination soared out of control as she heard his bed creak beneath his weight. What an unusual way for a man to sleep. Unusual and enticing. She could almost see the crisp white sheet against that mat of black hair on his chest. What a contrast his hard body would make against the downy softness of the bedclothes.

Mumbling an unladylike word under her breath, Ellen turned her back to the other bed and clamped her pillow over her head, as if she could block out the images inside her own mind.

Through the pillow she heard his muffled good night.

"Good night," she muttered in reply.

Good night, indeed!

CHAPTER 14

The breakfast buffet laid out
in the dining room featured eggs Florentine, eggs Benedict, coddled eggs, scrambled eggs, and omelets of every
description. The sideboard groaned with the weight of
sliced ham and bacon, pastries and fruit—fresh, sugared,
cooked, or compoted. It was truly an appetizing display,
a credit to the managers and owners of the Atlantic and
Mediterranean Steamship Line, as well as to the chefs.

Jordan had little appreciation of the buffet this morning, however, and less appetite. His eyes felt gritty, his
body stiff, and his temper frayed.

"Is that all you're eating?" George asked. He stood
beside Jordan at the buffet table and looked down at the
lonely egg and single thin slice of ham on Jordan's plate.
"At least take a pastry. These look delicious." He put an
iced sweet roll onto Jordan's plate, then took one for
himself. "You should lure this cook away from the *Mary
Catherine* and have her work at Endsfield."

"The chef is a man," Jordan said.

"No matter. Mother would be offended, but the domestics will have to answer to the new baroness now, won't they? I imagine Ellen will make a few changes around the place. Bring it up to date a bit. High time, too."

Jordan merely grunted. They took their plates outside, where tables had been set up in a protected area of deck adjacent to the dining room. The day was an incredibly fine one for mid-November.

"Have you ever seen such a beautiful day?" George set down his heaping plate and raised his arms joyfully toward the blue sky. "And here it is almost December in the middle of the Atlantic. It's a sign, I tell you—a sign that something is right with the world."

"Judging from your mood," Jordan commented, "your world seems to be in good order."

"Couldn't be better." George sat down and dug into a heaping pile of eggs. "It's amazing what a good woman can do for a man's perspective," he said around a mouthful. "I must admit I was a bit nervous about the whole idea of marriage. The commitment, you know. It is a frightening responsibility. But I believe it's going to work out very well indeed." He chuckled contentedly to himself. "Very well indeed."

"I'm glad to hear it," Jordan said sourly.

"You're looking somewhat haggard this morning, brother. Not much time for sleep last night?"

Jordan resisted the urge to put his fist into George's knowing grin, for George didn't know the half of it.

"I must say I didn't think you had the nerve to do it."

"Do what?" Jordan growled.

"Marry Miss O'Connell, though I think it was a very good notion. She's an original. No one can argue that. Mother is going to tear you limb from limb, you know.

She'll be so furious with you that she'll scarcely take note of my inappropriate alliance."

His mother's reaction was the least of Jordan's concerns at the moment. For the next few weeks—until he had done his duty by Ellen and given a certain credence to this marriage—he had to think of a way to keep his hands off of her. His hands, his mouth, and all the other body parts that were itching to touch her.

He hadn't thought it would be this difficult. Actually, he hadn't thought much at all past convincing her to marry him, and his motivation for that was beginning to be suspect even to him. Perhaps, somewhere deep in his mind, he'd pictured them cavorting through the next few weeks like newlywed lovers until it was time for him to return to England, when Ellen would cheerfully wave good-bye. She would keep his name and protection for her child while he sailed back to England to enjoy his new status as unavailable. Surely even his unconscious mind couldn't be that stupid.

Or maybe he was that stupid. Damn, but all desire for Ellen should have died after he discovered her secret. She was the victim of another man's lust, a woman who needed his help, not his passion.

"Are you going to eat that slice of ham?" George asked. His fork was poised, ready to spear the meat off Jordan's plate.

"Go ahead."

"Usually I don't have such an appetite so early in the morning," George said with a grin. "But this morning I could eat a ton."

"Isn't that what you're doing?"

"Do you know what Jane told me last night?"

"I can't imagine."

"She cooks. She *likes* to cook. Do you believe that?

Said she'd make me her special Yorkshire pudding for Christmas, as if I can't afford to employ proper help in the kitchen, and rest of the house as well. I plan to put a house on my property down in Cornwall, for she likes it there, and perhaps buy a place in London. And I'll make sure she has the best of everything. She won't have to lift a hand unless she wants to. Not to say she can't cook or sew or such if it amuses her."

He helped himself to Jordan's pastry. "She is absolutely the sweetest girl I've ever known, Jordan. When I first saw her, I really thought her rather plain, can you believe? But those eyes of hers, and that smile. I must have been blind. Her soul shines through her face, and it's the best and purest soul any woman could have."

Jordan sighed.

"What's more, she's kind. How many beautiful women do you know who are actually kind? Most of them are too concerned with their own reflection in the mirror to be mindful of anyone else, but Jane has . . ."

". . . the best heart of any one I know," Jane said with an ecstatic sigh as she and Ellen sipped tea in the sitting room of Jane's suite. "He's so kind and considerate. I was a bit embarrassed last night, I'll admit—well, any bride would be. But he made everything seem so right, so natural, not embarrassing or shameful at all."

"That's wonderful," Ellen told her. She wondered if a plea of returning seasickness would spare her from the rest of Jane's testimonial to married love. It wasn't that she begrudged her friend's happiness, but Jane's glowing rapture was a bright counterpoint to her own dark mood, and the contrast made things seem that much worse.

"He is so beautiful," Jane gushed.

Ellen got up from her chair and went to the suite's porthole to gaze out at the calm blue sea. It wouldn't do for Jane to see her face. Tired as she was, Ellen didn't have the strength to hide her emotions.

"Who would have thought that a man could be so beautiful?" Jane wondered dreamily. "Even . . . well, *that* part of him. Ellen, did you know what men really look like before you were with Henri?"

"I went to medical school, Jane."

"Well, yes, I know. But I mean, what they really look like when they . . . uh . . . you know."

"Yes." Ellen sighed.

"Well, I didn't. I didn't know any of it."

"I should have talked to you, I suppose."

"Not at all. It was quite all right, really, although I was a bit surprised! Actually, I was scared to death at first, and when George told me what men and women do together, I thought he was joking. In very poor taste, too. He laughed, bless him. But he was so sweet. And it didn't hurt at all—well, not very much, at least. And at the last . . ." Jane sighed. "I've never in my life felt like that. Afterward, we lay together for the longest time, hugging and talking. It was wonderful. Absolutely wonderful. You should have told me, Ellen, that loving a man is so grand."

Ellen hadn't told her because Ellen hadn't known. She had been with Henri but once, and that experience hadn't exactly been grand. As she remembered, it had be painful, embarrassing, and very messy. After his passion had been spent, Henri had collapsed to one side, naked and clammy with sweat. There he had snored the night away, leaving Ellen to her own confused thoughts until well after dawn, when he had awakened and displayed considerable surprise at finding her in his bed.

She should have left well before daylight, he'd complained, so that no one would see her coming out of his lodgings.

At that time, Ellen had been contrite for embarrassing him. Green and unsophisticated, she hadn't known the rules. Now she found herself resenting that she would never know the bliss that Jane knew on this morning.

Jane fell into silence, and when Ellen turned away from the porthole, her friend was regarding her curiously. "Ellen, dear, are you and Jordan getting on all right?"

"Yes, of course."

"Was he kind to you last night?"

"Very kind."

Jordan had let her be after they went to their separate beds, and though she'd heard his restless tossing and uneven breathing the whole night through, he'd made no more attempts to exercise his husbandly rights. When she had awakened from an unsettled doze shortly after dawn, he'd been gone, and she was safe from his attention. That was what Ellen wanted, wasn't it?

"Why would you think Jordan was other than kind?" Ellen asked.

Jane shrugged, still looking suspicious. "You have a peculiar air about you this morning."

Ellen put on a faint smile. "I'm tired. That's all."

"I think it's wonderful that Jordan has taken on responsibility for the baby. Not that you don't deserve such a wonderful outcome to your situation. He must love you very much."

Ellen could only look at the floor as Jane took her hands and turned them around the room in a spontaneous little dance. "Love is a miracle," she sang. "A wonderful miracle that can make anything happen—make barriers disappear, make sadness become joy." She collapsed on the love seat, glowing. "But you've been in love before, so you knew all along this was true."

Ellen smiled weakly. "Yes. I suppose I must have."

Ellen could put up with Jane's cheerfulness for only so long. After one cup of tea she made excuses to return to her own suite, where she opened the door furtively, like a thief, then breathed a sigh of relief when she discovered that Jordan had not returned. She wasn't up to facing him. Hell, Ellen thought, she wasn't up to facing the rest of her life. Somehow the bleak future had been easier to face when she'd been on her own, and before she'd had to listen to Jane rhapsodizing about love and passion. Accepting Jordan's proposal was supposed to make things easier, not harder.

What she needed, Ellen decided, was rest. She hadn't slept more than a quarter hour the night before. Jordan's restlessness had kept her awake, and in the rare moment he was still, she'd been forced to listen to her own meandering thoughts and endure her own feelings—none of which had been conducive to sleep. Surely after she'd slept an hour or two, the world would look brighter.

Still, she couldn't very well sleep with the bedroom in such disarray. Jordan's shirt from the night before hung from the back of a chair. His trousers lay in a heap at the foot of his bed, and a silk dressing robe was precariously draped over the top of the privacy screen. Obviously, the man was accustomed to having maids pick up after him. It was too much for Ellen's innate sense of neatness, developed from a childhood spent keeping house for her clutter-producing father and twin sister.

When she picked up her husband's shirt and shook it out, a faint aroma of Jordan clung to the material, a not unpleasant scent that combined sea breeze, liquor, and a warm muskiness that produced a peculiar tingle deep in Ellen's belly. She rememberd how it had looked hanging open to reveal a virile chest beneath white linen, and the memory made her swallow hard. Almost against her will, her fingers caressed the material that had lain against his body so intimately. Closing her eyes, she could almost feel hard muscle warming the soft cloth, almost see the seams strain when he flexed his shoulders.

Suddenly filled with contempt for herself, she threw the shirt on the bed. What kind of woman was she, anyway, lusting after one man while carrying another man's child?

Jordan is your husband, a voice in her head tempted. *Is it so wrong for a woman to desire her own husband?*

Their marriage was a business arrangement, Ellen reminded herself. His peace and freedom in exchange for her respectability. They weren't really husband and wife.

That wasn't what your wedding vows said, the voice argued. *That wasn't what the marriage certificate read.*

With a groan, Ellen dropped into the chair and hid her face in her hands. She could argue with herself all day and only come out the loser. It was true that Jordan had said they wouldn't live "in each other's pockets." Did that mean, as she had taken it at the time, that he intended a marriage in name only? It was also true that he had desired her last night. Was she unjustly depriving him of his rightful privileges, repaying his kindness—and he had been kind—with a cold shoulder and impossible expectations?

Ellen sighed. Her thinking was in a dreadful muddle. Even Jordan had agreed that complicating matters would do neither of them any good. But she had seen his face when she'd asked him not to embarrass them by leaving. The expression had combined pain with determination. He'd been a man girding himself to face the impossible. Was it so hard for him to sleep in the same room with her and leave her untouched?

Slowly, Ellen got up, walked over to the bed, and picked up Jordan's shirt once again. If she was honest with herself, she would admit the desire to experience lovemaking with Jordan Chesterfield—right or wrong, wise or foolish—further proof, if any were needed, that she wasn't a particularly virtuous woman. If she was truly in love with Henri, as she'd once thought, she wouldn't feel what she felt for Jordan. If she had any delicacy at all, she would swoon at the thought of making love with a man when she was carrying another man's child.

But God help her, she needed a bit of tenderness to last her for a lifetime that promised to be sterile and lonely. If Jordan didn't love her, at least in bed he would make her feel loved. Ellen knew he would, because she felt loved even when he did nothing more than kiss her.

She sat on the bed and hugged his shirt to her, hot tears running down her cheeks. Virtue and delicacy, she decided, were highly overrated in this world. To hell with them.

The captain of the *Mary Catherine* was not normally a man given to joviality, but the honor of officiating at the downfall of two such prestigious bachelors as Lord Chesterfield and his brother had put him in an expansive mood. As the two newlywed couples took their places at the captain's table that night at dinner, he beamed at the four of them like a father well pleased with his sons, starting a round of applause that was soon taken up by indulgent gentlemen and soulfully smiling matrons all over the dining room. Jordan saw Ellen bite her lip and grow pale at the attention as he seated her, and he himself felt his face grow a bit warm, an unthinkable lapse for someone who'd been in the public eye all his life. George and Jane were faring a bit better. George, always one who basked in notoriety, waved to the well-wishers, while Jane blushed prettily and hid her eyes behind lowered lashes.

"Haven't seen these fellows or their brides all day," one man at their table teased. "Had to surface for sustenance, did you?"

Jordan quelled him with a steely glance. "Mind your manners, Mr. Ferron. There are ladies at the table."

"And very lovely ladies they are, too," said another.

The matron sitting beside Ellen, a Mrs. Collins, joined in. "What a lucky girl you are, Miss O'Connell. But of course, it's Lady Chesterfield now, isn't it? How dreadfully exciting to be whisked off and married aboard ship. Did you plan to be wed aboard the *Mary Catherine*, or was this a spur-of-the-moment inspiration?"

Jordan felt Ellen tense, so he stepped into the conversation with a practiced smile. "I fear the unconventional wedding was my doing, Mrs. Collins. When Lady Chesterfield finally agreed to be my wife, I was taking no chances on her changing her mind."

"How wonderful!" Mrs. Collins darted a glance at her husband. "What a shame that more men don't have your romantic impulses, Lord Chesterfield."

"It's the ladies who inspire romance, madam. We poor men simply respond."

Ellen rolled her eyes in a manner reminiscent of Prissy, and Jordan's smile was genuine this time. It was good to see her showing a bit of spirit again.

"And you, Mr. Chesterfield?" a woman down the table asked George. "Did you come on board with plans to marry?"

George charmed the woman with a wicked grin. "Not at all, Mrs. Bates. I simply followed where my big brother led. I always try to follow the path he lays out for me." He raised Jane's hand and kissed her fingers. "But from now on, I plan to follow only where my lovely wife leads."

Jane smiled happily, and Jordan could see George's heart in his eyes. If George and Jane had been alone at the table they couldn't have been more wrapped up in each other. A pang of pure envy cut through Jordan like a knife. He'd never shared such a thing with Mary Catherine, or with any other human being. He'd never wanted to, and now he wondered what he had missed.

He dared a glance at Ellen to find her also watching his brother and Jane. Her lovely green eyes were misty with . . . with what? Who could understand what went through a woman's mind and heart, especially Ellen's? She turned her head quickly and caught his eyes fastened upon her. Her cheeks turned pink.

"She's still blushing," Mrs. Collins gushed. "Isn't that sweet!"

Jordan sighed. It was going to be a long, long dinner hour.

After dinner, the four of them made an appearance in the red salon to dance to the orchestra.

"Are you feeling well?" Jordan asked Ellen as he led her onto the dance floor.

"I'm fine, thank you."

Her waist was still small, her form supple. She fit naturally into his arms and effortlessly, instinctively followed his movements as if their bodies were linked by some invisible bond. Making love to her would be similar to dancing, Jordan sensed. Their bodies were in tune, slaved to the same rhythm.

Holding her, knowing he would never experience loving her, was paradise and purgatory rolled into one. Had he known what he was letting himself in for when he proposed? Jordan wondered. Just how much of a marriage had he intended? He'd been seized with an idea—almost an obsession—and had taken it to completion without thinking it through. Very uncharacteristic of him. He'd been a cautious planner all his life—until Ellen came along.

Ellen fanned herself with a napkin when they got back to their table, where a waiter had placed port for him and sherry for her. "I . . . I think I'd like to retire early, if you don't mind."

He gave her a concerned look. "Are you all right?"

"I'm fine. Quit asking me if I'm all right. I'm just tired."

She didn't look sick. At the moment, she didn't even look tired. Her eyes were bright, her color heightened. She looked beautiful, Jordan thought. And nervous.

"Would you like me to walk you to the suite?"

"Yes, please. If you don't mind."

"Of course I don't mind."

They were silent as they made their way toward the bow, where the family suites were located. Ellen radiated a tension that precluded casual conversation, and Jordan supposed he wasn't exactly giving off signals that would put her at ease. No doubt she was girding herself to fend him off once again. He meant to reassure her on that point when, at the door of their suite, he gestured her inside while remaining in the hallway.

"I think I'll go up to the Gun Room for a while," he told her. *And stay there,* he added silently.

She didn't look a bit relieved. In fact, she appeared distressed. "You're not coming in?"

"I'll be in shortly." *Maybe at the end of the voyage.*

"I . . . I . . ." Whatever word she groped for didn't come. With a frustrated sigh, she grabbed his hand and pulled him into the sitting room. "Jordan. We need to talk."

Talk was the last thing he was interested in at that moment. "Ellen, we're both tired. Perhaps we should put this off until later."

"It won't wait." She darted around him and closed the door, then stood against it as if to block his escape—or to hold herself up. Face pale, hands shaking slightly, she did appear in need of being propped upright.

He surrendered with a sigh. "All right, we'll talk." He took off his coat and hung it over the back of the chair. "What are we talking about?"

"I've had quite a few hours to think today."

That could be dangerous, Jordan thought.

"It occurred to me that we got married in a great hurry."

"True."

"You were very persuasive in your proposal, and"—a smile lifted one corner of her mouth—"I was quite readily persuaded. But we never talked about quite a few things we should have talked about."

Jordan lowered himself into the nearest chair and sat back, beginning to be curious about where she was going.

"It occurs to me that I owe you an apology for last night, Jordan."

"Really? In what way?"

"I . . . we . . ." She bit her lip, then plunged on. "We never really discussed the details of our arrangement. For some reason I assumed you wanted our marriage to be in name only. Perhaps . . . perhaps I assumed wrong."

What a bizarre scene this was, Jordan mused. How many men sat down with their brides and discussed sex like two businessmen hammering out the details of a contract? The notion inspired him to smile, but the anxious look on Ellen's face made the smile fade. "To tell the truth, Ellen I'm not even sure myself what I intended. Usually I'm a man who thinks things through before I act—thinks them through to exhaustion, according to my brother. This time I didn't."

"I see." She sighed quietly and intertwined her fingers in a tangle of white knuckles.

"Ellen, I'm very sorry if I frightened you last night. I didn't intend—"

"No," she denied, cutting him off midapology. "No. You didn't frighten me."

For not being frightened, she was very pale, but Jordan let her continue.

"We are two reasonable, mature adults. I see no reason why . . ." She glanced downward, and long lashes hid the emotion in her eyes. ". . . why you should be . . . should be denied the rights of a husband."

The words sounded rehearsed and stilted, spoken at great price. A moment passed before their meaning sank in. When they did, however, something warm began to blossom inside Jordan, and the warmth had nothing to do with sexual hunger. Ellen was trying so hard to not look nervous, not seem frightened—like a young girl facing her first ball or London soiree.

Except that this was much more serious than a ball or an evening of gossip.

Jordan sat forward on his chair and regarded her thoughtfully. "Ellen, you have no obligation to sacrifice yourself to my . . . uh . . . masculine desires. I assure you that I'll survive."

She gave him a nervous laugh. "But I'm not sure that I will, Jordan."

Narrow-eyed, he scrutinized her face for signs she was teasing. That wasn't Ellen's style, but he found this other almost equally hard to believe.

"Aren't you . . . aren't you going to say something?"

He got up. She fought an obvious battle to keep from darting away as he approached. "That puts an entirely different slant on matters."

"I know I'm being terribly forward . . ."

"Feel free to continue being forward," he urged with a smile.

"And I know we've many things left to discuss . . ."

"They can wait." He reached out and untangled her hands, gently liberating each finger one by one, then intertwining them with his own. "But let me understand this perfectly, Ellen, so I don't make an unforgivable mistake. You truly are inviting me into your bed?"

She swallowed hard. "I think so."

"There's usually very little thinking involved in making love. You must make up your mind one way or another. Either you want me there—not out of obligation, or duty, or whatever other martyrlike reason you might concoct—but because you truly wish to be intimate with me. Or you don't want me there. All or nothing."

She took a deep breath, and exhaled a soft "I do" along with the air.

"You're very sure?"

"Yes. I'm sure. Very sure."

"And making love with a man won't hurt your pregnancy?"

"Of course not." For an instant she sounded like the old confident, give-'em-hell Ellen. "I wouldn't do anything to hurt my baby."

"I know you wouldn't."

Mary Catherine had left his bed the day she discovered she was pregnant, and refused to so much as sleep by his side, as if a caress, a kiss, a mere lustful look would be inappropriate in her delicate condition. Suddenly Jordan found himself wishing it had been Ellen he had married in those days when he was young, idealistic, and looking for a lifelong partner. A passion was building inside of him that he wasn't sure he could contain, once he let it loose.

He still had her hands in his, and she glanced down at them uneasily. "You haven't given me an answer," she murmured.

"What answer?"

She flashed him an annoyed look. "Are you going to make me ask outright?"

He almost laughed, but doubtless she wouldn't have forgiven him for that. "Dear Ellen, how can you imagine that my answer would be anything but this?"

He put his arms around her, still holding her hands so that her arms were trapped behind her back. And then he kissed her.

CHAPTER 15

Ellen's initial hesitation melted slowly under the warmth of Jordan's kiss, and when he released her, the color had returned to her face with some to spare. She had made her decision in the light of logic and fairness, with a touch of loneliness and desperation to help make up her mind. But now Jordan added that golden spark of passion, as he always did when he touched her this way. It traveled in a warm river through every nerve, melting the icy apprehension that had frozen and imprisoned her spirit.

Yet a hint of doubt stirred uneasily as she looked up into his eyes. A man like Jordan Chesterfield would expect sophistication and skill in a woman. Suddenly she couldn't bear for him to be disappointed in her. "I'm not sure I know how to go about this very well, Jordan. Don't forget that I warned you about my lack of talent in these matters."

He threw back his head and laughed while his big, warm hands rubbed up and down her upper arms. "Dear girl," he said when he subsided. "In lovemaking, there

are certain advantages in artistry, sophistication, and experience. But believe me, enthusiasm and willingness
are by far more important." He sobered, and sharp gray
eyes searched her face. "Are you sure you want to do
this, my love?"

His endearment sent a shiver of pleasure straight to
her heart, even though she knew it to be a figure of
speech. "I'm very sure, Jordan. If we insist on keeping
ourselves apart in this way, then we'll always feel as
though something between us wasn't expressed, something that needed to be expressed." She grinned, feeling
suddenly like the Ellen of old. "Affection and respect,
as we said last night. Isn't that what this is all about?"

His eyes became molten in their intensity, and he gave
her a slow smile. "Affection and respect it is. I promise
to be most respectful, and very, very affectionate."

A new tension in his stance told her that some threshold had been crossed. She bit her lip, wondering what to
do next. What did he expect?

"Come here, Ellen."

She hesitated.

"Come here," he repeated patiently.

"I'm already here."

He unfastened the pearl buttons of his waistcoat and
took it off. "Closer. You're a whole foot away."

Hesitantly, she complied.

"Lovemaking is generally accomplished in fairly
close quarters, you know."

She breathed deeply. "Naturally. I knew that."

He fingered the poufy bow at her neck, then unfastened it and tossed it aside. "I want you to notice how
respectful I'm being. A less civil sort of man would have
this clothing ripped off you in no time."

He peeled off her little beaver jacket with its brocaded

velvet and satin sleeves, then deftly attacked the fastenings of the gown itself.

"Wait." Suddenly she felt shy. "I can do it. I'll just go behind the screen and—"

His grin was positively wicked. "I don't think so. Turn around."

She obeyed, but jumped when his clever fingers loosened her bodice, then the little brown velvet belt at her waist.

"Seeing you revealed layer by layer is a rare joy I'm not willing to forego. In a most respectful fashion, of course."

"Of course." She was breathless when he turned her back around.

"You're clinging to that dress as if it were a suit of armor, Ellen. Here, let me help you."

"Shouldn't we be doing this in the dark?" Ellen asked, backing away. Henri had made sure the room was dark before he'd so much as touched her, but then, she didn't want to think about Henri right then.

"Why should it be dark when two people make love? Are you shy?"

"Perhaps a little." Her back met the door. She could retreat no further. "I warned you I wasn't very good at this."

He chuckled. "You're wonderful, charming . . ." He plucked her hand from the bodice of the dress so that the whole ensemble slithered down around her ankles, leaving her clad only in her embroidered batiste chemise and satinet drawers. "Beautiful," he whispered, almost reverently.

"I . . . I don't wear a corset."

"So I see."

"An eighteen-inch waist is medically unadvisable, you know, even though it is the height of fashion."

"Is that so?" Gray eyes met hers, and there was a twinkle of amusement in their depths. At the same time, with one finger Jordan traced the lacy neckline of her chemise, his light touch blazing a trail of shocking fire across the swell of her breasts.

Ellen tried to catch her breath, but she couldn't. This was not at all what she had expected. The shameless appreciation in Jordan's eyes made her stomach do somersaults, and the practiced delicacy of his caress was setting every nerve ablaze—even so small a thing as he was doing, and the blaze burned hotter when he pushed aside the strap of her chemise and pulled down the soft material to reveal one naked breast.

Jordan's breath rushed out as his hand closed over her, and Ellen's whole body turned to water.

"You are perfect," he breathed. The hard palm of his hand was an erotic contrast to the tenderness of her skin. She closed her eyes and let the feeling take her, then cried out as warm breath tickled her nipple and an even warmer mouth engulfed her. She would have sunk to the floor if his hands hadn't grasped her waist and held her in place.

"God help me," he groaned against her breast, "I want you so much it hurts."

Pinned against the door, she couldn't move when he placed her hand between his legs. His erection strained the buttons of his trousers. Her heart skipped a beat. The medical texts really had very little to say about this particular phenomenon. She closed her eyes and surrendered to the urge to caress him there, where he was so very different from her.

His breathing caught for a moment, then escaped in a quiet groan. "Don't stop," he whispered.

Ellen had no desire to stop. A strange and wonderful elation made her feel as if her feet were about to lift from the ground.

His fingers tangled with hers as he swiftly unfastened the buttons of his trousers. "Yes," he groaned as she touched him with only the soft cotton of his drawers to fend her off. "Lord, woman, you're going to kill me."

He put his hand over hers, held it still, and pressed it against himself, his face rigid with the effort to hold himself in check. "I thought you were shy."

"I am."

"I thought you weren't good at this."

"I'm not."

"For a smart woman, you have very faulty notions of what you are." With what seemed like an effort, he lifted her hand from him, then led her to his bed. "Lie down and let me look at you while I get rid of these clothes."

At that moment she would have laid herself on a bed of hot coals had he asked it of her. Without taking his eyes from her, Jordan shed his boots, trousers, and shirt. Then without hesitation or modesty, he took off his drawers and threw them in a careless heap with his other clothing. Ellen tried not to stare, but it was impossible not to stare. Her husband's statuelike masculine perfection was marred only by a state of arousal that no sculptor would have dared depict in plaster or marble, but which would have been very educational for the female of the species. Ellen felt deliciously wicked, staring and being stared at. She was flooded with cravings and desires she hadn't known existed, and urges that were downright abandoned—like wanting to run her fingers through the mat of black hair on Jordan's chest and exploring the hard contours of his muscular arms. At the same time, she wanted to spread herself before him like a feast waiting to be devoured. She wanted to toss the last shred of modesty to the wind and bare her enticements to the warm perusal of those molten eyes, to tempt him past where he could hold himself in check.

Only a lifetime of being proper and modest—by her lights, at least—kept her from following her desires. But Jordan must have seen the craving in her eyes, and he had no modesty at all, so he helped her.

When he walked toward the bed, like a tiger stalking his prey, Ellen thought the time had come. Now the pleasant playing was over, and they would get down to business. She was wrong. He smiled wickedly, his eyes glittering, as he sat on the bed at her feet.

"You forgot your shoes." He remedied the oversight by unbuttoning her high top kid boots and sliding them off, then slowly rolling down the silk stockings—her only pair—and dropping them with her garters beside the bed.

He ran a warm, hard hand up and down her bare leg, from her ankle to her knee, then higher as his hand slipped beneath her drawers. "You have beautiful legs, Ellen."

He reached the apex of her thighs, and she moaned, torn between modesty and desire.

"You're so soft. So warm."

The edge of his voice betrayed his rising urgency, but he was painfully patient. He slipped off her drawers and parted her legs. Breathing in jagged spurts, he worked magic on her most intimate flesh, teasing, tantalizing, thrusting inside and then tickling with fingertips and hot, tempting breath. Sinful. Joyous. Ellen thought she might burst as need swelled within her, blocking her vision, squeezing breath from her lungs. Then his hands traveled upward, splaying over her stomach, sliding beneath the thin chemise that was the only garment that remained. He cupped her breasts and lowered his mouth to hers in a devouring, all-absorbing kiss. Then, somehow, by some slight of his hand, the chemise was gone, and his bare chest rubbed against her tender breasts, the mat of hair abrading and caressing until Ellen thought she would scream for him to fulfill her body's craving.

"Please!" she groaned.

"Soon," he promised. He rose above her, his eyes feasting upon her nakedness, traveling slowly from her touseled hair to her bare toes, visibly enjoying every inch of the journey. "I had to see you like this," he whispered. "I've imagined how you would look lying on a bed, naked and wanting me, but you surpass my imagination."

She closed her eyes as he moved over her.

"No," he ordered. "Look into my eyes as I come into you. See what I feel, what you do to me."

She felt her flesh part to take him. He was rock hard and very large, but she wanted all he had to offer. She lifted herself to meet him as he sank deep within her. All the while he held her eyes with a steady look that was every bit as demanding as his body. His gaze was molten steel, fusing, burning, then hardening to a sharp edge that cut deep into her soul, as deeply as he pierced her body. She felt utterly consumed, yet more completely safe than she'd ever been in her entire life. Need swelled and thickened in time to the rhythm of his thrusts, and she rose to meet him with increasing urgency. Her world narrowed down to include only her need, herself, and the man who suddenly was such an integral part of her, flowing through her like blood, beating within her like a second, vital heart.

Then time stopped, and the two of them filled the entire universe. Ellen's cry was descant to Jordan's guttural shout. The sound rang with base and divine, animal and angel, and it echoed in Ellen's ears like a voice from another world.

For a moment it did seem she was in another world. But slowly, the reality of the bed, the cabin, the gentle hum of the ship's engines came into focus again. Jordan was still cradled between her thighs, his weight supported on his elbows, his head lowered so that his brow rested against hers. They shared the same air, breathed in the same rhythm, still interlocked in some mysterious unity.

"Jordan?" she whispered.

Her only answer was a contented, drawn-out sigh.

How nice it would be to sleep this way, Ellen thought in lazy bliss. Surrounded by Jordan, still a part of Jordan. She was warming to the notion when Nature took a hand and began to separate them. Jordan groaned quietly, opened his eyes, and looked unerringly into hers.

His smile was indolent and replete. "My lady wife. If it was only affection and respect you craved, we may have gone a bit overboard."

Laughing seemed a very irreverent thing to do directly after experiencing such earth-shattering passion, but Ellen couldn't help herself. Her laughter separated them once and for all.

"Now see what you've done?" Jordan complained.

"You made me do it!"

"Woman's cry from time immemorial."

A great yawn took her by surprise, and suddenly she was too tired to keep her eyes open. The last thing she felt as sleep claimed her was the brush of Jordan's hand across her cheek as he pulled up the bedclothes and tucked them securely below her chin.

When Jordan woke, the light of a new day streamed through the porthole. Beside him, Ellen still slept. She'd thrown off part of the covers during the night, exposing a bare shoulder and breast to the cool air. Gooseflesh raised small bumps on the creamy skin and puckered the rosy nipple, but the cold wasn't enough to wake her. Unable to resist temptation, Jordan cupped his hand just above the flattened mound of her breast. A scant half inch lower and he would touch that lush flesh and feel the soft protrusion of the nipple against his palm. She would wake, and he would take her again—bury himself between those sweet legs and feed on those tender breasts and succulent lips until she surrendered her very soul to their passion. The very thought made him grow hard.

He didn't have the heart to wake her, though, so deeply and peacefully did she sleep. Instead, he contented himself to merely watch the skin warm beneath the umbrella of his hand. The gooseflesh disappeared. The nipple expanded and relaxed like a thing with a life of its own. Jordan smiled and pulled the covers up to shelter her, then settled back onto the bed.

He had slept well for a change, and he felt more alive than he had in days. The world seemed fresh and new, and he felt strong enough to conquer it. He was familiar with the delusion and the cause—a round of exceptionally good loving could make a man think he could fight dragons and win. He'd had the feeling once or twice in his life, but that was all.

Most of his intimate moments with women had

been—if not exactly lackluster—at least routine. The first night he'd been with Mary Catherine he had thought they'd found heaven, until she made it clear that the angels certainly hadn't sung for her and that no decent woman could truly enjoy such a foray into base passion. After the honeymoon she had dutifully let him into her bed once a week and expected thanks for her generosity. It wasn't a situation that encouraged grand explorations of paradise.

Since his wife's death, a few discreet alliances with ladies who were interested in companionship rather than marriage had served his needs well enough. The relationships had been pleasant and entertaining, but no fireworks had showered the bed in live sparks during their most passionate moments. Not as they had last night. Not as they had with Ellen.

He stole a glance at her sleeping face. She was an enigma—a chimera he had possessed in the most intimate possible way, yet she remained just out of reach. Why had he married her? While he thought of himself as a decent enough fellow, he wasn't generally given to such broad gestures of benevolence. And while it was true that an arrangement with Ellen would save him his mother's nagging and the relentless pursuit of matrimonially ambitious females, it raised as many problems as it solved.

One of the problems was his growing obsession with this woman. He was actually looking forward to being her champion before the world, fending off slurs cast upon her name as a swordsman would parry blows directed at his lady fair. Most uncharacteristic of him—so much so that the notion was almost frightening.

Surely by the time he had Ellen settled somewhere close to her family, secure in the respectability of marriage and no doubt eager to get him out of her life, his interest in her would have faded to mere friendship. He would visit her upon occasion to make sure all her needs were met. To put a good face on their relationship, she could come to England a time or two with the child. They would be friends, but not lovers. No need to complicate an already complex situation, after all.

But for now, until the obsession faded. . . . He smiled and wound a strand of her hair around his finger. He could lie in bed all day and admire the curve of her lips, the faint blush on her cheeks, the endearing upturn of her nose. How many secrets did he still not know? How many faces did she hide beneath the face she showed to the world, to him?

As if nudged by his scrutiny, Ellen's eyelids fluttered briefly and closed again, and the graceful wings of her brows puckered. Finally her eyes opened, jewel green in a frame of lush black lashes. Were they brighter and clearer on this morning than they had been in the past, or was he merely flattering himself?

"Good morning," he said softly.

She raised herself on one elbow and looked at him blankly for a moment, as if surprised at finding him in bed with her. Then the muzziness left her expression. Her eyes widened, and she blushed. One hand came up to partially cover her face. "Oh my God."

He gently pried her hand from her face. "How are you this morning?"

"Oh, I'm . . ." She laughed in chagrin. "I'm . . . embarrassed."

"Embarrassed? The woman who rides bareback like a Cossack over hedges and ditches? Who lets fugitive foxes use her as a stepping-stone to freedom? Who elbowed her way into the male medical fraternity? This woman is embarrassed?"

She grabbed a pillow and hugged it to her. "Quit! This is different! I didn't mean to be so . . . well . . . forward. I didn't know making love could be like that." Smiling shyly, she finally met his eyes. "You took me by surprise."

"Did I?"

"Yes. You did."

He couldn't resist leaning down to taste those warm, beautiful lips. He had to tangle his hand in the bedclothes to keep from doing much, much more. "I rather took myself by surprise as well," he said in a husky voice.

Self-consciously, she drew back. Her diffidence and embarrassment made him wonder about what sort of experience she'd had in the past. That thought led to the question that had been inexplicably nagging at him since he'd proposed. Reluctantly, he settled back to his own side of the bed.

"Ellen—the baby's father. Were you terribly in love with him?"

There was little overt change in her expression, but he could see the withdrawal in her eyes.

"It's not really my business, I realize. But the question has been on my mind since I first learned you were carrying a child."

A muscle in her jaw twitched, and her eyes flickered downward. "I suppose you have a right to know the circumstances."

"I know the circumstances. Henri Chretiens, a physician at the clinic where you studied."

She threw him a shocked look.

"Jane told me. Don't resent her for betraying a confidence. She was vehemently defending you at the time. I know what happened. What I'm curious about is—did you love him?"

"Why would you think I didn't?"

"For a woman who is carrying the child of a man she loved, you seem fairly uninitiated into the joys of passion."

She hugged the pillow more tightly. "I warned you that I hadn't much talent in that area."

"You have so much talent in loving, my dear Ellen, that you showed me a place in paradise I didn't know existed. That isn't what I meant."

Her mouth curved hesitantly upward. "I did?"

"You did indeed. What I meant was—you seemed like a child with its first taste of candy. Don't tell me that you are a victim of the ridiculous notion that decent women don't enjoy lovemaking."

"No, of course not. My father and stepmother seem to enjoy each other very much, and Olivia is the most decent woman I've ever met." She sighed and lay back, still clutching the pillow like a shield. "It only happened once between me and Henri, and that certainly wasn't planned—at least not on my part. It was quick, messy, and painful, and afterward, Henri seemed more disappointed than satisfied. He said I was green, that I would be better at it the next time. There wasn't a next time, though. Part of me wanted to please him so much it hurt, but I was ashamed of what we'd done. Every time I saw him, I expected him to propose, but he didn't. Finally, I started avoiding situations where I would be alone with him. By then he'd caught the attention of Lady Patricia Fulton. She was the daughter of a count, very beautiful, and in line to inherit a ton of money. The family has land all over France and Germany, and some in Switzerland as well."

"Did he not know about your condition?"

"He knew. When I learned I was carrying his child, he was the first I told. Henri offered the services of another physician to rid me of the burden, and I refused."

"And you left."

"It was one of the clinic physicians who examined me, so my condition was a matter of record. I couldn't stay, of course. I'll admit I was fairly frantic. Jane, bless her heart, pulled me back together and offered to keep me company on my trip home."

Her voice was matter-of-fact, but he heard the pain behind the words. She hadn't looked at him once during the recitation of pathetic facts, but instead stared at the ceiling as if she were reading from an account written there.

"You didn't answer my question."

She sighed. "Didn't I?"

"You know you didn't. Were you in love with this Henri Chretiens? Are you still?"

She frowned silently at the ceiling for a long while, and when she finally gave her answer, there was an edge to her voice. "I loved him. I must have loved him, or what I did would be not only foolish and wrong, it would have been sluttish. I'm not a slut, Jordan."

"I didn't mean to imply that you are."

"As for now . . ." She bit her lip and sighed. "I used to think when a person fell in love, that love was forever. My father would have loved my mother forever, if she had lived. I'm sure he'll love Olivia till the day he dies. That's the way love should work."

"Unfortunately, many things in this world don't work the way they should."

"I guess not. But I'd like to think my love isn't so shallow that it dies the minute I find my beloved to be a blockhead."

That wasn't exactly what Jordan wanted to hear. He didn't know what he wanted to hear, exactly, but it wasn't that. As if sensing his disappointment, Ellen glanced his way.

"I don't know, Jordan. These last weeks I haven't understood just how I feel or even who I am. I used to know without a doubt, but not now."

He couldn't help but be moved by her honesty, and her pain. "I know who you are, Ellen."

"Who am I?"

"You're a smart, beautiful, and loving woman who as of the day before yesterday is my wife, and who right now is in my bed. And those two circumstances are giving me ideas of how to spend an entertaining morning."

Her brows flew up in surprise. "In broad daylight? You must be joking."

"I'm not known as a man with a sense of humor, wife."

"What about breakfast?"

"I'll send for a tray. Later."

"But if we're not at our table, everyone will think we're . . . we're indulging in some kind of newlywed shenanigans in our room."

"And they'll be green with envy for me."

"You're serious."

"I'm more than serious," he told her. "Just lying beside you has made me hard enough to drive steel."

She laughed at the preposterous image, and a rush of color heated her cheeks. The tense melancholy of talking about the past dissolved. "But what if I'm hungry?"

He swooped down to bite gently at her shoulder. "Then I'll show you what appetites are for."

"You're a beast!" She laughed.

He growled and dove under the pillow to attack a breast. Her laughter trailed away into little gasps of pleasure as his mouth found one nipple and his seeking hand paid homage to its twin. Jordan wanted to glut himself with her tempting body. With other women he could keep himself under control, hold back part of himself. Not with Ellen. With Ellen he could go from laughter to passion in an instant. Desire spurred him with rowels of fire, making him long to taste every part of her, touch her inside and out, and drive her again and again to a spike of passion where the burning in her eyes was all for him. Only the need to bring her with him, joyous and unafraid, into that world of erotic gluttony made him slow his pace and hold himself marginally in check.

Her hands were in his hair, combing and toying with a touch that sent shivers of carnal hunger shooting down his spine and into his loins. He threw back the bedclothes, baring her flesh to his pleasure. Her ribs begged to be marked by his teeth, her navel invited his tongue. He took it all. Every inch of her that he could find with his seeking mouth was captured in his feast, while she twisted the bedsheets in her fists and uttered little cries that urged him on. His tongue drew circles around her knees, explored the indentation of her calves, caressed the arch of her foot. Then the inside of those slim, long thighs, and the sweetest, tenderest flesh of all.

Her gasp was torn between delight and horror. "What are you doing?"

Choked with the intensity of his own need, he couldn't speak. He merely rose above her and thrust inside, blind to everything but her moist, welcoming warmth and the feel of her tightening instinctively around him. Her legs gripped him and urged him closer, deeper.

He was in heaven, and he wanted to stay, but the end, bright and hot, rushed toward him. Not yet! Not yet! He pulled free, tumbled her onto her stomach, then lifted her up to hands and knees.

"It's all right," he breathed against her neck as she cried out. "Trust me."

Forcing himself to be gentle, he entered slowly from behind, touching her much more deeply than before. She gave a little squeak of surprise, and as he thrust more forcefully, gasped his name in pleasure.

They climaxed together, a long, intense spasm that brought joy almost to the point of pain. When they finally sank to the rumpled bed, she made no move to escape his grasp, but snuggled more closely against him as he pulled up the sheets to cover their sweat-damp bodies. When he could breathe normally once again, Jordan kissed the tousled black mop of her hair. She brought his hand to her lips so he could feel her smile.

"That," she whispered against his fingers, "was the most spectacular breakfast I've ever had."

CHAPTER 16

Ellen had always known she didn't like New York City. The noise, the dirt, the crowds of downright rude people. For a girl from Montana whose idea of a crowd was three people in the same room, New York City was just too much.

Now, however, she had a few other reasons to loathe the place. When the Statue of Liberty came into sight through a haze of fog and city smoke, the fantasy world she had shared with Jordan came to an end. The open sea was an ideal place to forget reality, and that was exactly what they had done in the three days since their wedding. They had made love, danced, made love, taken walks with George and Jane, made love, held hands on the moonwashed deck, and made love again. Conversation was always in the present, for theirs was not a marriage founded on the future. New York City, however, was the beginning of the future, and reality crashed down upon them with a vengeance.

Ellen had hoped they could escape the city quickly, but Jordan had business contacts in New York who were expecting him. Consequently, her escape from the crowded buildings, noise, and dirt was not to the west, as she'd hoped, but east to Long Island, to the posh residence belonging to Spencer Crabbe, Jordan's partner in the Atlantic and Mediterranean Steamship Line. It was there that she discovered what made her uncomfortable in New York was not so much the buildings standing shoulder to shoulder or the constant noise and traffic, but the people. And from the New Yorkers there was no escape, for Spencer Crabbe threw wide his doors and invited the well-heeled and well-connected to a reception for Jordan and his unexpected bride.

The gathering was a harsh dose of reality. The food, the obsequious servants, the glittering guests, the lavish decor of Crabbe's Long Island mansion—everything annoyed Ellen on this evening. She didn't want to share Jordan with these rich, fawning New Yorkers. She wanted to be back aboard the *Mary Catherine*, gazing at the moon while Jordan held her hand, or in their little bedroom that rocked in time to the rolling seas and vibrated with the hum of the ship's turbines—and their passion.

Jane touched her shoulder, distracting her from her mope. "Smile," she advised. "You look like you've lost your best friend."

Ellen managed a grin. "I haven't." She squeezed Jane's hand. "You're still here."

"That's better." She surveyed the glittering crowd with twinkling eyes. "These people are outrageous, aren't they?"

Ellen didn't think they were much more outrageous than the upper crust of England, but she supposed Jane had a different point of view. The English woman was accustomed to people who were so steeped in their own pedigrees, it wouldn't occur to them that anyone would doubt their superiority. The New York upper crust—at least the part of it who milled through Spencer Crabbe's ornate residence—were the new rich, people whose grandfathers or fathers were shrewd enough and hard-working enough to carve fortunes from the brawling cities and wild frontier of a young and burgeoning country. Now their sons and grandsons lived in mansions like Crabbe's and labored to convince themselves they were far removed from the dirt and sweat that had produced their family fortunes.

"I thought you told me that Americans are unpretentious," Jane accused with a smile.

"These aren't Americans," Ellen countered. "They're New Yorkers."

"Don't let Mrs. Wright over there hear you say that. She told me that New York is the center of the universe."

"She didn't say that!"

"Those weren't her words, but that was what she meant."

Ellen chuckled. "I'll bet she believed it, too."

"Oh, she did!"

"Where is George? I haven't seen you two apart since the wedding."

Jane's smile took on a dreamy quality at the mention of her groom. "He's gone off somewhere with Jordan and Mr. Crabbe. I think he's taking an interest in Jordan's shipping business. He said Jordan has offered him a share and he's considering taking him up on the offer."

"You're going to reform the rake," Ellen teased.

"He doesn't need reforming. He's already the smartest, sweetest—"

Ellen cut her off with a good-natured groan. "I know.

I know. The handsomest, most considerate, most refined . . ."

"You forgot talented."

"All right, talented." She grinned. "You'd probably claim he's a genius except for one thing."

"What's that?"

"You know that *I've* seen inside that handsome head."

Jane laughed, then looked abashed. "Am I that bad?"

"No," Ellen assured her. "I think it's sweet."

Jane took Ellen's hand and squeezed it gratefully. "What would my life have been if we hadn't met in Paris? None of this would have happened. I never would have met George. I never would have made such a happy marriage. My life would have been spent keeping house for my father. Here I thought to help you by going to Montana, and you end up transforming my life so much for the better."

"I hope you can still say that when you go back to England and face Lady Chesterfield."

"But *you're* Lady Chesterfield now. I should start addressing you as Ma'am and My Lady."

Ellen rolled her eyes. "I mean the real Lady Chesterfield."

"Lady Chesterfield!" came a cry from behind them, like an echo of their own conversation.

Ellen grimaced. People had been addressing her as Lady Chesterfield all evening long. She felt as uncomfortable in the pretentious title as she did in the very fashionable silk, velvet, and lace gown that Jordan had purchased for her at an uptown clothing establishment. She was the proverbial sow's ear masquerading as a silk purse. And as for being a lady, she wasn't a lady in any sense of the word.

"Lady Chesterfield! I've been trying to break away all

evening to give you my best wishes for your marriage. What a surprise when Jordan told us that he'd taken a bride!" Alicia Crabbe—Spencer Crabbe's plump, pretty, socially correct wife—was given to gushing, Ellen had noticed. Especially when she thought she addressed a social superior.

If she only knew, Ellen reflected with wry amusement.

"And George as well! Now there was a surprise! Jane, dear, you must be an absolute magician. But of course we all knew George would settle down sooner or later. Young men will sow their oats, after all."

Since George wasn't the titled brother, Jane didn't rate quite the degree of obeisance. The difference was a subtly noticeable one in Mrs. Crabbe's voice.

"It was very thoughtful of you to include George and me in your invitation," Jane said.

"But of course you were included! George is Lord Chesterfield's brother, after all, and the baron is almost family to us. But come, my dears. You mustn't stand over here by yourselves and deprive us of your company. Everyone is anxious to meet you, and dear Lord Chesterfield charged me especially with seeing that you were made to feel welcome."

Ellen followed Mrs. Crabbe reluctantly. She could have felt welcome at a barn raising or a town hall dance in Willow Bend, but she doubted she would ever feel welcome at an affair like this. Too large a gap yawned between these people and herself. She could dress up in a fancy evening gown, drink champagne, and wear fancy jewels, but she would never be one of them. Not that she wanted to be. Lately the vast difference between Jordan and herself had become unclear. Now it was being redefined with a vengeance.

Their hostess guided them to a group of ladies and gentlemen who regarded them with avid interest. "Lady Chesterfield, Mrs. Chesterfield, may I present Mr. and Mrs. Worth and Mr. and Mrs. Goodenow. Mr. Worth is president of one of New York's largest banks, and Mr. Goodenow is a partner in the Atlantic and Mediterranean Line, though of course his holdings in the company don't match Lord Chesterfield's or Spencer's."

The gentlemen hid their speculation behind chivalrous half bows, and the ladies cooed and twittered.

"So this is the lucky girl who stole Jordan Chesterfield's heart." Mrs. Goodenow's smile was not nearly as genuine as the diamonds that clustered at her throat. "Such a sudden marriage! Do tell us all about it. I'm sure the story is terribly romantic."

They hoped the story involved juicy scandal or intrigue, Ellen knew. If she told them the truth they would probably faint dead away.

"It wasn't so sudden as it seems," she lied. "I spent several weeks with Jordan's family in Staffordshire before sailing. Jordan decided to join me on the crossing. He proposed, and we both preferred the simplicity of a wedding at sea to the terrible fuss we would have had to endure back in England."

Terrible fuss was an understatement. If the dowager baroness had gotten hold of Ellen before the wedding, England would have witnessed a row that would have made a catfight look tame.

"How economical of you," Mrs. Worth remarked. Her tone equated economical with plebian. "And you also, Mrs. Chesterfield. I understand George is independently quite well off. Here I thought all young women dreamed of a gala wedding. I know I certainly did."

"And you certainly got your wish," Mr. Worth commented dryly. "We've been married fifteen years and people still talk about it."

Mrs. Goodenow was not about to give Mrs. Worth the floor for long. "That is certainly a lovely gown you're wearing, Lady Chesterfield."

"Thank you. My husband chose it for me."

"What an extremely fine eye he has for fashion. And it sets off your exotic coloring so well. I do envy you that complexion. I had a friend from Spain who has a similar cast to her skin. Do you by chance have ties in Spain? It's such a lovely place."

"No. My father is Irish, and my mother was of the Blackfoot people."

Eyes widened. Brows raised. Mouths fell open without words coming out, but words would certainly be in plentiful supply when that tidbit hit the gossip mill. Ellen knew that in this company she should have been more discreet about her heritage, but she didn't feel like being discreet. She supposed pregnancy was exacerbating inbred Montana orneriness, but the more out of place she felt here, the more she wanted to proclaim her differences.

Mrs. Crabbe was the first to recover. Though she looked as though she'd bitten into a green apple, she bravely carried on. "There are the Gibsons!" she exclaimed with forced enthusiasm. "You ladies simply must meet them!"

Thus Ellen and Jane were hustled off to be displayed to another set of people Mrs. Crabbe wanted to impress. Nothing was said of Ellen's mixed blood, as if glossing over the subject would make the facts disappear. Obviously, Ellen was no social prize in herself. Quite the contrary. But she and Jane both reflected their husbands' aristocratic grandeur, and everyone wanted to claim their acquaintance. For America's moneyed class, who did not have the validation of generations of pedigreed fore-bears, rubbing shoulders with European and English aristocracy was a validation in itself, even if that "aristocracy" was an American half-breed who had somehow married herself an English baron and an English nobody who had managed to marry above her class.

Ellen and Jane—mostly Ellen, for she, after all, was the one with the title—were fawned upon and speculated about. Their histories were probed under the guise of friendly interest. Their clothing was scrutinized, their manners surreptitiously examined, and their good fortune constantly commented upon. The eventual revelation that Ellen was a physician was greeted with expressions that ranged from blank to curious to horrified. It was another thing she should have kept close to her chest, Ellen told herself, but she'd be damned if she was going to try to pass herself off as someone these professional socialites would approve of and accept.

Jordan and George were not around to take the heat off their brides, for they had disappeared with their host shortly after arriving. Ellen didn't blame them. If these leeches fawned on her to such an overwhelming degree, how must they behave with Jordan, the genuine English peer?

The reception was interminable, and swiftly became intolerable after Jane was pulled off in another direction and Ellen was left alone with her hostess and the current set of pseudo-admirers. She felt like a doe surrounded by wolves—wolves who smiled and simpered but who had sharp teeth and deadly intentions nevertheless. Pleading a need for fresh air, she finally escaped through a set of French doors to the garden. There she inhaled deeply of the cold, tangy Long Island air, wishing she could escape for an hour instead of just a moment—until she spotted the greenhouse at the end of the garden path where the lawn met the woods. The greenhouse was almost as big as a house—a normal house, that is, not one of the cavernous mansions in which these people preferred to live. And it would be filled with plants and blossoms, growing things to soothe the soul.

Ellen gave in to temptation, took off the delicate kid slippers that matched her gown in both fashion and practicality, and ran down the moonlit path to the greenhouse door. It was unlocked, so she invited herself inside—just for a moment, she told herself. A moment to enjoy solitude, a moment to breathe air breathed only by plants, a moment to sit among all these lovely growing things and soak up their silence.

The air was warm inside, and the quiet plash of water only seemed to deepen the tranquillity. This was not an ordinary greenhouse, Ellen saw. It was a rich man's jungle paradise. Paths wound through hothouse blossoms, ferns, bamboo, palms, and lush trees imported from all over the world. Flowers hung from every corner and crossbeam. Marble benches hid among ferns and broad-leaved tropical vegetation. An artificial waterfall spilled into a stream that babbled in tortuous courses beside winding gravel paths in the greenery.

Ellen puffed out a sigh, dropped onto a bench, and leaned back to stare upward into a tangle of palm fronds. Moonlight gave the artificial paradise a sheen of reality. She could almost convince herself she was alone in a tropical rain forest with the moon gleaming overhead and the warm air steamy and laden with the scent of vegetation.

How nice it would be to escape so easily, to walk

through a door and be someone else, someplace else, leaving her woes behind. The more she tried to solve her problems, the more complex they became. Shortly she would be with her family once again, the at once longed for and dreaded reunion. How could she tell them about Paris? How could she look at their faces and read the disappointment there? Yet she had to tell them. For the sake of her child, she could lie to the world about her marriage and the baby's paternity. But she couldn't lie to her father and Olivia, and Katy would see through a falsehood before the fabrication was out of Ellen's mouth.

Now she had dug herself in even more deeply. Like a giddy adolescent, she was allowing herself to become attached to a man she couldn't have. Jordan. She had his name. She had his friendship. But they had an agreement. He didn't want a full-time wife. She'd assured him that she didn't want a husband. On the ship they had playacted, but sometime in those few days, the play had become more real than acting.

Stupid, stupid, stupid! Ellen closed her eyes, still scolding herself, when a voice spoke her name. She opened her eyes to find Jordan smiling down at her.

"I thought I might find you in here." He held up the slippers she had discarded on the path. "Did it get too much for you in there?"

Ellen smiled sheepishly. She felt like a child caught playing hooky from the schoolroom. "I'm afraid I'll never be a social success."

"I wouldn't say that. If being a social success means making a big splash in the pond, you've certainly done that. The subject of conversation in the house seems to be what an extraordinary bride I've taken."

"I'd wager 'extraordinary' isn't the word they're using."

"As long as I'm within earshot, they'll not be using anything less complimentary, I can assure you."

A momentary flash of steel in Jordan's eyes told Ellen that she had a staunch defender, and a surge of warmth for him banished her gloominess. "You really are a sweet man," she told him.

"Sweet? Good heavens!" He grinned. "Don't go spreading that rumor, I beg you."

"I suppose you've come to fetch me back."

"Not necessarily." He pulled her to her feet. "Though the hard part is over, really. The dancing has begun, and that distracts the sharks from cutting one another to ribbons."

"Sharks, hmm? I rather thought they were more like wolves, though perhaps that's a disservice to a noble beast. Remember, I grew up with a wolf as a pet, though he was my sister's more than mine. I've missed him terribly since leaving."

"And I thought you were enamored only of foxes."

She laughed, then wondered at the way his eyes seemed to feed on her face. He took her hand.

"May I have this dance, my lady?"

"What . . . ?" She frowned quizzically.

"Listen."

Sure enough, faint strains of music drifted from the house.

"This dance floor is assuredly less crowded than the other," he said, taking possession of her waist and pulling her against him.

They danced, winding along the gravel paths, twirling across the picturesque wooden bridges that crossed the stream—he in black evening habit with its silk braid and white gloves, she barefoot in silk and velvet with ostrich feathers in her hair.

"You're going to ruin the image of the dour Englishman," she warned him lightly.

"You think so?"

"Dancing in a greenhouse in the moonlight—with a barefoot half-blooded savage, no less?"

"I'll deny it to my dying day. After all, there's no one here to see us."

"That's true."

They executed a quick turn, and Ellen found herself backed up against a wall of ferns and bamboo. The floor beneath her feet was mulch with a soft carpet of fallen leaves. The stream gurgled a few feet away, and as the vegetation closed behind Jordan, the path disappeared from sight.

Jordan's hand roamed over her hip and came to rest on her backside. "There is no one here to see us," he reminded her softly.

"Baron Chesterfield, you are the very devil."

"Only with the right woman." His fingers deftly released the rear fastenings of her gown.

"You can't be serious!"

"You think not?"

He kissed her, pressing against her to demonstrate just how very serious he was. The kiss was not gentle or courtly. It was hot with passion and expectation, rough with quick-rising desire.

"You are serious!" she gasped when he released her. Already her heart pounded, the blood rushed through her veins, and she ached with an emptiness that longed to be filled. How quickly her body responded to meet his demand!

"Get rid of it." He pulled the poufed velvet sleeves

off her arms and the gown slithered down to her knees. She obeyed. Gown and petticoats gone, she stood in the middle of Spencer Crabbe's artificial jungle in only chemise, drawers, and stockings. Jordan took a moment to appreciate the sight before he pressed her down onto the soft mulch.

"This is very wicked," she said with a soft laugh.

"It's all your fault," he complained. "You have me wanting you every minute of the day, and when I've so little chance to get you alone, I have to resort to wicked displays of lust in out of the way corners."

He demonstrated by nuzzling her breasts through the filmy material of her chemise. His mouth was fire, the hands that stroked her legs, hips, and stomach kindled an escalating passion that goaded her to match his impatience.

"Don't wait," she gasped. "Please don't wait. I've been wanting you too—so very much."

Jordan needed no further invitation. Within seconds, her drawers hugged her ankles and his fancy dress trousers were down around his knees. She rose to meet him as he thrust. Hard, fast, and efficiently he brought them both to a quick crescendo, then sent them hurtling over the edge. They clung to each other, lost in a world exclusively theirs, until George's unexpected call shattered the dream.

"Jordan? Ellen? Are you two in here?"

The voice was like a dash of ice water. Ellen gasped, but the sound was smothered by Jordan's hand.

"Jesus!" he groaned quietly. After taking several deep breaths, he shook his head and grinned ruefully. Suddenly, Ellen had a wild impulse to laugh. She bit her lips to keep the sound inside while Jordan rose from between her legs and straightened his clothes. With a look back that was meant to be stern, but only struck Ellen as funny, he left her alone in the little grotto.

"What the hell are you doing here?" she heard him demand.

"Looking for you. Ellen here as well?"

Ellen heard the wicked smile in the question. She grinned. If Jordan occasionally cracked the dour Englishman mold, George had shattered it long ago.

In the momentary silence, Ellen heard Jordan weighing his options. "Yes," he finally said. "Ellen's here as well."

"Splendid!" Enjoyment rang in George's voice. "Everyone's been wondering where you two are."

"So you set out to find us."

"Not without good reason, brother. A telegram came for you. From our dear mother."

Ellen grimaced. The dowager baroness had a long arm.

"And that momentous event led you to seek me out?"

"That and the hope of catching you red-faced. There's been little enough opportunity in the past, so I thought I might take the chance to enjoy it."

"Satisfied?"

"Immensely. By the way, you'd best brush the mulch from your knees before coming back to the house," he advised cheerily. "Good-bye, Ellen dear."

"Good-bye, George," she called, laughing.

Later, in the guest suite where they were to sleep, Jordan explained. "I telegrammed my mother of our marriage when the ship docked in New York."

Ellen sat at the vanity brushing out her hair. Jordan's warm woolen robe shielded her from the cold air whistling in around the windows. Spencer Crabbe's mansion was spectacular, but drafty. "You didn't waste any time telling her."

He dropped into a chair and kicked off his patent leather evening shoes. "As I said, I'm tired of her plots and scheming."

"Poor Hillary."

He laughed. "Don't waste your sympathy on Hillary Moorsmythe. She may appear the noodlebrain at times, but she's not, and she is certainly not and never was in love with much more than my title. Even before I left, she'd made sure that she was being pitied as the innocent victim and I was being castigated as a rake and a libertine." He came up behind her and took the hairbrush from her hand. "Did you know that your husband is a seducer of innocent maidens?"

She smiled at him in the mirror. "It doesn't surprise me one bit."

Jordan began brushing her hair, and in his hands, the brush became an instrument of sensuous pleasure. "You have beautiful hair," he told her. "Women spend hours with a curling iron trying for this effect, I suspect. Just enough curl to twine invitingly around a man's fingers."

"Mmm." She tilted her head back under his ministrations. "That feels so good." For a moment she let herself simply enjoy, then she forced herself to open the subject that she knew had to be dealt with.

"Jane offered to continue with me to Montana," she began.

Jordan chuckled. "Do you feel we need a chaperone?"

"No. It's just that . . ." She turned to face him and took the brush from his hand. How was she supposed to be coherent when he was so close to her? "You married me, gave me your name, and established with a host of witnesses that we are indeed man and wife. If you don't want to go with me to Montana . . ."

"Of course I'll go to Montana. I said we wouldn't live in each other's pockets. I didn't say I was going to leave you at the church steps and go on about my business."

"But . . ."

"Jane should stay with George."

Ellen smiled crookedly. "I'm sure George would trundle along with us. He's not going to let Jane out of his sight for very long."

"And I'm not letting you out of my sight until you're settled and established in whatever it is you want to do. Are you so anxious to get rid of me?"

"No!" she cried, then more calmly: "No."

She wrapped his robe tightly around her and crossed to the window. The dark panes reflected Jordan's face as he came up behind her and circled her waist with his arms.

"Is your mother very upset?"

He laughed. "You might say that. Although George and Jane got off lightly. With me to rail at, she'll likely leave them alone."

Ellen bit her lip.

"Is that what has you looking so melancholy?" He turned her to face him, keeping her within the circle of his arms. "Don't worry about my mother. She is a blustery old dragon, and her schemes are an annoyance, to be sure. But beneath all the spitting and hissing, she truly loves her sons. George will build his house in Cornwall and live there for a while, and then Mother will forgive him. She'll forgive me, too, after a time. She has no choice, you know."

Ellen sighed. "It seems as though you're putting up with a lot for my sake."

"Believe me, I'm not putting up with anything I don't choose to put up with. Is it such a sacrifice to cross this beautiful country and see a place I've never seen, to meet new people, or to claim a beautiful, intelligent woman as my wife?" He tilted up her face so she had to look at him. "I wouldn't have missed knowing you, Ellen." His grin was devilish. "In all senses of the word."

She smiled.

"As I've said before, you are an extraordinary woman."

Her smile turned wry. "I'm extraordinary, all right."

"You should stop blaming yourself so much for succumbing to Henri Chretiens. An innocent, loving girl like you—Ellen, you didn't have a chance with a rake like him after you. Your child is going to be beautiful and fine, like you, and there's going to be nothing of Chretiens in it. I am your child's father. Remember that."

A tear slipped down her cheek.

He brushed it away, but another followed. "What if the baby is a boy? What of the legalities, with your title, your family?"

"Don't worry about the Chesterfield title and estate, Ellen. If that becomes an issue, we will take care of it. You just worry about having your baby and making sure both of you live the lives you want to live."

The sigh that escaped her felt as though it came from her very soul. She leaned into him, resting her brow against his chest. "You are a friend," she whispered. "Thank you for being such a friend."

He drew her closer. "I can be very friendly indeed."

His hand cupped her bottom, and she laughed. "You're also a satyr, Jordan Chesterfield."

"Lately I have been."

She wanted to give in. Loving him always made the world go away. But it always returned. Sooner or later she had to put a stop to her growing need for him. "This is foolish, Jordan. We're fools to play the part of true husband and wife when soon we'll have so little part in each other's lives."

He touched her damp cheek. "Yes. It's foolish. And we are fools. Conceived in foolishness, born into foolishness, and likely to die from foolishness of some sort. We should take every opportunity to take comfort with another fool, don't you think?"

She couldn't resist him. She was cold, and he was fire. She was empty, and he could fill her. Fools they were indeed, but right now she couldn't think on it.

Someday, a small voice whispered at the back of her mind. *Someday she would have to.*

CHAPTER 17

Two days later, after bidding George and Jane godspeed on their trip back to England, Ellen and Jordan left New York behind. They did not, however, make a beeline for Montana. Though Jordan had traveled to five continents in his lifetime, on North America he was acquainted with only the eastern seaboard. He wanted to see some of the sights between New York and Montana, and Ellen wasn't adverse to showing off her country.

Their first stop was Washington, D.C., where they made the usual tour of monuments and sat in the gallery to watch the Congress meander through the lawmaking process—not so different from Parliament, Jordan declared, though a bit more down to earth. They rode a tour boat down the Potomac to look at Mount Vernon, which Jordan politely commented was very imposing for a relatively new house. When Ellen raised quizzical brows, he reminded her that many parts of Endsfield Park were standing a century before Mount Vernon was built. Feeling the pressure of patriotism, Ellen replied that Mount Vernon, at least, had not been built on the backs of struggling serfs and tenants. Jordan promptly pointed out the slave quarters behind the main house, and Ellen had to concede.

When they strolled along the Tidal Basin the next day, a sudden snow flurry coated the bare cherry trees in white. Ellen assured Jordan that he hadn't seen a real snowstorm until he'd experienced a Montana blizzard. The thought made her homesick, a malady which, curiously enough, she had not experienced much lately. But now the cold wind and stinging snow were tactile reminders of the biting, blustery winters of her home, and the lively conversation, debates, chess games, laughter, and loving that had always made the O'Connell home such a lovely warm contrast to the bitter elements outside.

Would that warmth and love also keep out the bitterness she brought home with her? Ellen wondered. In a way she feared putting it to the test. Perhaps that was why she was content to wander across the country with Jordan instead of heading directly for Willow Bend.

From Washington, D.C., they took the train to Chicago, a city raucous with industry and rough vitality. It was quite a contrast to the genteel marble city on the banks of the Potomac. Chicago was the home of her brother-in-law's family, Ellen told Jordan. When he suggested they pay a call, however, she refused. She had met Jonah Armstrong's mother and sister only once—at Katy's wedding. They were pleasant people, but she had no desire to subject her growing waistline to their knowing, feminine scrutiny. Now in her fifth month, Ellen was having more and more difficulty concealing her condition. A husband at her side might make her pregnancy socially acceptable, but it didn't relieve her own feelings of guilt or make her want to parade herself in front of family connections.

From Chicago they traveled to St. Louis, where Jordan was suitably impressed with the vast Mississippi River, then to Denver, where Ellen at last began to feel she was on home territory. In the near distance to the west, mountains serrated the sky in jagged splendor, and to the east stretched the vast plains that had been first spanned by the railroad only thirty years before. Here at last was her beloved West, with clear, sharp air and deep blue skies, where a man could still walk for days without seeing a house, a barn, or another human being.

"Quite impressive," Jordan admitted, looking at the distant mountains from their hotel window.

"Compared to the mountains in Montana, those are mere hills," Ellen boasted.

He put an arm around her. "Seems I've heard that refrain more than once in these last few days. Does anything compare to Montana?"

She laughed. "No. Nothing compares to Montana. You'll see."

His hand moved from her waist to her abdomen. "You're beginning to swell quite impressively, my sweet."

Ellen's buoyant mood deflated a bit. "That is what happens."

He moved behind her and splayed both hands across her rounded stomach. Up until now, she might have passed her belly off as a bit of gained weight, but no longer. She was lucky to have concealed her condition for this long.

"Our child," Jordan reminded her. "Yours and mine. Remember."

"I remember." She let her head drop back against his

chest. Jordan's support warmed her heart, but already she wearied of a deception that would have to last a lifetime.

"Are you sure you want to tell your family the truth?"

"Very sure. We've never lied to one another about anything. Even if I wanted to, it wouldn't work. The rest of the world is easy to deceive. Not them."

"I see this eating away at you, Ellen."

"It would eat at me regardless." She turned in his arms and smiled up at him. "You don't know them. It will be fine. I'll be fine."

Ellen prayed that it would be fine, but three days later, as their train approached Willow Bend, her heart was in her throat. She had not suffered morning sickness at the very first of her pregnancy, as most women did, but the last two mornings she had been unable to hold down her breakfast and had little appetite for lunch or dinner. Her medical instincts told her that nervousness, not pregnancy, was at the root of her discomfort.

She remembered how, during her first weeks in Paris, she had dreamed of the joyful homecoming that awaited her after her year's planned study. Now all that was spoiled by her own foolishness. It had not taken nearly a year for her to make a total fool of herself, and her homecoming would be anything but joyful. The thought made her angry at herself, and the anger made her feel even worse.

"Are you sure there's a town out here?" Jordan asked as he looked curiously out the window at the rugged, unpopulated countryside. The trains had become noticeably less luxurious as they had traveled west. From New York to Washington, D.C. they'd ridden in their own private compartment. Now they endured a poorly heated coach with hard seats, smudged windows, and a leather-goods salesman snoring in the seat in front of them.

"It's here, though it's not very big, I'll admit." She smiled. "My brother-in-law Jonah calls it a relic from more colorful times. He wrote a couple of articles about it for the *Chicago Record*."

"That interesting a place, is it?"

Ellen laughed. "You probably need a trained eye to appreciate it."

"Is your father's place close to town?"

"Pa's property starts about five miles outside of town and covers—well, it covers a big piece of land, although some of his cattle graze public range. My stepmother has a medical clinic in Willow Bend, but my father prefers to live in a place where you can look in every direction and not have anyone in sight. I guess he's a bit of a relic himself." She laced and unlaced her fingers nervously. "I hope someone comes to the station to meet us."

Jordan captured one of her hands and twined her restless fingers with his. "I can't imagine them not meeting you. The telegram you sent from Denver told them when we would arrive."

"But we're late."

"It's been my experience in this country of yours that the trains are always late. Do you expect your family to not greet you just because we're a half day off schedule?"

"No, no, of course not." She was fretting from simple nervousness, and Ellen knew it only too well. She'd sent her father a telegram when they landed in New York telling the family of her marriage, then another from Denver giving their schedule of arrival. Her family would be waiting all right, full of questions she didn't want to answer. They would want to know why she had left Paris in so unexpected a fashion, and of course they would demand every detail of how she had met Jordan and come to marry him so suddenly.

If Ellen was lucky, Katy would be in Alaska where she and Jonah had settled, or in Seattle, where they spent most of the winter months. One part of her longed to see the sister who'd been the other half of her when they were growing up, but another part dreaded facing her.

As the train rounded a low bluff, Willow Bend finally came into sight. In spite of her mixed feelings, Ellen felt the tug of affection. The few dusty streets and low buildings certainly weren't much to look at. In fact, the town was little more than a blemish on the beautiful intermontane valley where it was situated. A backdrop of mountains and the vast Montana sky made it seem even smaller than it was. But Willow Bend was home. She knew every soul who lived here, every rock and tree.

"Quite a place," Jordan commented as the train pulled to a huffing, squealing stop. His gaze swept past the town to the rugged scenery. "I can see why you thought the English countryside so tame."

She stood and gripped her small valise in a white knuckled grip and wrapped her coat around her to conceal her expanding waistline. There was no sense spoiling her very first moments home with an explanation of her pregnancy. "Here we are."

"Here we are," Jordan agreed with a smile. "And if you don't move we'll be continuing on to Missoula."

Ellen had scarcely stepped off the train when her valise was grabbed out of her hand and she was crushed in a bear hug against a familiar cowhide jacket.

"Ellen, girl! Welcome home!"

"Pa!"

Engulfed by her father's familiar scent—dust, leather, and clean male sweat—and with his hearty voice declaring how much he had missed her, Ellen felt like a little girl again. The feeling didn't last long, however, for the man who descended the steps behind her was undeniable proof that she was indeed a woman. Her father's eyes narrowed as Jordan put a possessive hand on her shoulder.

"Ellen?" Jordan prompted.

The glint in her father's eyes was a dangerous one. Ellen hastened to make introductions.

"Pa, this is my . . . my husband, Jordan Chesterfield. From England. Baron Chesterfield, actually. Jordan, this is my father, William Gabriel Danaher O'Connell."

The two men regarded each other cautiously. Ellen was surprised to find her husband every bit as tall and broad shouldered as her father. She'd always regarded Gabriel O'Connell as one of the most physically imposing men she knew, and he still was. When she'd described her father as a relic, she'd been talking about his attitudes, not his physique. His hair was as black, his eyes as vivid green, and the muscle that filled out his frame as hard as it ever had been. Her father had led a hard life that had made him a hard man, and few men cared to stand in his way when he had his back up.

"I'm honored to meet you, sir," Jordan said. His tone was politely respectful, but his stance was just as territorial as her father's. When Jordan held out his hand, Gabe took it in a firm grasp. The grips of the two men became firmer as they shook hands, and neither set of determined eyes left the other. Nervous as she was, Ellen couldn't help but be amused at the show of masculine rivalry. Some things certainly didn't change through the ages.

"Pa, quit!" she scolded. "You, too, Jordan."

"What?" her father asked innocently. With a final hearty squeeze, he released Jordan's hand.

"You're both behaving like cave men!" Ellen whispered intensely.

"We were merely shaking hands," Jordan commented.

"I know what you were doing. No more. Where's Olivia and David?"

"Olivia is delivering Mrs. Robert's baby."

"Jed Roberts got married?"

"It happens," Gabe said with a laconic glance at Jordan. "Married a girl from Bozeman."

"Where's David?"

"Home with Katy, Jonah, and Ty. Mouse is about to foal, so they stayed with her. She's too valuable to let her deliver by herself. You know anything about horses?" Gabe demanded of Jordan.

"A bit."

"Jordan has a stable full of horses that would put Mouse to shame, Pa."

"Is that so?" Gabe was clearly unimpressed.

"And dogs, too. Maisy's the best pointer in the county." Ellen didn't know why she felt the need to brag about Jordan, but suddenly she did. Her father clearly did not recognize what a worthy fellow Jordan was, and his attitude rankled.

"Ellen exaggerates a bit." Jordan gave Ellen a private smile of encouragement. "She helped deliver Maisy's pups, and she may feel some proprietary prejudice."

"You don't say," Gabe commented blandly.

As they gathered up the baggage and walked down the street toward the livery barn and their buggy, Ellen attempted to point out the meager local sights—the candy store, the barber shop, the Watering Hole Liquor

Emporium. All the while, Gabe sized up Jordan with what appeared to be a good deal of reserve. In Ellen's experience, very little ever got by her father's scrutiny, and from his attitude toward her husband, she wouldn't be surprised if he had taken note of her condition even through the concealing wrap.

"Your telegram saying you got married came as a fair surprise," he told Ellen.

"We . . . uh . . . met in England, when I stopped over to visit Jane Browne."

Jordan stepped into the awkward pause that followed. "Your daughter was kind enough to help my brother after he was accidentally shot."

"You got married after you left Paris?"

"We would have waited," Jordan explained with smooth evasiveness, "but I fear my feelings for Ellen took me by storm."

"In a hurry were you?" Gabe inquired. His tone was superficially polite, but the hard stare he gave his new son-in-law had sent more than one man scurrying for cover.

Jordan merely raised an aristocratic brow. His eyes were as flinty as Gabe's. Ellen had to give her husband credit. Few men could stand up to Gabriel O'Connell without at least a flinch. She certainly couldn't. A spark of indignation began to overshadow her nervousness. Her father had no right to conduct this inquisition. She remembered quite clearly the winter he and Olivia had spent in the little cabin at his mine above Elkhorn. He hadn't been married to Olivia, but that certainly hadn't held him back. If he was suspicious of the motives for her hurried wedding, he had very little room to complain of their behavior.

Besides, Ellen had every intention of revealing the

whole messy truth, but not before she could tell Katy and Olivia at the same time. She wasn't going to tell her father the news right there and treat the whole town to the sight of him blowing up like a lit stick of dynamite.

"Pa, we'll tell you everything you want to know back at the ranch. Right now, I'm tired. Could we go home, please?"

The sharp glitter of Gabe's eyes softened for Ellen, and the smile that slowly mellowed the harsh planes of his face was the smile Ellen remembered and loved. "Of course we can go home, sweetheart. Just let me hitch old Sadie to the buggy."

It took most of an hour to travel from town to O'Connell land and another thirty minutes to reach the Thunder Creek ranch house, a sturdy, spacious log house surrounded by corrals and outbuildings. The wide valley wasn't green, as it had been when Ellen had left in early summer, but it was a beautiful sight just the same. A welcome peace spread through Ellen's soul at the familiar scene as they came over the last hill and the house came into sight. Cattle dotted the valley, scarcely distinguishable from the brown grass. A mile or so east of the house two riders rode among the cattle at a leisurely pace. Four horses dozed in the corral beside the barn.

"This is it," she told Jordan. "Thunder Creek Ranch."

She almost expected some derogatory comment. Compared to Endsfield Park or any of its stately neighbors, her home was a mere rustic shack. But Jordan's voice held a note of sincerity when he said, "It's beautiful, Ellen. I see now why you keep telling me that nothing in the Old World or New compares to your Montana."

He squeezed her hand, and her heart swelled in unexpected affection. In spite of her father giving them the steely eye, she brushed a light kiss across his cheek. "Thank you, Jordan."

Jordan had to admit he was having the time of his life. He was a well-traveled man, but he'd never before seen such space and distance, such uncrowded majesty as Ellen's Montana. He could understand why a person raised in this beautiful, uncompromising land would be impatient with the inanities of society, with the crowds and squalor of civilization. He could understand a bit of what had molded Ellen's unconventional forthrightness and independence.

When the Thunder Creek Ranch buildings came into sight, Jordan felt a tug of affinity. What man, somewhere deep inside him, would not like to be master of a place such as this? The ranch perfectly fit the man who owned it—rough around the edges, but well suited to its setting.

Jordan liked Ellen's father, despite the man's cool greeting. It was only natural for a man to be protective of his daughter and wary of the stranger who'd stepped so abruptly into her life. In his position in society, Jordan seldom came across a man who would meet him eye to eye with uncompromising challenge. Those who weren't intimidated by his name and title were awed by his wealth. Gabriel O'Connell wasn't well acquainted with those details about his new son-in-law's stature, but Jordan suspected that his manner toward him wouldn't have altered in the slightest. Ellen's similar disregard for the customary obsequiousness was one of the things that had first fascinated Jordan about her. Now he realized she came by her attitude honestly.

Ellen squeezed his hand as they drove beneath a rustic wooden arch that announced they'd arrived at the Thun der Creek Ranch. "Brace yourself," she warned in a whisper.

A moment later he understood what she meant. Out of the main ranch house spilled a horde of welcomers. Actually, they weren't quite a horde, but they were enthusiastic and overwhelming enough to seem like one. Before anyone could get down from the buggy, a pint-size version of Gabriel climbed aboard and engulfed Ellen in an awkward embrace that lasted only a half second before he bounced to the ground and smiled a cherubic smile. "I missed you!" the boy said with a delighted laugh.

Ellen's smile matched the boy's. "This is my brother David," she told Jordan.

"I'm seven," David announced proudly as Jordan climbed down from the buggy.

"I see that you are." Jordan tried to sound suitably impressed, and won a grateful look from Ellen for his effort.

Jordan reached up to help Ellen from the buggy and found himself competing with another set of sturdy arms lifting toward her for the same purpose. Gabe glared at him briefly while Ellen glanced from one of them to the other, obviously wondering what to do. Jordan knew he should back off. Gabriel was her father, after all, and he hadn't seen his daughter in months. Jordan was but a passerby in Ellen's life. Nevertheless, Jordan stayed rooted to the spot and was inordinately pleased when Ellen took his hand instead of her father's. He couldn't resist giving his wife a brief, possessive hug once her feet were on the ground.

"Gabriel!" chided a soft feminine voice from behind them. "Behave yourself."

"Olivia!" Ellen launched herself from Jordan's arms

to the embrace of one of the most striking women Jordan had ever seen. She was in her late thirties, he would guess, but her eyes still shone with the luster of youth and her smile produced girlish dimples in her cheeks. Though lovely, her features were strong rather than beautiful. Jordan got the impression just from looking at her that she was more than a match for the hard man she'd married.

"Ellen! You look wonderful! It's so good to have you home."

"I thought you were delivering a baby!"

"It's a boy. Seven and a half pounds, healthy as a horse, and already as obstinate as his father. I got back just an hour ago."

"I've missed you so much!"

There was a desperate note in Ellen's voice that brought a tiny pucker to Olivia's brows. She looked her stepdaughter up and down, and though she missed nothing, Jordan suspected, her welcoming smile didn't falter. It was equally friendly when she greeted him. "You must be Jordan. This is quite a surprise—our Ellen coming home with a husband."

Her quick, friendly scrutiny missed nothing about him, either. Jordan began to understand why Ellen had said she couldn't successfully keep a secret from her family.

"Quite a surprise," Gabe echoed ominously.

Olivia smiled at her husband in a clear message to behave. "I'm sure you're both tired," she said. "Train trips can be such a chore. Come in and sit down, and we'll talk."

Before they reached the safety of the house, however, a thunder of hooves and a shriek riveted their attention to the road from up valley, where a rider sent up clouds of dust galloping in pursuit of a dog. No! Jordan thought incredulously. Not a dog, a wolf! Unbelievable though it seemed, the creature galloped full speed into the ranch-yard and headed with savage intent at Ellen. Feeling as though he'd somehow stepped into a nightmare, Jordan moved to push his wife aside and meet the beast's attack. A firm hand grabbed him and held him back.

"I wouldn't, if I were you." Gabe's eyes crinkled with amusement.

Jordan was about to wrench free when Ellen's crow of delight stayed him. She actually laughed as the huge creature launched himself at her. Jordan watched in absolute amazement as the wolf put his huge paws on Ellen's shoulders and licked her face, all the while whining with happiness. Ellen hugged the beast as enthusiastically as she'd hugged her little brother.

"Stop, you fat old wolf! You're going to knock me down!"

The rider who'd followed the wolf careened into the yard and pulled to a halt. Before the horse had fully stopped, the rider jumped from the saddle and joined the wolf in a raucous greeting.

"Ellen! Ellen! I just went out for a short hour, and you choose this time to drive up! God, it's good to see you!"

"I thought you were in the barn with Mouse."

"She delivered early this morning! A beautiful stud colt! Wait till you see him!"

A moment passed before Jordan realized the newcomer was a woman. At first he'd thought it was a young boy, an understandable mistake given her trousers and flannel shirt. But no boy looked quite like that in pants. He got another shock when the grinning women faced him, side by side. He was astonished enough to forget all pretense of manners.

"Good Lord! There's two of them!"

Gabe and Olivia both laughed. Knowing their girls only too well, they understood the dismay.

"Didn't Ellen tell you she had a twin?"

"A twin, yes. A carbon copy, no."

Ellen's sister was her mirror image come to life, albeit a somewhat scruffy image. Glossy black hair curled in exactly the same way. Bright emerald eyes looked out at the world with a mischievous twinkle. The elfin oval face perfectly blended Indian beauty and Irish leprechaun charm.

She examined him with a forthright intensity that was startling in a woman. Apparently satisfied with what she saw, she announced, "I'm Katy."

"So I gather. I'm pleased to meet you, Katy."

"And this is Hunter."

"He's a wolf!" little David supplied proudly.

"A very impressive wolf," Jordan agreed.

The wolf had stood looking at him with a reserved hauteur that seemed to disavow all knowledge of his earlier unwolflike display. His muzzle was somewhat gray with age, but he was a beautiful creature. Jordan couldn't resist an animal that displayed so much devotion. He squatted down to the wolf's level and smiled. "Hello, Hunter."

Hunter allowed himself to be petted and gave Jordan a quick lick that was apparently a stamp of approval, for Katy grinned.

"Has Pa beat the stuffings out of you yet?" she asked impishly.

"Katy!" Ellen and Olivia both chided.

Katy's grin did not fade. "That's what he did when he first met Jonah. Though Jonah at least gave as good as he got." She eyed Jordan speculatively, as if estimating his chances.

"Enough of that!" Olivia scolded. "Let's go inside and have some coffee and cake."

At the promise of cake, David took Olivia's hand and tugged his mother toward the house. Katy grabbed Ellen's arm and immediately started chattering about Mouse's new foal, leaving Jordan to walk with Gabriel, not the most happy pairing.

"Beat the stuffings out of Katy's husband, eh?" Jordan asked cautiously.

"At the time, it seemed he needed it." Gabe's smile was a bit grim, as if he was still making up his mind if Jordan deserved a similar introduction to the family.

This was going to be one hell of a visit, Jordan concluded.

Coffee, tea, and slices of delicious devil's food cake were served in a parlor that was comfortably and warmly furnished. Most of the furniture was crafted from pine and aspen and upholstered with leather or sturdy tweeds. No velvets and satins here. Photographs of a prosperous-looking older couple decorated the top of a grand piano. The floor was softened with several good-quality Oriental-style rugs. Once again Jordan felt an affinity for this place and these people. The grandeur of Endsfield would never be this comfortable or welcoming. And surely his own mother, though she loved both her sons in her own reserved way, would never greet either of them with the unqualified affection with which Ellen's family had engulfed her.

"This cake is delicious, Dr. O'Connell. You must be an accomplished cook."

"Please call me Olivia, Jordan. I'm afraid I can't claim credit for the cake. I'm accomplished at some things, but cooking isn't one of them. Sarah Mulholland keeps house for us. She went into town today, but left a few treats behind, fortunately. Ellen is the one who's a really fine cook."

"I'm sure he's discovered that," Katy said proudly. "Ellen makes the best sourdough biscuits in the West."

"Actually, I've never cooked for Jordan," Ellen admitted.

"Of course," Olivia said. "You were married on the ship, weren't you? And back in England I'm sure a member of the peerage has a cook and housekeeper to take care of such things."

"Yes, ma'am."

"A baron, eh?" Ellen's father said, clearly unimpressed.

"Yes, sir. My father was the eleventh of the Chesterfield title, and my mother is the youngest daughter of a prominent Irish banking family—the Flynns. I believe she was quite impressed that Ellen was of Irish descent."

"Your mother's Irish, is she?" Gabe raised one brow. "Well, now, that's a point in your favor."

"Maybe Pa won't beat on you after all," Katy speculated, eyes twinkling.

"I would appreciate that," Jordan said half seriously.

Everyone laughed except Gabe and Jordan. The inquisition was going to get a good deal more serious very shortly, Jordan sensed. He felt for Ellen, knowing how hard it would be for her to tell the truth, and knowing also how deeply she felt that she owed the truth to these people. In this, there was little he could do to help her. He reached for her hand and squeezed it, and she sent him a nervous smile.

"Where are Jonah and Tyrell?" Ellen asked Katy.

"Jonah went over to Tad Barton's to deal for a horse," Katy told her.

"And Tyrell's asleep," Olivia supplied.

"And hopefully will stay that way for another hour." Katy rolled her eyes. "I never would have guessed that a one-year-old kid could put such a crimp in your life."

"And you love every minute of it," Olivia teased.

A sudden pause in conversation resulted in awkward silence. Jordan felt Ellen tense as Olivia's mouth tightened into an unhappy line.

"We're all anxious to hear about your wedding, Ellen. And about Paris."

If Ellen squeezed Jordan's hand any tighter, she might have broken bones. It was all he could do not to wince.

"But I'm afraid I have some bad news to impart before we get into that," Olivia continued.

"Bad news?"

"Your grandmother is very ill. We've only been waiting on you to go to the reservation to visit her. I think it will be our last visit," she said gently.

"Squirrel Woman ill?" Ellen's voice shook. "What is it?"

"I believe it's a cancer of the pancreas, though she hasn't let me examine her, of course." One corner of Olivia's mouth lifted in a wry smile. "She's always trusted the traditional medicine more than anything I could do for her, though in this case I couldn't have done much."

Jordan could see the pain in Ellen's face. Obviously, all thoughts of her own situation had fled her mind.

"When are we leaving?" she asked.

"Now that you're here," said Gabe, "we'll leave tomorrow morning. If that's all right with you, of course," he inquired sardonically of Jordan.

"Of course."

"You might find the reservation interesting."

Jordan detected a gleam of wicked satisfaction in his father-in-law's eyes. No doubt he felt an Indian reservation was just the place to test the mettle of the uppity English lord who had so precipitously married his daughter. This little sidetrack in his life was getting more complex by the hour.

CHAPTER 18

The Blackfoot lands in Montana were near the Canadian border, well north of Willow Bend, and the train trip there was indirect and tiresome. Ellen's admiration for Jordan grew apace with her gratitude for his aplomb in dealing with the cold, sooty train ride, the unexpected alteration of his own plans, and not least of all, her family.

Ellen thought of her family as special. Someone less emotionally involved might think them eccentric. Her father was a man who had once been hounded across the face of Montana for murder. Her stepmother was a woman physician, which was enough, in the thinking of many people, to make her an offense to nature, and Ellen herself had followed in her stepmother's unconventional footsteps. Sister Katy, who most of the time wore trousers, could outride and outshoot most men in the state. The only normal person among them was Katy's husband Jonah, and the longer he was married to Katy the less normal he became.

Though she loved her family dearly, Ellen was surprised that a man of Jordan's background tolerated them so well, especially since interrogating, pestering, teasing, and otherwise bothering Ellen's new husband proved to be the family's chief distraction on the tedious trip.

He bore it all with good grace and met their blatant attempts to probe into his background, financial circumstances, and his history with Ellen with a hint of amusement in his eye. David roped him into reading several stories aloud before Olivia corralled her son and diverted him with other amusements. Katy's husband, Jonah, felt Jordan out about politics, social philosophies, and his taste in everything from literature to sports before sharing the story of his own explosive first meeting with Gabriel O'Connell.

"It wasn't *my* fault," Jonah told Jordan in an oft-repeated protestation of innocence. "Katy dragged me to the Klondike, not the other way around. And we would have been married long before Gabe caught up with us if she hadn't been such a stubborn little blockhead. But *I'm* the one who got his clock cleaned when her father came steaming up the Yukon River looking for his little girl!"

"You're just lucky I took you to Dawson with me," Katy declared with a laugh. "Otherwise you'd still be stuck writing stories for that newspaper in Chicago instead of watching the gold come out of our claim in Skookgum Gulch."

"Not to mention he wouldn't have such a charming wife and handsome son," Jordan added with a twinkle.

Men usually didn't hesitate to admit Katy was beautiful, but not many went so far as to call her charming. Ellen could see that Jordan's choice of compliments tickled her sister's fancy. And of course anyone who recognized baby Tyrell's beauty won the mother's instant approval. Jordan clinched Katy's wholehearted support, however, a few minutes later when Ty baptized his new uncle's lap with an overflow from his diaper. Jordan weathered the aromatic accident with good humor.

"You're a damned good sport," Katy told her new brother-in-law as she handed him a towel for his lap. "Most men will wade through the muck of a stockyard pen without flinching, but touch them with a thimbleful of baby pee and they act as though they've been poisoned."

Katy threw Jonah a telling glance, and Jordan and Ellen both laughed. Ellen felt her heart soften with a warmth that was downright dangerous. How different this Jordan was from the haughty, stiff aristocrat she had first encountered at Endsfield Park. Had he actually changed? Ellen wondered. Or was the apparent change just another layer she had uncovered by knowing him better?

Katy cleaned up her overflowing son with quick efficiency—she'd become as adept with a diaper as she was with a rifle. Handing him to Jonah to cuddle, she dug into her bag of baby underthings and infant accessories and came up with a deck of cards.

"How about a game of poker, Jordan? Help pass the time?"

Jordan laughed. "I can think of about a hundred safer ways to pass time. Your sister cleaned me out once, along with several other gentlemen who thought they were devils with cards, and she tells me you can play circles around her."

"At last she admits the truth." Katy gave Ellen an approving grin. "You cleaned them out?"

"I didn't," Ellen denied. "I relieved them of a few pounds, is all. Just to show them they weren't as smart as they thought they were."

Katy chuckled. "Good for you!"

Jordan gave Katy her game of poker, but only after she agreed to set a nickel limit on the bets. His caution made Katy unbearably smug, in Ellen's opinion, so she gave her husband some help in defending his nickels. Quickly enough she discovered that he didn't really need her help, but propping her head on his shoulder and occasionally whispering in his ear was so pleasant that she continued in the role.

Ellen wondered if it was her pregnancy that made her so susceptible to Jordan's appeal. It was the common opinion that women in the family way lost whatever small amount of reason they had, and though she certainly didn't subscribe to that school of thought, Ellen did admit that she'd been very emotional lately. The night before, she'd almost wept when Jordan had shown an extraordinary amount of thoughtfulness for her ragged emotions. After an evening spent reminiscing about her grandmother and the "old times" before Ellen had left for medical school and Katy had run off to the Klondike, Ellen and Jordan had retired to Ellen's old bedroom. The curtains Ellen had made still covered the windows, and the quilt that had taken her two years to complete was spread upon the bed. Surrounded by the treasures of her youth, she'd felt like a much younger and more innocent Ellen. When Jordan had pulled her close in bed, the idea of making love hadn't seemed right. Her body had wanted to respond, but the awkwardness of their surroundings made her stiff.

Without Ellen saying a word, Jordan had seemed to understand. Hard with his own desire, he had nevertheless given her just what she needed—comfort and cuddling—and no more. When the dawn had awakened her, she woke in his arms feeling safe and cared for.

Why hadn't she had the good sense to fall in love with a man like Jordan Chesterfield instead of Henri Chretiens? Ellen asked herself, though she wondered which man her husband really was—the stiff-necked English lord or the amiable, understanding fellow who tolerated babies, nosy in-laws, and a moody, unpredictable wife? Maybe both personas were an act.

Whoever Jordan was, she probably didn't deserve him, Ellen mused morosely. She had thought she was being so brave and forthright by insisting that her family know the truth, yet she had seized upon the first excuse—the confusion of their departure for the reservation—to not tell them. Soon she was going to have to tell them something, for if their sharp eyes had been deceived so far, and she wasn't at all sure that they had been, it was only because of their preoccupation with Squirrel Woman's illness. Very soon she would need to find the courage to confess.

They arrived at the Blackfoot Indian agency at noon of the second day. Compared to the countrysides of England or France, compared even to the rest of Montana, the reservation seemed an empty place, just over two thousand Blackfeet were accommodated on a million and a half acres of land. When Ellen was a young girl visiting her relatives here, the place hadn't seemed so deserted. Then the People had still lived in hunting bands, most of which set up their encampments on Badger Creek near the old agency. In the short time it took Ellen to grow up, the way of life had changed, however. Hunting bands were useless when game was nearly impossible to find. Agriculture, both communal and indi-

vidual, had failed miserably. The Blackfeet were
uninterested in farming, and the land was unsuitable for
most crops. In the last three years, however, the People
had found an aptitude and interest for ranching. A fine
herd of nearly 12,000 cattle grazed the communal grass-
lands, and the families, instead of living together in the
traditional hunting bands, spread out over the reservation to tend the herds. They set down roots and moved
out of their tipis into small round log cabins or, sometimes, neat clapboard houses such as the white men
built.

Ellen's grandmother Squirrel Woman still lived in her
traditional tipi, a thirty-minute wagon ride from the Indian agency. In a log cabin only a stone's throw from
the tipi lived her son Crooked Stick and his wife Big
Nose. Crooked Stick possessed a herd of fine horses that
made him rich, by Blackfoot standards, and also enough
head of cattle so that he and his family no longer depended upon the agency-issued food rations to survive.

Crooked Stick greeted his nieces and Olivia with a
broad smile, Gabe with a brotherly embrace, Jonah with
a friendly nod, and Jordan with suspicious caution.

"Crooked Stick is my mother's brother," Ellen explained to Jordan. "Mother's name was Many Horses
Woman, and she was the most beautiful girl for miles
around, wasn't she, Crooked Stick?"

"She was. Before your father won her, many young
men wanted her as wife. She was beautiful, talented, and
virtuous also."

"As are her daughters," Olivia claimed.

"They are," Crooked Stick agreed solemnly.

Not true, Ellen chided herself. She had no intention
of being overly honest with her uncle and grandmother,
however. The Blackfoot people set great store by a wom-

an's virtue. She would not burden her grandmother in these last days of her life.

"How is Squirrel Woman?" Olivia asked Crooked Stick.

He shook his head. "She is alive still. That is all I will say."

"I know she won't let me treat her, but would she go to the hospital at the agency and let another doctor help her?"

"The medicine woman called Spotted Horse in the Water comes every day. My mother is content with that, even though she complains that Spotted Horse does little but give her bitter tea to drink."

Olivia sighed, and Gabe put an arm around her shoulder.

"Big Mouth Woman," Crooked Horse said gently, using the name he had given Olivia on the first day they had met. The name had long ago lost its derogatory edge and become a symbol of affection between them. "It is Squirrel Woman's time to die. She complains that she has already lived past her time and seen things she should not have lived to see. She waits only to say good-bye to her granddaughters and the husband of my sister Many Horses. The old die, and that is as it should be. We should not dispute the commands of nature."

Olivia smiled wryly. "It is a physician's job to dispute the commands of nature."

"That is your way," Crooked Stick reminded her. "It is not ours."

While Gabe went into the tipi to greet Squirrel Woman, the rest of them waited in Crooked Stick's log cabin. Though a primitive-looking dwelling, it was comfortable and surprisingly roomy inside. The dirt floor was packed hard and swept clean of debris. Mats were scattered here and there for sitting and sleeping. On a hearth in the middle of the cabin burned a low fire that provided enough heat to keep the cabin comfortable as well as rather smoky. One small glass window admitted little light, but kerosene lanterns hung from the low rafters and made the interior quite pleasingly bright.

In spite of her name, Crooked Stick's Gros Ventre wife was quite pretty. Crooked Stick had married only two years ago, when Squirrel Woman's failing health had forced him to stop his habitual wandering from the reservation. Big Nose was not much older than Ellen and Katy, but fortunately for her husband, was of a much milder temperament.

"I have made tea," she announced as they sat down upon the mats by the hearth.

"Tea?" Jordan asked. His tone was politely bland, but Ellen detected the caution.

"Big Nose makes tea from rose hips and mint," Ellen explained. "It's very good for you."

"Yes. Of course." He took a polite sip from the steaming cup Big Nose handed him. One brow lifted approvingly. "It's very good."

Big Nose nodded and smiled.

"I thought among your people that a man did not speak to his wife's mother," Jordan commented to Crooked Stick.

Ellen gave him a surprised look, which he answered with a shrug. "I have been reading about the Blackfoot people and their history."

"When did you start this?" Ellen demanded.

"The first time you told me your mother was a Blackfoot woman."

Crooked Stick nodded approvingly. "A husband

should know everything he can about his wife. It helps him to manage her."

"You have a point," Jordan agreed.

Katy snorted indignantly, and Jonah chuckled.

"Since Ellen's father is in the tipi speaking to Squirrel Woman, I take it the ban of a man speaking to his wife's mother doesn't apply in a situation like this."

"That is not true," Crooked Stick told him. "They do not speak. Many times exchanging feelings does not involve words."

Jordan nodded. "You're right. Sometimes words just get in the way."

As time passed, they drank tea and mostly kept to themselves, as people tend to do in the face of death. David napped with his head on Olivia's lap. Katy held on tightly to Jonah's hand and stared at the dirt floor, her eyes far away, no doubt focusing on memories of summers spent with Squirrel Woman and their mother's relatives.

Ellen wished she could lose herself in fond remembering as she suspected her sister was doing. But until the present was resolved, memories of happy times in the past brought more pain than comfort.

Gabe walked into the log cabin and sent Olivia to see Squirrel Woman. "No doubt the old lady wants to tell Olivia just once more how to be a good wife to Many Horse's husband," Gabe said when Olivia had left. "No one could ever persuade Squirrel Woman that she doesn't know better than everyone else how to run their lives."

Jordan chuckled and looked at Ellen. "Does that remind you of another old lady you've met?"

The thought that Jordan would compare an old Indian woman to his imperious, sophisticated mother brought a smile to Ellen's lips. "Your mother could probably learn something from Squirrel Woman about being a tyrant, but underneath it all my grandmother has the biggest heart in the world."

Olivia returned shortly and gave her stepdaughters a sad smile. "I'm afraid she doesn't have very much time left, girls. You should go in to see her now. And, Ellen, don't try to diagnose your grandmother," she warned. "And don't waste your time thinking up ways to ease her, for she won't listen. Use your time to give yourself a good memory."

Ellen followed Katy into their grandmother's tipi, which was brightly painted with symbols that were a part of the old way of life. Squirrel Woman's only concession to the changing times was to cover her dwelling with canvas instead of the hides of buffalo cows. The buffalo herds were long gone, and with them went the traditions that had been the foundation of Squirrel Woman's life.

The old woman lay on a mat by the central fire. The last time Ellen had seen her, Squirrel Woman had been stooped with age, but still lively and full of energy. Now the only life was in her eyes, which still sparkled like two onyx gems shining from the mass of wrinkles that was her face.

The girls knelt beside the mat, and Katy took the old woman's hand. "Grandmother."

"White Horse Woman."

Squirrel woman had never called her granddaughters by their white names. She had always regarded them as Blackfoot girls who just happened to live with another hunting band far away. She held out her other hand to Ellen. "Lights up the Sky. It has been many seasons since I have seen the daughters of Many Horses. Have you found husbands yet?"

Ellen stifled a smile. She should have known that was the first thing the old lady would ask.

"I have a fine husband and a son," Katy told her.

"Your husband is a white man?" It was more of a resigned statement than a question.

"Yes, Grandmother, but he is strong and honorable. And rich," she added.

"He has fine horses?"

"The finest horses anywhere," Katy told her with a fond smile. Horses would mean more to Squirrel Woman than Katy and Jonah's gold claim in the Klondike.

Squirrel Woman squeezed Ellen's hand. "And you, Light up the Sky?"

"I have a husband also."

"No son yet?"

Ellen hesitated and bit her lip. Katy's eyes rested on her face curiously. "No," Ellen finally said. "No son yet."

The old woman focused intently upon her face, and her gaze made Ellen want to back away, but she didn't. Finally, her grandmother sighed. "I will not die just yet, though I am ready to travel to the land of the dead. My husband Walks Straight will meet me there, and things will be as they once were. The buffalo will stretch as far as my eyes can see, hiding the sky with their dust. The People will be strong, and no white men will tell us that we shouldn't dance the Sun Dance, or pray to our own gods, or dress and talk as we like. There will be no one to take our children away and teach them our ways are evil, so that they come back talking and thinking as white children.

"I am anxious to go, but I will stay awhile, because there is still something I must do."

"What is that, Grandmother?" Katy asked.

Squirrel Woman merely huffed in reply. "When you were small I told you stories of what was expected of a virtuous woman of the *Siksikauw*. Most important is being a good, faithful wife to your husband. Are the daughters of Many Horses Woman good wives to their husbands?"

"Yes, Grandmother," they both answered.

"Do you obey your husbands?" The old woman targeted Katy with her eyes. She knew her granddaughters well. "Are you meek and willing workers?"

"Grandmother," Katy replied, rolling her eyes. "I am every bit as meek as you ever were."

The old woman's lips twitched in a smile. "I expect better, White Horse Woman. Lights up the Sky, you have always been a good girl. Does your husband treat you kindly?"

"Very kindly, Grandmother." More kindly than she deserved, perhaps.

"Does he own many horses?"

"Beautiful, strong horses, Grandmother. I wish you could see them all."

Squirrel Woman nodded. "You will bring your husbands here so I can meet them."

Ellen hadn't anticipated this. Poor Jordan. After all her posturing about being honest with her family, she was putting him through this charade. She felt like the lowest worm for imposing on him and lower still for deceiving Squirrel Woman. Yet burdening her grandmother with disappointment—one the old lady had no part in and could do nothing to help—would be a selfish piece of unnecessary honesty.

Jonah came in first, carrying Tyrell. Jordan followed, looking around the interior of the tipi with considerable interest. He took Ellen's hand when he knelt next to her beside the old lady's mat.

Squirrel Woman scrutinized both men with merciless intensity as Tyrell wriggled in his father's arms and fussed to be put down.

"Show me your son," the old woman commanded Katy.

When Squirrel Woman touched the boy, he grew quiet. She looked at him long and hard, then smiled her approval. "A fine son, White Horse Woman."

She handed the child back to its mother, then locked her gaze onto Jonah. Katy's husband didn't flinch. Ellen had to give Jonah Armstrong credit. Squirrel Woman had been known to stare down some of the strongest men on the reservation. One Indian agent, in particular, had taken to giving her a wide berth. But Jonah was having none of it.

Of course, Ellen reflected, the man had to have nerves of iron just to have won and wed her sister.

When Squirrel Woman's challenge shifted to Jordan, Ellen's hand tightened involuntarily on his, but he didn't need her help. His experience with his mother stood him in good stead.

Finally, Squirrel Woman nodded, as if satisfied. "My daughter's daughters are prizes who deserve men of very strong medicine," she declared. "When I look into your eyes, I see strong men. But I see only white men. Not good enough."

Jonah looked as though he'd heard something like this before—probably from Katy. Jordan merely raised one unperturbed brow. Ellen doubted, given his looks, money, abilities, and rank, that he had ever been told he wasn't good enough for anything. All things considered, he was taking it rather well.

Ellen didn't take it well, though. Somewhat to her own surprise, she found herself growing a bit steamed that anyone, even Squirrel Woman, would not see Jordan's obvious worth. She opened her mouth to protest, but a sharp warning from Katy's eyes forestalled her.

"You must prove yourselves worthy to be men of the People," the old woman continued. "You each will go alone to a place where you will not eat or sleep, and there you will seek the approval of a spirit who will give you the power to be worthy of Many Horses' daughters. When you have done this, come back and look into my eyes so that I may see who you are."

Jordan smiled. "I would be honored, dear lady."

Jonah grimaced when Katy poked him in the ribs. "Yes, ma'am. Whatever you say."

"Jordan, you do not need to do this!"

Jordan watched as his wife paced the hard-packed dirt floor of her uncle's log cabin. Ever since the interview with her grandmother, Ellen had been bursting with objections and excuses, but not until now, an hour later, had they found a moment of privacy in which they could talk freely. All that time Jordan had imagined he could see the words swell within her until she was ready to come apart at the seams.

"Don't worry about it," he advised her. "If this will set your grandmother's mind to rest, it's worth doing. I went through worse rituals in the school my father sent me to."

"You don't understand. My people are very serious about receiving medicine power from spirits. It is not something to be laughed at."

"I'm not laughing."

"Saying you did it and lying about the results would be worse than telling her you refuse."

"Why would I need to lie to her?"

Ellen raised her brows in disbelief. "You actually intend to sit in the freezing woods and fast and meditate until you find a vision?"

Her skepticism goaded him into a grin. "I'm looking forward to it."

"You're crazy, Jordan! It's December, and this is not the gentle English countryside. This is Montana!"

"How do the Blackfoot men manage?"

"They are accustomed to going for long periods without food, and they know how to take care of themselves in any conditions. Squirrel Woman was wrong to ask this."

"As I recall, she didn't ask. She commanded. In some ways, meeting your grandmother made me homesick."

"Don't change the subject."

"Yes, my lady," he said with a smile.

"You don't need to do this."

"To tell the truth, Ellen, I rather want to do it. The culture of your people is fascinating, you know. I admire their spirituality. It seems to me that while our civilization is certainly more sophisticated about things, your so-called savages may have the advantage over us when it comes to matters of the heart and spirit."

She stared at him. "You constantly amaze me."

"I rather amaze myself at times."

"I don't know whether you're an idiot or a savant."

"Given that limited choice, I vote for savant."

Ellen laughed, then sighed in frustration. A confused mix of emotions showed in her face. Jordan reached out and touched her cheek.

"This is an adventure for me, my love. Don't make it into something it's not."

Her hand came up and caught his, and her eyes pulled him toward her. But before Jordan could move, the cabin door opened to admit Katy and Jonah. Ellen jumped as though they'd been discovered in something much more dramatic then merely exchanging a look.

"Hello, you two," Jonah greeted them. "Has your wife been more merciful than mine, Jordan, and granted you a reprieve?"

"I've been trying," Ellen said, spearing Jordan with a sharp glance.

Jonah grinned at Katy. "My wife should be so generous! You see, Katydid? Your sister loves her husband enough to spare him turning into a block of ice—and a starving one at that—for some equally hungry bear to come along and have for a snack."

Katy winked at her sister. "Ellen always was a pushover."

"And my husband is a moron. He insists on going."

"An Englishman with Blackfoot medicine power." Katy's eyes sparkled with mischief. "You could write about that, Jonah."

"Not if I lose all my fingers to frostbite."

"This'll be good for you. Besides, ever since that visit to your family in Chicago last summer I've been looking for an appropriate revenge. I would say three weeks with your mother is worth at least three days fasting in search of a spirit dream."

Jonah shook his head. "When I married you, Katy O'Connell, I figured the price was going to be an adventurous life with an early death. I just didn't know how early."

Katy grinned. "You asked for it."

"I did, didn't I?" His eyes crinkled in silent laughter. "Welcome to the family, Jordan. It appears we're both about to prove ourselves true men, Blackfoot fashion."

Blanket wrapped around her head and shoulders against the cold, Ellen worried a path around the twin pines that stood behind her uncle's cabin. She felt like fretting, and she couldn't fret properly with Big Nose and Olivia looking on, with David following her about wanting to know what she was up to, with Tyrell fussing by the hearth where he was supposedly taking a nap. A person needed privacy for a proper fret, and privacy was a rare thing around here.

Ellen couldn't believe Jordan had been gone two days—two cold, blustery days with the sky spitting snow and the wind sharp as a well-honed knife. It was unfair that her people were putting him through this. It was unbelievable that he'd consented. He was an English nobleman, for mercy's sake! He'd lived his whole life in a land where one could scarcely ever get out of sight of a dwelling or another human being. And now, because of her grandmother's old-fashioned notions and his own warped sense of adventure, he was sitting somewhere in the middle of a Montana winter, waiting for lack of food and exhaustion to give him a glimpse into a spirit world he didn't even believe in.

Ellen couldn't believe he had gone. She couldn't believe her father and Olivia had supported—had even been grateful for—his decision. And she couldn't believe, after just two days, how much she worried about him and missed him. Since they'd come to Montana, they hadn't made love or had any of the intimate moments that they'd indulged in before. They'd scarcely had the privacy for so much as a kiss. But a connection existed on a deeper level. She had felt his silent support each time she thought the stress of reunion with her family or the anguish over her grandmother's illness might overwhelm her. Jordan seemed to read her mind and see into her soul. At times she thought she could see into his. Maybe if she ignored the uneasiness that clouded her thinking, she could even understand his trek into the woods—the pride, the perverse sense of honor that in England would earn him the title stalwart. In Montana he would be called stubborn and downright ornery. Montanans admired that sort of thing.

When had she let herself become so dependent on Jordan? A wedding didn't create this. Sex didn't either. She'd submitted sexually to Henri; she even carried his child. Yet she had never felt this kind of connection with him, even though she must have loved him.

Ellen closed her eyes and prayed that Jordan would come back from this ordeal whole and healthy, and that she could somehow find a way not to care so much when they finally took separate paths to live the lives they both had to live.

Her prayer was interrupted by a muffled curse from behind a screen of scrub oak. Ellen recognized both her sister's voice and Katy's favorite cuss word. She pushed through the brush to find Katy herself fitting a stone into the pocket of a rock sling, which had always been her favorite weapon, despite her proficiency with a rifle.

"Still practicing?" Ellen teased. "I'd think you would have it down by now."

"Very funny." Katy let fly at a rusted can that sat on a stump a good distance away. The can shot off its perch and bounced along the ground.

"Is that what you were aiming at?"

"You know it is."

Ellen sat on a log and watched as Katy continued to fling stones at the downed can. Each shot bounced the can farther away. Finally, she threaded the sling through her belt and joined Ellen on the log.

Ellen smiled at her fondly. "You'd think a person who owns one of the richest gold claims in the Klondike wouldn't need to bring home squirrels for dinner by conking them with a rock."

"The talent's sometimes useful for other things," Katy said with a grin. "I conked Jonah with it once."

"I remember the story."

"Besides, I don't want all that money to go to my head. It's bad enough we bought that house in Seattle to spend the winters in." Katy gave Ellen a canny look. "It appears you've done pretty well for yourself along those lines as well. An English baron, no less. How rich is he?"

"I have no idea. It's none of my business."

"He's your husband. Doesn't that make it your business?"

Ellen silently cursed her sister's nosy instincts. She hastily changed the subject. "Do you think they're all right?"

"Jonah and your baron?" Katy chuckled unsympathetically. "Sure they are. Crooked Stick and Pa are keeping an eye on them.

"Did they tell you that?"

"No, but I know they are. Haven't you noticed how often they've been absent the last couple of days. Not that they need to baby-sit our boys. Jonah can take care of himself. He just pretends to be a citified greenhorn because I made such an issue of it when I first met him. Actually, he's tough as nails. And your Jordan seems like a man who knows what he's about."

"Jordan's an Englishman, for heaven's sake!"

Katy shrugged. "Jonah hails from Chicago, and it didn't make him a weakling, though I admit I took my own sweet time realizing it. I've learned that if a man's got backbone and brains, it doesn't make much difference where he comes from."

"Jordan's a good man," Ellen said with a sigh.

"I like him," Katy declared. "Though he's a bit on the stuffy side. Is he prim and stuffy in bed?"

"Katy!"

"Well? You *are* married."

Their old habit of sharing absolutely everything was going to prove her downfall, Ellen thought. Her face heated uncontrollably. "Jordan is . . . very competent."

Katy grinned wickedly. "Competent, is he?" Her eyes darted to Ellen's waist, which had been assiduously concealed with aprons, overcoats, blankets, dish towels—any handy and plausible camouflage Ellen could find—since arriving in Willow Bend. "When are you going to break the news?"

Ellen gusted out a sigh. She should have known she couldn't hide anything from the nosy little weasel. "When all this is over."

"Aren't you happy about it?"

"Of course," Ellen said unconvincingly.

"How far along are you?"

"A little more than five months."

"Lucky you! You don't show all that much. I looked like a whale at five months. Or at least, I felt like one."

Ellen bit her lip.

"Don't pull such a long face," Katy advised. "Pa and Olivia aren't going to make a fuss about your falling into bed first and marrying second. Not that it's the way things should be done, but it's not the end of the world.

Olivia could have ended up the same way." Her mouth twisted in wry humor. "For that matter, I could have, too. And I didn't even feel guilty about it."

"You hardly ever feel guilty about anything, Katy."

"That's true. And you were always such a model of virtue. You felt guilty about everything."

Ellen had to chuckle. "That's true, too."

"The important thing is that you love the man, and he loves you."

Ellen tried to keep her smile from faltering.

"You do love him, don't you?"

"Of course I do." Once the words were out, Ellen wondered if they just might be true. How did one know when passion and caring deepened into love? What exactly was love, anyway? She missed Jordan when they weren't together. Her spirit brightened whenever she saw him. She craved his touch. His smile made her glow. His kiss made her knees weak and her head light.

Was that love, or was it some disease that no one had yet described? And if it was love, then what was it she had felt for Henri? Dashing, clever, sophisticated Henri, who had swept her off her feet and then dropped her back to earth with such a thud.

Ellen admitted total confusion. The business of love, she reflected, was certainly oversimplified in song and poetry.

CHAPTER 19

The physician in Ellen couldn't believe that Squirrel Woman was still alive. The old woman's heartbeat was irregular, her pulse thready, and she'd taken only water, no food, in the last two days. The part of Ellen that was Blackfoot knew the power of the spirit though. Her grandmother would not die until she willingly released her spirit from its earthly bonds, and that would not be until she was good and ready.

Someone was with Squirrel Woman around the clock, and Ellen volunteered for more than her share of vigils. She didn't mind. Sitting beside her grandmother's mat, the woman Ellen had become—sorrowful, mistrustful, and bitter—fled before the bright and confident girl she once had been. Even though Squirrel Woman spent most of her time sleeping, the old woman's very presence took Ellen back to a time before she had gone to Europe, before she had met Henri Chretiens and realized she could fall as far and hard as anyone else, with disastrous results.

Ellen was in Squirrel Woman's tipi when Jordan returned, three days after he had left to prove himself worthy to be Ellen's husband. When she heard Olivia cry Jordan's name, Ellen shot up to go to him, but Squirrel Woman reached out a clawlike hand to grab her arm.

"Stay!" she commanded.

"But Grandmother!"

"He will come here—to me. Then we will see what this man of yours is."

Ellen couldn't go without wresting her arm from the old woman's grasp, so she sat back and waited impatiently. As Squirrel Woman had predicted, Jordan came straight to the tipi. He looked only at Squirrel Woman as he knelt down beside the mat, but Ellen felt his awareness of her like a palpable thing. That awareness had a tension to it she hadn't felt before.

"I have done as you asked, madam."

"Didn't ask," Squirrel Woman rasped. "Commanded."

"As you say."

For a moment the old woman gazed intently up at him. Ellen was surprised she had such concentration left in that frail, failing body. She wondered what her grandmother saw in Jordan's eyes, in his soul, for she had no doubt that the old woman could see into a person's soul. Jordan was dirty, noticeably thinner, pale, and very weary looking, but his eyes met Squirrel Woman's gaze with steady purpose.

"You were successful," Squirrel Woman finally said.

Jordan didn't answer.

"It is good that you are silent, for when a man finds his medicine power, it is for him alone. I can see that you are not just a white man."

Jordan seemed to sag as the tension in the tipi eased. For the first time, his eyes turned Ellen's way.

"Welcome back." She didn't mean to put so much of her heart into the words, but she heard it there, just the same. Embarrassed, she tried to look away, but couldn't. His gaze seemed to devour her.

"Are you all right?" she asked anxiously.

"I'm fine. Just tired."

He held out a hand to her, and she started to rise, but once again, Squirrel Woman held her back.

"Go," the old woman ordered Jordan. "She will come to you in a while."

Jordan obeyed. Ellen fretted. "Grandmother . . ."

"You have many seasons to be with your husband, Lights Up The Sky. You have only a little time to be with me."

Ellen's gaze flashed to Squirrel Woman in instant concern, but the old woman's eyes were still bright with life as she squeezed Ellen's hand.

"Your husband is a good man. He is strong, and he knows where his center is. Your child will be strong as well."

Ellen sighed disconsolately. "You know." It didn't occur to her to deny the truth.

Squirrel Woman grunted. "I am old. I am not blind, or dead. Not yet."

Ellen felt something snap loose inside her. She was so very tired of deception, of lies, of evasion and hiding. "Grandmother . . ." Her hands came up to cover her face. "Grandmother, forgive me. The child is not Jordan's."

The old woman did not seem surprised. "Your husband knows this?"

"Of course he does! It's the reason he offered to marry me. That, and . . . It's complicated." Tears ran down her cheeks. She impatiently brushed them away, ashamed both of her undisciplined emotion and her lack of virtue.

"Lights Up The Sky," Squirrel Woman said in a calm voice, "I have time to listen."

Knowing her grandmother would ferret out the last ounce of truth anyway, Ellen told her the whole story, from beginning to end. She spared herself nothing, made no excuses for her weakness, and forced herself to look her grandmother in the eyes during the painful confession. At the end, Squirrel Woman nodded.

"This Paris must be a very strange place," she commented. "You should not have gone there when you were so young and stupid."

More tears overflowed onto Ellen's cheeks.

"Our people can be strange, also. When an unmarried woman opens her legs to a man and he plants a child, the people always blame the woman, and not the man. This is wrong, even though the people do it. I think it is wrong."

For a few minutes Squirrel Woman lay in silence, and Ellen wondered if she'd gone to sleep, but a close look showed the black eyes still gleaming deep within the wrinkled old face.

"Jordan is your husband now," she said abruptly. "He is your child's father."

Ellen shook her head. "He's going to leave."

Squirrel Woman reached out a shaking hand and put it on Ellen's stomach. "He is the father. Sometimes something strange happens, and the father of the spirit is not the father of the flesh. You must open your eyes and see what you hold in your hand, Lights Up The Sky. You no longer know where your heart is."

That was true enough, Ellen thought miserably.

"You must forgive yourself, and then your courage

will return. You are a smart woman, and a brave one. Like your mother Many Horses. Like your mother's mother Squirrel Woman. But you have forgotten who you are."

Ellen bit her lip in an attempt not to cry. "Do *you* forgive me, Grandmother?"

"I do not need to forgive you. You did nothing to me. You did something to yourself." The old woman squeezed her hand. "Go to your husband now. Remember that he is worthy to be a Blackfoot, just as you are."

Ellen rose, but before she lifted the blanket flap that blocked the door, Squirrel Woman called her name softly. "Nothing is easy," she said when Ellen turned. "All in life must be won with sweat and endurance. Remember that you are strong."

"Thank you, Grandmother."

Ellen hoped she was as strong and brave as Squirrel Woman thought she was.

Jordan was not in Crooked Stick's cabin when Ellen looked for him there. Katy was, however, with Tyrell and David.

"Jordan went down to the creek to wash—and did he ever need it!" Katy grimaced. "I told you he would be all right."

"Jonah hasn't come home yet?"

"Jonah will come. Don't worry about it. Pa's keeping an eye on him."

"Where's everyone else?"

"Olivia and Big Nose went to the agency. Olivia wanted to take a look at the new hospital, and Big Nose wanted to get some flour and bacon. Crooked Stick went to sit with Squirrel Woman for a while."

"Well, if nobody here needs me," Ellen said with a slight blush, "I think I'll go say hello to Jordan."

Katy's eyes twinkled. "You do that. Take an extra blanket with you. It's cold out."

Ellen found Jordan's clothing a quarter mile upstream from the family encampment. When she looked around and saw no sign of her husband, she grew worried. Then his head popped through the surface of a quiet pool at the far side of the creek.

"Jordan! That water's freezing! You're going to give yourself pneumonia."

"At least I'll be clean when they haul me off to the hospital." Jordan stroked to shallow water and stood up, unabashedly naked. "Don't get too close to those clothes. The smell alone could probably start an epidemic of some sort. Do you know how dirty a man can get sitting around the woods for three days meditating?"

Ellen smiled. "Yes, I do."

"It's not a pretty sight, or a pretty smell."

Jordan, on the other hand, was a very attractive sight as he walked through ankle-deep water toward the bank. They hadn't been alone together in a long while, and Ellen had almost forgotten what all that muscle and masculinity could do to her equilibrium. She tried not to stare as she handed him the blanket.

"Bathing naked in a freezing creek, Lord Chesterfield? Coming to America has certainly made you uncivilized."

"Is there anywhere else to bathe around here?"

"Not for about ten miles."

He used the blanket to dry himself, but he didn't seem in a hurry to cover himself with it. "You're blushing, Lady Chesterfield."

"I am not!"

"Then it must be the cold air turning your cheeks so red." His eyes crinkled with silent laughter. "There's a nice embankment over there in the trees that provides good shelter. I've just recently learned how warm a person can be on a cold day if he huddles somewhere out of the wind."

"Didn't you bring any clean clothes with you?" she said tartly.

He pointed to folded denims and a woolen shirt on a bush behind her.

"Well, put them on! You're going to catch cold. And you need to eat, and rest, and—"

"I'll tell you what I need." He wrapped the blanket around his lean hips. "In fact, just come over to that embankment with me and I'll show you what I need."

Her brows shot up as she caught the glint in his eye. "Out here in the cold?"

"I'll keep you warm," he offered with a smile.

"In broad daylight?"

"There's no one here to see us." He took her arm and led her to a brown, grassy hillock that did indeed shelter them from the cold wind. A few scraggly trees crowned the crest, and at the base, a bed of dead leaves awaited them. The air did seem much warmer out of the wind. In fact, when Jordan wrapped the blanket around both of them together, Ellen found herself getting quite warm indeed.

"This is not a good idea," she warned.

"Making love to you is always a good idea."

His kiss eliminated any need for further conversation. Together they sank down onto the bed of leaves. With an urgency that seemed almost desperate, he devoured her mouth and her throat. Touched by a kindred desperation, Ellen helped him unfasten the buttons of her shirt and push down her chemise to let him suckle at her breasts. Each stroke of his tongue sent a river of desire pulsing through her veins. Each touch of his hand made her ache with need, until she couldn't keep her own seeking hands from his naked body. When she found the center of his passion, he was hard and huge and hungry.

He groaned in both pain and ecstasy when she released him to try to wriggle out of her dress. "Don't stop now!"

"I want to undress."

"No. You'll get cold," he warned with a slightly mocking grin.

"And you're not?"

"I assure you, my lady, right now I am anything but cold."

She reached up and touched his cheek, running her finger over the black stubble that remained from his three-day vigil. "I want to feel you next to me."

"You will," he promised softly.

Arranging the blanket so it covered them both, he pushed up her skirt and ran his hand along her naked thigh. Her muscles clenched, then turned warm and liquid with the sheer joy of it. When his fingers eased inside her in intimate exploration, she was more than ready for him.

"Lord but I need you," he groaned. He kissed her with a hard urgency and entered her fully in one imperative thrust. Closing her eyes, she moved with him, soaring, gliding, higher than the clouds and warmer than the sun itself. Every empty space in soul and body was filled, every feeling nourished by a rain of joy. The journey was timeless, yet not long enough. The end was a bright culmination of emotion and fervor, but it was still an end. As they settled slowly back to the real world, Ellen held to Jordan as if he would slip out of her arms, and of her life, if she let him go. His face was buried in her hair, his body still buried in her flesh, when the cold finally started to intrude.

He wrapped the blanket more securely around them. "Are you chilled?" he whispered.

"No," she lied.

His hands still wandered over her hips and thighs, as if he couldn't get enough of the feel of her.

"You're tickling," she warned.

"Don't laugh. No! Ah, damn. You know what happens when you laugh."

Her laughter sputtered to a halt. "Jordan, I'm so glad you're back safely."

"So am I." His hands kept roaming. "You are getting very round, you know? Just how far along is this child of ours?"

Her face and feelings instantly fell.

"Our child, Ellen," he reminded her. Patting her stomach fondly, he speculated. "I can see her now, a dimpled little girl with glorious black hair and jewel-green eyes like her mother's, ready to twist every man's heart around her little finger. She'll have your looks and spunk, and—"

"And your name," Ellen finished with a wry smile. "And what if the baby's a boy?"

Jordan grinned. "If he's lucky, he'll be handsome and smart like me."

Ellen groaned with laughter, suddenly wishing with all her heart that the child she carried within her had grown from Jordan's seed. *Sometimes the father of the spirit is not the father of the flesh*, Squirrel Woman had said. That was a comforting notion, if a medically improbable one. But then, what did medicine know of the spirit, after all?

Suddenly, she wanted very much to believe what Squirrel Woman had said. "Jordan?" she asked hesitantly.

"Yes?"

"I have something to ask you—something big."

"All right. Ask."

"Will you stay with me until the baby is born?"

The silence made her heart drop.

"I know we've no plans to really live together, and you probably need to get back to England, but—"

A gentle finger across her lips stopped the flow of words. Jordan smiled down at her. "Of course I'll stay until the baby's born. It's what I always intended."

"Thank you," she breathed. "Thank you."

Jordan's hand continued to caress her belly, as if he could communicate somehow with the child that rested there. "It's quite daunting, really, to see this expand, week by week, and know there is an actual human being curled inside you, getting ready to start its life."

"It's already alive. I can feel it move inside me."

"It seems you should be much bigger."

"I will be," she told him ruefully. "I've seen plenty of women who scarcely show at all for months, then suddenly blow up like a whale."

"We're going to have to tell your family something before that happens."

"I'll tell them the truth soon. Katy already knows. Squirrel Woman also. That old woman has a way of weaseling things out of a person."

He chuckled. "She's remarkable."

"Yes, she is. She lived her whole life in a tipi, sleeping on the ground, cooking over an open fire. She's never seen a city, never been inside a church, a library, a museum, and can't even write her own name. Yet somehow she smarter and wiser than us all. Have you noticed that in all the distress and confusion surrounding her imminent death, she is the only one not confused or distressed?"

"You will miss her terribly, won't you?"

"I will. So will we all." Ellen grimaced, thinking of all the times she had taken Squirrel Woman's wisdom and guidance for granted. "She thinks you're worthy to be a Blackfoot, you know. That may not mean very much to an English baron who lives in a mansion with everyone around him addressing him as "my lord," but in Squirrel Woman's world, that's quite a compliment."

"It means something. Believe me."

To Ellen, just lying there with Jordan beneath the little hill with its scraggly trees, drawing in his warmth, inhaling the freshwater-clean scent of him, was almost as intimate as the act of love they'd just performed. Squirrel Woman was right. Jordan Chesterfield was a good man, and a strong one.

"What did you find out there in the woods?" she asked quietly. "Did you find a spirit totem to give you power?"

He was silent for a long moment, staring up at the winter-blue sky. Finally he smiled and drew her once again into his arms. His lips touched her ear in a soft whisper as his leg moved against her in intimate invitation. "Someday I'll tell you what I found out there, nosy woman. But right now I have other matters on my mind."

Jonah returned that evening, and though Katy had tried to hide any concern about her husband's absence, Ellen knew that her sister was relieved when he walked through the cabin door. Gabe returned a discreet two hours after Jonah. He held a brace of squirrels aloft as his excuse for being gone, but everyone knew that he and Crooked Stick had secretly kept watch over the twins' husbands, even as they had always tried to keep watch over the twins. Katy also seemed to be relieved when Squirrel Woman announced her approval of Jonah as a worthy mate for White Horse Woman.

"He is one who can bridle the wind," the old woman declared. "And the other is one who can look at still water and see more than his own reflection. Many Horses' daughters have found worthy husbands, and I am pleased."

Those were the last words Ellen heard her grandmother speak. Throughout the night Squirrel Woman would have no one in the tipi but her son Crooked Stick. By morning her spirit had traveled to the Sand Hills, where the Blackfoot go after death to take up a life much like the one they leave behind. Ellen hoped her grandmother would be as well loved in the next world as she was in this one.

Both Crooked Stick and his wife Big Nose cut their hair and smeared themselves with white clay from the creek bank. Only Jonah's intervention prevented Katy from doing the same. Ellen mourned in her own way, filling her mind with memories of Squirrel Woman as she helped Big Nose and Katy dress the old woman in her best clothes and prepare the body for burial. Gabe kept a confused and fussy David out of the way, and Olivia took charge of Tyrell while Katy did her last painful duty to her grandmother.

Squirrel Woman was laid to rest atop a grass-covered hill that looked out upon the mountains to the west and the plains to the east, where herds of buffalo had once provided Squirrel Woman with all she needed, and dictated the comings and goings of her life. The buffalo were gone, and now Squirrel Woman was gone as well. Somehow Ellen felt as though her grandmother's passing was the death knell of more than one old woman.

January hit Montana with a vengeance, sending air that was too cold and dry for snow whipping down from the arctic. It froze the ground, the creeks and lakes around Willow Bend, and the hands and faces of any who dared to venture out into its bite.

Fortunately, the foundation for the Chesterfield house was laid before the cold turned the ground hard as rock. The house was protected from the noise and bustle of town by a thick stand of pine trees, and it was only a short walk from Willow Bend's one hospital, which was owned and run by Dr. Rachel Olivia Baron O'Connell.

The cold did not stop the walls from being raised nor the roof laid, and many willing hands from Willow Bend volunteered to help with the labor. One week after New Year's Day, a house-raising party went to work before the tardy winter sun rose above the horizon. They swore they would have the walls and roof in place before the sun set in midafternoon.

Ellen and Olivia worked to prepare a communal meal at the home of a neighbor who had volunteered her spacious kitchen and dining room. A small army of women worked beside them. Katy sat on a stool at the kitchen table, occupying herself with tasks that didn't require any talent at cooking. She and Jonah had decided to stay in Montana until the birth of Ellen's baby.

The week they had gotten home from the reservation, Ellen had confessed—confessed to being pregnant, that is. Though she had vowed to be honest with her family, when she saw how happy everyone was with the prospect of another child in the family, she couldn't bring herself to tarnish their expectations with the ugly truth. The deception weighed on her heart, however. Squirrel Woman had expected her to be brave and true. Jordan had, also, though he didn't say a word about her lie of omission. She had disappointed them both. Worst of all, she had disappointed herself. She could rationalize to herself from dawn until dusk about sparing her family the grief, sparing her child the stigma, and the overrated value of stark, merciless truth, but the fact of the matter was that she was a coward, and she felt cowardly clear through to her marrow. She didn't know how she could put up with herself.

"Hey!" Katy objected. "Leave some potato when you peel those things. I'm the one who's supposed to be ham-handed at this, not you."

Ellen looked down at the fat potato peelings in the bowl and the brutally scalped potatoes on the platter. "Oh. Sorry."

"You all right?"

"Of course I'm all right. Why wouldn't I be?"

Katy shrugged. "When I was pregnant with Ty, sometimes it knocked me off center. I remember one day at the mine I was trying to fix a wagon wheel on one of the ore wagons, and I couldn't 've hit a nail on the head if I'd had a hammer the size of a steel plate."

"You shouldn't have been doing that kind of work while you were pregnant."

"Yeah? Well, I'm thinking you shouldn't be allowed to wield a knife while you're in the family way."

"Oh bother! I need to take a walk anyway!" Ellen

pulled on her coat and huffed out of the house, Katy's puzzled frown burning a hole in her back.

She walked the short distance to the half-built house, hoping the cold air and exercise would clear her mind. But seeing the construction only dampened her already low spirits. Jordan had insisted she needed a house of her own, and not just any house—one that was worthy of the Chesterfield name, or at least as worthy as possible in a place like Willow Bend. Ellen had told him she didn't need a house. A house, the clothes he'd bought her in New York, the money he'd deposited in her name in the bank—none of that had been part of their original bargain—a bargain in which she had bartered away her soul, she'd begun to think.

He wouldn't listen to her protests, of course. In some ways he was as stubborn as a Montana mule. She was his wife, he constantly reminded her, and he wouldn't have his wife being dependent on her relatives, even if she had taken a partnership in her mother's medical practice and would be earning her own way.

Of course, the family believed Ellen would be living in that new house with Jordan. They thought Jordan was staying, and Ellen didn't acquaint them with the impossibilities of that. He had neglected his estate, his business, and his political aspirations to deliver her home, and she knew he was sorely missed. Since returning from the reservation, he had received at least one telegram a week as well as several letters—one from New York, one from Endsfield Park, and the others from London. Ellen hadn't pried into what these communications said. It wasn't her affair, and she tried not to be concerned.

She was concerned, though. She was concerned that she was imposing on him far too long. She was concerned that he would unravel the fabric of her life when he left.

How would they explain it, she wondered, when her husband left? Would they stage a huge argument and have him stalk away, vowing never to return? Or would they simply say he needed to tend business in England? When he'd been gone long enough, everyone would slowly come to realize that something was wrong and he wasn't coming back. Or, if he did return, it would be a duty visit only, with no intent to make his home here.

Such thoughts made Ellen downright ill. Wearily, she sat herself on the stump of a pine tree near the construction and watched the men work. It was a rough and burly crew—friends and neighbors who had learned to love Olivia and respect Gabriel, who wanted Gabe's daughter, the new doctor in town, to have her own home. Amazingly enough, Jordan worked enthusiastically alongside them. If stuffy old Codgkins, the Chesterfield butler, could see his master now! He was laying tarpaper on the roof, crawling on hands and knees. His face had acquired a new crease or two since coming to Montana, creases from the glaring sun—bright even in the winter—and a wind that turned most men's faces to leather before they were forty. His exposed skin had turned brown, and his neatly tended hair had acquired the wind-blown look that was unavoidable in Montana. Ellen imagined that his laughter was heartier than it had been in England, his eyes brighter. Jordan looked, in fact, as if he'd been born and raised a Westerner. His gait had taken on a free-swinging, purposeful stride. He rode a western stock saddle as though he'd been doing it all his life. He had even gone so far as to rope a steer or two, with Gabe's coaching, and to beat Jonah at poker, which took very little talent but seemed to make Jordan proud all the same.

Ten more weeks she had with him. Ten more weeks until she would birth her baby, and he would have fulfilled his promise to stay. She would miss him terribly, Ellen acknowledged. His companionship had become too vital. Reaching for him in the middle of the night had become too much a habit.

"Haalloo over there!" came a call from the roof. Jordan had looked up from his work and spotted her.

She waved.

"When's dinner ready?" he shouted, and the shout was taken up by a dozen hungry men.

"Soon!" she assured them.

So down-to-earth, this scene. So full of camaraderie. It was enough to warm one's heart, if one really belonged here, if one weren't a false-hearted coward who didn't deserve all this kindness and warmth.

Ellen wrapped her coat around her and trudged toward the neighbor's house and its platoon of friendly, honest, hardworking women who had welcomed her back to Willow Bend because they didn't know what she really was. With every day that passed she was digging herself deeper into deception. Soon she wouldn't be able to look at herself in the mirror.

Lord but she wished she had never come back home.

From the half-finished rooftop of the house, Jordan paused in his labor and watched his wife trudge away. A solitary figure leaning into the cold wind, she looked lonely. He toyed with the notion of climbing down from the roof and going after her, but there was much work to be done if the house was to be finished before Ellen delivered.

"Don't worry about her so much." Jonah clumped up and sat down beside him. "Those girls are tougher than they look. Ellen's quiet. She doesn't toot her horn quite as much as Katy, but she'd made of the same stuff."

"She's tough, all right."

"Katy almost ran me ragged before she had the mercy to marry me. She didn't think much of a greenhorn from Chicago."

"I think it's safe to say that Ellen didn't think much of a stuffy baron from Staffordshire."

Turning his attention back to the job at hand, Jordan drove a nail, straight and true. He was constantly surprised at the satisfaction that went along with such a simple, mindless task. Holding up another nail, he told Jonah, "I never in my life drove a nail before I came here. Can you believe that?"

"I can believe it."

"That bad, am I?"

"On the contrary, you show rare talent as a common laborer."

Jordan laughed. "Four months ago if someone had made that statement, I would have counted it a mortal insult. Now, surprisingly, I find it quite gratifying."

"Amazing the changes that come to a man's life when he marries an O'Connell woman." Jonah picked up a nail and regarded it speculatively. "I've been meaning to ask you, Jordan. I do free-lance pieces for the *Chicago Record*, and the story of an English peer's impressions of one of the last outposts of the Old West would make a fine article. Especially since that lofty Old World personage married the daughter of a Montana ex-outlaw. That's the kind of stuff that the readers love. It wouldn't have to get too personal if you don't want, but I'd like to include something about you on the reservation. It's not every Englishman who'd sit under a tree with no food for three days just to please a dying old Indian woman."

"That's true," Jordan agreed. "Most Englishman have more sense." He sent Jonah an amused look. "Most Chicagoans, also, I'd wager."

Jonah grinned. "*Record* readers would rather read about an Englishman, believe me. The story would make damned good reading."

"More than you know," Jordan said cryptically.

"Think about it." Jonah patted the roof of the house. "I know where to find you."

A good story, indeed, Jordan thought as Jonah clumped off and he went back to work nailing tarpaper. He just wished he knew how the story was going to end. The old ending didn't fit anymore—the one with him going back to England to enjoy the advantages of being officially unavailable, and Ellen staying in Montana with the security of her status as a married woman. That logical, sane ending didn't take into account the feelings that had ignited inside him the time Ellen had first stumbled into his life, wet and bedraggled as a half-drowned cat, feelings that had grown every time she had confronted him, stood up to him, or extended the hand of friendship. He had fooled himself into believing that he had married her for practical, benevolent reasons. A ridiculous notion, really, but living in English Society made one rather good at fooling oneself.

The self-deception might have continued indefinitely if not for those three dreadful days under a pine tree on the Blackfoot reservation. It was amazing what a man discovered when he was isolated for such a long period with only his own thoughts for company. No Indian totem or spirit had stopped by to make his acquaintance, and his only visions were those prompted by hunger—usually visions of Cook's steaming kidney pies or a sizzling beef roast just out of the oven.

In spite of his inborn English skepticism, however, he had eventually been forced to look inward. While keeping company with oneself under those circumstances, hiding becomes impossible. He made some discoveries that surprised him—about himself, his life, his ambitions, what was important, and what wasn't. What he hadn't learned was how to act upon those discoveries.

He'd better learn, he told himself as he drove another nail. Ellen's house would be completed in a few weeks, and Ellen's time would come in a few weeks more. He could fall back onto the old plan—inadequate, but easy. Or he could make some changes and take some chances.

Either way, he didn't have much time to decide.

CHAPTER 20

The month was late January and the day was the coldest day of the year so far. Willow Bend's hospital had been quiet all morning. With the temperature at fifteen below zero and the wind lively enough to kick up whirlwinds of dry snow and snap the flag at the train station back and forth like a whip, most people had decided that their ills could wait for a warmer day to be treated.

There were a few brave exceptions. Olivia had done a tooth extraction that morning with Ellen assisting. Willow Bend had no dentist, so the O'Connell doctors had to fill in where needed. Since starting to work in her stepmother's practice, Ellen had needed to round out her medical education by digging into texts on dentistry and veterinary medicine. Sometimes it seemed as though she treated more horses than people.

The morning's only other patient was a man who had sliced his knee open with an ax. Ellen had cleaned and stitched the wound under Olivia's watchful eye, then sent the fellow home. That left them with an empty waiting room and not much to do. Of the ten beds in the hospital, only two were occupied, and those patients required more rest than medical care.

"Why don't you go back home and keep Katy from destroying the kitchen?" Olivia suggested to Ellen. "She said something about fixing dinner for the men, since this is Sarah's day off."

"Heaven forbid. It's a good thing Katy and Jonah found gold in the Klondike. It gives them enough money to hire household help so Katy doesn't have to cook and clean."

Olivia smiled. "Katy's talents lie elsewhere. And speaking of talent, Ellen, that was a fine job you did on Mr. Grayson's knee. I couldn't have done it better myself."

"Thank you."

"I'm really glad you're back. Your father and I miss you girls dreadfully. It's going to be wonderful to have at least one of you settling down close to home. I understand Jordan is interested in investing in the railroad system."

"That's what he says. His mother despairs of his interest in business. Among their set, making money from business and trade is considered quite plebian, you know?"

Olivia laughed. "You don't say! When I studied in Paris, I didn't get to mingle with the nobility. And here you up and marry one."

"Yes," Ellen replied softly.

"Jordan seems to be a very fine man, though. Even your father has warmed up to him, and unlike Jonah, it didn't take a fistfight to win him over—thank heaven!"

"Jordan is a good man. You wouldn't believe how good." A train whistle lured Ellen to the window to watch the noon train roll into the station. The engine belched great billows of steam that froze instantly to anything it touched. The whole area around the station was coated in ice.

"I don't really feel up to the ride back to the ranch right now," Ellen told her stepmother. "Why don't I stay here and you go back to save the kitchen from Katy? When Mrs. Eldridge comes this afternoon, I'll ask her husband to drive me home."

"Are you all right?"

"I'm fine. Just not used to carrying this much of a load with me every day." Ellen patted her stomach fondly. Sometime in the last month she had come to think of this child as hers and Jordan's. Not because she was delusional. Unfortunately, she remembered every unpleasant detail of the baby's conception, but she had come to realize the wisdom of Squirrel Woman's words. A moment of selfish passion did not constitute fatherhood. By giving the child a name and the dignity of legitimate birth, by standing beside her and watching the baby make its presence known week by week, Jordan had earned the right to be considered the child's true father. Even when he left to go back to England, he would be more her child's father than Henri Chretiens ever would be.

Olivia put on her coat, gloves, and hat. "If you'd rather stay, Ellen, that's fine. As quiet as it is today, maybe you can get a nap. That's more than you'd be able to do at home with David and Tyrell underfoot and the men debating what kind of flooring should go into your new house. I'll bring in some wood for the stove before I go."

"I can do that."

"No, you can't," Olivia said sternly. "You're going to

start taking it easy if I have to tell Jordan to tie you to your bed."

"Oh, he would love that!" she blurted out, then promptly turned red.

Olivia laughed. "Jordan, too? I thought your father was the only man who found pregnant women attractive."

After Olivia had gone, Ellen checked on the little hospital's two current patients, a woman with pneumonia and a man whose arm had been amputated by a whipsaw. They both slept. The temptation to do the same was irresistible. It seemed to Ellen that she'd been tired for at least a month. From scarcely showing her pregnancy at all at five months, she'd blown up to whale proportions at six, or so it seemed to her. Her feet and back constantly hurt. She was always hungry, frequently cranky, and her energy bounced between frantic and none at all. Right now she had none at all, so a nap would be in good order.

She put more wood into the cast-iron stove and was turning down the bed in Olivia's office when she heard the door to the waiting room open.

"Wouldn't you know?" she grumbled, pulling her apron back on.

The man had his back to her when Ellen walked into the waiting area. He was looking out a window at the town, which on a day this cold was so quiet it could have been a ghost town. He wasn't a local, Ellen noted. No one in Willow Bend would wear such an elegantly cut suit or the fine wool overcoat and expensive homburg that hung on the coat tree.

"May I help you?" she inquired.

The man turned, and Ellen's jaw dropped.

"Hello, Ellen. You're looking very well."

Ellen's mouth flapped several times before she could get a word out. "Henri! How . . .? Where . . .? What on earth are you doing in Willow Bend?"

His smile was just as charming as it had ever been, and his eyes twinkled as they regarded the pearlike shape she could no longer camouflage. He had a boyish insouciance about him, even though he was in his mid-thirties. When they had first met, that devil-may-care manner had reminded Ellen of her father. The difference, she had discovered, was that Gabriel O'Connell had character beneath his careless boyishness. Henri didn't.

"What are you doing here?" she demanded more firmly.

"That should be obvious, my love. I just came in on the train, searching for you. Willow Bend, Montana, is certainly out of the way, isn't it? But it's charming, in a rustic sort of way. Is it always this cold?"

"Of course it is, Henri. We have our Fourth of July picnics ice skating on the pond over there."

He didn't bat an eyelash at her caustic tone. "Still sharp-tongued and sharp-witted, I see. That's my Ellen."

She raised one brow.

"Aren't you going to offer me a seat?"

Ellen folded her arms across her chest and regarded him uncharitably. "Sit if you like."

"Ah. Thank you." He dusted off a wooden chair—as if it needed it—and sat. "I can understand why you're not greeting me with open arms. I fear I treated you quite badly. There's really no excuse for it."

"You're a worm, Henri."

His expression was a study in artful regret. "An overly colorful description, *peut-être*, but I suppose my behavior merits it. Aren't you going to sit?"

"No."

"You look quite uncomfortable, *cherie*, standing there like that."

"I'm fine. Are you going to tell me why you've come looking for me?"

"*Vraiment*, Ellen, I had an attack of conscience. After you left I realized not only how wrong I'd been, but how much I had lost with you gone. I have missed you terribly."

"Is that so?"

"*Oui*. That is so, *mon coeur*. I bid farewell to Patricia and investigated the clinic files to discover where you would go. I eased my conscience, and my heart, by taking a vow to find you and make things right. You are carrying my child, after all, and you have had possession of my heart since the day we first met. In brief, *ma cherie* Ellen, I've made the journey here to seek your hand in marriage."

Six months ago his proposal would have been Ellen's dream come true. Three months ago it would have been a shaky port in a very stormy sea. Now, she not only didn't want Henri, she didn't believe him.

"You want to marry me," she summarized dubiously.

"It is what I just said, *non*? I will kneel before you if you like." He regarded her quizzically, as if he didn't understand why she wasn't weeping with joy. Then he smiled in comprehension. "Poor Ellen. I can understand your anger, but you must believe I will make it up to you—everything I've put you through."

"You broke off an engagement with the heiress of your dreams in order to run after an unsophisticated, unconnected American whom you bedded once and declared laughably inept as a lover."

"Ellen, you mustn't speak so of yourself."

"I didn't. You did."

His smile was becoming strained. "It was only a bit of fond teasing. A tasteless joke, I'll admit."

In Ellen's opinion, Henri himself was a tasteless joke. Why had she ever thought this man attractive? He was as easy to see through as a glass window. "I think I know why you're here, Henri."

"Of course you do, *mon coeur*. I just explained."

"Patricia found out what kind of man you really are, didn't she? Since my condition is a matter of record at the clinic, maybe she even found out you'd gotten one of your students pregnant. She broke off with you, didn't she, you horse's ass!"

"Horse's what? Really, Ellen—!"

"Didn't she?"

"What does it matter who broke off with whom?"

"Then you went searching through the clinic student files and discovered that my father owns one of the larger private holdings in Montana and my sister has an address in Dawson, which is in the middle of Canada's richest gold territory. You thought you could recoup what you'd just lost. Isn't that it?"

"One in my position must always pay attention to financial advantage, Ellen. It's true I've had some expenses. A gentleman must maintain a certain way of life, you know, if he's not to be written off by Those Who Matter. But truly, *mon amour*, the money was secondary. If you hadn't a cent, I would still stand by you. You must believe that."

It was Ellen's turn to smile. "It doesn't matter what I believe, Henri. I'm already married."

Henri's expression hardened to disbelief. "Married? How could you be married?"

"It's done in a ceremony with licenses and witnesses and the like." Ellen was beginning to enjoy herself.

"Who would marry a woman who is pregnant with another man's child?"

"Someone kind and honorable."

"Unforgivable! You didn't tell him, did you?"

"I told him."

"And he married you? I don't believe it. No man would marry a woman still wet with another man's seed."

Ellen clenched her teeth at Henri's vulgarity. Suddenly the sound of his voice made her ill. "Get out. Get out now."

He stood, his back stiff as a ramrod. "I do not think so. Not just yet."

"I said get out."

"I have not traveled halfway around the world for a bride to go away empty-handed! I offer you my name and my honor, and you give me insults in return. How could you marry another man while you carried my child? What kind of woman are you?"

Ellen shook her head. "I don't believe this."

"Well, *ma petite*, believe this. I can make life very uncomfortable for you. *Oui*! I can."

"What are you going to do, Henri?"

"You think you are safe behind another man's name? You think you will fool people into believing you are a chaste, respectable woman? I will ensure you fail. I will embarrass you. I will embarrass the man who was fool enough to marry you. And I will embarrass your family. Who knows, I might even decide that I would like to have my offspring. Children are a man's immortality, after all. I'm not sure I want a child of mine raised in such an uncouth place as this."

Ellen's stomach knotted. "You *are* a pathetic worm."

"I am not a worm! I am a man scorned! You have betrayed me, Ellen, and I will have my revenge."

"You have a twisted view of just who betrayed whom. But I suppose you know how illogical your accusations are, don't you. All these histrionics are simply leading to money, aren't they?"

He looked down his nose in supercilious condescension. "I might consider settlement of my debts a just recompense."

"And those debts amount to how much?"

"In the dollars of *les Etats-Unis*, twenty thousand."

Ellen stared at him in horror. "Twenty thousand dollars? Where do you think I would get that kind of money?"

"Your father, I'm sure, would want to preserve his daughter's reputation and keep his grandchild near."

"Leave my father out of this. He doesn't have that kind of money."

"Your sister, then. She has a gold mine?"

"My sister would probably shoot you rather than pay you, Henri. And I'm not sure I wouldn't help her hide the evidence."

"Where you get the funds is not my affair, *cherie*. I have said what must be said. Now I will leave you to think upon your choices. Tomorrow at this time I will attend you here to receive your answer. Until then, *au revoir*, Ellen."

She watched him march out, then collapsed into the nearest chair. What in heaven's name was she going to do now?

It was dark when Mr. Eldridge, the husband of the hospital's night nurse, dropped Ellen off in the yard of the

Thunder Creek Ranch. At this time of year, the sun set in the midafternoon, and the night seemed to stretch on forever. Ellen felt as though the dark night of her life was stretching on forever as well. Just as she began to think dawn was within reach, it wasn't. Right now, Ellen felt as though her sun might never again rise.

"There ye be, Dr. Chesterfield." Mr. Eldridge chuckled. He'd known Katy and Ellen since they were thirteen, and he thought it a great jest to address each of them by their grown-up titles. "Ye get some rest now, gal. Ye're lookin' poorly."

"Yes, Mr. Eldridge. Will you come in for a cup of coffee?"

"Naw. I'll be gettin' back to the hospital and haulin' in some wood for the missus. Cold weather like this, a body needs to keep that stove roarin'. You just say heidee to yore ma and pa fer me."

"I will. Thanks for the ride."

"Anytime."

He clucked to his team and headed toward the road. Ellen watched until the darkness swallowed the wagon and mules, then she turned to face the house, wishing for an excuse—any excuse—not to go in. She'd spent the whole day since Henri's visit watching nightmare visions march through her imagination. Jordan's gesture of marrying her was going to be for naught; her reputation was going to be shattered into a million pieces. Her mother's medical practice was sure to suffer. Her whole family would be the brunt of jokes from Montana to St. Louis. Worse, Henri might try to take her child. A father's right to his child was held to be sacred by many courts. He might succeed if he tried. She could bear embarrassment and humiliation, but she couldn't bear to lose the little life that was growing inside her.

Now she had no choice but to tell her family the entire truth. She had her back against the wall, and there was no place to go. No escape.

You will find your courage, Squirrel Woman had predicted. Ellen didn't feel a shred of courage within her, only desperation.

Olivia greeted Ellen in the entry hall with a cup of hot chocolate. "Heaven's sake, Ellen. You're white as a sheet! You're not frostbitten, are you?"

"No." She took a grateful sip of sweet warmth.

Katy came out of the living room, Tyrell riding one slender hip. One look at Ellen's face brought a scowl to her face. "What's wrong? What's happened?"

Trust Katy to know instantly that something was wrong. "Are Pa and Jordan here?"

"They're upstairs with Jonah, washing. They just came in from the north pasture."

"Would you ask them to come down? I . . . I have something to say to all of you."

Olivia shot her a worried look. "Let me get you another chocolate while you take off your things."

"Thank you," Ellen said listlessly. Feeling numb, she peeled off her coat, gloves, and woolen scarf and went into the living room to wait.

Once they were all gathered, the silence in the room could have been cut with a knife. Beside her, Jordan raised a quizzical brow in her direction. She tried to smile at him, but she couldn't. Unable to meet his eyes, she took a deep breath and launched into the recital she had rehearsed at least a dozen times on the wagon ride home.

Telling her family how severely she had stumbled was one of the hardest things Ellen had ever done. She spared herself nothing and presented Henri's threat as unemotionally as possible. Though she tried to paint Jordan's part in the drama in a positive light, her family shot him cool looks as she explained the circumstances of their marriage. Naturally they would be hurt that the man they had begun to think of as family had married her as a convenience—no matter that the marriage had been of more benefit to her so far than to him.

At the end, she was proud of herself for getting through the grim story without tears, and ashamed that she hadn't had the courage to reveal the truth earlier. Her family was silent and stunned. Jordan sat beside her looking grave. Ellen knew if she stayed with them one more minute she would disgrace herself with a flood of tears. Mumbling an inarticulate plea to be excused, she fled.

Alarmed, Jordan shot up to follow Ellen, but Katy got to the door first. Ellen's twin was so like her, and yet so unlike her, that Jordan always felt a bit unnerved in her presence—a feeling that was rare for him. The cool look Katy gave him as she blocked the door from the living room let him know he was no longer on her list of favorite brothers-in-law, even though he was her only brother-in-law.

"I'll go to her," Katy told him. "She needs *me* now."

Jordan didn't dispute her. Ellen needed the reassurance of her family more than she needed him. From him she needed protection, and he bloody well intended to provide it.

Apparently he was not the only one who felt that way. As Katy ran after Ellen, Gabe rose slowly from his seat. This was a Gabriel O'Connell Jordan hadn't seen before. He and Ellen's father had had their tense moments, but he'd never seen the man look quite so deadly. Jordan understood finally why Ellen had called her father a relic. He certainly wasn't a relic in age or infirmity; he was a throwback to a time when a man didn't survive in this country without having a gun on his hip and steel in his soul.

"I'm going to take that French pissant sidewinder apart with my bare hands," he said in a chillingly matter-of-fact tone.

Olivia was apparently undaunted by the violence in her husband's eyes. "No you're not, Gabriel. If you can't confront the man without resorting to your fists or a gun, then let someone else confront him."

"Let me handle him!" Jonah offered grimly. "I've got a lawyer friend back in Chicago who'll know the lay of the land as far as whether or not this snake can really get his hands on Ellen's baby. And he'll know what we can do about it if he tries." He grinned. "Sometimes it takes a big city boy to deal with another big city boy."

"I think perhaps Ellen should go with Katy to your place in Seattle," Olivia suggested to Jonah. "I don't want her to be within reach of this Frenchman. She's had a hard enough time of it as it is."

For a few minutes the three of them tossed suggestions back and forth. Not once did anyone ask for Jordan's input, but he was not about to be ignored. Ellen was his wife, and no one threatened what was his without hearing directly from him.

"I think you're forgetting who has the most say about where Ellen goes and what steps are taken to protect her."

Three sets of eyes turned on him. Olivia frowned speculatively. Gabriel scowled. Jonah's expression was merely cautious.

"I'm not entrusting my daughter's protection to a stranger," Gabe declared.

"I'm not a stranger. I'm her husband."

Olivia's tone was friendlier than Gabe's, but still cool. "You must admit, Jordan, the circumstances of your marriage cast some doubt about your commitment to Ellen."

"Anyone who knows me well would never doubt my commitment to anything that is mine."

"She's not the hell yours!" Gabriel proclaimed.

"The bloody hell she's not."

Olivia regarded Jordan thoughtfully. "We'll see. Maybe we should ask Ellen just what she wants to do about this."

Jonah grinned. "Ask Ellen. That's a novel idea."

"It would be better done tomorrow," Olivia advised, "when she's calmer and more rested."

Gabe glared at Jonah, then turned his ice chip eyes back to Jordan. Jordan almost smiled. He couldn't fault Ellen's family for wanting to take Henri Chretiens apart both legally and physically. But he had no intention of letting anyone but himself deal with the miscreant. He'd been wanting to get that jackass within reach for a long time.

Ellen threw herself on her bed and gave vent to feelings she had held inside all day. Amid streams of tears, she sobbed, she beat the pillows, she kicked the mattress with her feet—a good, old-fashioned tantrum like the ones she had thrown as a little girl. Or so she was told. She didn't remember, because she hadn't exploded like this since she was five. Right now, though, she deserved a tantrum, and she was damned well going to indulge in a good one.

When it was over, she felt marginally better. At least the tears were gone, the anger and frustration vented.

She hugged a pillow to her and buried her face in its downy softness. It smelled of Jordan—a comforting, welcome, even arousing scent. How would he take this turn in events? she wondered morosely. His reputation would be caught in a bind almost as much as hers if the world found out he had knowingly married a woman who carried another man's child. Henri might even go so far as to dun Jordan for money once he found out just whom Ellen had married.

She moaned as a fresh wave of self-disgust washed over her. How had she ever believed herself in love with Henri Chretiens? He was handsome and clever. He was—in spite of his lack of character—a talented physician. He was well read, well spoken, well educated, well bred, and a total, absolute, unrelenting libertine. Why hadn't she seen that? Henri had never loved her, not even a little. He had merely used her and thrown her away. It was her fault. She had allowed it. She had thought she was in love.

Love! She hadn't known what love was. Love was not handsome, clever, or witty. Love was not flowers and romantic poems. Love was not stupid declarations of fate and passion. Love was steady, kind, and caring. Love could read your heart and mind. Love was— Jordan.

All this time she had believed she couldn't be in love with two men at the same time. She was right. Henri had never owned her heart. That's why she had given it to Jordan. She had thought it was friendship she felt for her husband, a particularly warm friendship paired with an impossibly eager passion. Perhaps that's what love was, after all. Friendship wedded to desire.

She loved Jordan. Her heart had known for a long time, but she had refused to admit it to herself. There was nothing complicated or confusing about it. She loved Jordan Chesterfield. Not that it mattered much. He cared for her, Ellen was sure, but they had their bargain, and he'd only stayed with her this long because he was kind, and she had practically begged him to remain until her child was born. What would he do now?

"Is the tantrum over?" asked Katy's voice.

Ellen lifted her tear-stained face from the pillow. Her twin stood at the door. "For now it is," Ellen replied with a sorry attempt at a smile.

Katy came in and sat down on the bed. "You want to talk?"

Ellen sighed and sat up. "What is there to say? I really messed up."

"Well, yeah."

"You used to tease me for being such a smug little Miss Perfect. Remember? You said I was too cowardly to ever do anything wrong."

Katy gave her a twisted smile. "I only said that because I was too cowardly to ever try doing something right. At least, I was afraid to try the things *you* did right. Things that women were supposed to do."

"We were a pair, weren't we?"

"Still are," Katy said firmly.

"Who would have thought that I would be the one to make all the mistakes? You were always the wild one who had everyone tearing out their hair."

"You don't exactly have the market cornered on mistakes," Katy reminded her.

"At least you never made a total pathetic fool out of yourself."

At that statement, Katy laughed heartily. "You don't think so? Don't say that to Jonah! I acted like such a jackass around him before I finally admitted that I loved him. And that I needed him."

"And now you have a beautiful son—and a husband who adores you."

Ellen felt the pressure of renewed tears at the sympathy she saw in her sister's face. Katy reached out and pulled her against her shoulder.

"Go ahead and cry," she advised. "You have a right."

Ellen didn't need the invitation. She was already making a wet mess of Katy's shirt. All the time they had been together, they had argued, celebrated, argued, plotted together, argued, worked together, and argued some more. They had delighted in taking potshots at each other's talents, character, intelligence, and ambitions. They had pulled each other's hair, and once Katy had blackened Ellen's eye. But they had always, always loved each other. And never had Ellen looked at her sister's face and seen pity there. Never until tonight, that is.

"Ellen, you're going to have a beautiful baby," Katy said. "And if that frigging Frenchman lifts a finger to make life difficult for you, I'll personally introduce him to Montana justice."

Ellen's tears dribbled to a halt. "Katy, you'll do no such thing!"

"And I'll get rid of that egotistical Englishman as well."

"You leave Jordan alone!"

Ellen's fervent tone earned her an inquisitive look from her sister—and a satisfied smile. "So that's the lie of the land, is it?"

"What?"

"You're in love with him."

Ellen sniffed. "Jordan is not your business. He has

every right to go back to England alone, Katy. He married me because he didn't want a wife."

"That makes sense!" Katy scoffed.

"And I needed only a husband's name, not a husband."

"That was then," Katy reminded her logically. "And this is now."

"Leave Jordan alone, Katy. Don't bother him."

"Me bother Jordan?" Katy replied with an innocent smile. "I wouldn't dream of it."

CHAPTER 21

Next morning, the coffee steaming on the stove was only marginally hotter than the tempers at the kitchen table, where Jordan sat opposite Katy over early-morning coffee and toast. The rest of the house still slept, and outside the kitchen window, the predawn was black as night.

"I think it's the perfect solution," Katy insisted.

"It's a naive, childish, inadequate solution," Jordan said impatiently.

"Why? He's got to be hooked on gambling to run up all those debts, right?"

"Perhaps, but there are plenty of vices other than gambling that can put a gentleman in debt."

Katy waved those possibilities aside. "I'll simply dangle the chance to win a good amount of money playing poker with a local rube, lead him on for a few hands, then wham! I've got him where I want him."

"And where would that be?"

"If I had my way, it would be flopping like a fish at the end of a hanging rope," Katy said with deceptive sweetness. "But I'll settle for having him so far in debt to me that he'll swear to leave Ellen alone."

Jordan sighed. "First of all, Katy, I'd doubt you'd win, no matter how good you are. I have no doubt that a scoundrel of Henri's caliber cheats."

"You think I don't?"

He gave her a narrow look. "And even if you extracted such a promise, it would mean absolutely nothing. He wouldn't feel obligated to honor it."

"He'd have to honor it. In Montana we have ways of dealing with welchers, ways that encourage people to pay up."

"Henri's not a Montanan; he's a Frenchman. There's a world of difference."

"He's in Montana now. We don't pussyfoot around with scum like him. Hell! If I had my way, I'd stuff that cow turd in a feed sack, haul him up to the Stillwater Range, and leave him there. He wouldn't be nearly so feisty when he found his way out—if he found his way out."

Jordan sighed. "This isn't the Wild West anymore, Katy."

"The hell it's not!" she grumbled.

"You stay away from Henri Chretiens. You'll only get yourself into trouble and cause Ellen and your family embarrassment. I'll take care of the scoundrel, I assure you."

Katy's face reddened. She had never liked being told what to do, and being chided by Jordan Chesterfield, who had the temerity to use her sister Ellen as a decoy wife, didn't set well at all. If the man didn't have smarts enough to be head over heels in love with a gem like Ellen, then he was sorely lacking in both brainpower and guts—both of which were going to be needed to deal with this slimy Frenchman.

"Don't put yourself out," she advised snidely. "You've fulfilled your part of the bargain with Ellen, after all."

"Katy, whatever is between me and Ellen is not your concern."

"But of course!" she sneered. "*Your* lordly honor can be tarnished here as well, can't it? You wouldn't want it to get around that the redoubtable Lord Chesterfield took another man's leavings."

"That's enough, Katy. Show some respect for your sister."

"I have all sorts of respect for my sister. That's why *I* will deal with Henri Chretiens!"

"And I'm telling you to leave him to me!"

Ellen paused on the stairs, out of sight but definitely within hearing of the two in the kitchen. She had so many defenders, it seemed, that they were fighting over who was going to get the honor of protecting her. She stayed where she was as tempers rose and words flew, unwillingly to make the situation even more awkward by putting in an appearance. Silently, she turned and climbed back up the stairs to her room, where she curled herself into a tight ball upon her bed and wondered what to do.

The night had granted Ellen very little sleep. Whys and what-ifs had paraded through the darkness until she thought she might scream, and when she had finally dozed, even the warm reassurance of being safe in the circle of Jordan's arms could not keep the nightmares at bay. And now she cowered on her bed while downstairs, people who cared about her argued over how to handle her problems. *Her* problems. She was at the center of all this confusion and furor; she was the focal point of the threats, the disgrace, the anger, the sympathy. She, and she alone.

So why was she cowering like a rabbit in its hole? Why was she dumping her burdens on people who had no part in creating them? Why had she let one instance of naive stupidity—enormous blunder though it was— poison her spirit so that she sat helpless and crying while others shouldered the load she by rights should carry?

Reluctant to face herself, Ellen nevertheless stood up and gazed into the mirror. The face that stared back at her had once been vibrant and glowing. The eyes had shone with confidence and humor. The mouth had been so accustomed to smiling that it had naturally curved upward. Where was that girl—the Ellen O'Connell of a year ago—in the pale and sorry visage that stared from the mirror?

"You're a poor excuse for an O'Connell," Ellen told her reflection. "Or a Chesterfield, either, for that matter. To hell with all this pining. You're going to tell Henri Chretiens a thing or two, and he's going to listen, dammit. And then you're going to have this baby and be the best damned mother this side of the Mississippi River, and the best doctor. And if people want to turn up their noses at such a fine person, it'll be their loss, won't it?"

She felt a warm surge of life travel through her veins. She had let the current of her mistakes carry her, passive and self-pitying, far too long. It was past time to fight back.

Before she lost her newfound determination, Ellen gathered her heavy coat, gloves, and scarf. Willow Bend only boasted one hotel, so Henri wouldn't be hard to find—if she could just manage to slip away from the ranch without the two early birds downstairs noticing.

As dawn began to turn the sky a pale gray, Jordan and Katy still sat in the kitchen arguing.

"You are one of the stubbornest men I have ever met!" Katy told Jordan in a furious tone.

"And you have to be the most pigheaded female on this side of the Atlantic. With the possible exception of your sister," he growled.

"If you had really cared about Ellen you would have married her for real."

"Ellen and I are about as real as it gets."

"For chrissakes, you know what I mean!"

"Your sister didn't want a full-time, permanent husband, Katy."

"You should know better than listen to what she says!"

"This is getting us nowhere."

Katy gave Jordan an assessing look. He was a blockhead. Almost as much of a blockhead as her father and Jonah. Indeed, he had possibilities of fitting into the family just fine. "All right, let's compromise. I'll give you a chance to handle the French skunk. But if you don't send him running with his tail between his legs, then I'm taking over."

"Believe me, Katy, when Henri Chretiens slinks away from here, he won't have a tail to tuck between his legs. I'll see to that."

Katy suppressed a smile. Montana was definitely rubbing off on Ellen's husband.

"Now to find the sorry beggar."

"Willow Bend has only one hotel," Katy suggested.

"Take Hammerhead into town. He's fast. And he won't throw you in a ravine on the way."

Katy only smiled at the sour look Jordan sent her way as he marched out the door, looking ready to do his worst, whatever the worst was for an English nobleman.

"What do you know," she said to herself. "The fish is hooked without even knowing it."

When Ellen had been a girl, Willow Bend's Grand Hotel had seemed like the height of luxury. The lobby had claw-foot chairs with carved arms and velveteen upholstery; the floor was softened by a flowered wool carpet that stretched almost from wall to wall, and a huge stone fireplace boasted a split log mantel that was the prettiest thing she had ever seen. The mantel was still beautiful, Ellen noted, but now, to eyes that had seen truly grand hotels on both sides of the Atlantic, the rest of Willow Bend's only public accommodations looked sadly shabby.

"Ellen O'Connell!" The night clerk greeted her when she walked in. "Welcome home, girl. What brings you out this early? It's cold enough to freeze whiskey right in the barrel."

Seth Graham manned the desk, Ellen was relieved to discover. She had hoped it would be Seth, who'd been sweet on her since a certain barn dance at the McGrady's place seven years past. Seth Graham would probably stand on his head and whistle a tune if she asked him to.

"Hello, Seth. I had to come into town to check on a patient, and I thought I'd drop in and say hi." Ellen felt only mildly guilty about the lie. When she finished with Henri, he might well be someone's patient. "Actually," she admitted with a little smile, "I was hoping the hotel kitchen would be open so I could get some hot coffee. You're right about it being cold out there."

"I'll bring you some coffee," Seth volunteered eagerly. "You just set yourself and warm up a spell."

"Oh thank you, Seth!"

Once the clerk was gone, it took Ellen only moments to locate Henri's name on the register and find the extra room key behind the desk. When Seth returned with a cup of steaming coffee, she was seated innocently on the settee, congratulating herself on a well-executed piece of mischief worthy of the redoubtable Katy. She drank the coffee with aplomb, then excused herself to the facilities upstairs. Seth anxiously provided directions. After all, what man in his right mind would deny an obviously pregnant woman access to a water closet?

Ellen paused before the door marked 203, letting the anger that had been brewing for months—anger both at herself and Henri—come to a rolling boil. Then she carefully fitted her pilfered key into the lock and let herself in. Henri was sprawled across his bed in a tangle of bedcovers, his bare legs sticking out like hairy white pipe-cleaners below the hem of a rumpled nightshirt. The sight brought back memories that made Ellen's stomach rise into her throat. Standing as far away as the door, she could smell the soured liquor and cigar smoke on his breath.

Here lay the father of her baby. Here lay the man who had discarded her for a wealthier woman and made her feel like the world was coming to an end. How could she have been so stupid?

Of course, first thing in the morning isn't the most flattering time for anyone, but still, Ellen couldn't help compare Henri to Jordan. Henri, she concluded, was pathetic.

"Henri!" she said firmly. "Wake up, you jackass."

Henri grunted and rolled over. One eye slitted open.

"Wake up, Dr. Chretiens. We have a bit of surgery to do this morning."

"Eh?" The one eye opened wider. When he recognized her, Henri came fully awake with a visible start. "Ellen!"

"That's me."

"What . . . how did you get in? The door was locked."

She held up the key. "I stole it."

Henri grabbed the covers and scrambled up to a sitting position. He regarded her from suspicious, bleary eyes. "That was very quick, *ma cherie*. Have you the money so soon?"

"No, Henri. There will be no money."

He scowled. "Do not push me, Ellen."

"Don't push you. Really? You're doing a great deal of pushing. Why are you the only one allowed to have fun?"

He gave his head a quick little shake, as if to clear his ears. "You are not making sense."

"I'm making the first sense I've made in months," she said with a smile. It was amazing how good this felt—the confusion on Henri's face, the uncertainty in his voice. Ellen decided she could learn to enjoy being a bitch. "As I said, Dr. Chretiens, we're going to do a bit of surgery this morning."

"What do you mean?"

"I'm going to excise you from my life, Henri. Once and for all. Like a tumor. A malignant tumor."

The sudden light of fear brightened his eyes. He leapt from the bed and backed toward the wall. "What is your little mind thinking, *ma cherie*?"

She advanced on him mercilessly. "My little mind is

thinking what an overripe, stinking piece of filth you are. You use people as though they were put on earth merely for your pleasure and convenience. You've taken the gifts God gave you—intelligence, looks, health, and talent—and squandered them just so you could satisfy your lust, greed, and sense of self-importance. Henri Chretiens, you are a walking, talking lesson in the sad consequences of irresponsibility and self-indulgence."

He shrugged eloquently, calmer now that he saw her only weapon was her sharp tongue. "One has but one life, *non*? Perhaps what you say is true, *cherie*. But that does not remove us from the situation we find ourselves in."

"I'm removing myself from the situation. If you tell the whole world that you are the father of my child, then I will trumpet it even louder. Loud enough for the news to reach Paris, and all those rich society matrons who bring their ills and complaints to your private practice and send their friends, children, and husbands your way as well. They might turn a blind eye to a gentleman discreetly indulging himself in the demimonde, but I think they would find seduction and impregnation of one of your students to be quite beyond the pale. I doubt they would continue to patronize such a man."

"See here—!"

"I'm sure the clinic protected your good name even while they tut-tutted and moaned about my wickedness. After all, you are a noted physician, and more importantly, a man. But I assure you that I'll make sure everyone in Paris knows of your peccadillo."

"You—"

"Be quiet, Henri." Ellen was on a roll, and she had no intention of giving up the floor. "You've had your say. Now it's my turn. I'm being gentle with you right now.

But if you ever try to take my child or touch him or her in any way, I will make sure that you're left with nothing. No honor. No money. No practice. Nothing. Believe me, I will do it."

"And if she doesn't to it, I will."

Ellen whirled to find Jordan standing at the door. He had a calm, deadly assurance about him that was more frightening than any threat Ellen could think to throw Henri's way.

"Henri Chretiens, I presume. Professional jackass. And quite accomplished at it, I hear."

"Who the hell are you?"

"Jordan, Baron Chesterfield."

Henri's jaw dropped.

"You can call me Lord Chesterfield. And from now on I'll thank you to address my wife as Lady Chesterfield."

As Jordan advanced, Henri's face turned pale as a frog's underbelly. "Don't touch me!" the Frenchman warned. "If you do, I'll tell the whole world your wife is a slut and you're a fool who got cuckolded even before he was wed."

"On the whole, Monsieur Chretiens, I think my wife was dealing with you much too gently. You may trumpet your accusations to the world all you like and only make yourself appear the pathetic fool."

Henri groped for what remained of his dignity, drawing himself up and straightening his spine in an attempt to look imposing, though bloodshot eyes and knobby knees doomed the effort to pathetic failure. "So my Ellen married an English lord, did she? *Eh bien*, your high-and-mighty lordship, do you remember, each night as you bed her, that Henri Chretiens was there first? Eh? Are the English so lacking in manhood that they are satisfied with another man's leavings?"

"I thank God that you are such a fool," Jordan replied with icy calm. "It is my great good fortune that you were too stupid to recognize gold when it lay within your hand." He gave the Frenchman an infuriating smile. "One of the noblest things about gold, by the way, is that whatever abuse it endures, it never tarnishes. It remains bright, clean, and pure. As does my wife."

Henri sneered. "She tarnished well enough."

Jordan reached for him, but Ellen put a hand on his arm. "Don't, Jordan. You can't do half the damage to Henri that he has done to himself."

While Henri and Jordan had exchanged unpleasantries, Ellen had observed Henri with a discerning eye. He had changed dramatically since she had last seen him in Paris, and the changes were not solely due to the unflattering effect of an early-morning rising. He had always imbibed freely, but since Patricia had snatched her fortune out of his grasp, he must have been worshiping the bottle, and perhaps even deadlier intoxicants, with uncommon fervor. Unless she mistook the signs completely, his liver had just about run its course.

Ellen realized, with an odd detachment and an even odder touch of pity, that she didn't really need to worry about Henri's threats. Not in the long term, at least.

"Henri," she said gently, "you taught me some valuable lessons in life, and though you didn't intend it, you gave me a precious gift." She laid a hand on her protruding stomach and smiled. "So I'm going to give you a gift—in a much more charitable spirit than you gave this gift to me. Stop worrying about money and making threats, Dr. Chretiens, and look at yourself in the mirror."

Henri's ravaged expression told her he understood perfectly. Whatever else he was, the man was a competent physician. As she started to turn away, his face filled with rage, as though she were to blame for the fate he'd brought upon himself.

"Slut!" He spat upon the floor to punctuate the insult.

Jordan's fist caught Henri squarely on the jaw and sent him crashing against the wall, where the Frenchman slid slowly to the floor in a dazed heap.

"That felt good," said Jordan, shaking his bruised hand. "I've been wanting to do it for a long time."

"You've been around my father too long," Ellen observed with a smile. As Henri cursed woozily and glared, Ellen took Jordan's arm. "Don't bother to see us out, Henri. We can find our way."

Henri did not bother them again. Ellen wrote to a friend in Paris, an ex-patient at the clinic where she had studied, and asked for him to pass on any news about Dr. Chretiens. Whether she liked it or not, Henri was her child's father, and therefore a part of her life forever. A month later, she received a letter from her friend. An enclosed newspaper clipping included the obituary of Dr. Henri Chretiens, Paris physician, born 1865, died February 1900. The obituary didn't state the cause of death, but Ellen knew what had killed him. First he had killed his liver by tipping a bottle. Then his liver had killed him. Henri had done it to himself, and the thought made Ellen sad. What a mark he could have made if he'd been blessed with as much character as talent and charm.

"Why the long face?" Jordan asked as he came up behind her. She sat at the desk of her father's office, going through the mail that Katy had brought in from town.

Ellen handed him the clipping. "Henri Chretiens died three weeks ago."

Jordan's brows flew up in surprise. "Good heavens! I didn't hit him that hard!"

"No, of course not. He had a liver condition when he left here. It probably started long before I met him. He never passed a day without polishing off at least one bottle, and I think his drinking must have increased by volumes after Patricia broke off their engagement."

He put his hands on her shoulders and massaged. "Are you all right?"

"Of course I'm all right." She leaned into the massage. "It makes me sad is all. Such a useless waste. What should I tell my child about his real father?"

"You'll know what to say when the time comes, Ellen. It seems you always do."

Ellen chuckled. "After the mistakes I made in my life?"

"You haven't made many mistakes lately." He gave her shoulders a final pat. "Must get back to work. Your father is a hard taskmaster. He unlocked my slave shackles only so I could come check on you."

"How's the move going?"

"Splendidly. We'll be sleeping in the house tonight."

"I could do something, you know. I'm not helpless."

"If you lift more than a cup of tea, Olivia, Katy, and I are going to tie you to a chair, and probably your father will stuff a rag in your mouth so we won't have to listen to your objections."

"Oh all right! Honestly, I'll be so glad when this baby is born and everyone stops treating me like an invalid!"

"Be patient for another few weeks."

"Easy for you to say."

Jordan gave her cheek a chaste kiss. Ellen's response was just as chaste. Neither of them was willing to start anything they couldn't end, and since a session of gentle lovemaking two weeks previous had sent her into false labor, Jordan had refused to do anything more strenuous with her than cuddle.

Jordan headed for the door. "I'll see you later."

"Wait. Before you go, I think there's a letter here for you. Oops. No. There's two. Here they are."

She handed him two envelopes, and he stuck them inside the pocket of his heavy sheepskin jacket. "I'll read them later. Take care of yourself."

"As if I have any choice," Ellen complained to herself after he had gone. The last week she'd been allowed to do little besides sit and wait while everyone else worked to finish the house—all because she had slipped into early false labor a couple of times. The contractions hadn't been strong at all, and hadn't amounted to anything alarming, but Olivia had forbidden her to work at the hospital, Jordan and her father both had refused to let her help with the house, and Katy had threatened to tie her to a bed for the rest of her pregnancy if she didn't behave.

Ellen wandered into the kitchen to fix some tea. Perhaps she was wearier than normal, but she had a right to be tired. All in all, these last months had been enough to wear down an Amazon.

Everything was fine now, though. Her family knew the whole truth. Henri—God rest his soul—was gone, and the last month had been calm. She had little to do but think about the impending birth and try to come to grips with her future—a future not exactly without Jordan, but with a Jordan who would be a faraway presence. They would write, probably. He might visit to check up on her—he was too damnably responsible to not do that. She might visit England to put an acceptable face on their marriage. But it certainly wouldn't be the same as waking up to him every morning and falling asleep in his arms every night.

Shortly after her confession, Ellen had told her family that Jordan would be returning to England after the birth, and she forbade them from troubling him about his plans. She had not discussed the future with Jordan, as much as she longed to declare her love and beg him to make their marriage real in every sense of the word. Her pride was tattered, but it was still strong enough to keep her from imposing any further on a man who had already given her far more than their bargain required.

Olivia and Gabe still treated Jordan politely, but their lack of warmth made it obvious they didn't know quite what to do with him or how to place him in their lives. Katy teased and tried to bully him with the devil's mischief in her eyes. But then, few people understood Katy or why she did what she did. Jonah was the only one whose regard for Jordan hadn't changed since the great revelation. They spent a good amount of time together, as Jonah was writing an article for the *Record* centered on Jordan's impressions of the West.

How different things would be, Ellen thought as she took her tea to the table, if she'd made a normal, everyday marriage instead of this peculiar bargain with a somewhat peculiar Englishman. She had wondered a time or two if their bargain might be changed, but concluded that was unlikely. Ellen O'Connell, Irish-Blackfoot half-breed, woman physician, was hardly the sort who could play the role of baroness in English Society, and Jordan had proposed in the first place to avoid the entanglements of marriage and pursuing women. Obviously Jordan couldn't stay in Montana, even if he wanted to. He was an English peer, with a seat in Parliament and an estate to run, not to mention a thriving business that needed his attention. He seemed content to take a vacation from his life for a while, but it was still his life. No amount of hoping would change the situation, no matter that every time she thought of Jordan leaving, the pain became harder to bear.

Ellen knew that once Jordan was gone, life would continue. The sun would still shine. Birds would still sing. Children would still laugh. She would have a precious child and her beloved family.

But she couldn't have Jordan, and how empty life would seem without him.

Ellen jumped as the baby kicked her hard in the ribs. "Ouch, you little devil! That hurt." She put a hand on her belly, wondering how something that had caused such pain and turmoil in her life could still be so precious. "Settle down in there. It's not time yet. Give me awhile, will you?"

Give me awhile, Ellen thought, *to say good-bye to Jordan. There is so little time left. So little time.*

So little time before she would say hello to someone precious coming into her life and good-bye to someone precious who was leaving.

So little time.

CHAPTER 22

There was less time than Ellen thought, as it turned out. When her father drove her to the new house that afternoon, Jordan was on the doorstep to welcome her. He made a show of carrying her over the threshold to her new dining room, where a dinner prepared by Sarah Mulholland awaited along with Olivia, Katy, Jonah, David, and Tyrell, who slept peacefully in the cradle Gabriel had made for the soon-to-be new arrival. Olivia had decided that Ellen needed domestic help more than she did right then, so Sarah was on loan until someone could be found to take her place.

Ellen laughed at Jordan's gallant gesture. "You'd better put me down before you strain something," she teased. "I'm not a lightweight any longer."

"Wait a few weeks," Katy advised. "It'll take a crane to get you off the ground."

Jordan played the gracious host, and the family made an effort to be amiable to him. After dinner they christened the house by watching Gabriel and Katy play chess—not normally a rousing event, but it became one when the whole family took sides and tried to help their respective champions.

Through the evening Jordan chatted, tolerated Jonah's jokes about his not knowing how to set a plumb line, lost gracefully to Olivia at a game of hearts, read a story to David, and made appropriately admiring noises when Katy took Tyrell around to give everyone a good-night kiss. Ellen detected a certain reserve in his manner, however. Something was wrong, and apparently it wasn't something he wanted to discuss in front of the family. Her imagination went to work thinking on the worst possibilities while she waited for the family to depart and Jordan to spill the beans—whatever beans they were.

Tyrell's good-night kiss was the mutually accepted signal for everyone to leave. Ellen was anxious to be alone with Jordan, but she felt obligated to protest.

"Are you sure you won't spend the night?" she asked Katy. "The guest room is cleaner than it ever will be again, after all, and poor Tyrell is going to freeze going back to the ranch."

"No he won't," Katy assured her. She clucked at the baby. "You're a tough kid, aren't you, Ty?"

"You deserve some time alone to admire your new home," Olivia told Ellen when they kissed at the door. "Gabriel, are you coming?"

"I'm coming. I'm coming." Gabe tore himself away from admiring his handiwork on the kitchen shelves and followed his wife out.

The wagon rolled away into the cold night. The door closed, and finally Jordan and Ellen were alone in their new home. No. Ellen's new home. Not Jordan's.

Ellen wasted no time. She turned with her back against the front door and looked Jordan straight in the eye. "Tell me what it is."

Jordan sighed and dropped into the nearest chair—a pinewood rocker that Katy had made as a gift for the baby. He made no attempt to deny that something had changed. "Those letters you gave me today," he said. "One was from Chamberlain—he's the queen's foreign secretary—requesting my presence at a meeting April five. The other was from the Duke of Marlowe—you remember him. Tindale's father. Good man, in spite of the son. He's been lobbying for a year to get me an appointment in the foreign office. He warns me that an appointment may very well come out of this meeting."

Ellen released the breath she had been holding, feeling her spirit deflate as she did so. "April fifth! That's so soon."

"I would need to leave immediately."

A riot of emotion erupted in Ellen's mind. She wasn't ready to lose him yet. After all, she had just a few short weeks ago admitted to herself that she loved him. She had accepted him leaving shortly after their child was born—not her child, but theirs. But for him to leave this soon . . .

"You asked me to stay until the baby is born, Ellen . . ."

"Of course you must go," she heard herself say. "This is something you've worked hard for."

"I did promise you. If you need me to stay, I will. I might be able to make arrangements to delay the meeting."

"Don't worry about this." She patted her belly. "I can do this with my eyes closed. Really. Men just get in the way at birthings, anyway. I was just being silly, wanting you to stay."

"To have any hope of arriving in London on time, I'd need to leave for New York on tomorrow morning's train." His eyes searched her face, trying to read her true reaction.

Normally, her defenses melted whenever Jordan turned the full force of his scrutiny upon her, but not this time. She kept a cheerful mask in place to hide her dejection. This appointment was important to him. She'd been hearing about it ever since she met him. She didn't want to have its loss on her conscience. "It's all right, Jordan. You have to go. There's no question about it."

"I feel like a first-class heel," he said.

Ellen smiled. "You are definitely first class, Lord Chesterfield. But you're not a heel. You've given me much more than I bargained for in this marriage."

He smiled grimly. "The devil's bargain. And I was the one who proposed it." His eyes suddenly bore into hers with a searching intensity that made Ellen's heart jump. "We need to talk, Ellen. But now isn't the time. You have enough on your mind right now, and so do I. When I come back, we'll set some things straight."

"You're coming back?"

"Of course I'll come back. I want to see the finished product of this very curious process." He directed a smile at her stomach.

Her smile was suddenly radiant. It was all she could do to not demand a solemn vow on the ancient Chesterfield honor that he was indeed coming back. Regardless which matter between them he wanted to "set straight," it was enough to know he considered something between them unfinished.

That night, their first night in the new house—a house meant for Ellen, not for Jordan, would have been strained enough without it being one long, awkward good-bye. Ellen wished desperately that she could be granted one more night of making love with Jordan—a night to brand her heart and body, to remember during the lonely hours to come. She was more than eight months pregnant, however, and one night's joy was not worth the risk it entailed.

Jordan seemed less concerned with the parting than Ellen did, and she tried not to resent it. He had promised to come back, Ellen reminded herself. Even if he came for only a short visit, a token meeting with the baby, a quick check that everything was all right with her before going once and for all back to his own life, that would be better than nothing. This parting wasn't forever. She should have learned by now that nothing was forever.

As she lay on their bed, staring into the dark and trying to convince herself that everything was going to be all right, Ellen could sense Jordan's wakefulness. His quiet voice came from close beside her.

"Do you want a backrub, little mother?"

Her back did ache abominably, as it had for the last week. Never again would she tell a pregnant patient to relax and enjoy her pregnancy. Some things just could not be understood until they were experienced.

"Oh, thank you," she breathed as he began to massage her lower back. "If I can't make love to you, a backrub is certainly the next best thing."

He started to make a comment, but stopped, leaving the tension of unspoken words between them. "Who knows?" he said finally. "If you delay just a bit in having the baby, I might be back in time to pace the floor with your father and Jonah."

"Don't talk to me about delays." She groaned in pleasure as he found a particular tight spot. "This baby's coming out on time, or I'll demand to know the reason why."

He chuckled. "You are an original, Lady Chesterfield." He tipped her over onto her back, so she found his face hovering close above hers. "I would not have missed knowing you for the world, Ellen."

She reached up and touched his lips. "I wish . . ." What did she wish? That she had met Jordan before Henri? If not for Henri, she would still be in Paris studying clinical procedures. She never would have met Jordan at all, much less married him.

"What do you wish?" he prompted.

She smiled. "I wish I didn't feel so much like a turtle flipped on its back."

He kissed her, and she let herself sink into the sensual luxury of that kiss, to stamp the taste, feel, and sound of it in her memory.

"You don't taste like a turtle," he whispered in her ear.

She laughed quietly, then sobered. "Jordan?"

"Yes?"

"Thank you for staying with me until I found myself again. It took me a good long while, but now I feel like my old self."

"Really?" He gave her belly a fond pat.

"Well, almost," she conceded. "I'm not angry any longer. Or bitter. Or afraid. I know I can do anything."

His eyes roamed affectionately over her face. "Someday I'm going to put that to the test."

"What do you mean?"

"Don't worry about it. Go to sleep, little mother. Your baby needs the rest if he's to grow big and strong."

"Not too big, I hope." Ellen curled into a ball beneath the covers, and Jordan curved his hard, warm body around hers.

What more could she want? Ellen asked herself. Indeed, what more could she want? She didn't even want to think about it.

Jordan wouldn't let Ellen accompany him to the railroad station, though she insisted she was more than capable of a fifteen-minute walk through town.

"I would worry about something happening while you walked back alone."

"Really, Jordan! What am I supposed to do? Take to my bed for a month? Sit in the rocker and knit booties?"

"Yes," he replied. "I want your promise that you'll take care of yourself. Sarah will be here within an hour, and I'm going to stop by their place and ask her husband to drive out to the ranch with the news that I'm leaving."

"I'll be fine. Stop worrying."

Her expression was resolutely cheerful, and he felt like an irredeemable scoundrel. He damned Chamberlain for choosing the most inconvenient time possible for summoning him. He had been lobbying for this appointment for three years. Why did the call have to come now?

"Go on," Ellen urged. "You'll miss your train. Give my love to George and Jane."

He didn't want to give Ellen's love to anyone but himself, Jordan admitted as he finally walked away. He resisted the urge to look back. He would return as soon as he could. Not soon enough to bolster Ellen during the delivery, perhaps, but soon enough to settle things between them. He had wanted to speak to Ellen for the last week—tell her that they could find some common ground between their two separate worlds. He wanted to tell her that she had become a part of him he wasn't willing to leave behind, that marriage and love had taken on new meanings since he had been with her, that his life would not be complete without her in it.

He had clamped his jaw shut every time the words had tried to come out, however. Ellen had enough on her mind with the coming baby. Now was no time to ask her to wrestle with such a life-wrenching decision. He had intended to wait until the baby was safely delivered and Ellen was on the road to recovery, then discuss the matter with her.

His most reasonable plan flew to pieces when those bloody letters arrived, however. His political career hung in the balance, and he had no choice but to leave. He told himself that Ellen had her family around her. She would do just fine until he could come back. Then he would lay his heart on the floor before her and give her the chance to pick it up, or step on it, as the case may be. Whichever, his personal desires would have to wait.

Walking through the chill morning, his lungs hurting from the cold, his breath freezing in the bitter March air, Jordan thought of how different this world was from his own. In England he would have been driven to the station by one of the servants, who wouldn't have dreamed of letting him touch his own baggage or open a door for himself. Here, he walked, valise in hand, dressed in a sheepskin jacket that made him look like a cowhand and ready-made denims purchased from the local mercantile. He'd spent the last weeks acquiring calluses like a common laborer, and he didn't mind admitting that a certain amount of satisfaction came with the calluses.

Not that he wanted to spend the rest of his life here. He didn't. Much as he despised some of the sillier aspects of English Society, that was his world—the one he'd been born into and the one where he fit. He loved England, just as Ellen loved her beautiful, wild Montana.

If they loved each other enough, perhaps they could find a way to live in both.

Sarah Mulholland was just leaving home as Jordan stepped up onto her porch.

"Land sakes!" she declared when he gave her the news. "That's right poor timin'. But don't you worry, Mr. Chesterfield. We'll take fine care of sweet Ellen. Don't you doubt it for a minute. And I'll send Charlie over to Thunder Creek to tell Dr. Olivia and Katy. They'll keep a good watch over her."

"Thank you, Mrs. Mulholland. I'm exceedingly grateful."

"Don't mention it. Just hurry back, you hear?"

"I will indeed."

As the train steamed away from the station, headed east to Bozeman via numerous local stops, Jordan tried to think about what lay ahead. He would try to find a telephone in Bozeman and call Spencer Crabbe, who could make hurried arrangements for a berth on the soonest possible departure from New York. If he couldn't find a telephone, he would telegraph. He would telegraph his mother from New York, and George also.

There was no need to spend time planning what to say in the interview with Chamberlain. He'd thought about that for months. He should be excited and exuberant, grateful that his chance had finally come. No doubt the feeling of accomplishment would come once he was on his way across the Atlantic, but right now his heart pulled him backward, not forward.

The train was insufferably slow, making stops at every little town along the line and seeming to crawl through the empty stretches in between. When they arrived in the early afternoon at the rail station in Sappington, Jordan had a surprise waiting for him. As soon as the train stopped, a commotion began somewhere up the line of passenger coaches. From what Jordan could ascertain, the few passengers who were trying to disembark from the cars ahead were having to crowd their way past someone who had just boarded and was pushing his way rudely toward the rear of the train.

Not *his* way, Jonah was startled to note as the intruder marched into his car. *Her* way. Katy, wind-burned and red-faced, made straight for Jordan.

"What the bloody hell are you doing here?" he demanded. "You should be with Ellen."

"So should you, you jackass!"

"Katy . . ."

"Shut up and come with me." She grabbed his hand and pulled. Rather than make any more of a scene than they already had, Jordan allowed her to drag him along the aisle and down to the platform, accompanied by the glares and curious murmurs of the other passengers.

"What's gotten in to you?" he demanded once they were off the train. "I know Ellen didn't send you, so—"

"Ellen's having the baby!" Katy blurted out. "I rode the legs off two good horses chasing this damned train."

Jordan's heart lurched. "Ellen's having the baby? She can't be! It's early yet. It's too bloody early!"

"Tell that to the kid. She must've gone into labor right after you left, and not a gentle labor, either. Sarah found her on the kitchen floor, practically passed out."

"She's all right, isn't she?" Jordan took hold of Katy's arm as though he might break it in two if she didn't give him the answer he wanted to hear. "Tell me she's all right!"

"It's going to be hard, Jordan. Real hard. The delivery's not going well, and Olivia doesn't know if the baby can make it." Her mouth opened and shut. The next words had trouble coming out. "Ellen . . . Ellen's having a real tough time of it. She's out of her head some, and calling for you. Though I don't know why the hell she would! But I figured if it would ease her a bit, I'd drag you back no matter how I had to do it."

A stone the size of Gibraltar settled on Jordan's heart. Such a short time ago he'd left Ellen standing in the doorway of the new house. She'd been so adamant that she was fine, that she would be fine, and now she was struggling both for her baby's life and her own. Struggling, out of her head with pain, and calling for him. And he was miles away.

Despair crystallized to determination as he surveyed the rough country over which the train had just carried him. "How long did it take you to ride here?"

"Three hours and two horses. But you can't ride nearly as fast."

"Just watch me."

For Ellen, hours had stretched into an eternity. Despite her medical training and experience dealing with the sick and dying, never before had she truly appreciated the power of pain. It stretched minutes into hours and hours into days. It played tricks on the brain and reduced the mind to something animal and desperate. Sometimes she didn't know where she was. Sometimes she didn't remember who she was or what had happened to cause such rending, wrenching agony. When she wasn't confused, she was frightened—more frightened than she had believed possible. Before today, she not only hadn't appreciated the power of pain, she hadn't understood the real nature of fear.

"Drink this." Olivia's hand slipped beneath Ellen's head and lifted until her lips touched the cup of steaming tea. Ellen recognized a concoction that Blackfoot women used to facilitate birth. Trust Olivia to see the value of something most doctors would scoff at.

"I can't," Ellen protested weakly. "I'll throw up."

"No you won't. Just a little."

Ellen obeyed. She choked. Her stomach tried to rebel, but she refused to let it.

"Rest a few minutes, dear. Then you must push a bit more."

"I can't!" Ellen's voice was hoarse. She supposed she had been screaming. She didn't remember. The hours of pain were blending into a nightmare where nothing was quite clear. "I can't."

"You can. You're strong, Ellen. You can do this."

"This isn't happening the way it should."

"No. But it's happening just the same. You must get through it. Think of all the other things you have conquered in your life. Think of all the things we've gotten through together. We can get through this as well."

Weary beyond words, Ellen felt tears burn hot trails down her cheeks. She didn't have the strength to wipe them away.

"Do you want to see your father? I've practically had to tie him to the sofa to keep him out of here."

"No. Don't let him in. This is . . . a woman thing." She tried to smile, and failed. "I don't think I ever want to see another man."

"Well then!" came Katy's mocking voice from the bedroom doorway. "I rode a hell of a long way for nothing."

Jordan pushed through the door behind her. He entered the room as though he were staking a claim in it, asking neither permission nor pardon.

Ellen could feel his presence before she saw him. His

absence had made the room hollow and dark. His presence filled it with hope. The pain was still there. Fear was still a brooding reality. Nothing changed, really, when Jordan walked into the room. Yet everything changed.

He sat down on the bed as if he belonged there, taking her hand and fixing her with a stern gray gaze. "What is this, Lady Chesterfield? You promise to behave, and the minute I'm out of sight, you do this."

"Jordan . . ." she croaked.

"Don't mouth off to your husband," he warned. "You have work to do, I think."

"Please don't leave."

He squeezed her hand. "I'm here, Ellen. And I'm waiting to meet our baby."

Ellen woke slowly, remembering only pain and gut-twisting effort. The pain lingered, though it was much less intense. Her body felt as though someone had used it as target practice for a battering ram. Even the slightest movement caused acute discomfort.

As she surfaced from heavy sleep, the memory of grief added to her physical pain. Remembered grief gradually became real and present as it coalesced into a wrenching sense of loss for something she had scarcely even known—her child. She was alive, Ellen concluded—alive and alone. Unless . . . she recalled the sound of Jordan's voice. It had seemed so real. She remembered his voice and the feel of his hand clasping hers while she squeezed and screamed. Jordan. Had he been part of a delirium, or had he actually been there?

Ellen opened her eyes. At first she didn't recognize where she was, and then she recalled. They had moved to the new house, and Jordan had left to return to England. He wasn't really here. By now he was far, far away.

"Well, I see you're finally awake." Katy swaggered into the room, all smiles and jauntiness. "Do you want to meet your daughter?"

"My . . . my . . .?"

"Daughter," Katy supplied. "Girl baby. Yup. A real corker, too, though she's on the small side. Olivia says any kid who can holler so loud is bound to be all right."

"I thought . . ." Ellen's words faded into a huge smile as Katy laid a squirming bundle of soft blanket and red, wrinkled flesh on the bed beside her.

"What are you going to name her?"

"Name her? I . . . I thought I lost her."

"With Dr. Olivia in attendance? Not likely."

Ellen raised herself painfully on one elbow and looked at the little bundle. Carefully, she touched a baby cheek with her finger. "Oh, little one, you're so beautiful. Are you sure she's all right?"

"She's got all her parts, and a bit of good sense, too, 'cause as soon as she slipped out, she started squalling about how cold and unfair the world is. You were out of it, by then, so you didn't hear her."

Ellen let herself sink back onto the pillow. "Thank God."

"Yeah," Katy agreed. "Thank God, and Olivia . . . and Jordan, too."

Ellen came instantly alert. "Jordan?"

"Yeah. Don't you remember? He was the one who sat here all the time and wouldn't let you quit. I'll say one thing for the Englishman, he does know how to boss people around."

Ellen's heart began to beat faster. "Where is he?"

"He'll be in as soon as Olivia lets him up. Once the

kid came out and started squalling, he keeled over like a wind-felled tree. The old British stiff upper lip sort of caved in when Olivia said that you and the baby should be okay. Men really don't belong in a birthing room," Katy said with a superior smile.

"Is that so?" Jordan demanded from the doorway. "And who else was swaying on her feet at the end?"

"Not me!" Katy said defensively. Her vexation was all show, however. Before Jordan took two steps toward the bed, she made a fast retreat and left them alone.

Ellen reached up for his hand. "Like a wind-felled tree, is it?"

"You might say that." Without releasing her hand, he pulled a chair under his backside and sat. "I like that description—a stalwart, stately tree felled by a woman's tender hand. You've wielded a mighty ax on both my resolve and my prejudices, Lady Chesterfield."

"Strange that you should say that. It was because of a windfall we first met, remember?"

"It must be fate, then."

She smiled, but the smile faded when she remembered why he had left. "Oh, Jordan! You'll miss your meeting."

"Hang the meeting. And the foreign secretary. When I feel secure enough to let you out of my sight, I'll write Chamberlain and Marlowe with the news that my wife just delivered our first child, and I could meet them in two months or so if they were still interested in speaking with me."

She squeezed his hand. "I'm sorry."

"Don't be. Sometimes our priorities in life get rearranged for the better. When Katy found me in Sappington and told me you were in a difficult labor, I realized once and for all what was truly important to me.

No. Don't say anything." He laid a finger on her lips. "Let me have my say. It's taken me long enough to gather enough courage to say it. Those three days sitting under a pine tree on the reservation—freezing my back-side to the ground—gave me a new insight into what I want in life."

"What do you want in life, Jordan?"

"You, Ellen O'Connell Chesterfield. I thought when I came back from England would be a better time to con-vince you, but Mother Nature had her own ideas about my leaving, it seems."

Ellen opened her mouth to speak, but Jordan fore-stalled her with a raised finger. "I'm not through yet, my love. I would like it very much if you would return to England with me, to be my wife in every way, to eventu-ally give this little girl here brothers and sisters. I know the medical establishment there is very stuffy about non-British medical educations, but we'll find a way for you to continue to practice." His smile had all the arrogance and confidence of the tyrant she had once assumed him to be. "After all, what use is being a peer if one can't exert a bit of influence here and there sometimes?"

The confidence vanished, suddenly, and in its place, a painful vulnerability softened the steel of his eyes and subtly altered the curve of his lips.

"I love you, Ellen. Give me a chance to make you happy. We can find some common ground to build a world where both of us will be at home. What say we divide our roots between England and Montana? After all, now we have homes in both countries."

Ellen closed her eyes, savoring the words she had thought to hear only in daydream imaginings. Her body was still weak, but her spirit soared, giving life to a smile.

"I'd make a dreadful baroness," she said.

"You'll break the dusty old mold and cast yourself a new one. Probably you'll become all the rage, and you can laugh at how silly Society is."

"And there's your mother."

"Ah, yes. The dowager baroness." Jordan grinned. "I will savor the look on her face when you walk into Endsfield Park as its new mistress."

"She'll have a heart attack."

Jordan laughed. "She's stronger and more resilient than you think. A little churning about of her nineteenth-century ideas will make her young again. This *is* the first year of the twentieth century, after all."

Ellen opened her eyes and met his gaze with a twinkling blend of love and mischief. "I suppose I should consider the few things I do like about England."

"Indeed you should."

"The beautiful horses in your stable."

"They are very fine."

"Maisy and her pups."

"One of which belongs to you, if you'll remember."

"Prissy and Andrea."

"Who need a woman's hand to guide them."

"And, of course, there is Lord Chesterfield himself."

Jordan raised one brow. "I've heard he's a bit stuffy."

"He's terribly proud," Ellen agreed. "And much too arrogant."

"A sorry fellow, in all. No doubt he needs some good woman to reform him."

"Sounds like a challenging task." Ellen smiled gently. "I'd tell you a secret, but I think you already know."

One big hand curling gently around the baby's tiny head, Jordan leaned close to Ellen's lips to whisper. "What secret do I know?"

She reached up and, with very little effort, brought him down to her lips for a kiss. "This Chesterfield fellow," she whispered back. "He is stuffy and stubborn, and haughty as hell. But I'd follow him anywhere."